WHAT DOES IT MEAN TO HAVE A FAMILY?

Singer and Lisa Thurman did everything right for their entire childhood. Their mother wanted a perfect life, and they knew how to fit that vision.

Then they grew up. Singer came out of the closet and Lisa joined a cult.

Singer and his partner are adopting a son. Unfortunately, all that practice being the perfect child didn't prepare Singer to be a merely adequate father. Lisa's just trying to get through the day. After three years in a cult, it's almost impossible to leave her bedroom, so redemption is going to have to wait.

WHAT DOES IT MEAN TO BE A FAMILY?

When their mother shows up and attempts to reclaim the illusion of her perfect family, old lives clash with new ones.

Recovering from perfection is messy, complicated, and fraught, but the riotous clan that rises from the ashes is full of joy—and the best kind of trouble.

A groundbreaking, honest, and provocative novel, *Kith and Kin* is contemporary family drama that grafts an entirely new species of family tree.

FAMILY IS WHAT YOU MAKE OF IT.

KITH AND KIN
S + J
by Crisripper

THE HELLUM AND NEAL SERIES IN LGBTQIA+ LITERATURE

Documenting Light by EE Ottoman
The Mathematics of Change by Amanda Kabak
Grief Map by Sarah Hahn Campbell
Kith and Kin by Kris Ripper
Abroad by Liz Jacobs

ALSO BY KRIS RIPPER

Queers of La Vista

Gays of Our Lives
The Butch and the Beautiful
The Queer and the Restless
One Life to Lose
As La Vista Turns

Scientific Method Universe

Catalysts
Unexpected Gifts
Take Three Breaths
Breaking Down
Roller Coasters
The Boyfriends Tie the Knot
The Honeymoon
Extremes
The New Born Year
Threshold of the Year
Ring in the True
Surrender the Past
Practice Makes Perfect

New Halliday

Fairy Tales
The Spinner, the Shepherd, and the Leading Man
The Real Life Build

Take the Leap

The Home Series

Going Home
Home Free
Close to Home
Home for the Holidays

Little Red and Big Bad

Bad Comes First
Red Comes Second

The Erotic Gym: Training Mac
The Ghost in the Penthouse

KITH AND KIN

KRIS RIPPER

THE HELLUM AND NEAL SERIES IN LGBTQIA+ LITERATURE
BRAIN MILL PRESS | GREEN BAY, WISC.

Published in the United States by Brain Mill Press.
Print ISBN 978-1-942083-66-5
EPUB ISBN 978-1-942083-67-2
MOBI ISBN 978-1-942083-68-9
PDF ISBN 978-1-942083-69-6

Cover art by Cindy Bean.
Cover design by Ampersand Book Covers.

www.brainmillpress.com

This book could only ever be dedicated to my brother.

For Mark. I'm so glad we lived.

KITH AND KIN
S + J
by Kris Ripper

PROLOGUE

SINGER
20 DAYS BEFORE MILES

In the middle of yet another incredibly loud debate, Singer Thurman's doorbell rang. The familiar voices continued in predictable movements of attack and retreat as he rose from his chair and answered the door.

For a second—half a second—he didn't recognize the woman on the front porch. Until he did.

"Lisa?" It was as if she were somehow insubstantial, as if this image of his sister, with the forbidding dark nimbus around each eye and shoulders rounded defensively, wavered over his mental picture of Lisa as he'd last seen her: self-assured and defiant, clothes and makeup her armor against the world. His popular, unassailable older sister, whom he hadn't seen in three years.

He blinked, but of course she was solid. And increasingly awkward. She dropped her eyes, murmuring a vague, "Hi, Singer," almost under her breath.

The boisterous group in the living room erupted (*Did he just say "Lisa"?*), but Singer was only aware of Jake stepping up to his side and holding out a hand to her.

"Hey. You probably don't remember me. I'm Jake Derrie. Singer's boyfriend."

She frowned. "I remember. Sorry."

The Lisa he'd known never apologized. And she really didn't look right. She looked almost … scared. Singer turned his body so as to invite less interference from the living room and gestured her into the house. Their house. His and Jake's now; his and Lisa's growing up. "Come in. I didn't realize you were, um, visiting. Do Mother and Dad know you're here?"

"Yeah." She shook her head. "I'm tired. Would it be all right if I went to bed?"

Why on earth are you asking my permission? Before Singer could say anything, Jake joined him in physically blocking off the rest of the house, and smiled at Lisa. "Definitely. Half my cousins are in the living room, sorry. I'll make them go out back so they don't keep you up."

She started down the hall. "Oh, no, it's okay——"

"Seriously, they're obnoxious. It's no problem."

"And we enjoy herding them," Singer added. "Let me get you sheets and blankets."

When he returned, Jake was helping with the sofa bed. Lisa accepted the stack of linens without looking up, and she seemed a little pale. Sweaty, even.

"Good night." Singer shot a look at Jake, which he greeted with a very slight shrug.

"Nice to see you, Lisa."

"You too."

They went out, and she closed the door very quietly. Something scraped along the ground, something heavy. It landed with a thump, making the door rattle.

Jake mouthed, *Oh my god.*

Laughter from the living room drew their attention, and they went to shoo the Irregulars outside, where they'd only annoy the neighbors.

Lisa was home. She'd spent three years in a cult, five days with Mother and Dad, and now she was here. Once reassembled out back, the gathering dropped all previous debates in the name of exchanging wild theories about what had precipitated Lisa's sudden arrival, but Singer mostly remained silent. He'd never known her well. He had no idea what would have made her come home.

Or if she even considered this her home.

*

Hours later, Singer stood in his kitchen, rinsing the last of the dishes. The night's guests had at long last gone home. Jake had seen everyone out before heading to bed, but Singer had lingered. He enjoyed the sanctity of the house when it was quiet after being filled with voices, perhaps especially tonight.

He listened for a moment in the hallway outside Lisa's room. As far as he could tell, she hadn't made a sound since she blocked the door. And, well, he was pretty used to Jake's relatives by now, but he couldn't fault the instinct to bar the door against them.

Jake came from a big family. A big, tight-knit family of siblings and cousins, full of people who spoke loudly, laughed even more loudly, and never stopped poking into each other's business. In high school he'd watched from afar as the Derries moved in a group, a herd, their volume making them impenetrable. These days he was frequently swept up in their wake.

He slipped quietly into the master bedroom and went to the alcove where the bathroom was, smiling helplessly at the inevitable mess Jake made rinsing his face. How one person could splash quite so much without meaning to was beyond Singer.

"Hey." Jake caught his eye in the mirror. "What'cha thinking?"

"That sometimes it'd be nice to have a drawbridge between us and your family."

"Oh my god, only *sometimes*?"

Singer smiled. "I love the Derries."

"You have the luxury of being able to pretend you aren't stuck with them." Jake picked up his toothbrush. "Note I said 'pretend.'"

"You don't think I could do something so horrible your family would disown me?"

Jake laughed out loud and wiped his mouth with the back of his hand. "Ha. They'd ditch me before they'd ditch you. Anyway, speaking of family, did you call your parents?"

It wasn't really the same, Singer didn't think, but he played along. "No. Was I supposed to?"

"Well, yeah, considering Lisa just sort of showed up here. You didn't want to find out what the hell happened? It's been, what, less than a week since she got out of her cult?"

Singer sank down on the bed, Lisa's silent presence heavier than it had been a minute ago. "True. I'm not sure what I'd say."

"Well. You could start with, 'How'd you guys screw up so badly you sent Lisa packing already?'"

He shot his boyfriend a look. "That does not sound like something I'd say to my parents, Jacob."

Jake smirked, as he nearly always did when Singer took a tone with him. "Ha. It's weird. I don't think your family has more money or more, like, rich white people entitlement than my family, but I always feel like a Dickensian waif around them."

"A Dickensian waif."

The smirk cracked into a smile. "Okay. That might have been an exaggeration. Definitely they think you're settling, though."

"You only met them once."

"Once was enough. And I don't hear you arguing with my assessment."

They didn't think of Jake as "settling." They didn't think of Jake at all. But Singer wasn't prepared to follow that train of thought to any of its logical conclusions. Still less to explain it to Jake.

"New topic, please. Frankie lived with us for a year and a half. How long do you think Lisa will be living in our scrapbooking room?"

"We have a *scrapbooking room*. How has Frankie never made fun of us for this?" Jake finished at the sink and walked over to sit beside Singer. "Listen, I feel a little bad. About Frankie, and generally my entire gene pool. We can tell them to hang out somewhere else. I'm pretty sure Lisa's not going to want to be around *that*. All the time."

"It's not your entire gene pool. Just … a lot of it."

"And Alice and Emery, don't forget."

"My fellow honorary Derries. They haven't made it into my mental roll call yet." Singer groaned. "Oh no. I just realized something."

"What?"

"If Lisa's staying, we need to call the social worker. She'll want to do another home visit."

Jake's face contorted. "That sucks. I keep thinking they're gonna figure out there's like no way we could be parents and reject us."

"We passed all the classes and read all the books. They already approved us."

"Yeah, but that doesn't mean we can't still mess this up somehow."

Singer pressed a hand to Jake's chest, pushing him down on the bed. Even now he watched carefully, ever wary, waiting for the pulling-back in Jake's body that had been a hallmark of their early relationship.

Not tonight. Jake stretched his arms over his head and assumed an expression that Singer found immediately suspicious.

"What?" he demanded, kneeling with legs on either side of Jake's.

"Nothing. Just waiting for you to reassure me."

"Excuse me?"

"Now you say, 'But Jake, we'll be fabulous parents!' and I say, 'You don't know that!' and you say—"

"I can't recall a single time I've used the word 'fabulous' in the last five years."

"Remember when you used to talk extra-gay?"

Singer allowed himself to fall forward, deeply pleased when Jake's arms wrapped around him. "I did not."

"You did! I remember."

"By the time we met—"

"Not when we met again, I meant in high school. I was thinking about Lisa and the cheerleaders, because Frankie always mocked them relentlessly, like to the point where we'd tease her that she secretly wanted to *be* a cheerleader because it was the only way to shut her up. And I have this memory of you, at a football game, doing that snap thing—remember? Snapping back and forth, like to make a point?"

"I did not."

Jake grinned up at him, arms still draped over his back. "I thought you were so, um, desirable. And brave."

"I wasn't, really. Not the way you mean. I just couldn't be anything other than what I was."

"Yeah. That was pretty attractive."

Singer caught his breath, trying very hard not to be visibly flustered by his boyfriend calling his much younger self "attractive." "I'm sorry I don't remember you that clearly from back then. Do you hold it against me?"

"I'm relieved. I was scared all the time. Totally not cool." Jake allowed his arms to flop back. "When I think of us having a kid I get scared all over again, except now I have backup."

"I will be your backup any day. And we're going to be great." Singer took advantage of the bedroom—and its accompanying looser physical boundaries—and kissed Jake. "You're going to be a completely amazing dad."

Jake gulped. "I'm glad one of us thinks so."

"Trust me."

"I *totally* trust you. It just feels like there should be a test, like for driving."

"Like, you'd get your parenting permit, and then when you demonstrated you knew what you were doing, you'd qualify for your license?"

"Well…yeah." Jake's left hand idly rested on Singer's arm, stroking the skin. "What if we don't know what to do?"

"I'm not too worried about it. I mean, my dad was never around, and is still basically a stranger to me, so as long as our child—or children—know that we're here for them, that we care about them, then I think everything else will work itself out."

"Huh. I guess I'm kind of the opposite. I think if I'm like my dad, I'll be okay. I'll just keep thinking, *What would*

Dad do? That's good. I can try that. I mean, if we, you know, eventually have a kid placed with us." Jake glanced up, just for a second, eyes barely meeting Singer's before sliding away again. "I used to do that with you. If I didn't know what to do in a situation, I'd think, *What would Singer do right now?* and it made it easier."

Singer kissed him. "I didn't know that."

"It's kind of silly. But I either don't stop to think before doing something, or I stop to think and then can't do anything. Like when your parents moved down south and wanted you to take over the mortgage. Remember?"

They'd stayed up half the night in his old closet-sized apartment in the Castro, drinking wine and making up lists of pros and cons, complete with mortgage calculations scribbled in the margins. "Well, that wasn't purely a financial decision."

"I know you were mostly trying to help your parents out, but still. You're so good at like ... triaging what's important, what needs to be done, and then doing it."

"Thank you. Though that's not what I meant." Singer allowed his fingers to drift along Jake's jaw, heart stuttering at Jake's convulsive swallow. "You were here. And I hadn't been sure how to bring up moving in together. So my parents deciding that retirement means creepily stalking their oldest child just kind of ... gave me a good excuse. To con you into living with me."

Jake glanced at the closed bedroom door. "I used to feel a little guilty that Lisa joining a cult was basically the best thing that ever happened to me. If she hadn't, we wouldn't have moved in together. At least, probably not for a long time. I guess I still feel crummy about it. I, uh, can't imagine being in a cult."

"Me neither." It had seemed like a joke, at first. Lisa, looking more confident about this than anything she'd ever done, unemotionally announcing at Thanksgiving dinner with Mother and Dad that she never planned to come home again, that she had a new family now, and she didn't need her old one anymore. As if it were out of a movie: she was reading her lines from a script and no one else had a copy. But—also like the movies—it had seemed pointlessly melodramatic and temporary.

Until she hadn't come home.

Jake blinked up at him. "I guess I didn't think about it that much when she was inside, but now I wonder what it was like."

"I have no idea. Mother has theories, but I'm not sure how factual they are. We'll probably never know."

"Huh."

Silence aside from the occasional car driving down the street outside, or dog barking in the distance.

Singer slid to the side and laid his head on the pillow beside Jake's. "Is it weird that I hardly ever thought about her?"

"I don't know. I guess I always thought about Carey, even when we weren't talking. Even when he was in New York. I don't know if he always thought about me, but knowing him, he probably did. He's only been back like three months, but now I think it'd be weird to go longer than a few days without seeing him."

True. The relationship he and Lisa had wasn't really comparable to the Derrie brothers, who had spent most of their lives incredibly close. They resembled each other superficially—pale skin, brown hair, brown eyes, Jake a little taller, Carey slightly broader—but it was more that they aligned in some subtle sense, clearly connected.

He and Lisa had been the negative ends of two magnets, repelling each other so completely they hardly ever crossed paths.

"Anyway." Jake settled lower in the bed. "I'm glad she's safe. Even Frankie's glad she's safe, which is saying something."

"I always wondered why Frankie hated her so much. I don't remember her bothering to hate anyone as much as she hated Lisa."

"Oh. Uh."

Jake's tone made him raise his head. "What?"

"So probably I could tell you, and it'd be fine, but do me a favor and ask her yourself. Is that okay?"

Singer blinked. "Of course. Is there— Did Lisa do something—"

"No, no. It's all Frankie. But it's, I don't know, kind of a thing. Or maybe it's not and I'm making it a big deal, but anyway, let her tell you why she hates Lisa. And I'm not sure it's hate as much as Lisa was that girl, in school, who lived like every day was her own personal *Dawson's Creek*, or something. And Frankie was Daria."

"Frankie *was* Daria. I can't believe I never made that connection before! Only her hair was very Jane."

"Oh my god, Singer, did you watch *Daria*?"

"Didn't you? Come on, Jane's brother was hot."

"Emery kind of looks like him. With the soul patch or whatever."

"And the 'I'm so hot I don't even have to try' deal he has going with his hair."

"It's shiny."

They grinned at each other.

For the most part, they kept affection locked down in the presence of other people. Jake was a little more relaxed around Frankie, who'd lived in the guesthouse for a while, but otherwise he never touched Singer if anyone else was near them. It might have felt stilted, or worrisome, if it weren't for how intense it made the moments when they were finally alone.

"You ready for bed?"

"Unless you have better ideas."

Ever since the beginning, since the first early dates after they met again seven years ago on a street corner, even before Jake was out to his family—this part had always made sense. The two of them alone in the dark, communicating through fingertips and murmurs and pleasure.

There was nowhere else in the world Singer would rather be.

1

SINGER
7 HOURS UNTIL MILES

Singer's phone rang as he was staring deeply into his empty coffee pot. Every now and then his eyes slid to the note hastily held in place with the sticker from the side of an avocado:

No coffee. My bad. Will stop on the way home. SORRY.

The **SORRY** was appropriately retraced in order to signify contrition.

Damn. The phone. He really needed his coffee.

"Hello?"

"Hi, Singer, it's Brandi Leone from Social Services. Is Jake with you?"

Everything stopped.

"He's at work."

"Rats, I was hoping he'd be there. Listen, I have a foster placement and you're the first family I'm calling, but I need a commitment from you right away. Ten-month-old African American boy named Miles, drug exposed at birth, but developmentally on target. I'm really looking for a permanent placement for him. Reunification with Mom was terminated a month ago and his recent placement had some complications, so I'm only looking at adoptive placements right now. I need an answer from you, ASAP."

All the websites, all the books talked about this. *Don't let them rush you. Don't let them pressure you.* Singer, heart pounding, forced himself to be reasonable.

Termination of reunification. "So is Mom out of the picture? There's a TPR?" Questions. Ask questions.

"Mom didn't follow through with her plan, and she's missed more visits than she's showed up for. We've still got one or two scheduled, so hopefully she'll make it." Brandi didn't sound all that hopeful, but Singer cautioned himself not to read into her tone. "It's still too soon for the Termination of Parental Rights, and I'd like to have him nice and settled well before then. I completely understand if the risk feels too high, Singer, but I need a yes or no."

Singer and Jake didn't want foster placements. They wanted an adoptive placement with a TPR on file. Singer closed his eyes.

Nine months. This was the first call in nine months for a kid less than a year old. And it had hurt to say no to the three calls they'd gotten for older kids.

"Can I have fifteen minutes?" he asked.

"Fifteen, okay. Then I start calling other families because I need a home for this kid pronto."

"I understand. I'll call you back."

"Thanks, Singer."

His "No, thank you" was lost to the *click* of the line disconnecting.

Oh my god. Oh my god, oh my god. With shaking fingers he hit Jake's number and waited. *Please pick up, come on, I know you're in the office somewhere, pick up.*

Voicemail.

He dialed again.

Ten-month-old boy. Ten months. Not talking, but maybe crawling? He'd have to look it up.

Voicemail.

No, don't look it up. Don't get attached to the idea. It's a bad call. Wait for a kid with a TPR, or at least with a permanency order. Wait for a kid who's available for adoption. Except what if one never came? What if the people who fostered those kids snapped them up the second they could?

Jesus, it wasn't like foster kids were limited-edition flatscreen televisions on Black Friday, available while supplies last, except everything in the adoption process made him feel like they were. The system was sick. Or maybe that was Singer.

If Jake were here, he'd be jittery and freaked out, but he'd probably want to go for it. If Brandi had called Jake instead of Singer, Jake would have said yes.

He tried one more time and left a fourth voicemail message. Then he dialed Brandi back.

"When?"

"This afternoon."

"We'll do it. We'll take him." Singer braced one hand on the counter and tried to breathe slowly.

"Great. I was hoping you'd say that. Now I need you to have a crib and a car seat on hand, obviously."

Brandi kept talking for a few minutes, but Singer lost track of what she was saying while he scrambled for something to write with. He ended up with a whiteboard marker and the glass carafe of the coffee maker: *crib, car seat.* What else had she said?

"Fantastic. I'll see you around four."

"Wait. Did you say there are visits scheduled?"

"One, next week. Um, Tuesday at 10 a.m. here at Social Services."

Singer added that note to the carafe. "Okay. So, what happens now?"

"Now you get ready to meet Miles. I'll see you at four."

"Okay. Thank you."

Brandi laughed. "Thank you. This is exciting!"

Click.

Singer bent all the way over and fought a wave of nausea.

Exciting. Terrifying. *Oh my god.*

He tried Jake again, left another voicemail, then contemplated taking a shower. But no. He had to actually say this to someone or it wasn't real.

He'd be thinking so much more clearly if he had coffee. He could run to the store. No. He couldn't possibly. Certainly not without showering.

He should shower. Then buy coffee. Then make coffee. And at some point in all that, surely, surely Jake would get his damn voicemail messages.

A thump somewhere in the house abruptly reminded him he wasn't actually alone. Lisa was here. And he'd have to tell her eventually, considering this would impact her, too.

Singer walked down the hall and stopped outside his sister's childhood room. They'd never been close. He knew he was her last choice of refuge. Still. She was here.

He knocked. "Lisa?"

"Singer?"

Like they were neighbors who barely knew each other.

"Yeah. Hi." Was she going to open her door? In the three weeks she'd been in the house, he'd only seen her a couple of times, when he surprised her in the kitchen, or when they had the bad timing to pass through the hallway at the same moment.

Rustling. The drag of something heavy on the ground. The doorknob turned and he could see half of her face. Not the makeup-shielded face she'd had as a teenager, before the cult. An older, longer face. No makeup, no defenses.

"Hey, so, I just got a call. It looks like our worker at Social Services found a placement for us. For Jake and me."

"A placement? Is that like a kid?"

He winced. "Sorry. Yes, a kid. A little boy. He'll be here this afternoon." *Oh my god, he'll be here this afternoon.*

"Huh." Lisa pushed her hair out of her face, eyes landing somewhere on the pictures lining the wall behind him. "Then … congratulations. That's what you wanted, right?"

"Yeah. We've been waiting for months."

"Okay. Well, good. That's … good."

Another awkward beat passed, and Singer shifted on his feet, wishing she'd at least look at him, or smile, or do something that answered the intense swirl of his own emotions.

"Yeah. It's good."

"That's cool, Singer. So, I'll see you later." She pulled back into the room, and the door slid shut. The sound of dragging furniture again. A slight thump. Then nothing.

I'm going to go crazy if someone doesn't get excited about this really fucking soon. Singer walked back to the master bedroom, already dialing Alice. In a world where the Derrie brothers were inclined to get married, Alice would be his sister-in-law.

In this world, they pretended.

"We got a call," he said when she answered.

And Alice, being Alice, jumped right in. "Oh my god. Is this happening?"

"It's happening." Relief flooded him. "I can't get Jake on the phone. I just did this whole thing by myself and I keep leaving him messages. Oh my god, Alice."

"I'm coming over. You want me to leave Care and Emery here?"

"No, bring them. And coffee. We're out."

"You're *out of coffee*? Sweet bleeding Jesus, why didn't you say something? We'll be over in a minute, and then you'll tell me *everything*."

"Nothing much to—"

Click.

Between the hanging up in his ear and the door shutting in his face, Singer was going to get a complex. Were parents allowed to get complexes about silly things? Probably not. They had to be responsible. They had to be adult. Parental.

He braced himself on the bathroom mirror and stared at his reflection. He'd apparently slept on his right side, facing Jake, judging by his hair. Also, his eyes were a little wild. He looked as freaked out as he felt. Was that a bad thing? He smoothed his hair down, but there was nothing he could do about the crazy expression in his eyes.

It took roughly ten minutes for Carey and Alice to drive from their new place. A quick shower, then. One of the advantages of being enmeshed with Derries was that you only had to deliver big news to one person, and soon everyone would know. Of course, that was the downside as well. Still, the entire network would know that he and Jake were about to be foster parents without Singer having to make another phone call.

Parents. Oh my god.

Nine months of waiting. It was as if he'd been staring at a locked door for nine months and now he'd heard the key turn, the lock disengage, but he was suddenly afraid to open the door.

He and Jake were going to be foster parents. This was happening.

Of all the days to be out of coffee.

2

FRANKIE
49 DAYS BEFORE COMING CLEAN

Frankie was just leaving the bookstore when the text came in. It was shocking enough for her to stop at the front.

Logan, anticipating her, had already found some books to shuffle beside the cash register. "You around later?"

"Apparently not." She held the phone out so he could see Carey's message: *Baby news. Hit Thurman House after work.*

"Whoa. That means Jake and Singer…?"

"You know everything I know."

"Listen, if they get a little Asian baby, can I be the kid's fake godfather? I'm just saying, I could be helpful."

She made her voice deadpan. "Because you're Chinese."

"Hey, I wouldn't be racist about it. I'd godfather a Japanese or Korean baby. Or any Asian Pacific Islander kid. Look, I'm just saying, I know from being raised by white people and there are some tricks the kid should learn." He smiled, and Frankie steeled herself against it, but they'd known each other too long, and he knew he'd gotten to her. His smile expanded in an irritating way.

"You're bugging me," she muttered.

"If you want to come over later to tell me the baby news, I'm off at six."

"I made your schedule. I know when you're off."

"I'm hearing that you memorize my schedule because you need to know when I'm available to nonsexually date you. And that is totally cool with me, FYI."

Frankie picked up the closest hardcover and threatened him with it. "Can it, bub." She glanced toward the back of the shop and called, "Izzy, I'm taking off! Fire Logan if you want, I don't care!"

"She didn't hear you," he said helpfully. "She's in the office."

"I swear to all the gods, I will fire your ass for insubordination."

"That might make our dates awkward."

"You mean *more* awkward."

"Oh, Frankie." This time he leaned over the counter. "I don't find our dates the least bit awkward. Anyway, if you want to stop by, you can."

She wanted to punch him. She also wanted to spend more evenings curled up on his couch watching anime with him. It was unsettling. "I can't believe this is my life." The book hit the top of the stack with a thud. "Shelve this. And everything else. I'm leaving."

"Bye! Remember to ask Jake if I can—"

"Totally not doing that!"

His laughter was cut off by the heavy glass door swishing shut. The thing about leaving Logan was that it always felt like an open loop. As if they should hug. Or wave. Or do … something to resolve the chord progression that always seemed to play in her mind when they were talking.

Frankie marched determinedly to her car. Screw all of it. *Stop thinking about stupid-ass Logan.*

There were more important things to think about. Like what qualified as "baby news"? Was there an actual kid? Or was this "maybe there will be a baby next month" news?

She pulled in behind Carey's car and did a mental roll call of who was likely to be inside. Only Carey's and Singer's cars, and it was just after noon. So: Singer, Carey, Alice, and probably Emery, who was kind of Alice's brother. Oh, right, and let's not forget Lisa fuckin' Thurman, emerged from the grave, or the cult, or Southern California, anyway. It was all basically the same.

Frankie headed for the door, wondering if she should have brought food. Did vague baby news have a traditional gift associated with it? Liquor, maybe? A stuffed bear holding a bottle of Xanax?

She knocked once and let herself in. "Hello? Is there a baby here right now, because I'm not changing fucking diapers!"

"No baby!" That was Carey's voice. Coming from the kitchen.

The living room looked normal enough, but when she pushed through the swinging door to the eat-in kitchen, it was clear that all hell had broken loose. The counters were covered in dishes and a seemingly random assortment of food and cleaning supplies. Every lower cabinet was standing open. She looked a little closer.

"Hey, is that door supposed to be hanging there like that?"

Singer turned from where he was affixing some sort of … plastic strap thing to the refrigerator. His normally combed hair was frizzy on one side like he'd been running his hand through it, and his eyes were wide. "If you don't have a way to fix it, your observation is useless to me."

"Whoa, nellie." She glanced at Carey, who minutely shook his head. *Don't fuck with Singer right now. Got it.* "What can I do?"

"I need Alice's help with that cabinet. She brought her toolbox. Can you—" He waved toward the rest of the house.

"Sure, I'll grab her."

"Thank you, Frankie."

She saluted.

Alice and Emery were attaching some sort of brightly colored mobile to the ceiling right in front of the window of the nursery. Alice had attained honorary Derrie status by hooking up semipermanently with Carey; Emery seemed to have … followed them all the way from New York.

"This ladder was not made for fat girls," she was mumbling as Frankie walked in. "Oh, Frankie, thank god. Will you stabilize me?"

Emery shifted the foot that was currently braced on the windowsill. "I could—"

"No, I need you right where you are, Em. Frankie has it."

"I got it." The ladder was dusty and cobwebbed; she tightened her grip. "Damn, where'd you dig this out from?"

"It was in the rafters in the garage. No black widows so far."

Frankie froze, torn between her stabilization responsibilities and jumping back.

The ladder shuddered when Alice laughed. "Shit! Sorry, no, I swear, no spiders at all. Only webs."

Emery shook his head. "You're such a jerk."

"I really am. Okay, let's finish up."

Frankie peered around the ladder to make sure no spiders were lurking. "Singer broke the kitchen, so he needs you."

"Got it. Just have to—" The drill hummed, stopped, hummed, stopped, hummed again. "There. This is *never* coming down."

"Isn't the mobile supposed to be over the crib?"

"Technically." Emery, balanced between a dresser and the sill, lifted his chin in the direction of the ceiling. "Unless you make it out of glass and live in earthquake country."

Frankie giggled. "Alice, you did not make a baby mobile out of glass." But sure enough, it wasn't just glass, but *broken* glass. Thick shards, which Alice had painted all different colors, with swirls, and designs, then mounted on a disk of wood so they'd all hang at different heights. Was it a mobile if it didn't move? Not that it mattered. Frankie was *never* having kids.

Although, considering the mobile or whatever was currently making rainbow splinters of sunlight dance across all the walls, she had to admit it was a cool idea.

"In my defense, I've never lived in earthquake country. Where I'm from, if you put something on the ceiling, it stays there."

"Unless it falls," Emery added.

Alice revved her drill at him. "Honey, when I install something, you better believe it doesn't fall. I'll leave you guys to clean up while I go fight crime and home improvement failures elsewhere."

"You're the sweetest!" he called after her, before offering a shrug to Frankie. "Sorry."

"No worries. I mean, better to be in here than out there, anyway. Singer's on a hair trigger. Where the hell is Jakey?"

"On his way home from work."

"Huh. I'll get the floor if you want to get everything else."

"Sounds good."

Emery was uncomfortably good-looking. From his perfectly mussed black hair to his body to his overall demeanor. He had dimples. And he never seemed fazed by anything. Not even Derries.

She steadied the dustpan to finish sweeping the bits of drywall on the ground. "Does anything ever surprise you?"

"Surprise me?"

"Yeah, you know. You hang out, but you never seem all that shocked by anything. Most people who spend time with us get a little green around the gills."

Emery huffed a laugh. "You guys don't scare me. And I don't know. I can't remember the last time I was really surprised by something."

"What about the tattoo parlor? Don't people shock you?"

"Never. Probably when I'm there longer and get more interesting jobs. Right now it's mostly drunk college kids who want Chinese calligraphy they don't understand."

"You ever give them the wrong word as a joke?"

Another laugh. "I respect the ink more than that. But I've definitely been tempted." He brushed his hands over the trash can. "What do you think? Clean enough for a kid?"

"Hey, you're asking the wrong person. I don't know anything about kids."

"Alice and I used to watch my neighbor's kids a lot, but I still get confused about which age is doing what. Singer said ten months, so I think we're good."

"Take your word for it."

They carried the garbage can, broom, and dustpan out to the kitchen, where things were still chaotic but Alice appeared to be taking over. In the bustle Frankie heard her phone ding a notification.

Logan. *Baby or no baby?*

No baby, she sent back.

Carey looked up. "Whoever that is, tell them to pick up coffee. We were supposed to but got distracted, and all Singer has is instant."

"Instant *isn't* coffee." Another ding.

Looking forward to being a godfather. I could be an Asian godfather to any kid, you know. The kid doesn't have to be Asian...

She bit back a smile. *You are not the kid's godfather. Get over it.*

"Who is it? Are they bringing coffee?"

Frankie focused on her cousin, feeling vaguely guilty. "No one. And no."

His eyes sharpened. Hell.

Before he could ask, she retreated—or, no, fled. She fled to the bathroom, turned her phone to silent, and stayed there until conversations in the kitchen had time to roll in directions other than hers.

Carey knew Logan. He didn't remember him from school, but he knew him now, as Frankie's coworker. Everyone knew Logan. It wasn't incriminating that Logan had texted, or that she texted back. They were friends; friends texted each other.

Damn Logan for making everything weird.

She emerged into the hallway and stood there for a minute, listening for signs it was safe to return to the kitchen. More whirling drill noises, Emery's voice, then Singer's. It was probably fine, but she hesitated.

Thurman House wasn't all that sentimental. There were formal graduation pictures, one for Singer, one for Lisa, in the living room. And a family portrait taken when they were both early teens, maybe. But every other picture in the house was right here, in the hallway.

It was like a timeline of their perfect lives, tracing from Lisa's birth on one end, through Singer's, and then their various sports and activities, family shots at the holidays, all the way until sometime in middle high school when the Thurman elders had either stopped taking pictures or at least stopped framing and hanging them.

Singer had done plays all through high school, always starring as a quirky side character. In the sparse later-years section of the wall Frankie found only two pictures of Singer's biggest extracurricular, one of which she remembered because it had been in the program (*Our Town? Annie Get Your Gun?*). The other was Singer and Lisa in the lobby of the theater, standing beside one another, he still in his costume.

Each of them was slightly turned away, like they'd been pulled together at random, not like they were brother and sister. But the smiles on their faces were identical.

Frankie shivered. The past was creepy as shit. She listened for a minute, trying to hear any proof that Lisa was alive, but if she made noise it wasn't enough to rise above Thurman House's current level of aural chaos.

The brightness of the kitchen was a relief. "Singer, what's up with your sister?"

"Hmm?"

"Your sister, you know, the madwoman in the scrapbooking room?"

He shot her a look. "Do you have a point?"

"Well, yeah." She cleared a spot of counter and hopped up, almost toppling a domino line of spray bottles with brightly colored fluids inside. "Does she ever come out of her cave?"

Singer glanced back toward the hall and shook his head. "I think she waits until Jake and I are out of the house. I haven't really seen her that much."

Ha. That got Carey's attention, though Alice and Emery were still staying out of it. Like amateurs.

"She's been back for weeks." Care raised an eyebrow. "You haven't seen her at all?"

"I saw her earlier today, when I told her about—about the baby. But not as a general rule, no. She stays in her room." Singer tried to sound defiant at the end there, but Frankie wasn't fooled. He felt guilty. She could spot that one a mile away.

Totally not her goal. She could tweak Singer's guilt some other day. Time to slightly redirect the conversation. "I didn't like the old version, but the new one's kind of freaking me out."

Carey got to his feet, brushing down the knees of his jeans. "Three years is a long time to be in one place. And then to be completely cut off from it. I'm sure there's some kind of culture shock thing there."

She poked him. "Is that what it felt like moving home after New York?"

"Probably more like how it felt to move to New York when I was eighteen. Everything was a little surreal, like I was living someone else's life." His hands spread. "Then again, Lisa came back here. That's gotta be even more disorienting. All right, Singer. Cabinets are done. What's next?"

Frankie paid half-hearted attention to the plans for the rest of the day, though it was hard to stop thinking of those identical perfect smiles in the pictures on the wall. Who was Lisa Thurman under all that bullshit? Did she even know?

It was so sick and wrong, feeling sorry for Lisa Thurman. Frankie resented the hell out of it.

3

SINGER
3 HOURS UNTIL MILES

The text came while Singer was washing bottles. Dozens of bottles, it felt like. All different types.

Cathy and Joe had gone shopping. When Singer started hyperventilating, staring at everything they'd bought, Joe had gently steered him toward the kitchen.

A somewhat hysterical part of his mind had registered that this was not the first time Joe had steered a panicking member of his family toward the kitchen. Singer was going to have to draw the line if his de facto father-in-law started preheating the oven or searching for cupcake tins, but he hadn't.

"Coffee fixes everything that parenting unravels," he'd said, shaking coffee grounds into the filter. Then he'd glanced over, with a small smile. "And anything coffee doesn't fix, wine does. Words to live by."

"I'll keep it in mind."

That's when the first load of bottles—unwrapped by the living room contingent—made its way to the kitchen. Alice offered to wash, but Singer had declined, grateful for something to do.

He still had a full sink of brightly colored kid dishes, utensils, and bottles left, but he looked at his phone when it chimed anyway.

I'm in our bedroom. DON'T TELL ANYONE. Also: hi. I'm in our bed.

Singer rinsed his hands, glanced toward the living room, decided they could all take care of themselves, and slipped through the back door to the hallway, past the bathroom, past Lisa's room and the nursery.

The lump on the bed, fully under the covers, had to be Jake.

"Are you hiding?" Singer inquired, trying not to smile.

"How are you *not* hiding? Oh my god, what is happening?" A dark patch of hair emerged, followed by only the topmost quarter of Jake's face, eyes wide. "I'm freaking out. Is that okay? Do you have time for me to lose my shit?"

"I think I can pencil you in." Singer contemplated the bed, and the fact that they had company. A lot of company. Then he locked the door and pulled off his trousers. "You snuck in the back?"

"I parked down the street and crept through the hedges. That's, uh, more hot than neurotic, right? Imagining me going all James Bond?"

"Definitely." The bed was welcoming in direct proportion to how risqué it was to slide under the sheets in broad daylight with a house full of Derries. Singer shifted closer, tugging Jake against him.

Jake buried his face against Singer's shoulder. "I'm sorry I took so long. I got caught up in trying to make sure everything was ready for me to be gone for eight weeks, and I had to sign those papers— Wait, you should have papers. Did you need us to drive into the city? We might not have time—"

"They sent me a PDF. Jake—"

"And then I realized eight weeks is a really long time, but it's also a really short time, like it can't possibly be long enough to bond with—with a baby—a kid—is ten months a baby or a kid? And then I started thinking about, like, spending *all day* with him, like what will we do?" Jake's much-beloved face, creased in worry, turned up toward Singer's from where he was lying on his pillow, pouring all of his fears out to the ceiling. "Do you feel ready?"

Singer leaned down for a kiss. "Your dad says coffee and wine fix everything."

"Ha. Which one do I drink right now?"

"Neither. I have some ideas for right now." In a move he wouldn't have dared anywhere else in the world, Singer extended his hand to cup Jake's cheek. "I don't think we can be ready. I'm already overwhelmed and the baby isn't even here yet, but I think that's probably how all parents feel."

"Really? I kind of can't breathe."

Singer smiled. "I know. I wish you'd seen your dad hauling all that junk into the house. He looked like the world's most bashful Santa Claus."

"God, they're overbearing."

"Yes. But now we have bottles, and dishes, and we're to call the second Miles gets here because 'there's a range of diaper sizes for a healthy baby' and your mom needs more information." His imitation of Cathy's tone got a reluctant smile out of Jake.

"I just can't believe this is happening. Does it feel real to you?"

Singer, allowing his hand to linger on the warm skin of Jake's cheek, shook his head. "Entirely surreal, I think. Like I'll wake up and it will all be a dream, except I wouldn't have imagined Alice making a crib mobile out of glass shards."

Jake's mouth dropped open. "She did not."

"It's actually beautiful." Singer kissed his boyfriend in their bed, behind a locked door in a house full of people. "You'll see. I don't think it will be easy, but I think we're up for the challenge." Each time Jake's confidence had faltered over the years, Singer's had more than made up for it. They were intelligent, capable men, and even if they didn't have a great deal of experience with babies, they should be able to manage.

"I'm glad one of us has it together." Jake took a deep breath. "But we don't have to go out there, right? I'm on the 'avoid Cathy and Joe at all costs' plan at the moment."

"Your parents have been nothing but helpful."

"That's what they want you to believe! It's not helpful, it's codependent, Singer. Don't let the Derries suck you in!"

The phrase hit both of them simultaneously, and they muffled laughter against their pillows.

Singer made his voice low and seductive. "There's only one Derrie I want sucking me in, Jacob …"

"Oh my god!" Jake laughed and blushed and tumbled Singer over. "You're not serious, though, right? Because actually I think that would be a really good idea, except for the fact that my parents and brother and Alice and Frankie are all out in the living room right now, but I'm sort of worried maybe this will be our last chance to have sex ever, so on the other hand—" He broke off when Singer kissed him again. "You're not worried about that?"

"I'm not worried about that."

"Okay, then. Good." Jake leaned his forehead against Singer's chest. "Sometimes I get so scared."

The perfect opening to wrap arms around him, hold him close. "I have you," Singer murmured.

"Thank god for that."

Something crashed in another part of the house, followed almost immediately by shattering glass. Both of them winced.

Frankie could be heard distantly. "It wasn't me! It *was not*, Carey, you jerk!"

Jake sighed. "God. How bad would it be if we just kept hiding?"

"No one even knows you're here. But I should probably go out and see what broke."

"I'm not sending you out there alone. What kind of man would I be if I did that?"

They traded smiles.

"Plus, any opportunity to fuck with Frankie should not be turned down." A quick kiss before Jake levered himself out of bed. "Our story is that I parachuted into the backyard. Got it?"

"You're afraid of heights."

Jake rolled his eyes. "Yeah, because *that's* the flaw in that story. If anyone asks, I took some really good antianxiety meds, and *then* I parachuted into the backyard."

"Your mom will want to know which meds." Singer ran his hands through his hair, sighting across the room to the mirror. "Carey will probably want to know if your company has skydiving as a perk, or if it's simply another mode of transportation, like the company car."

With a tremendous sigh, Jake paused, one hand on the doorknob. "Fine. We'll tell them I donned an invisibility cloak and walked right through the front door."

"That's much more believable."

They squared their shoulders and went to face the family.

4

SINGER
MILES.

Miles's arrival was somewhat anticlimactic.

"He is so ready for his bottle." Brandi was young and white, with an air of tarnished good intentions about her. Right now she just looked tired, shoving a bag into Singer's hands. "Okay, who's taking him?"

They both froze. Then Jake, without a bag, shrugged. "I guess I am."

Miles had tears in his eyes but wasn't actively crying. Apparently, it had been a rough drive. Jake settled him somewhat awkwardly against one shoulder, bouncing him a little.

At least one of them had, at some point, been around a baby.

"If you give him a bottle, he'll go right to sleep. Here." She handed over a canister of formula. "This one's open, but there's another in the bag. Do you have bottles?"

Thank god for Cathy. "In the kitchen," Singer said. (All freshly sanitized and arranged in some kind of bottle organizing contraption Cathy and Joe had bought, which took up a significant chunk of counter space.)

"Good. Okay, then." Brandi tweaked Miles's nose, but he dodged away, leaning into Jake instead.

Jake's eyes widened fractionally.

"Singer, you're my victim. Here." Brandi passed him a pen. "Let's do paperwork."

He thought he'd done paperwork before, and he had. Astounding amounts of paperwork. Applications, reports, questionnaires. But Brandi had brought with her a heretofore unexamined treasure trove of paperwork. An entire ream, it seemed.

"Do, uh, I have to sign all that, too?" Jake shifted on his feet, jiggling Miles in some kind of dance designed to either make both of them more comfortable or possibly just to do something that wasn't standing there still.

"Nope. Only need one."

Page after page, some with cute names—a health passport?—most boring. Singer's hand wasn't exactly cramping by the end, but his signature was less and less namelike.

"Perfect. All right, then. Any questions for me before I go?"

Any questions? Singer almost blanked out, but rallied. "We'll need to know more about his parents, Brandi. This isn't exactly how we pictured it."

"Well, like we always say, anything can happen."

"Can you tell us more about his family?" Miles. Miles's family. Miles, who'd gone from being a name in his ear this morning to a child—an actual human child—in Jake's arms tonight.

"Not much more than I've already told you. Dad wants nothing to do with anything baby. Mom's struggling. He was drug-exposed in utero, but so far he's developmentally solid. Mom hasn't followed through with her reunification plan, and Grandma's not able to provide a safe environment for a growing boy."

"Wait, there's a grandma?"

"That's where he's been until today, isn't it Miles? You and Nana, hanging out."

Singer blinked at Jake. This was the nightmare. Relative placements always took higher priority than nonrelative placements.

"Can I ask why he's not with her now?"

"You can ask, but there's not much I can tell you. Suffice it to say that Grandma's got some medical issues—nonhereditary, from an accident a few years ago—that keep her from being able to look after Miles."

"But she wants to? His grandma wants to keep him?" *Did we just steal a baby from his grandmother?*

"In a perfect world, sure. But in this one, there are a lot of complications." Brandi contemplated for a second, then shrugged. "There's some kind of back thing, and it affects her mobility. Some days she can barely leave her bed, other days she looks fine. I can't actually share more with you than that, but the important thing is that it's not genetic."

Really? That's the takeaway here? His grandmother has medical problems so serious you're taking him from her, but we should just be happy she can't pass them down to him?

She tweaked Miles's nose again, and this time he smiled at her. "There's the kid. Sorry about the drive, pal. I know it's been a long day. Listen, why don't I leave so you guys can get settled? And I'll try to get Mom to confirm the next visit so you don't drive all the way out to Richmond for nothing. Good-bye, Miles. You'll like Jake and Singer, they're pretty cool."

Small talk, nose tweaking, promises to call in the morning.

And then it was the two of them. With Miles. Who was somehow being entrusted to their care.

"Oh god. I screwed this up." Singer shook his head. "I'm so sorry, I did everything we swore we wouldn't do."

"You didn't screw anything up. Come on, look at this face. This is not the face of a screw-up."

Which was true. Miles had big cheeks and all-seeing eyes.

"Sorry, Miles," Singer said. "I didn't mean you. Obviously. Jake, should I have said no?"

"Nope. You should have said yes, and you did, and here we are."

God, he was so certain. Was this how Singer had sounded over the last year since starting the paperwork? Certain of the process, in total faith that it would work out for them?

Jake shifted Miles to the other arm. "Man, I don't know what I expected, but you're heavy, Miles. Also, your hair is tickling my neck." He glanced up, banishing Singer's fears with the openness on his face. "So, um, do you know how to make formula? Because I really don't."

"Remind me why we asked your mom to stay home?"

"This would be so much worse if she was here. Um." Jake blinked at Miles, who was looking at him with placid acceptance. "Shouldn't he be crying?"

"I don't know, but I guess we should, you know, make a bottle, in case he starts." Good. A plan. "There are directions on the can, I think, and I know you aren't supposed to do it in the microwave, but Alice said we just have to be careful, or use room-temp water." Singer realized he was in danger of babbling again. "Oh my god, Jake, this is happening. For real. Right now."

"Is it? Because it doesn't feel real. Like, at all. So you think they'll have another huge stack of paperwork like that if we end up adopting him?"

"I'm pretty sure I just signed away our lives. Maybe our souls. And—yeah, probably."

They smiled at the same time.

"Shit, okay, I'm totally freaking out." Jake leaned in for a slightly awkward kiss around Miles. "Holy crap. Uh. You want to hold him?"

"No. I mean yes, but no, he's happy with you right now, so we might as well leave him." *What if I drop him? What if he cries when I touch him?* "I can make a bottle, though. I watched a YouTube video."

"You did not."

"I really did. More than one, actually."

Jake laughed. "God. I love you. Okay, demonstrate your bottle-making skills for me, then."

"It just got weird to me that someone trusts us with a baby." A real baby, not the idea of a baby, a vague baby-concept in the future. But an actual flesh and blood child, staring at the side of Jake's face with concentration.

"Ha. Do you want me to give you the lecture on how straight fertile people don't have home studies or have to fill out forms or write essays to get their kids? What are you always saying? We've been vetted way more than most people."

"I guess so. But it's still weird to me that someone thinks we could look like parents."

Jake carefully shifted Miles to his other arm, while Miles, dark brown skin, owl eyes, short curly hair, switched to watching Singer's hands. "Yeah, I definitely don't look like a parent right now."

"Oh, I don't know. You've got a baby in your arms. You look parent-like."

"*You're* making a *bottle*. That's totally parent-like."

"I'm making a bottle. Wow." Formula scooped in. Water to the line. Shake. "Oh damn. I think I was supposed to stir, not shake."

"Why does it matter?"

"Um. Gas, I think? Something about air in the formula and if he drinks it he'll get gas?" Singer looked over at Miles. He was dressed in a pale green onesie with a pair of brown sweat pants pulled up over his diaper. "Oh god. Diapers. We have to find out what size he wears and call Cathy."

"Why don't we just go to the store?"

They stared at each other. Then both of them looked at Miles.

"Call Mom," Jake said. "I'm still scared of the car seat."

"Will you find out what size he wears? Is that how you say it? 'What size he wears'?"

"I think maybe there's something in this bag ..."

Jake investigated diapers, Singer possibly overtested the formula's temperature (his arm was dripping, but at least he was certain it wouldn't burn Miles), and Miles *watched*. Singer thought babies were supposed to be in constant motion, but Miles was a still, silent spectator in Jake's arms, while everything went on around him.

Cathy and Joe promised to be over with diapers in the appropriate size in a little while, so they sat down on the sofa. With Miles. And a bottle.

"Um. So I guess I ... stick it in his mouth?"

"I guess so."

Jake picked up the bottle, but before he'd gotten it halfway to Miles, chunky baby fists had grabbed it and slammed it home. Jake laughed. "Oh my god, Miles. Hungry?"

Hungry and exhausted. Miles's eyes were rolling back in his head after only a quarter of the bottle.

Neither of them spoke. They watched him fall asleep, fingers still tensing and relaxing on the side of the bottle, eyelashes fluttering. Singer could hardly breathe.

A baby. Not their baby, no, but at least temporarily in their care. Their responsibility. Theirs to watch fall asleep just like this.

"Oh my god," Jake whispered. "That was—"

"Yeah."

Time must have passed, though Singer didn't notice it. Cathy and Joe arrived. He let them in quietly and stepped aside so they could make a beeline for Jake and Miles.

"Oh, look at him." Cathy, clearly itching to give Miles a full exam, kept her distance, only reaching out once to touch his feet. "I love baby socks. Joe, look."

"I know. I can't believe our kids are old enough to have kids."

"More than old enough." She glanced at Singer. "Everything okay?"

"We navigated making a bottle. That's pretty much all we've done so far."

"Change his diaper when he wakes up."

"What do we— I mean— What time should we put him to bed?" Singer floundered.

"Yeah, Mom. He's ten months old. We don't even know what that means."

"It means you cut food very small before you give it to him and watch him like a hawk. Do you know if he's crawling at all?"

They shook their heads.

"You'll learn. You'll learn all of it. I gestated two of them, and there's not a book in the world that can tell you how to parent, boys. Learn as you go." She kissed Jake's forehead, then Singer's cheek. Then she leaned down to kiss Miles's forehead too. "I can't wait to meet you, kiddo."

Cathy had tears in her eyes. Joe reached for her hand.

"Don't cry in front of the boys," he whispered. "We're supposed to be pretending it's all easy, Cath."

"Right, I forgot. Wouldn't want anyone to know the truth." She offered a slightly watery laugh. "Sorry, I'm trying not to plan too far into the future, and I know it's complicated, but you two have to understand that you just made us grandparents." This time she shook her head. "Anyway, we only came to drop off diapers. Call us if you need *anything* else."

Jake smiled up at them. "Don't you guys have jobs?"

"Hush. I will walk out of the ER in the middle of my shift if you so much as need a box of Kleenex."

"Liar," Joe said. "But she's right. We'll bring food over tomorrow in case you don't want to leave the house. And we'll tell everyone else to leave you guys alone."

Alone. Such a strange concept, applied to the three of them. Alone together. Alone together with Lisa silently living in her cave down the hall.

Singer tried to pull himself back into the room. "Thank you so much."

"Don't be silly. Call for anything."

"Cath, they know."

"Doesn't hurt to remind them."

He walked them out. When he came back in, Jake was maneuvering to stand up.

"What're you doing?"

"I thought— Shouldn't I put him down? Do you think?"

"Oh. In his crib?"

"Yeah, but Singer, I don't get how to do that. Do you think my arms are long enough? How do I not drop him?"

They slowly walked to the room they'd made over. It had been Singer's growing up, then an impersonal guest room, and now was an impersonal guest room with a crib and a dresser and Alice's painted-glass mobile, which splintered little patches of colored light all over the walls.

"But." Singer studied the angles, and the high side of the crib. "But it must be doable. People put sleeping babies into cribs all the time."

"Um. How?"

"I have no idea."

"Maybe it's easier if they're smaller?"

Sorely tempted to call Cathy, or Alice, Singer pulled himself together. Self-sufficiency, dammit. "Okay. We can do this. No, you know what? It's not even nighttime yet. This is a nap. What if we put him on a blanket on the floor?"

Miles sniffled, and Jake urgently bounced him until he settled again.

"My heart's pounding," he whispered.

"This is highly stressful. Blanket?"

"Yeah. I might be able to do that."

Singer spread out the quilt Alice had given them, folding it in half to make it a little thicker over the carpet. He stepped back.

"I'm so fucking scared," Jake said. "And I don't know why. If he wakes up, he wakes up. That's okay, right?"

"What if he cries?"

"Singer, you're supposed to say yes, of course it's all right."

"Of course it's all right. But seriously, don't wake him up, he might cry."

Jake huffed a laugh and knelt down, slowly lowering his arms and trying to keep Miles cradled in closely. "Fuck, fuck, fuck, fuck," he whispered.

"That's a very original lullaby."

"Shh."

Watching Jake put Miles down was like watching him try to diffuse a bomb. People did this multiple times a day? How did all parents not have bleeding ulcers?

After an extraction Singer held his breath for, Jake sat back. "I'm exhausted. Do we get naps, too?"

"I think we actually do, at least for a while." Singer turned to the baby monitor helpfully unpacked by their earlier guests. "I guess we should set this up?"

"Yeah."

With a minimum of beeps and feedback (Singer made a mental note to never turn it on while the receiver was next to it again), they managed to back out of the room secure in the idea that if Miles woke up, they'd hear him.

"Bedroom?" Jake whispered.

Singer nodded and followed him in.

"I can't believe we're doing this. Is it too soon to say 'dad'? It's too soon, right?"

"It feels too soon." *Dad.* The enormity of it washed over Singer, leaving him shaky. "Oh my god, Jake."

"I know." Jake lay back on their bed. "Oh my fucking god, we have a kid." He waved. "You know, for however long. We have a kid. But I don't know, Singer. He just, like, fell asleep. In my arms. I'm pretty sure Will once puked down my shirt when he was a baby, but that wasn't really a bonding experience."

Singer smiled and sat beside him. "But Miles falling asleep in your arms was?"

"Oh yeah. Man. I could seriously watch him sleep. You, uh, think I'm making this stuff up because I want it to be true?"

"I don't think you can make that up. You feel what you feel."

"Do you feel it? I mean, not like it has to be the same. Obviously it won't be the same. Never mind. Sorry. I know we read all the books but I totally wasn't prepared to feel this way."

I was. And I don't. But all that would come, in time. That's what the books said. Singer forced his mind away from needlessly worrying and stretched out, letting his arm touch Jake's. "What do you think we do with him when he wakes up?"

"I don't know. Take him around the house? Introduce him to Lisa? Hey, did you call your parents?"

"No. I will, in a few days. But right now I don't want to hear their indifference, you know?"

"If only. Indifferent parents isn't actually a topic I can relate to." Jake turned his hand over, letting his fingers play with Singer's. "Do you remember when we first started talking about this?"

"How could I forget? I think I blacked out from shock."

"Shut up. Though I do remember all the blood draining from your face like I just proposed we have sex in the middle of the Folsom Street Fair." He leaned up, bringing both of their hands to Singer's chest. "I thought you figured I was too big a mess to have kids with."

"I never thought that. Ever."

"Singer, come on. I was totally a mess."

Singer brushed hair back from Jake's face and tried to remember him younger, earnestly talking about children, as if coming out to his family had opened all the doors to the future and he wanted to walk through every one of them. "You weren't a mess. You were … it was more like you'd never let yourself hope for things to be good. And then you did."

"Yeah. Well, because of you."

"Jake—"

"We're lying here right now because you asked me out." Jake nodded to the wall they shared with the guest room. "We have a foster son in the next room because you didn't give up on me. That's all I'm saying." He leaned down. The kiss was brief, but Jake kept his face pressed against Singer's, cheek-to-cheek.

Singer's fingers drifted across Jake's neck. "I love you."

"Oh god, I love you so much. Thank you. For believing in me."

"Always."

A sound over the monitor. A gurgle. A something. Both of them sat upright.

"Oh shit, what do we do?"

Miles seemed to go back to sleep. They flopped down again.

"You know…" Jake rolled to lie on top of him. "I'm feeling exhilarated suddenly."

"You're really worried we're never going to have sex again, aren't you?"

"Shut up. I can be, um, amorous just because." As if to prove it, Jake kissed him again. "But yeah, a little. The books talk about that. People lose their connection. I don't want us to lose our connection."

Singer tugged him down. "We won't."

They didn't have sex. They made out and gazed at each other and kept their clothes on. When Miles eventually woke up, Jake went to him and Singer assembled diaper things. They fumbled through their first diaper change, laughing, and when Jake picked Miles up again, Singer let him.

He told himself he'd have time to hold Miles later, even though the truth was that since Miles arrived, he'd felt far more shaky than expected. Singer had assumed the confidence that had carried them through until this moment would … keep them afloat. But he found himself strangely insecure instead. They'd read about this sort of thing, so it would undoubtedly pass. Singer just hadn't thought it would happen to him.

Despite his sudden uncertainty, there was still something arresting about seeing Jake with a baby in his arms. Something completely and totally *right*.

5

LISA
29 DAYS SINCE LEAVING GRACE

The snakes were spinning, spooling, twisting. Lisa woke up with her legs trapped in the sheets, seconds away from screaming.

You're safe. You're in the house with Singer.

She was safe with Singer. And a glance reassured her that the side table was still firmly up against the door.

The snakes. She forgot about the snakes.

Lisa scrambled out of the bed and shook out the sheet, the blanket, the light coverlet.

No snakes. Right. It was a dream.

She peered at the phone Mother and Dad had bought for her. Half past two a.m. Saturday morning. At the farm she'd still be asleep right now. She should at least be able to sleep here, where no chores awaited her, where no voices called to her. No one watching everything she did.

Sleep, in a bed, in a room of her own, with walls, a door that closed against outsiders. No hope for a warm body nearby, but no fear of one, either. No dread of exclusion.

Lisa tried to go back to bed, but it was almost impossible. It wanted to be a den of snakes now. She could feel the snakes, even though she could see they weren't there.

Definitely not a good sign.

After an indeterminate amount of time—she was sweating now, stiff as a board, trembling with the chill of cool air on sweaty skin—she got back up.

Her hoodie felt right on her shoulders, hood pulled tight over her head. Yes. This was good. If she were back home—no, not home, back at the farm—she'd pull this on first thing in the morning, every morning. There was always moisture in the air that close to the coast.

For a vivid, horrible moment, she missed it. The coast. Smelling the air in the morning, dawn breaking over fields they worked with their hands. She tried to kill that feeling with every ounce of her energy. No one forced her out; she chose to leave. She couldn't miss it. Missing it was the worst betrayal.

Lisa had hated gardening before she went to the farm. But she'd been terrible at recruiting on the streets, and by the time she was given farm duty, it was a relief.

"Just be yourself," Anthony Grace had said, touching her cheek. "You're so beautiful you glow, Lisa. Be yourself and that's what will convince them that they want to join us." He hadn't known Lisa didn't exist. That she was a false front. That all her life she'd painted over herself to be whatever other people needed her to be, and now she was nothing at all.

She looked at her phone again, but it was too early to catch the street teams on Twitter. That had been the last time she used a phone so much it felt normal in her hands. Once she'd started working at the farm, she'd turned her phone over to whoever took her place. Of course it hadn't been *her* phone. The way her clothes became communal clothes. Sometimes she'd look down and realize she wasn't wearing a single thing she'd arrived with. Or she'd look over at Abigail and realize she was wearing an entire outfit of Lisa.

It had been a soft joke between them. A silent one. On a bad day they'd switch clothes completely.

There had been bad days. She could remember that now. For so long she'd told herself she just needed more practice finding the good. But no. Some days had been bad.

Even pulling the blinds all the way up didn't let any light in. Not close enough to dawn yet.

The bed still wanted to be snakes, so Lisa sat in the chair instead.

She'd gone through every inch of the room when she first arrived, every bit of paper, every sticker, every unused stamp, every blank scrapbook. Mother had intended to chronicle *something* in this room, but Lisa had no idea what. She'd found a box of snapshots high up in the closet, pictures from when she and Singer were young—probably rejects from the hallway—but they were still in their little drugstore envelopes, with the negatives stuck insecurely in the front.

Lisa looked at the pictures, searching for the moment she'd transformed from a child into a pretty picture of the popular girl. Mother had dressed her up, starting when she was a baby. Perfect little dresses, perfect little bonnets and bows. Like a doll.

She shivered and pulled her knees up to her chest. Still too early to see them on Twitter, but she booted up the ancient laptop anyway. She'd found it in the bottom drawer of the desk and still couldn't imagine what Mother was doing with a hidden computer. Nothing important or she would have brought it with her to Southern California.

Maybe it was just old, replaced by something new, but still functional.

Slow. She took deep, steady breaths, waiting for Windows to stabilize enough so she could open a browser.

The farm was not a cult. At least, she'd been sure it wasn't a cult when she first left. You couldn't leave a cult, right? She knew she could leave the farm. All she had to do was walk away.

Mother had taken her to three "specialists" in five days, men who wanted to talk about "deprogramming" her like she had an operating system malfunction, like she only needed to be rebooted and everything would be fine. But Lisa had never been fine in the first place. The character she'd played in high school had disintegrated when she landed in college, and then she'd floated, trying to find her true self underneath the tatters of all that pretending. She'd thought Anthony held the key to who she was. It took a while to realize that he made everyone feel that way, as if even a smile from him was enough to make them real.

Now she was nothing at all. Not the popular girl, not the glowing girl, warm in Anthony's gaze.

Singer remembered the popular girl. So did his boyfriend, and the rest of them. The Derries. They remembered her as the Lisa who blew kisses to her basketball coach and dated boys on the football team. That was the Lisa she'd been, but that Lisa had died years ago.

Died. Dead. Blown away on a slight breeze, insubstantial and featherlight, leaving nothing behind but a husk.

Time for another search. They always turned up the same things, but as long as she wasn't asleep, she might as well do this.

She typed "praise for anthony grace" into the search engine and waited for the ancient computer to load results.

Very few people named their pasts. The same six hits came up again, and Lisa clicked on the four relevant ones.

She hadn't known any of these people. In the three years she'd spent on the farm, she'd seen two people leave. She'd turned her back like everyone else as they walked down the long road, never dreaming she'd do the same. She'd pitied both of them.

At least neither of them had a blog.

Still, she found four, four faceless people online who talked about recovering from their time with Anthony Grace as if he was a disease they'd had for a while, then been cured of. As if their recovery had been long and hard, but eventually complete.

Lisa wanted desperately to be cured. To no longer wake up twisted in her snakes, or worse, consumed with desire. So much worse.

"I can still smell his skin. The way I used to salivate for it. Crave him. I'm so ashamed I needed him that much. I can't tell anyone, not even my therapist, how deeply I needed him, how I thought I'd starve without his smiles."

Lisa shuddered and skimmed down. Yeah, this was the part she wanted. The author, who called herself Xfamily, talked about getting a job, how hard it was at first, how she didn't want to leave her house. How she stayed in bed all day because it was the only place that felt safe. Lisa lost herself in reading more stories, and it didn't matter how ugly they were. She was ugly, too.

Down the hall the baby started to cry, jolting her out of a daze. Not quite asleep, not quite awake. It was such an anomalous sound Lisa thought for a minute Singer and Jake were watching a movie about babies. A very loud movie about babies.

The door to Mother and Dad's room—now Singer and his boyfriend's room—opened. The door to Singer's room—now the baby's—opened. Low murmurs. Probably both of them. They both got up most of the time.

For a stunning, absurd moment, Lisa imagined herself standing, shifting the side table away from the door, turning the knob, stepping out. She would go to the doorway, ask if they needed anything. The farm had a few younger kids, a few babies. She'd been saying she hated kids her whole life; it had been weird to realize she didn't. They were fun, in a limited way. Also, they were fun in an unlimited way, when they got older and could run around. Lisa's shifts childminding had been some of her favorites.

She hadn't seen Singer's baby. She'd been hiding. He'd knocked once to tell her a baby was coming, and again to apologize in advance for any crying.

So like Singer to apologize in advance, a little bit wryly, as if he were offering a stock apology and they both knew she would offer a stock acceptance.

Lisa's stomach grumbled. She'd snuck out late on the night the baby showed up to make some sandwiches—four, maybe?—and she still had a quarter of a sandwich left, which meant she'd eaten three and three-quarters sandwiches over the last five days. That definitely fell under the header Not Good. She couldn't go out now. Not with Singer and/or Jake and/or the baby awake.

She kept promising herself she wasn't going to do this anymore. But she checked the time, and the street teams would be on the move, which meant they'd be on the phones. She unwrapped the quarter sandwich and opened Twitter in her browser.

Carefully, very carefully, she typed "#praiseforanthonygrace" into the search bar.

Just after four a.m. the hits started coming, and she refreshed, and refreshed, and refreshed. Everyone was there. Talking to each other. All three teams were getting ready to hit the streets, one in Santa Monica, one in Pasadena. Her old team was in Long Beach.

@rm_pfag: Gonna be a gorgeous day in LB. #praiseforanthonygrace

@ap_pfag: @rm_pfag Light seen in darkness transcends sight. #praiseforanthonygrace

@rm_pfag: @ap_pfag Also, the weather report calls for sunshine. #praiseforanthonygrace

@dd_pfag: Levity has no place in worship, @rm_pfag @ap_pfag #praiseforanthonygrace

Despite herself, Lisa smiled. She could hear their voices. Ray's wry, Angel's willing to be drawn into the joke, Di's severe. She kept the search tab open and added a new search, typing quickly. #fail_pfag

@rm_pfag: The weather really does call for sun. #fail_pfag

@ap_pfag: Stop making me laugh, she's staring right at me. #fail_pfag

If she refreshed again, they would be gone, deleted as quickly as they appeared, leaving no trace. (Of course they left a trace—on Twitter's servers, if nowhere else—but the system had not yet failed the youngest members of the family, the ones who knew the secret, irreverent hashtag, the one you deleted a careful thirty seconds after you'd used it.)

Alone in a room far north, Lisa realized she was crying. A cult? But that implied, what, poisoned Kool-Aid and locked doors? There was no Kool-Aid. There were moments of joy and laughter. And when she'd finally decided to go, no one stopped her. No one spoke to her. No one met her eyes at all. They turned their backs as she walked the long gravel road through the farm, holding nothing in her hands, carrying nothing with her but grief, thick and cloying on her skin.

She hadn't turned back, no matter how much it hurt. Most of them stopped long before they reached the gate and the roads beyond, stopped and came home, begged forgiveness, made amends. But Lisa's two legs, strong after all the field work, in shoes worn from walking the streets searching for believers—or those who wanted to believe— kept going until she was outside the gate, on the main road, past the scattered ranch-style homes, as the lot sizes got smaller and smaller until she was inside the city limits.

It was like that old kids' movie, the one with the alien on the bike. *Lisa phone home.* She'd called Dad's cell phone collect. She hadn't even known collect calls still existed. And he accepted the charges.

Lisa wiped her tears and crumpled up the plastic wrap. She hoped Singer would take his new family out somewhere today. She needed to stock up on supplies. A glance at the bed confirmed that, in near-morning light, it no longer wanted to be snakes.

She curled into her pillows, twisted the sheets around her neck, and fell asleep.

*

Eleven a.m. More people were in the house. Lisa lay in bed with her eyes closed, listening to their voices. The baby gathered "ooh"s and "ahh"s, and she wondered what he thought of it all. Did he really want a bunch of strangers staring at him making noises? Probably not. Though he didn't seem to cry, so that was good.

Unless he was numb. Lisa ran through her body seeking numb spots. Sometimes she … lost parts. She'd be lying there, flat on her back, and suddenly she no longer had a chest. Or an arm. Sometimes she lost the length of one thigh, or a large patch of her right shoulder. Numbed out, nerves silent, no longer reporting for duty.

When she concentrated very hard she could feel herself fading. She pictured her body flickering, the numbest parts blinking out. She knew she couldn't actually become invisible, but sometimes it seemed like it might be worth a try.

The realness of this feeling—this flickering—started to feel more like a weight. She forced herself to get out of bed.

Car doors slammed outside. No engines started. She peeked around the edge of her window (far too obvious to pull the shades now), and yes, they were outside. With …Jake's parents? Was that his brother? Hard to tell them apart from far away. And there was a stroller. Taking a walk?

The baby was black. That was surprising. The brother holding the little black baby was probably Jake, and Singer was dabbing something on the baby's face. Oh, ha, the baby wasn't a fan of that. Singer jumped back, but Jake laughed.

God, it was weird to see Singer like that. Part of this huge group of people. He looked even more out of place than his little black baby in a sea of white faces.

Yes. Taking a walk. Okay. Lisa waited until they'd moved beyond the hedges, mentally planning her attack. She'd make six sandwiches this time. And look for fruit. She needed bananas. Bananas would stay good for a few days. Apples would work alone, though if she had her own peanut butter to keep in her room, that would be better.

Singer probably didn't randomly have extra jars of peanut butter living in his cabinets, but she'd look. That'd be the last thing she did, after making and storing her sandwiches, and trying to track down some fruit that didn't need the refrigerator. Then she'd turn to the pantry in the hopes of finding doubles. She could eat beans out of the cans, as long as they had pull tabs. Add "spare can opener" to the list of things she'd forage for.

One more check out the front window. No one.

She had to be fast.

Lisa shifted the side table out of the way and opened the door. Bathroom? No. Food first. The bathroom was right across the hall and slightly easier to use when there were people in the house. And she was hungry.

Straight to the kitchen, then. Coffee. She could smell coffee. Coffee would wreck her body after this long, but suddenly she wanted it even more than a sandwich.

There were people in the house.

"We haven't met. I'm Alice." The woman in her kitchen—tall, fat, with hair like Shirley Temple—held out her hand. When Lisa didn't take it, she made it into a wave. "You want coffee? Also, this is Emery."

Dear god, the man on the other side of the butcher block island was hot. Shiny dark hair cut to his jaw, a little messy, blue eyes, dimples, little soul patch beneath his lip. These people were definitely not Derries.

Emery held up a hand. "Hey. Good to meet you."

She should probably say something now. She didn't.

Alice opened one of the cabinets. "Let me get you coffee. It's the least we can do for being here. But seriously, have you ever taken a walk with Cathy and Joe? They're hikers. I have some hope they won't take the stroller too far off-trail, but I couldn't wrangle a commitment out of them, so I decided to save myself and stay here. This fat girl don't hike." As she spoke, she poured. Then she set the mug on the counter near Lisa, but didn't make her take it.

She had an accent. But it felt shifty. East Coast, definitely, though Lisa couldn't get more specific.

"Shouldn't we be building something?" The guy's voice was also underlain with an accent, a little grit between his consonants. "I thought that's the excuse you gave Mama Bear?"

"We'll build in a few minutes. Though I think building a plastic playhouse for a kid who can't even crawl is doing too much."

Lisa reached for the coffee. The mug was wonderfully hot, too hot, but she gripped it in both hands, trying to suck the heat all the way into her bones.

Steam misted her skin. Coffee. An addictive substance, so no one drank it on the farm. The emphasis on clean living was one of the things she'd been so drawn to in the beginning. Sweet Angel talking about how she'd never felt as high on drugs as she did breathing fresh air and eating homegrown food. Abigail, holding up a squash like she'd conjured it, grinning, more excited to harvest vegetables than Lisa had ever been on Christmas morning.

The first sip scalded her tongue and burned down her throat. Lisa's eyes watered, so she closed them and took another sip.

"I knew what I was getting into when I moved out here," Emery was saying.

"That doesn't mean you should let him take advantage of you."

"Don't be dramatic. He's giving me lousy shifts because I'm the new guy."

"You should be doing a lot more than inking butterflies on drunk college girls, Em."

"When you want to do the back piece, babe, you let me know."

"Soon, I hope. I'd rather not be living off my man and spending my savings on tattoos."

"Please, your man loves my work. I bet if I asked, he'd buy it for you."

"*Do not* ask Carey to buy my ink, Emery. I will knock your ass flat so fast—"

"Okay, okay."

Their voices misted her like the steam, absorbing through her skin without any conscious effort. The coffee was too bitter and yet it tasted miraculous. She hadn't missed coffee, not really, but standing in Mother's kitchen feeling hungover from bad sleep, it felt like time had folded. She was her old self and her new self and the farm had never existed. Maybe she was just here for a visit, to see the new baby. She wouldn't want to hike either, so she'd stay back with the fat woman whose name she'd already forgotten, and Emery of the glossy black hair.

She wanted to touch his hair. The thought invaded, twisted, sinking into her guts.

Praise for Anthony Grace. Anthony. With his wild Jesus locks and his mischievous eyes that were always a little sharper than Lisa expected them to be. Anthony was love, love was Anthony, but Anthony (like God) was always watching.

What was she doing standing here drinking coffee? They could be back any minute. All those people, filling the spaces, their voices far too loud.

Lisa, hands shaking, set the mug back on the counter and turned to get out her bread.

Six sandwiches. Three bananas taken from a six-banana bunch. Would they mind? No. Singer had offered her food. What else? No secondary jar of peanut butter, but she did find a crummy old can opener. If she brought beans to the bedroom, she'd also need a spoon. Eating them cold didn't sound terrible, but it didn't sound good. And what would she do with the liquid? She could rinse them in the bathroom, but that was almost as tricky as coming out to the kitchen to do it.

"There's leftover soup and cupcakes in the fridge."

It took a full minute for Lisa to realize the woman was talking to her. She turned just enough to look up. "What?"

"Leftovers. Soup, cupcakes, maybe lasagna. If there's lasagna, you should have some. Cathy picked it up from Genova's." The woman crossed the room, never coming too close, and checked in the refrigerator. "God, Lisa, let me reheat this for you. It'll only take a minute. Do you eat meat?"

Lasagna? Lisa's mouth watered. "Yes."

"I'm cutting you some. Give me like two minutes in the microwave. You keep doing what you're doing."

She hadn't even thought about how she might look to them, with her twelve slices of bread, her production line of peanut butter and jelly. Lisa hastily wrapped everything up and took it back to the bedroom, adding two apples at the last minute. Apples weren't her favorite food, but they were better than nothing.

She contemplated hiding. But the microwave went off and drew her back to the kitchen (after a check out the window; still no one in sight).

And the smell. The melted cheese, the sauce, the meat.

"Here. Try it. If you don't want it, Emery will eat it. Won't you, Em?"

"It's not Mrs. Murphy's, but it's good."

"Here, here. No lasagna can be as good as Mrs. Murphy's. I think because she poured all of her passion and suffering into making it." The plate, too, was placed on the counter.

Lisa wished she remembered the woman's name. "Thank you."

"No problem. You want anything to drink? Heavy cream, maybe?"

"Alice, quit it." Emery sighed. "I love how you'll gut anyone who polices your body, but you feel free to police everyone else's."

"What? Listen, not everyone can be as healthily round as myself, but I'm saying I can see bones."

"Excuse Alice. She has no manners."

"I have tons of manners."

Alice was the woman's name. And Emery's dimples drew Lisa's attention like headlights on a dark night. She focused on her lasagna.

Anthony never had to warn them about lust for other men, because the women all tried to outdo one another's devotion to him. There had been no question that they all wanted him. At least, almost all. She fought a sudden memory of Abigail's eyes, imploring her to please take her place, and please, *please*, don't tell anyone. Anthony had never seemed to notice who arrived, and maybe she should have made more of that at the time. Were they all inter-changeable to him?

Stop it. Eat your lasagna and stop thinking about him.

The reheating was spotty, still cold in some places, fiery hot in others. It didn't matter. Lisa devoured the lasagna, mixing the flavors in her mouth, trying to chew it until it had no structure so she could better taste it. They'd had good, clean food at the farm, but they hadn't had anything indulgent.

This lasagna, with its stringy melted cheeses, its intense-ly delicious tomato sauce, was indulgent. No one needed to eat like this, but oh god, Lisa couldn't stop herself. No flickers, no numbness; food this heavy tied her to the world.

In the background Emery and Alice continued to argue about Emery's job, their voices a pleasant static soundtrack.

As Lisa was scraping the last of the cheese off her plate she heard a low bell sound.

"And that's Care. Fair warning, Lisa, the hikers are re-turning."

That was to her address. Oh, right. The hikers. The people. Singer's people.

She moved to wash the plate, but the woman, Alice, waved her off.

"Oh, let me. I'm the one shoving food at you. I guess you aren't coming out for fireworks tonight?"

"Fireworks?"

"Fourth of July." When Lisa shook her head, Alice laughed. "Yeah, didn't think so. Singer and Jake and Miles are supposed to pick us up at seven, so you'll have the place to yourself for a while, at least."

She could shower. She might even be able to shower without thinking someone had been in her room while she was gone. But how could this strange woman know she was desperate to be alone? Telepathy wasn't real, was it?

Lisa, suddenly overwhelmed, mumbled, "Thanks again," and got back to her room before the front door opened.

Her heart didn't stop pounding until the side table was once more pushed up against the door and the blinds were pulled all the way down and tightened until almost no light got through.

The bed looked safe, like the absolute only place in the world she could be. She tumbled into it, a little too warm in her hoodie after the lasagna, and curled into a ball.

No snakes. No ropes. No niggling feelings she couldn't explain. It felt good to be full. She couldn't remember the last time she'd felt sated, and she wanted to keep the feeling as long as she could, wrapping her arms around her legs like she could hold it inside.

6

SINGER
8 DAYS WITH MILES

Miles's mom did not show up for the visit. His grand-mother did, instead.

"You don't have to go through with it." Brandi's fore-head was creased in irritation, aging her at least five years. "I should have known Mom wasn't gonna show. She does this every time. Anyway, you only have to have visits with Mom, not Grandma."

"But his grandmother is here?" Singer looked at Jake, who was batting Miles's hand away from his nose.

"Yes, but like I said, you only *have* to let him visit with Mom, since that was our agreement." She glanced at her watch. "I need the room in twenty minutes, so …"

Jake just slightly raised his eyebrows. They had driven all the way to Richmond. And Miles looked cute and not covered in food yet.

"Miles can see his grandmother," Singer said. Jake's smile was all he needed to know they agreed.

"Well, then." Brandi didn't exactly flip her hair, but Singer felt it was implied. "Follow me."

They waited, standing in the small room (two-seater sofa, upholstered in some kind of plastic; cheap round table; three mismatched chairs).

"I'm nervous." Jake shifted Miles to his other arm.

"I'm sweating through my clothes. You can't smell me, can you?"

"No, Singer——"

Brandi reentered, followed by a short, slightly stooped woman with skin every bit as dark as Miles's. Singer had expected an old woman, but Marie couldn't have been older than midforties. Younger than either his or Jake's parents.

"Jake, Singer, this is Marie, Miles's grandmother. Marie, Jake and Singer. I need the room back in fifteen minutes." Without waiting to see how the introduction went over, or to acknowledge the enormity of it ("This is half of your potential son's biological family"), she was gone.

"Good to meet you," Jake said awkwardly, trying to hold out a hand. At that moment Miles dove, and Jake pulled back to catch him right as Marie was reaching out.

Singer winced.

"Sorry," Jake murmured.

"Give that baby to me. You come see your nana, boy." She made an air sound with her teeth. "Which one are you?"

"I'm Jake. This is Singer." They'd agreed, before they ever started the process, to never refer to each other with any of those dreadful nonspecific terms people used: lover, partner, significant other. Even though they could choose to get married now, those words still felt like cheap imitations of "husband."

"Huh." Which was all the response they got. Miles began to whimper, and Marie shushed him, turning away, bouncing him and speaking quietly. She went to the small sofa and took a seat, turning him so he faced her.

Singer thought he could see stiffness in the way she moved, but he might simply have seen what he expected to see. And they could hardly ask, *So, exactly how debilitated are you? How likely is it you'll spontaneously recover and want Miles back?*

It felt wrong to be standing there. Intrusive. Unwelcome. Singer frowned, and Jake offered the barest hint of a shrug. What else could they do? Miles put his head down on his grandmother's shoulder and sighed, as if he was smelling her, soothed by her.

He had never put his head down on Singer's shoulder like that, but it had only been eight days. It wouldn't even be healthy attachment if he felt that comforted yet. He'd known his grandmother his entire life. Could he really smell her? Probably. They—someone scientific, Singer forgot who—said scent was the strongest human sense, and the one most tied in to memory.

"His mama's a real chatterbox." Marie's hand rubbed up and down his back, occasionally pausing to pull his onesie straight again. "Last time she came for him she never stopped talking. Probably hurt his ears, listening to her go on and on like that."

"He's been, uh, trying to crawl, some," Jake offered.

"I know that," Marie snapped. Her jaw tightened, and when she spoke again, she was clearly making an effort to control her tone. "She never wanted to put him down, either. I told her he needed to strengthen his muscles, but did she listen? Huh. Does she ever?"

The last question was directed down at Miles, who now watched his grandmother's face with intensity, one hand waving around, the other winding in her sweater.

Jake swallowed and tried again. "My mom—she's an ER nurse—says he's right on target. She said most people pressure babies into crawling and walking too soon, anyway."

"Hm." Marie's tone was tense and tight. "So you two trying to take him for good?"

"We'd like to adopt him." Jake shot Singer a look. Before Miles, it had all been Singer's area: he'd filled out the forms, made the phone calls, set the appointments. But now he was tongue-tied, vocal cords paralyzed.

"He has *family*. You're not his family." She bent her head, pressing her face against Miles, eyes shut hard.

To see your grandchild, your blood, and know you couldn't keep him—it must be like someone giving you visitation for a limb, how unnatural. Like you weren't whole without it.

Singer bit down on his lip and Jake moved closer, their hands brushing, neither saying a word.

Brandi showed up in the doorway a few minutes later, sticking her head in.

"Almost ready to wrap it up?"

"I want to take my grandson home." Marie looked up at Brandi with her face set once again in an angry, desperate glare.

Neither of them moved, but Singer could feel his heart start racing like the one and only time he'd tried ecstasy and the world tumbled over and over again until it was unrecognizable, all the edges blurred, all the colors too loud.

"Marie, we've been over this. I can't place him with you again. It's not gonna happen."

"My health is improving."

"We tried, Marie, but it's too much for your back. Between the bed rest and the meds, you know you can't be hauling him around all over the place. And look at this boy, he's only getting bigger, aren't you, Miles?"

"We could try it again," Marie said, and the urgency in her voice turned Singer cold. What did he think? That they'd adopt a kid whose family waved cheerfully as they drove away?

"This visit is over. You have Regina contact me, Marie. You know I'm supposed to make sure she's here when she says she'll be here." Brandi glanced at her ever-present watch. "Miles is going home with Jake and Singer. He's safe with them."

"They're not his *family*." Marie held Miles a little tighter.

"I know." Brandi's voice softened, and she came into the room, standing right inside the door. "I know you wish you could take him, and god knows I wish I could place him with you, but this is what we got, Marie. Let Miles go home. Then you get his mom to call me to set up the next visit, okay?"

"None of this is okay. It can't be right, taking a baby from his family, giving him to strangers." She kissed Miles, and her tears fell on his head. "You be good, boy, you hear me? You listen to your nana and be a good boy."

Jake stepped forward, like a pale ogre, stealing away Miles from his grandmother's arms, and they followed Brandi back out of the maze of rooms and cubicles.

"You won't need to deal with her once the adoption is finalized," Brandi assured them in an undertone as they reached the door. "I'm sure she won't try to get visitation. Regina wants Miles to go to a good, stable home. Marie knows she can't provide that for him, she's just having trouble accepting it."

God, it was all so *casual*. And what did *I'm sure she won't try to get visitation* mean?

"Sorry about how hectic it was today." She opened the door and called, "I'll be in touch."

And then, just like that, the visit was over.

"I'm gonna cry," Jake murmured. "That was awful."

"Do you get the feeling what she tells us and what she tells Marie are very different things?"

"He's falling asleep. Maybe he'll sleep in the car." Jake looked over, troubled. "Singer…are we doing the right thing?"

Singer unlocked the doors and didn't answer right away, stowing the diaper bag while Jake plugged Miles into his seat. But the extra time to think didn't help much. Was there even a "right thing" here? Maybe Marie couldn't take care of Miles by herself, but was this the best the system could do? Take him away? Hand him over to two white men with money, who could send him to the best schools and love him like their own, but who could never replace his grandmother? *You won't have to deal with her after the adoption.* How many children disappeared into wonderful homes after assurances just like that one? If this was the "right thing" to do, Singer only knew it made him feel ill.

"That was awful," he finally agreed. "It must get better from here. Right?"

"God, I hope so. We need coffee."

"We really do. Drive-through?"

"Add shots all around."

Singer put the car in gear and pointed them in the direction of caffeine and clear-headedness, trying to forget the way Marie's voice broke when she said, *You aren't his family.* What if they never were? Or worse, what if Jake and Miles became a family, and he was forever on the outside, looking in?

7

FRANKIE
40 DAYS UNTIL COMING CLEAN

Frankie had lived in the guesthouse out back for almost two years. She'd seen Jake and Singer in every permutation of their relationship, from harmony to what passed for a raging fight. Singer went dark when he was upset; Jake removed himself before he could say things he didn't mean. She thought she'd seen every flavor of their occasional angst, but this was new.

In the past it was usually Jake who went off the deep end and had to be reeled back in. But this time? This time Singer was the one she watched, waiting for him to do or say something that would clarify what the fuck was happening. Because something was up, and even though she couldn't point to any specifics, she could feel it.

Aunt Cathy had dropped off more cupcakes, Alice had brought over more lasagna—which Frankie was currently availing herself of—and Carey and Jake were now sitting with Miles on the floor, where he was delighting in an avocado. He seemed under the impression that avocado was an artistic medium instead of a food, and Frankie didn't like kids much, but Miles squeezing avocado between his fingers was pretty hilarious.

Singer wasn't laughing. He was washing dishes. When he was done with the stuff in the sink, he went to the refrigerator and found a few more dishes he could clean, scraping old leftovers into the trash.

Yeah, no, this wasn't even gonna fly. Frankie finished off her lasagna and dutifully carried her plate to the sink.

He reached for it. "I'll get that."

She held it a little too far away. "Not until you tell me what the fuck is wrong with you right now."

"What are you talking about? Nothing's wrong." He stretched farther and took the plate out of her hand.

"You're a fucking bad liar, Singer."

"I'm not lying."

She backed against the counter so she could shamelessly stare at his face, waiting for some hint. He avoided looking at her, but he was out of dishes again. Laughter erupted from the avocado section of the kitchen, and Singer's jaw tightened.

What the hell? For real.

She nudged him and kept her voice low. "Something's up with you. I can always tell."

"Nothing is up with me. Are you especially bored for some reason?" Now he looked over. "How's the new apartment?"

"Well, it's not *boring*. It's a fucking nightmare. Every second I spend there fills me with rage. My roommates are meatheads, and I'm pretty sure they only accepted my application to move in because they thought they'd score with me." Her body tensed in anticipatory disgust, but she thought she hid it all right. "Anyway, my shoddy living situation aside, is there anything I can do to help?"

"Help with what?"

"Fine. Pretend nothing's up. Even though something is."

He relented, shaking his head. "Nothing's up, I swear. Everything's good. Obviously."

Lies. All lies. But maybe he was lying to himself instead of her. Which was worse.

Alice started slicing another piece of lasagna. "I'm offering Lisa food while it's still hot."

All heads in the kitchen (except Miles's) turned to her.

She raised her eyebrows. "What?"

"You're"—Frankie paused for effect—"going to knock on her door?"

"Yeah. Why are all of you acting like she's a leper? The only thing she eats is peanut butter and jelly sandwiches. The girl could use some lasagna."

Singer brought a plate over. "That's very nice of you, Alice. Thank you."

"I'm not doing it for you. Though I guess you're welcome." She glanced at Carey and Jake. "What is it with you guys? What am I missing about her that makes everyone so content to pretend she doesn't exist?"

Jake refocused on Miles, but Care shrugged. "I don't think it's that we're pretending she doesn't exist. It's more like—when I knew Lisa, before, she was not someone who seemed to need help. Or maybe she always did, I don't know. Either way, she wouldn't have welcomed it."

"Well, she doesn't have to welcome lasagna, but I'm offering it anyway."

"I'm so gonna watch this." Frankie grabbed a bottle of water. "I mean, I'll bring her some water."

"Frances—"

But she ignored Singer and followed Alice to the hall of perfectly framed memories.

Alice knocked; after a brief sound of something heavy being dragged across the floor (she and Alice traded a look), Lisa cracked the door.

"I know you like this lasagna." Alice held out the plate.

"But … isn't it old, by now?"

"Hon, no. This is leftovers from the dinner you didn't come out for last night."

Lisa seemed to contemplate that for a long moment, while Alice didn't quite wave food around right in front of her face. Slowly, as if against her will, Lisa opened the door enough to fit the plate through. "Oh. Um. I don't—" She took the plate. "It does smell good."

"It's bliss, babe. Enjoy. And Frankie brought water."

Oh, right. "Uh, yeah, here, Lisa. The lasagna's kinda … hot." In other words: *I totally didn't follow Alice in order to gawk at you, because that'd be rude.*

"Thanks."

They stood there, a tableau of awkward silence, good intentions, and Frankie's insatiable curiosity.

"The leftovers will be in the fridge," Alice said. "You should eat more. Anyway, have a good day, Lisa."

"Oh. Um. You too." Lisa withdrew, a turtle pulling back into her shell, and Alice pushed Frankie in the direction of the kitchen.

Frankie jumped up on the counter. "Whew. Damn. Lisa is … damn."

"She's what?" Carey asked.

"Nothing. I mean, she's …" The dark hallway, the dark silhouette of Lisa in the slim space she'd cracked her door open, the sound of her voice when she said, *It does smell good.* As if she meant to say no, but didn't. "I think she's so sad. I don't know."

"Well, obviously." Alice rolled her eyes. "Does that really surprise you? Wouldn't you be sad if you were her?"

"I just didn't know Lisa Thurman had a 'sad' setting, that's all." Frankie glanced at Singer, who was frowning. "Anyway, it's cupcake o'clock. Should we have told her there were cupcakes?"

"She'll find them if she goes looking for more lasagna."

No one said anything for a long moment. Jake cleared his throat. "Are we going for a walk?"

Alice nodded. "Sounds good to me."

Singer went into action, grabbing a pastel, baby-soft cloth, getting it wet, wiping Miles down.

Not saying anything. That was the weird thing. He did all that and everyone talked around him, but Singer said nothing.

Frankie decided she was gonna keep tabs on old Singer, and followed the rest of them out the door.

8

SINGER
10 DAYS WITH MILES

Denial was a strange, slippery companion.

An hour might pass during which everything seemed fine. The weight of Miles in Singer's arms seemed right. His babbling, while not resolving into words, nonetheless seemed like a dialogue.

Then something would happen. Something small and insignificant. Singer would fumble resnapping the onesie after a diaper change. Or he'd attempt a jar of food, and Miles would delight in rejecting it.

All normal, he kept telling himself. Perfectly appropriate. He was new to parenting; Miles was ten months old. No part of this was mysterious, or ominous. Everything was just fine.

Right up until Jake walked into the room and … did not fumble. When Miles spit food out at Jake, Jake made him laugh and shoved it back in his mouth. How did he know to do that? They'd read all the same books. They'd visited the same websites, often together, taking pleasure in the process of discovering the ways they wanted to parent. They'd relished even the trickier conversations (Jake was adamantly against raising children in the church; Singer thought finding a church might not be a bad thing).

All of it had felt like a way to build up to this moment, when they actually had a foster child. When they could begin to practice all the things they'd only read about. But despite having invested so much time in building, brick by brick, their ideas of themselves as parents, somehow none of that mattered. Singer's confidence, shaky to begin with, eroded steadily. He didn't mean to hand Miles off each time he cried, but Jake soothed him so much faster.

Of course it would take time. He knew that. Mostly. But each day came with reminders that his learning curve was Sisyphean, while Jake's was an anthill.

*

Singer escaped to his car with ignoble relief and drove down the street before pulling over until his hands stopped shaking.

He had to stop in at work. And when he said *had to* he should probably revise that to *volunteered to*. Eagerly. Each of them had eight weeks of family leave from their jobs, followed by half-time with work-from-home flexibility built in "for as long as you need it, up to six months"—wonderful, progressive policies they'd been thankful for when they'd made all the arrangements months ago, to be put into effect when they got a placement.

He'd had no idea that driving to the office would seem like an oasis. Or that he'd feel so inescapably trapped at home.

The previous days ran through his mind like an unrelenting film reel of his personal failures as he drove into the city. He dreaded being the one closest to Miles when he needed something, dreaded that moment when Miles

74

would lean all of his weight Jake-ward, holding his arms out, willing to topple out of Singer's grip as long as it meant Jake picking him up.

No one's fault, of course. Maybe it was as simple as that first moment, when Brandi handed him to Jake while Singer signed the papers. Or maybe it was Jake's comfort with children. Maybe Miles sensed he was safer with Jake, that Jake understood how to take care of him better than Singer did.

It was later than usual, and he had to park a few blocks away from work. It was good to walk. To breathe. To be outside.

To be alone.

"You coming in today? Singer?"

He'd walked past the side door to the office building, all the way to the corner where everyone smoked.

Not everyone right now. Only Victor. Of all people, Victor, the straight Republican Christian. The only person Singer knew from normal life who'd adopted kids from foster care.

If there was such thing as signs, this was undeniably a sign. Singer's chest constricted with restrained emotion. "Sorry," he said, to the entirely wrong person.

Victor waved a hand, smoke trailing from the cigarette. "I was just going to get coffee. You want some?"

"I should go up ..." To more responsibilities, more expectations.

Victor took a long pull on his cigarette and held the smoke in, a gesture Singer was far more accustomed to seeing while smoking other things. But no, it was clearly a normal cigarette.

A Pigpen-like cloud marked the movement of Victor's head as he looked up in the direction of the office windows. "You'll go up and they'll all crowd around, demand pictures, ask you if it's the greatest thing that's ever happened, if you're a different person. They'll mean *better* person, but they won't say it." He glanced over again and stubbed his cigarette out on the sole of his shoe. "I almost asked Jerry for your phone number the other day."

It might have been the most Victor had ever said to him in the three years they'd worked together.

"Is all the paperwork in place yet, or … not?"

Singer sighed. "Not. Maternal grandmother was his first placement, and we only have some vague thing about medical reasons why she can't keep him."

"Risky." But it didn't sound like disapproval the way Victor said it. Acknowledgment, maybe.

"I swore—we both swore—we wouldn't go forward, but—"

"I know. I remember. That's how it was with Rachel. We were so desperate, it felt like if we said no, they'd never call again. Let's get coffee, Singer." Then he started walking.

Singer glanced up at the windows one last time before he followed.

"Ten months is a great age," Victor said, once they'd settled into a spot at the counter. "Is he crawling? Ty, our youngest, had a little trouble crawling because he hadn't used his muscles much. Rache was the opposite—she'd been left to her own devices and was close to walking by ten months."

"He's squirming. Jake's mother is a nurse, so as long as she doesn't look worried, I don't worry."

"That's good. Worry is anathema to good parenting, I think."

Maybe that was Singer's problem. While he wasn't worried about Miles crawling, he was definitely *worried*, in general.

"Jake's family is nearby? I know Jerry and Meredith were saying your parents are in Southern California."

"Jake's entire extended family with few exceptions live within ten minutes of us." Singer realized belatedly that it might sound … bitter. Or like a complaint. "They've actually been wonderful."

Victor offered a dubious eyebrow raise but didn't speak.

"It really has been nice." It sounded weak, even though he meant it. Sure it had been nice. For distraction, if nothing else. By now Jake must know that, in this area, regardless of Singer's many other offerings, he was a complete dud.

A dud for a dad. Oh, god. It was a clear indicator of his distress that his brain was forming bad plays on words.

"So, scale of one to ten, how freaked out are you right now?"

The question jolted his focus. "Um, a six? Well, seven. Maybe." *Closer to nine.*

Victor nodded. "That might be your new calm, Singer."

"For how long?" *God, no. No.*

"Oh, depends on how it all happens." Victor's fingers twitched, like he wished they were holding a lit cigarette. "We got burned once, before Rache. So with her, we were panicked for, I don't know, three years maybe, thinking someone would take her from us. Until the paperwork was signed and sealed and the judge congratulated us, and for another six, maybe nine months after that. Dull panic can be a hard habit to break."

That was a warning. Probably a good one. Singer nodded.

"We should get back."

"I haven't even made it to the office yet."

"If you have pictures, get them ready now."

He had pictures. Lots of pictures. Miles with Jake, Miles with Frankie, Miles with Alice and Carey, Miles with Cathy and Joe, Miles with various other Derries, Miles with Jake, Miles with Jake, Miles with Jake. Singer could click pictures with his phone all day long and call it fatherhood.

Right before they stepped into the stairwell, Victor stopped. "Listen, get my phone number before you leave. Call if you need anything, Singer. Even when you're surrounded by people, this process can make you feel pretty isolated."

Isolated. The word careened around in his skull until he nodded, shaking it loose. "Thank you."

"Of course."

Everything Victor said came true. They gathered and cooed and asked what felt like more-personal-than-casual questions, though he was surely being oversensitive. After years working in the same big room, hadn't they earned personal? He assured everyone that Jake's phone had dozens of pictures of him with Miles.

It didn't.

*

He'd received two voicemail messages from Dad and seven from Mother. He hadn't mentioned Miles. The vast hollowness of their reaction to the news that he and Jake were planning to adopt—in contrast to the near-intervention Cathy and Joe had staged in their living room, with cupcakes, followed a day later by more cupcakes and expressions of total support, with previously stated reservations held in check—made telling them about Miles difficult.

And, if he was being honest, it didn't feel real yet. Why invite the horrible sucking sensation of parental ambivalence if it didn't even feel like the truth?

Mother called again, when he was almost home. He pulled over to talk to her. Anything to put off the inevitable moment when he'd have to muster a smile and pretend everything was just fine. And Mother was the perfect practice.

"Your sister won't answer her phone, Singer. Are you certain she's all right?"

"She got out of a cult a little over a month ago. I'm certain she's not all right, Mother, but I'm not sure what I can do about it."

"Are you *trying*? Do you even talk to her?" The low mumble behind her was censure from Dad, but she brushed it off and persisted. "I mean, it's like you kids are completely unreachable!"

"We're living in the house, Mother. How unreachable can we really be?" He bit his tongue, sparking just enough pain to distract him from the rant he wanted to launch into. "I'm sorry. I'm not sleeping much. Lisa's safe, Mother. I'm not sure what else you want from her."

"I want her to be like she used to be!"

Conceited, obnoxious, self-obsessed. "She was there for three years. I think it's going to take more than a month for her to ... move on."

"Maybe I should come up there, Singer. You shouldn't be responsible for your sister—"

"I'm not, Mother. She's responsible for herself. You have to give her time."

"You sound just like your father!"

Singer rubbed his eyes. "I'm sorry she won't talk to you, but there's nothing you can do about it. I'll mention your concern to her when I see her." *If she ever leaves her room.* "I have to go now, Mother."

"Fine. Good-bye, Singer."

"Bye, Mother."

A sharp pulse began to beat at Singer's temple. Home. Go home. Kiss Jake. Smile at Miles. He wasn't sure what to do about Lisa, but at least he knew he could smile and nod at everyone else. And that was going to have to be good enough.

9

LISA
37 DAYS SINCE LEAVING GRACE

In the dream Anthony was looking at her and his mouth was moving, but it wasn't his voice she heard. It wasn't a voice at all. It was a dull thumping sound, perfectly in sync with his lips opening, like a fish.

He was trying to say something, and she could tell he was getting frustrated that she didn't understand, but she couldn't, they weren't even words, they were just sounds, noises, thumps, thuds, knocks—knocks—

Knocking. On her door. She opened her eyes and there was no Anthony, only scrapbooking and the laptop, ever-open, on the desk.

And knocking. Don't forget knocking.

She heaved the side table out of the way, and it must have been audible because the knocking stopped.

Lisa cracked the door, still rubbing her eyes. What time was it? She had no idea.

The boyfriend. Jake. And the little black baby.

"Sorry, can I come in?" His voice was barely a whisper, with a harsh edge.

No, no, no. She was already moving over so he could step inside, but when he closed the door she slid all the way back to the desk and folded her arms so they'd stop shaking.

"We gotta get out of here." The baby made a sound, and Jake glanced over his shoulder at the closed door. She had a weird vision, suddenly, of that Princess Leia projection where she was kneeling to talk into R2-D2 and looked back over her shoulder like she was being chased. "Lisa?"

"Sorry. What?"

"Your mom is here." He bounced the kid a little. "Singer thought you might want to be—somewhere else."

"My mom? Mother?"

"Is sitting in the kitchen with a cup of coffee. And Singer."

She frowned, still trying to process.

"Listen, he told her you were at the store and said to get you out of here. But we can go hang out, if you'd rather—"

"Mother is *here*? In the house?" This made no sense.

Jake rolled his eyes. "Oh my god, the two of you. Yeah, she's not an apparition, she's really here. But if we're gonna make a break for it, we should probably go now. I don't know how long he can hold her back."

Mother. The days after leaving the farm came back to her in sudden flashes of specialists and shopping trips designed to make her the girl she'd been before. That had been Mother's idea of returning her to factory settings.

"Lisa—"

It was weird to be this close to one of the Derries.

"What should we do?"

Jake blinked. "We're gonna run. You guys have, like, no sense of drama. You and me and Miles are gonna sneak out through the master bedroom and drive somewhere.

Anywhere. The grocery store, the library, I don't care. Wherever you want."

Sneak out? "We're going to hide?"

"See, now you're catching on. But faster. Get dressed and meet me in the bedroom. And try not to make noise; Singer's pretending we're already gone."

Gone. Out. The grocery store. The library.

Lisa's stomach knotted. "I'm not sure——"

"Or we go in and have coffee with your mom."

The knot twisted. "I'll be ready in five minutes."

Jake grinned. The baby—Miles?—waved a hand at her. "Aw, look, Aunt Lisa's gonna be a refugee with us, Miles. We'll meet you by the back door in five."

"Okay."

Jake snuck very quietly back out again, and she pulled on jeans and her hoodie before stuffing everything she owned into her backpack and hefting it to her shoulders.

For years she'd considered sneaking out of her childhood home an art form, but she'd definitely never done it by going through Mother and Dad's room. She closed the door, wincing at the little *snap* it made, and turned to find Jake trying to do everything one-handed while still bouncing the baby.

"Can I help?"

"It's just that you have to take, like, everything, in case you might need it. Here, can you grab him for a sec? Miles, this is Lisa. You're pretty chill about new people, so let's hope today——" As he started the transfer, Miles kind of squawked. "Dude, work with me here. No?"

"It's okay. Tell me what else you need."

"I don't know. Maybe shove everything else into the diaper bag and we'll call it good."

She packed the bag fast, then swung it— Or, okay, maybe it weighed twenty pounds. "God, Jake."

"I know. I only have an unopened can of formula back here. And there's two water bottles at the bottom. Sorry."

Sounds, out in the hallway. Both of them froze and looked over.

"Mother, she's a grown woman." Singer's voice was unnaturally loud, clearly warning them. "You can't go into her room—"

"I own this house, Singer. It's technically *my* room."

"Mother—"

Jake nodded his head toward the open slider, and Lisa tried not to feel the straps of both bags like snakes sliding over her skin. She followed Jake and the kid outside, temporarily blinded by how bright it was.

She hadn't been outside since she got here.

Don't think, keep moving.

"Okay, that was invasive. Has she always gone into your room like that?" Jake asked. "If they're in your room, we can go all the way around the back. But there's still a chance they'll see us through the windows. Are the blinds closed?"

"Yeah."

"Thank god." He picked up the pace, and Miles watched Lisa over his shoulder. "We used to play spies all the time when we were kids. I'm having some kind of memory-related adrenaline rush right now. That's crazy, right?"

"I just feel sick."

"Yeah, I felt nauseous before, but now my brain's tricking my body into thinking this is a game. I mean, Lisa, we're in our thirties and we're sneaking out of your house to hide from your mom. And we have a baby with us." He glanced back and caught her eye as they slipped through the gate in the side yard. "I mean … come on."

Despite the snakes, despite Mother's voice echoing in her ears, Jake had a point. "This is ludicrous."

"Exactly. Now, um, let's try to get to the car really fast so they don't catch us. Miles, man, you gotta be on the team. No flailing around today. Let's go get donuts. Do you like donuts?"

When Jake pretended to tiptoe down the driveway, Miles started to…talk. Chatter. Not words Lisa understood, but like he was playing along.

"I know, right?" Jake said to him. "One of these days I'm gonna know what you're talking about. Here. In you go."

They strapped themselves (and Miles) in as quickly as possible and started driving. In the excitement of escaping, Lisa forgot to be afraid.

Donuts and coffee. She could already feel her body responding to the wild toxic rush of sugar and caffeine.

Singer's apparent stupidity was a good focus for the wave of restless energy. "So he just didn't tell her that you guys kind of have a kid?"

"See, that's the thing."

They were sitting in the car. Miles was passed out in his seat, so Jake had run in for breakfast while Lisa sat with Miles and hoped he stayed asleep.

If she only concentrated on watching Jake's face while he talked, she could forget that the entire world was on the other side of a little bit of glass and metal.

"Miles isn't ours permanently yet. I think Singer's— afraid to commit, if that makes sense. And I get it. Like, the idea that Miles could be taken away from us is terrifying. But when I look at him…" Jake wiped sugar off his top lip and took a sip of coffee. "It's weird. I'm usually the one holding back. Anyway, yeah, Singer didn't tell your parents we had a baby living with us. He's probably doing that right now." He glanced at his phone again.

She wanted Jake to keep talking. Partly as a distraction, but also partly because she was beginning to think she liked him. It was the strangest sensation. He was kind of goofy, and not nearly hot enough (he looked down-to-earth, like a regular guy, boring short brown hair, unremarkable brown eyes, average height, a little skinny). In high school she wouldn't have looked twice at him.

"Sorry. I'm sure you don't care about any of this."

"I do," she said without thinking.

Jake raised his eyebrows. "So."

"What?"

"Well, this is the first time you've left the house. What do you want to do? There's gotta be stuff you need, Lisa. Should we, I don't know, go to a store?"

She shook her head. "I'm not even sure I could get out of the car. I— When I think about trying to walk into a store, I can't— My heart pounds like I'm—" dying. *Don't say that.*

"Huh. Panic attacks, huh? That sucks. Okay, no store then."

Lisa frowned. "What do you mean?"

"Isn't that what you're saying? Heart pounds, can't breathe, the whole universe pressing down on you until you feel like it's crushing you? Panic attacks." He offered a slight smile. "Anxiety is sort of a family hobby. I don't get panic attacks, but my brother does. And fully half the cousins. Don't worry about it. But we do need a system. Where's your phone?"

"In my backpack." When people said *panic attack* she always thought they meant, you know, they freaked out.

Not they freaked out and literally thought they were dying. There was a word for this? This happened to other people often enough for Jake to talk about it so casually?

"Okay, so, save my number, and if you need anything, text me. Right? Seriously, I'm good for anything." He paused. "No, I think I'm good for anything. Like if you want tampons I'm gonna be pretty uncomfortable with that, but I could do it without having a panic attack, I think. So yeah. Let me know."

Lisa tried to burn off her twitchy fear that this was a trap, that anyone this nice had to be laying groundwork for something. She took another sip of coffee.

"Phone, Lisa Thurman." Jake held out his hand. "Everyone in my family called Singer 'Singer Thurman' for like two years when we were first dating. Probably to be jerks, because I was still in the closet at first. I think they were making the point that they didn't buy we were just friends." His fingers wiggled but weren't snakes yet.

"You tried to pretend you were just friends?" The phone was stored in the bottom of the zipped compartment in the smaller pocket of her pack. It was off. She handed it to Jake, who powered it on.

"Not really. I mean, we're having a kid together now and if you saw us in public you'd still probably think we were two guys who hang out and watch football. But I never got the whole public displays thing. Why would I want people looking at me and thinking about sex?"

"I don't think it's actually about sex. I think it's—" What? No public displays at the farm, not between anyone. She'd missed that. "I think it's belonging. You hold someone's hand and it's a way of showing you belong to each other, you know? You're not afraid of it."

"Huh. I was always afraid of it. Anyway." The phone vibrated to life in his hand. "Oh my god, what is *wrong* with you guys? Lisa, you have like ten messages and a bunch of texts from your mom. You know, if you or Singer actually talked to her, we might not be invaded right now."

Lisa stared at his fingers, nimbly swiping away notifications. Not snakes, dammit.

"Um. The most recent one's from Singer." Jake glanced up. "Apparently your mom says she's planning to stay for a while. To help you?"

Lisa sank into the passenger seat and allowed numbness to overtake her body, from her toes and fingertips to her heart. "Oh shit."

"Oh shit," Jake repeated. "Yeah. Um. This seriously has the potential to get awkward."

"You already have me living with you."

He waved a hand. "You're not awkward, you're fine. Your mom, though. I don't think she likes me. We only met once, but she sort of acted like I was the help."

"That's just how she acts." Numb, numb, numb. She took a small bite of donut and the sugar woke up her taste buds. Did she want to be numb or awake? She couldn't decide. "I'm so sorry, Jake."

"For what? This is proof your instincts were right about hiding from her in the first place. I mean, not that I can talk about overbearing parents. You may have heard mine loudly telling us what to do pretty much all the time." But he smiled when he said it. He smiled when he thought about his parents. "Okay. Well fuck it. Singer can deal with her right now. We're gonna have a nice breakfast of food *my* mom would definitely lecture us for eating, and if Miles gets wiggly we'll start driving again."

"So we're just putting off the inevitable?"

"We are. Here. I saved my number under my name, which should be pretty easy to find since you only have your parents and Singer in there, and sent myself a text message so I'd have yours, too."

"Okay." Was that enough? "I don't really like to use it."

"Huh. See, I figured you for a phone person."

"I was. I guess." A phone person. The popular girl. Skins she'd shed to become whatever she now was.

"Well, if you need anything, text me."

Miles yawned, throwing his arms and legs out to the widest reach of his safety seat.

"Time to ride." Jake shook off crumbs and reached for his keys. "I can't believe your mom's here. She took a plane, Lisa. She took a plane and showed up in a cab. Singer says she plans to use the Volvo while she's here."

"Does the Volvo even run? It's been sitting in the garage for … years." Time was still hard. Five years? But no, she'd been at the farm for three. No one had taken the Volvo out since Singer bought himself a car after high school. Ten years? If she was thirty-four, that made Singer thirty-two, which meant the Volvo had been sitting around for fourteen years, apparently waiting for Mother to spontaneously show up and decide to use it.

"God, I hope so. I hope it purrs like a kitten and she wants to drive it a lot, to faraway places. And thank god for the guesthouse. If your mom was gonna be inside all the time, I'm pretty sure we'd have to move."

"Don't leave me with her."

He grinned. "Yeah, that'd be fucked up. Okay, where to? Let's go see how many entrances to Mount Diablo we can hit before he really wakes up."

"Okay."

Lisa cradled her coffee in her hands and sat back. Driving through hills and fields sounded perfect. No people, no cars. Just trees.

And coffee.
And, okay, one more donut.

10

SINGER
13 DAYS WITH MILES

Singer stood in his kitchen, coffee cup in hand, ghost of Jake's kiss still on his lips: a pillar of strength. "I didn't know we were expecting you this morning, Mother." He sounded firm. He sounded unmoved by Mother's rather horrifying appearance at eleven o'clock on a Sunday morning.

It all went downhill from there.

He gave them an hour before texting—begging—Jake to come home. He added, *Joking.* He doubted that Jake missed the real message, which was: *So not joking.*

Jake replied, *Donuts and coffee. Requests?*

He thumped his head against the wall of the bathroom, where he was—okay, be honest—hiding from his mother. Had it really only been an hour? It felt like he'd been having the same awkward conversation with her for weeks.

There was nothing for it. He declined donuts and forced himself to go back to the kitchen. Where Mother was inspecting the refrigerator, providing a running commentary about the state of their produce, questioning its origins, and considering the quality of the stores from which it had come.

Oh, god. Mother. What was she doing here? And, alarmingly, why did she have luggage with her?

*

Half a pot of coffee later—which Singer drank himself, because the coffee wasn't fair trade, and Mother declined—he worked out the real reason she was there.

"You aren't taking care of things, Singer, and somebody has to."

"And by 'things,' are you referring to my sister?" In his entire life, he'd never thought of Lisa as "my sister" as frequently as he had in the last few weeks of talking to Mother and Dad. It had never seemed like a word that described their relationship; sure, they were genetically related, but otherwise they'd always been satisfied as strangers. He could say the same thing about their parents.

He was a little surprised to find he felt … protective of Lisa.

"Singer." Mother's I'm-withholding-a-long-sigh voice. "You know that your sister is unwell."

"I know she's an adult, which makes her old enough to judge for herself when she needs help." Which was only a small lie.

"Of course she needs help. Anyone can tell by looking at her that she's not her old self. Have you seen the clothes she's wearing? She wouldn't even let me buy her anything but those jeans and *T-shirts*. I took her shopping more than once, and—"

"You thought *shopping* was an appropriate treatment for spending three years in a cult? Did one of your specialists suggest that?" Singer shut his mouth. He'd been spending way too much time with Derries. "I apologize," he managed to say after a moment.

"I don't know why you're being so hostile. I'm only trying to help."

"Will you be paying a third of the mortgage? Right now Jake and I split it and cover Lisa since she's not working."

Mother's eyes narrowed. "Are you trying to be funny?"

"I'm trying to understand what you think is going to happen here." He waved a hand, as if it would somehow conjure the right words. "You moved two and a half years ago, Mother. You asked me to leave the apartment I loved in the city so that you wouldn't have to worry about renting the house out, so I moved here. As a tenant. Are you kicking me out?" *And Jake, and Miles?*

"Of course not. This is your home, too."

But not Jake's. Or Miles's.

Singer forced his voice to remain steady. "I assume you'll be staying in the guesthouse."

Here at least she had the decency to look shocked. "I— I assumed— I suppose I *could*—"

"That would be best. There's something I haven't told you, and once I do, I think you'll prefer to be in the guesthouse. Or to go home."

"I hardly think there's anything you can tell me that will make me second-guess my desire to help Lisa."

"Jake and I are fostering a baby."

Surprise shifted to shock, then a gratifying second of outrage before settling into stunned.

"A baby? Here?"

"Well, Mother, my landlord didn't inform me she'd planned to move in on no notice. Of course here. This is where we live."

"Why didn't you tell us? Is it— Is that wise?"

"Wise?"

"You know what I mean, Singer. The two of you aren't married."

"The two of us were together before it was legal for us to get married. We haven't caught up to this newfangled thing all the kids are doing."

She sent him a look that communicated exactly how little she appreciated his attempt at humor.

His phone buzzed right as he heard a car pull up out front. *Oh thank god.*

"It sounds like they're home." He didn't quite jump to his feet. "I'll go check."

Mother did not, as he'd feared, follow him.

"I'm dying in there." He grabbed the diaper bag from Jake so Jake could unbuckle Miles. "I don't know how long she plans to stay, but it's already too long."

Lisa, whom he hadn't actually seen in daylight, froze. "What do you mean you don't know how long?"

"I don't think she has a return ticket."

It was odd, the two of them sharing a moment of panic. As adults, in front of the house in which they'd grown up. Lisa tapped nervously on her phone and glanced at the windows, as if she were waiting for some sign.

Miles started talking—making noises, anyway, that weren't cries—and Singer turned to Jake, expecting to see irritation, or annoyance, or at the very least some expression that would justify his guilt.

Instead, Jake was grinning at Miles, tugging on his ear, and the tail end of that smile caught Singer by surprise.

"So, time to hang out with the in-laws, huh? I mean, you've been stuck with, like, all of my people. It's only fair."

"This isn't really the same," Singer muttered, cheated out of his bad mood by Jake's lack of complicity.

"Okay." But clearly Jake—whose huge, loving, over-involved family was nothing like the Thurmans—had no idea what was wrong.

"So you think she's staying for a few days?"

He looked at Lisa, and at least she understood that now was a time for dire warnings. "I *hope* that's all she's staying."

She sighed, slipping her phone into her pocket. "All right."

Jake, still carrying Miles, trailed behind them while the Thurman kids squared their shoulders and prepared to smile at their mother. They knew how to do this. At one time, both of them had even been good at telling Mother exactly what she wanted to hear. Somewhere along the line, Singer thought he'd lost the skill. And he could tell by looking at her that Lisa wasn't better off.

This was going to be a disaster.

*

Derries to the rescue.

Singer's shoulders tensed. But the text message—from Carey, of all improbable people—said nothing else. Then the phone rang. The landline, which they only used for telemarketers and charities.

He excused himself from the stilted conversation in the living room. "Hello?"

"Singer, it's Cathy. Did I hear correctly that your mother is in town?"

In town. What a phrase.

"Hi, Cathy. Yes, she is. She arrived this morning."

"Joe and I would love to have all of you over for dinner."

"Oh, that's—very kind of you, Cathy." How could he decline? Or accept? Surely he had to decline.

There were voices on the other end, and Cathy saying, "Leave it."

"Excuse me?" Singer said, to fill space, give himself more time to think.

"Let us take care of entertaining tonight, Singer. Unless you want time with your mother, of course, and your sister—"

"No, no. I mean—" He broke off, grateful the doors were closed so at least he could sag back against the wall in relative peace. "No, Cathy, that's— I mean, thank you, so much, for the offer."

"Singer, I—" Cathy paused, and he closed his eyes, waiting for some platitude, getting ready to give some meaningless reply. "It's been a hell of a week."

Shocked into a laugh, he said, "I've never heard you curse before."

"Only when it's appropriate. Please invite your mother and sister over for an impromptu family dinner." All ambiguity was gone; that was Cathy's no-nonsense voice. "Carey and Alice will be here. Please let me at least try to help."

Singer straightened his back. No-nonsense deserved the same. "Thank you very much. I'll let you know our plans."

"Excellent. I look forward to meeting your mother. Don't think I haven't noticed the way you kept us apart all these years."

"No, I—" No-nonsense, dammit. "It should be interesting. Thanks, Cathy."

"Of course."

He stood there in silence for a moment after hanging up.

"He's asleep." Jake was standing at the hallway door, leaning against the jamb.

"I didn't know you were there. That was your mom."

"Yeah, I just got a cryptic message from Carey. What's up?"

While Singer outlined the conversation, Jake moved closer to him, standing right inside his reach. In other times, he'd close the distance, adjust Jake's shirt, brush something invisible from his collar. Now Singer felt glued in space, unable to move. Waiting to see what Jake would do.

Jake's phone buzzed, and he looked at it for a long moment. (*This is the opportunity*, Singer's brain informed his limbs: *this is when you make contact*.) "Okay. We'll take separate cars. You take your mom in your car and leave first, so Lisa can—I don't know—spontaneously combust or something."

Singer was so preoccupied with whether or not to reach out, it took him a full minute to understand. "Oh. *Oh*. Of course." He glanced at the door to the living room. "Was this the plan all along? It's a good one, but Cathy didn't mention—"

"No, Mom totally wouldn't." Jake held out his phone, open to a text message. *Tell Singer to say yes. But no pressure. We thought at the very least Lisa could use a break.*

"All right. Well, we should— I should tell Mother … something."

Jake's hand, in slow motion, descended on his wrist. "Let me. Mom would probably have asked me to do it anyway, except you're way more reliable." Then he smiled, an ordinary Jake-smile, one that held no special subtext or meaning.

Right now that smile made Singer want to cry like a little kid, off on his own, wallowing in self-pity and the knowledge that he didn't deserve Jake's smile, or Cathy's help.

"Once more into the breech." Jake let go. "I think Miles likes Lisa. Because she doesn't demand his attention, just watches him and lets him be."

"Really?" It was something he hadn't even considered, the relationship between their child and his sister. Until the last month, he had mostly written her out of his future entirely. She could still leave, obviously. Just like Miles.

Jake delivered the invitation smoothly, and Mother's innate politeness forced her to accept (on Lisa's behalf, as well, though he thought Jake might have winked at her when she opened her mouth to speak).

Lisa would be an aunt. He'd thought of Aunt Alice, joining the ranks of the Derrie aunts and uncles, but it hadn't occurred to him that Lisa would be as much his child's aunt as Alice was.

And Mother would be a grandmother. Singer glanced across the room at her perfect makeup and set shoulders and wondered if any of this would ever make sense.

11

VIV
107 DAYS UNTIL STARTING OVER

Viv was tired. She had imagined a quiet dinner at home with her children, but she could hardly turn down an invitation from Jake's parents. They lived in an upscale neighborhood she mentally dated back to the same era of her own house, though in a slightly less desirable area of town. She and Drew had seen a few houses nearby, if she remembered correctly. It was such a long time ago, of course; they'd been younger than Lisa and Singer were now.

Cathy and Joe Derrie matched their house: nondescript, ordinary. She smiled, shook hands, and thanked them for having her over on short notice. She also met the brother, Carey, and his partner, Alice. Carey shook her hand and mentioned that he'd been in Lisa's class in high school. He clearly hadn't been a friend, or even an acquaintance, but Viv nodded and smiled, as if this bit of personal trivia was as significant as he expected it to be.

Alice—and Viv wasn't sure what to make of the word "partner" in the context of a woman—had a pretty face, a loud voice, and a weight problem. Still, Singer seemed to feel comfortable around all of them, which was slightly disorienting.

She looked forward to asking Lisa about Singer's apparent newfound fascination with … chaos. Strange, considering he had always seemed so in control. Surely Lisa must be equally mystified.

Viv felt a sudden pang of regret. Had it been this way the entire time since Lisa returned home? Unexpected dinner parties she didn't feel she could turn down and overfamiliar strangers? Whatever had happened, Viv could start putting it to rights now that she was here. She turned to the expansive front windows in time to see Jake pull his car to the curb in front of the house. She hadn't really gotten a straight answer from Singer about why they'd needed to take separate cars in the first place, but at least now she could see Lisa for herself, even if the conditions were less than ideal.

Except Lisa wasn't there. It was just Jake, extracting the little boy from his car seat, fumbling with the diaper bag.

She fought a sudden irrational fear that something had happened to Lisa. Of course it hadn't. That was absurd. Which didn't explain where on earth she was.

"Where is your sister?" Her tone was light, but Singer immediately looked away.

"She's at home."

At home? But Lisa had been invited. They'd all been invited into this cluttered house, with its overstuffed chairs, its cupcakes—*cupcakes*—set out on the kitchen counter, a children's birthday treat presented like hors d'oeuvres.

Jake walked through the door and nearly tripped, losing his grip on the diaper bag, scattering its contents everywhere.

Singer dropped Viv's arm and went to help gather the bits and pieces, while Jake awkwardly attempted to get to his knees.

"At least you saved the kid." Alice reached for the baby. "Right, Miles?"

"It was a close thing." Jake shook his head, murmuring something to Singer, who didn't quite look up.

Who are these people? Singer's last boyfriend, or at least the last one she'd met, had been a quiet boy. Reserved. He'd suited Singer, she thought at the time. She wondered whatever happened to him.

The parents hustled and bustled around each other, trading smiles and stories, folding Singer and the little boy into their bewildering volume. The child assumed the glazed expression of a person overstimulated beyond reason, but Singer's behavior was far more confounding. He might be pretending out of politeness, which would at least explain matters, though if Viv were being honest, that wasn't what it looked like. He seemed genuinely … at home in the relative mayhem.

Viv found a safe corner and a glass of wine, making small talk with Joe Derrie while watching his son from across the room and trying to understand Singer's attraction.

Yes, she agreed Miles looked perfectly healthy. Of course she remembered the local athletic club, and no, she didn't realize it had finally gone out of business. It turned out they'd been house hunting right around the same time and had probably looked at a few of the same houses. And yes, that was quite the coincidence.

Dinner was served around a table that was nearly large enough to accommodate them all. Jake ate one-handed while the child drank a bottle on his lap. Cathy offered to fit the high chair in at the table, but Jake declined, choosing to defend his dinner from tiny fists while Singer attempted to keep the tablecloth and Jake's clothing free of food-covered handprints.

They laughed. They laughed at the baby's antics, at his expression when he managed to grab a handful of mashed potatoes. Cathy patted Singer's shoulder as she passed him and said, "Don't worry too much. There's nothing here that can't be cleaned, Singer."

Viv bristled at her presumption. Having been placed in a situation that almost guaranteed a mess, was it any wonder that Singer was trying to prevent it? But Singer only smiled apologetically and stood to follow Cathy into the kitchen. He helped with the dishes while she made coffee, both of them speaking in low voices.

Food soured in Viv's stomach, sitting at a table with people she did not know, unable to even hear her son's voice over the general babble of the room. It should have been easy enough to navigate a dinner party—even one as disorderly as this—but she felt an unaccustomed hollowness in her chest whenever she looked at Singer. How could her own son feel so foreign, so alien? She'd fed him and clothed him and raised him, and yet he was, if anything, more bewildering than the spectacle of Jake's family.

The disorientation was slightly dizzying.

But she smiled, and nodded, and agreed. *Yes, it is good to see the boys. Yes, Lisa looks very well.* Such small, meaningless words; she barely noticed herself speaking. When they were finally alone in the silence of the car, she waited for Singer to explain something, anything, about this night. Why Lisa was at home. Why he'd expected Viv to accompany him to this dinner party. He said nothing.

They were nearly back to the house when she couldn't contain her perplexity any longer.

"What happened to the young man you introduced us to a few years ago? I don't remember you telling us ..."—*anything*—"... whatever happened with him."

Singer looked over. It was possibly the first time he'd looked directly at her all night. "The young man I introduced you to a few years ago." His voice was perfectly flat.

Perhaps she shouldn't have asked. "I was wondering, but of course you don't have to tell me." Aware it was weak, she added somewhat defensively, "I was only making conversation."

"Mother, I've only introduced you to one—man. Person. Boyfriend. *Ever.*"

"Yes, I remember." Reserved, polite, a nice young man.

"I don't think you do remember, actually." Singer sighed. "That was Jake. Jake is the only person I've ever introduced you to, Mother. You just spent the entire evening with him."

"That's absurd. They're nothing remotely alike. The one you brought to dinner was ... He barely said a word the entire time he was with us." This had to be a joke. She opened her mouth to say something, but then she caught his expression.

Singer's lips pressed grimly together, and for a moment Viv lost sight of her son in the man sitting next to her. She sought familiar details—the small scar on his neck from where he'd picked at his chicken pox, the cowlick on the top of his head that could never fully be controlled—and to her relief he came back into focus. Her son, of course. An adult man who was still her son.

It had been such a long, long day. She sat back in the passenger seat of the car and wondered if she wasn't experiencing one of those troubling mental stumbles that heralded eventual dementia. That made more sense than crediting Singer's story as truth.

She tried to picture the young man from—what had it been? Five years ago? She couldn't remember anything about the boyfriend but an indistinct blur, who'd sat at her dining room table and said "please" and "thank you" in the correct places. She had still hoped, halfheartedly, that Singer would eventually bring home a girl. A wife.

Clearly that hope had died, but Viv wasn't archaic in her views. She didn't mind that Singer liked men. If he had to like men, though, why did he have to like this particular man, with this loud, exhausting family?

"Are you *certain* that you introduced us to Jake before?" It was a last effort to reconcile the jumble of the day.

Singer pulled into the driveway and shut off the engine, but made no move to get out of the car. "Mother, I've been with Jake for nearly seven years. He's the only serious boyfriend I've ever had. The night he met you, he wore a brown plaid shirt he thought was too preppy, and you treated him like you'd treat a plumber, or a car mechanic, with cold detachment."

She stiffened, stung by the censure in his tone. "I was perfectly polite. And I wouldn't invite a plumber to dinner, for goodness' sake."

"You didn't invite him, Mother. I did. The one time, in my entire life, I cared enough about someone to introduce him to you and Dad. And you didn't even recognize him when you saw him again." Singer shook his head and unbuckled the seatbelt. "Lisa is at home. The entire night was just an excuse to get all of us out of the house so Lisa could have a few hours of peace. That's how the Derries work: they heard she needed something, so they did it. They've never even met her, and yet they know her better than you do, Mother."

He left the car, snapping the door shut behind him.

That's not fair. How can you say that? You are so much like your father. But, also like Drew, Singer wasn't there to fight with. It was so easy for them to walk away, leaving her with all of her arguments loud in her head, unspoken.

The tightness in Viv's body was unfamiliar and unpleasant. None of this made sense. Everything she'd expected when she called for a car this morning to take her to the airport had fallen apart. She'd imagined arriving home, assessing Lisa and finding a new specialist, to say nothing of making a hair appointment for both of them, just like she used to do. At first, for a split second, Viv had felt hope. Lisa had smiled as she used to smile, like nothing could touch her, like she could have whatever she wanted. Viv had always thought a little bit of that triumph was hers, raising a daughter to face the world like she'd already conquered it.

But then she'd noticed the bags under Lisa's eyes, the way she couldn't quite hold her smile in place. She hadn't sat down, not even just to chat. She'd edged out of the room and down the hall. And Singer had pointedly offered the guesthouse. In her own home.

Or rather, her own backyard.

Jake's car pulled alongside, parking in the driveway. She should have looked away, but instead she searched his features to confirm what Singer had said. All she managed to accomplish was startling him when he spotted her still sitting in the passenger seat.

For a prolonged moment they stared at each other.

Who are you? Why are you in my house? Whose child is that? Viv looked away first, resentfully loosening her belt and going inside without a backward glance.

No sign of Lisa, and the light in her room was off. Viv had come all this way and had hardly seen her daughter at all.

She retired to the guesthouse, feeling almost unbearably exhausted. Surely that was part of the issue. It had been a long day, and while it hadn't gone as smoothly as it should have, all was certainly not lost. It would no doubt be easier to begin straightening things out after a full night of sleep. It always was.

12

LISA
41 DAYS SINCE LEAVING GRACE

Four days into Invasion Viv, the majority of Lisa's contact with the outside world came from random text messages, mostly from Jake (with a scattered helping of Singer, and Jake's cousin Frankie, who, last Lisa had heard, hated her guts). The most recent Jake text read: *V's getting her hair done. QUICK, EAT SOMETHING.*

Lisa double-checked the front yard, but sure enough, the Volvo was gone. Of course Mother was getting her hair done. She probably couldn't wait to tell her old stylist all about her wacko daughter's adventure in a cult. Mother's voice would lower as she spoke, like whatever she was saying was top secret, even though she was thrilled that everyone in the salon would be trying to listen in.

Not that it mattered. None of it mattered. Though apparently Lisa was still vain enough to hope no one she knew was there today. It was one thing to know the story would eventually spread; it was another thinking of some former friend or enemy hearing it directly from Mother's mouth.

Another text: *Donuts.*

That wasn't fair. Point to Jake.

She went to the kitchen, which was oddly empty. Since donuts did not make a meal, she added a chunk of something that looked like it had been a casserole (which she reheated while helping herself to the donuts) and two slices of some kind of fruity, nutty bread.

There were voices in the living room. Maybe the idea that Mother wasn't haunting every corner was a sort of dull intoxication, but instead of taking her food back to her room, Lisa went out to sit with Singer and Jake. And Miles, obviously.

Emery was a surprise.

"Lisa, hey," he said, and she tried to tighten her stomach against the whirlpool pleasure of his smile.

"Hey."

She sat on the armchair. Eating in the living room was a new phenomenon. Had to be a Derrie tradition. The Thurmans never ate in the living room, which made it even more subversive to take the opportunity to do so when Mother could return at any moment.

"Miles, come on. Check it out, you can do this." Jake flopped onto his stomach and got closer until he and the baby were almost nose to nose. "I know your needs are totally taken care of and you have no actual reason to crawl, but think of the freedom, buddy. Think of the chaos you can cause. All those cabinets to break into, all those electrical outlets to stick your fingers in—"

Emery laughed.

"Jake." Singer's repressive tone sounded, actually, a lot like Mother, though he was trying not to smile.

"What? Listen, Miles, you gotta start crawling or Singer and I will get all lazy with the childproofing. It's your job to keep us on our toes."

"That's true." Emery raised a black camera and pointed it at Jake and Miles. "It's your grave responsibility not to let your dads get lazy."

Whoa. Dads. Singer went stiff; Lisa could see it from across the room.

Jake had started playing a game where his fingers inched forward, then back, then forward, and Miles watched with rapt attention. When they moved too close to him, he giggled.

"Who needs toys when you have hands, right? I'm gonna get you, Miles. Gonna get you—"

This was apparently the funniest thing Miles had ever seen in his short life. Jake moved faster and closer and started making noises for his fingers in response to the noises Miles made, which just cracked Miles up more.

Emery kept taking pictures, but Lisa hoped he was keeping Singer out of them. Singer still looked frozen. He was smiling, but not-smiling. Lisa was familiar with that expression. It was a mask. To think they'd known each other their whole lives and she never realized that she and Singer had the same mask.

She finished her meal and stood up to leave, but Emery caught her attention.

"What about a few pictures with Aunt Lisa? Always easier to take pictures when a kid's actually having fun than try to initiate having fun in order to take pictures."

Miles was definitely having fun now. He'd collapsed and rolled to his back, and Jake had upped the ante by crawling his fingers over Miles's stomach and up his chest while Miles laughed himself hoarse.

"I don't think we should be using words like that." Singer's tone was repressive, but Lisa thought he was trying to hold back his own emotions more than anyone else's. "It feels like inviting trouble."

"Jesus, Singer." Jake walked his fingers all the way up to tap Miles's nose. Miles guffawed. "He's been here three weeks. When do you want to start acting like we're his family? At six months? A year?"

"When a judge tells us we're his parents."

"That could be two years from now. Or longer."

"Fine. But I'd like to at least meet his mom before we take everything Brandi says as gospel."

"I don't take anything she says as gospel, but what's the harm in saying 'aunt'? Lisa doesn't mind, right?"

Caught. Lisa accidentally met Emery's eyes in an effort to avoid everyone else's, and he mouthed, *Sorry.*

"Can we not put Lisa in the middle?"

"I wasn't. I just think we don't gain anything by being detached with him. Or I guess I think it's kind of selfish. If someone takes him away, I want him to know that right now we played and I was having fun and that's good enough."

"If someone takes him away, he'll never even remember you."

Jake swallowed, fingers going flat over the baby's chest. "Fine, Singer. You do it your way. Hey, kid, I think you could use a diaper change. All that formula. Maybe you should have some more avocado later, Miles. Remember avocado? It's green and squishy and you can paint the table with it?" He scooped Miles up and carried him down the hall.

"Apologies," Singer murmured. He hesitated, like he was going to say something else, then appeared to give up and went to the kitchen.

Emery grimaced. "Shit. Sorry, Lisa."

She shook her head. "I'm not sure what that was."

"Definitely my bad, though. Damn." Emery pulled the strap of the camera over his neck. "So that goes down as not one of my best jobs."

"Is that what you do? Take pictures?"

"It's one of the things I do." He flashed a smile. "I'm a man of many talents, Lisa. I also do tattoos, and more artsy photos than this."

"Artsy?"

"Some of them might be nudes—but *tasteful* nudes, I swear. Anyway, how are you doing?"

"Fine. You?" Nudes? Wait, nudes like what? What did that mean?

His smile turned into a smirk like he knew what she was thinking, and damn, those dimples. "I never see you out in the house when I come over."

"Yeah, I mostly stay in my room. Especially now that Mother's here." She checked the front windows for the Volvo, though from here she'd certainly notice Mother pulling into the driveway. Jake was now parking on the street, which probably made sense but also was kind of irritating. He was paying half the mortgage. Shouldn't he get the better parking spot?

Jake trundled Miles back into the room, now in a onesie and a diaper. "Hey, you know what you need, Lisa? A lock."

"A lock?"

"Yeah. So you can leave your room without worrying your mom's going to go through your stuff again. A lock."

She blinked, not quite sure what to say to that.

"Oh, lock shopping." Emery's eyebrows rose. "Doorknob lock? Hollow-core door?"

"Probably. Can we get a keyed lock for a hollow-core door?"

"Sure. Not one that will hold up to a determined thief, but I assume you're more looking to send a message."

"Yeah," Jake said. "Like 'mind your own business,' which is what I really wish Singer would tell her. Sorry, I'll shut up about your mom."

Lisa shrugged. "Why? She's gotta be bugging you more than she's bugging me."

"I'm not sure we're ever going to have a loving in-law relationship. But I shouldn't talk shit about her. Anyway."

"We could go now." Emery cleared his throat. "To get a lock, if you wanted. There will be a few different kinds."

We? Lisa shook her head. "Oh, no, it's a— It's a nice thought, but I don't actually need— I mean— It's probably stupid that I—"

He held up both hands. "It's not stupid. Even if it is symbolic. Would it make you feel better to have a lock on your door?"

She could feel her vulnerability as she sat here, in the living room. Her backpack was in there, her hoodie. If there were a lock on the door, would she still feel this wide open?

"I guess so, but it's so stupid—"

"I could bring you one," he said. "If you don't mind me picking it out."

"Oh."

"Yeah, do that." Jake set Miles down beside the table so he could pull himself up and totter there. "Right, Miles? Because Aunt Lisa gets to feel safe in her own house, just like you do."

Lisa had always thought people who talked to children about things they couldn't possibly understand were deluded or foolish. But Jake wasn't either. He was simply including Miles in a conversation, and even though he didn't know what was going on, he still seemed to like being talk-ed to.

"I'll drop one off next week." Emery offered that heat-inducing smile again, and it coiled in Lisa's belly like it wanted to expand.

She didn't let it. "You really don't have to." He want-ed something, he must want something. She used to be so good at figuring out what men wanted, but all she got from Emery was that smile, and a light in his eyes that might mean flirting, or might mean he was humoring Singer's crazy sister.

"Hey, I like Home Depot. It's not a problem."

"Um. Thank you." *Thank you* was appropriate, proba-bly even if he was humoring her.

"Sure." He turned back toward Jake and raised the camera again. "Miles, look at me. Miles. Look at the weird black box. Yeah, there you go. Man, your eyes, Miles. Aunt Alice is gonna go crazy painting your beautiful eyes."

Miles cocked his head to the side as if he actually could understand.

"There, that's awesome. That's fantastic. You're sav-ing my whole job, Miles, yeah, look right at the big black box—"

Lisa went to rinse her dishes, expecting Singer to be in the kitchen. He wasn't. She finished up, grabbed a few ba-nanas and an armful of water bottles, dropped them in her room (a lock, a lock on the door so she could leave without imagining someone inside when she came back), then got to work gathering more supplies.

Emery's laughter joined Miles's. He had a great laugh.

13

SINGER
20 DAYS WITH MILES

This was ridiculous. Mother showed no signs of leaving any time soon, despite the fact that Lisa was avoiding her as much as humanly possible. Did she think if she lurked in the kitchen long enough she'd starve Lisa out? Even Mother had to sleep. Singer was almost certain he'd heard Lisa up in the middle of the night making sandwiches.

And that was nothing compared to Jake, who hadn't asked for this, who hadn't been born to it. Mother was coldly civil to him, but he had to know that she wasn't happy about his presence. Or Miles's.

Singer needed to say something. He was really only pretending to get ready for bed. Miles was asleep, the baby monitor hummed on the counter, and only the bedside lamps were still lit.

He had to say something, anything. There were probably many things, but he had to say *something* to Jake—about his mother, about his frustration, about, hell, anything at all.

Jake leaned out of the bathroom doorway. "You remember that time at your apartment, when I spent the night after you had everyone over? This is like that. Only it's not me wigging."

"I'm not—"

Jake grinned and pulled back into the bathroom.

"Oh, shut up." *That night*, the first time Jake had overtly stayed with him in San Francisco instead of slinking out to follow his cousins with a lot of halfhearted backward glances.

"It's kind of cool not being the one freaking out for once. It's usually me, Singer. It's probably just your turn."

"Stop being so *nice* about this." Singer got up, started pacing. "You should— You should be mad at me, or something, but instead you're being so *nice* about it."

"About what?"

"About *this*, this thing, where my mother shows up out of nowhere and apparently decides to move in, without asking, without giving any indication that she's ever leaving!"

"You think she's staying forever?"

"Or the way she looks at Miles, like he's just some fucking *set piece* in the drama that is Mother's life."

Jake dried his hands and moved to the bed, sitting at the edge of it, watching him pace. "Are we— Is this an air-your-fears moment right now? Or do you want to vent for a while?"

"Vent? My mother moves in with us without asking, treats *you* like an uninvited guest, and you think I need to vent?"

Jake raised his eyes and pulled his legs onto the bed to sit with them knotted in front of him. "Yes? Maybe? Venting might … help."

But now that he was thinking about it, that sounded so absurd. Singer sank down on the bed beside him. "I don't know how to vent, Jake."

"Want me to teach you?"

Singer shook his head. "Why aren't you mad at me?"

"Why would I be mad at you?"

It wasn't equivocation; Jake looked genuinely stumped. Which made everything harder. He could have kept up some of his anger if Jake had only—provoked him a little.

"My mother." Singer waved a hand. That should be enough, shouldn't it?

"Singer, if you want me to be righteously pissed at you because your family has slightly inconvenient timing once, in the seven years we've been together, I really can't. I mean, if we were doing that, you'd be pissed at me a hundred percent of the time. Right? I don't know if you know this, but my cousin lived in our backyard for a year and a half. Also, someone I'm related to 'drops by' pretty much every day."

"It's not the same."

"Why? Because you like them?"

"I don't— I didn't say I *dislike* my mother—"

Jake held up both hands. "Not what I meant. But sometimes I find all of them embarrassing. Sometimes I wish I was the one whose family kept a decent few hundred miles in between them and me. Not that it's been easy, I don't mean that either, but when Mom's on me about whether Carey's gonna have a kid and Frankie's dodging her parents— Sometimes it seems like your family is more peaceful."

"We just hide it better."

"I know that. Intellectually."

"I wanted this to be time for us, time for us to get to know Miles. I feel like my mother is cheating us out of this time we'll never get back with him. And she just *looks* at him. Like he's an intruder." He glanced over at the baby monitor, wondering if it would be weird to go check on him again. "She looks at you that way. It infuriates me."

"I know." Jake pitched his voice low. "And I'm not saying I dig being the proverbial dog shit on Viv's shoe. But I don't know, I think she might be a little adrift right now. I doubt she really wants to be living in the guesthouse, anyway."

"We *are not* giving up the bedroom."

"I'm definitely not suggesting that. But when she pisses me off, I remind myself that as screwy as she is, she had a part in you being you. Which I kind of have to support, you know? Because I really…like you. The way you turned out. Um." The light was too low to tell for sure, but Singer thought Jake was blushing.

"You like me so much you don't mind that my mother is in the backyard right now?"

Jake looked at the exterior wall, then at Singer. "I guess that means we should be very, very quiet."

"Jake…"

A pause, while they looked at each other.

"She wears earplugs to bed," Singer said. "And I think the neighborhood has enough white noise."

"Oh, good." Jake leaned in for a kiss, then pulled back. "Is this weird, with Miles asleep? I mean, is it super creepy that I'm, um, kinda in the mood?"

"It's really not creepy. I love it when you're in the mood. Plus, we said we wouldn't be those people who resent their child for demanding all their time." Another kiss, and with every touch Singer felt his load lighten. Maybe it had just been a tough week. Maybe everything *was* all right.

"We do not want to be those people," Jake agreed. "But what if he wakes up while we're…in the middle of things?"

"We'll hear him. Parents must do this. And it's not like he's in the room." Singer paused. "Actually, parents probably do have sex while kids are asleep in the room."

Jake shook his head. "I couldn't. I'm so glad Miles has his own room."

Turning off the lights almost seemed to rewind their lives—a month ago this would have been normal. A month ago making out in bed wasn't even remarkable.

And in the dark, with his eyes closed, Singer could remember what it felt like to believe in this. He banished all thoughts before he had the chance to feel that loss again. *Just feel. Think later.*

Just feel, he repeated to himself, and shut down his brain to everything but the sensation of Jake's skin on his.

14

LISA
47 DAYS SINCE LEAVING GRACE

Avoiding Mother was only possible in a limited way. Lisa could manage it, but she soon realized if she didn't make an appearance at least once a day, Mother started to get twitchy.

"Twitchy" was Jake's word for it. Jake was her newsfeed to the outside world, letting her know when he was going shopping, buying her peanut butter and bread she could keep in her room.

She still had to leave to get jelly, though he'd bought her an entire flat of water. She heard Singer and Mother fighting about it once when she was grabbing a few bananas.

"He shouldn't enable her like that," Mother said tersely.

"By buying her water? What would you rather we do, let her get dehydrated?"

"She needs help, Singer."

Singer said something to that, but Lisa had escaped back to her room and shoved the side table up to the door. She'd squished one of the bananas so hard it oozed through cracks in the peel. Nothing for that, so she ate it and plugged her ears with a roll of toilet paper she'd stockpiled for her more out-of-control crying jags.

Making an appearance in the morning seemed the best way to do it; when she got it out of the way early, sometimes she could return to her regular schedule of hiding in bed or haunting #praiseforanthonygrace on Twitter. Or rereading those blogs about how to get over yourself after leaving a cult. Not that reading seemed to have helped at all. Here she was, freaked out and sitting in her bed, knowing she had to leave the room at some point. Step number one for cult recovery: Leave your room.

How was she going to get a job if she couldn't even leave her room?

Just do it.

She gathered her composure and promised herself coffee.

Mother was sitting at the kitchen table, like anyone would sit at their kitchen table. But when she looked up, Lisa wished she'd gone back to bed.

"I'm glad you're awake," Mother said. "We have an appointment."

"An appointment?"

"Yes."

"What kind of appointment?"

Mother's eyes flicked up and down, and Lisa's entire body cringed away from her assessment. This was the woman who'd taught her how to apply lipstick and trace the outside of each lip with liner. This was the woman who'd taught her how to curl her eyelashes and straighten her bangs. This was the woman now eyeing her as if she had just jumped off a truck leaving the fields after a hard day of work.

Was that racist? Lisa half turned away, ashamed of herself for a kaleidoscope of reasons, some of which actually seemed to conflict. She washed her hands, which was a normal thing to do, except that seeing water running over skin reminded her of the time she and Abigail tried to make tamales for their dinner shift, how the corn husks hadn't held together and it all ended up being one huge mess. Still tasted pretty good, even if everyone had to scoop it into bowls.

Clara had nearly thrown a fit. Ranting about resources and planned menus and responsibility until someone (Di, maybe) stepped in. They hadn't used more than a meal's worth of food, after all. They hadn't done anything wrong, not really. Abigail had taken it hard. Abigail took everything hard, Lisa thought, standing in her mother's kitchen with the remembered feel of the farm's wood-grain countertops rough under her palms. They'd washed up—volunteered for it to get Clara off their backs—and she'd made Abigail laugh, tears on her face.

Was that it? Had that been the day she'd decided to do it? But that had been at least a year ago. She'd been okay for a while after that.

Not that any of it mattered.

"We'll leave in forty-five minutes. When you're ready."

Slight emphasis. She forced herself to translate: *Clearly you aren't ready to leave the house now, but forty-five minutes should be enough time to pull yourself together.*

Her internal Mother voice was such a bitch. She'd have to ask Singer if he had one of those, too.

"Fine," Lisa said. She could fight, but where would it get her? Did the Bay Area have cult specialists? She was probably about to find out.

*

The new specialist was a woman, which could have been okay. Except she bonded immediately with Mother. They spent the entire hour processing Mother's feelings about what she termed Lisa's "abandonment of the family," and in a way, it was interesting. She'd been so in love with Anthony, with the fantasy he'd offered of living on the farm, everyone responsible for everyone else, everyone in love, that she'd hardly blinked when they told her to write a letter withdrawing from her "baby family." *You're a grown woman now, Lisa. You don't need them to take care of you anymore. We will take care of you.*

Mother said reading that letter was like having her heart torn from her breast. She actually said "breast." If Lisa remembered how to laugh, she might have. It was probably good she didn't.

The therapist, whose name she didn't remember, was very sympathetic. She nodded a lot and asked Mother questions, drawing out her responses. Toward the end, the woman had looked at Lisa and asked if she'd known how deeply her actions affected her family.

For a second, she'd frozen. But this was an easy question, so she'd offered an answer.

"I guess it didn't seem like anything I ever did mattered before."

Mother had gasped and started crying again, which was weird. Lisa tried to feel bad, but she couldn't feel much of anything.

They left, Mother still dabbing her eyes, and once they were safely in the car, Mother said, "She's the first one we've seen who was helpful, don't you think?"

"I guess."

It was enough. Thankfully today Mother didn't insist on any further errands. Mental note: make Mother cry at therapy so she gets insecure about her makeup and doesn't decide to tack a Nordstrom's trip on after.

God, what a horrible thought. Lisa at the farm wouldn't have thought that way. For a brief moment, she'd been a better person. Was it only because of the structure? Was it only because of the pressure to be good? Was it only because Abigail used to look at her like she was good so she started to believe it?

Lisa turned her face to the window and discreetly bit down on three of her fingers. *Don't think. Don't.*

Her fingers wiggled—had she told them to?—and she realized they were snakes. She pulled them from her mouth, heart pounding. The strange girl in the reflection looked terrified. Was that her? Was she terrified? She could still taste her fingers. Not snakes.

She dug her nails into her palms for the rest of the ride home and chanted *no snakes, no snakes, no snakes* until they were nonsense syllables in her head.

15

EMERY
21 DAYS SINCE MEETING LISA

Emery arrived bearing fancy pastries from a Russian bakery in Berkeley, which he handed off to Carey at the door.

"We do have bakeries on this side of the tunnel, you know."

"You got poppyseed rugelach out here?"

Carey shook his head. "You may have a point. If we've got that—whatever it is—I haven't heard of it."

"You should be ashamed of yourself. Living in New York City that long and never having rugelach. Alice! Your man is a stunning disappointment!"

Carey laughed and led him into the kitchen. "She's making an egg bake for dinner. You have a job nearby in the morning?"

"Yep." A fetish shoot arranged by a dominatrix he'd worked with before, but Carey didn't need the details. "Thanks for putting me up for the night."

"I'd actually completely forgotten. Let me make up the sofa bed and clear out of the office."

Alice's lack of immediate appearance (or response to his shout) meant she was painting, so Emery took a stack of sheets and blankets and got to work while Carey shut down his computer and neatened the desk.

The first time they'd met, Carey had invited Emery to his apartment. Alice's comment to him was, *I like this one, Em.* A plea simultaneously for approval and a check on her judgment. Later, after they'd solidly established a friendship even apart from Alice connecting them, Carey had confided that her comment to Carey had been, *Em sees through people. You'll like him.*

The guy made okay money back home, but okay money still meant you had a fourth-floor walk-up and your kitchen was in a closet if you wanted to live in Manhattan. Emery had been struck by how *purposeful* Carey's apartment was. It didn't appear sparse, but everything had a place. Clearly he treated his office the same way, leaving it pristine at the end of the day.

Each of them was finishing up when Alice's studio door opened. "Where're my husbands?"

Emery made a sour face; Carey offered an apologetic shrug.

"Reconvening in the kitchen," Carey said. "Should I start prepping something?"

"Spicy sausage. Em can grate cheese." She stuck her head in. "I had a shit day in the salt mines. Remind me to pull out a picture I want later, Em. It's a beaut, but I need it at least five by seven, if not larger, so I can work with it."

"Oh, sure. Your wish is my command, Queen of Sheba."

"Go prep food for me, minions. I need to wash up."

Emery decided not to grate cheese. She'd been playfully calling him her husband for years—since long before Carey—and he'd halfway hoped that Carey would dislike it and demand she stop. Unfortunately, Carey wasn't the jealous type. Or the possessive type. Or even the strictly exclusive type, though Emery didn't think that he'd ever tested that last one.

Alice, who tested everything, had tried to hook up with another man exactly once since she and Carey got serious; she'd ended up leaving in the middle of her date and showing up at Carey's apartment. Emery grinned a little maliciously at the memory.

"What're you looking so smug about?" She deposited a block of cheese, a grater, and a bowl in front of him.

"Hey, remember that time you thought you were gonna fuck a CEO?"

Carey grinned. "Poor guy."

"He was a schmuck. Why isn't my cheese grated?"

"You don't deserve minions." But even as he said it, he was unwrapping the cheese. "Anyway, I thought I might pick up a lock for Lisa. A keyed lock, so she can leave her room without thinking someone's going to search it."

"Hmm." Carey drained the sausage and grabbed a pepper to chop. "Is that what she's afraid of?"

Emery considered it. He'd only met Lisa a handful of times, but he couldn't stop thinking about the way she'd looked while she drank her coffee: eyes closed, head tilted forward, lips…he probably shouldn't be thinking about her lips. And anyway, she'd looked the same with the lasagna, as if she hadn't really *enjoyed* anything in a long damn time. Not that enjoyment had anything to do with putting a lock on her door. "Jake thinks it's all about her mother, but I think she might be more generally jumpy than that. It might not be about *who* is in her space, but about the potential that someone could be."

Alice leaned against the counter where she could supervise both of them. "Cults aren't known for prioritizing physical boundaries. Could be she's extra paranoid."

"There was an incident with the mother, as well," Carey said. "Which isn't an argument against paranoia."

Emery met Alice's eyes across the room, both of them thinking about how weirdly sheltered the Derrie kids were. Even Carey, who had his own burdens, had a quaintly well-adjusted streak.

Emery shrugged. "If she grew up with that kind of thing, it probably wouldn't be all that disturbing to her now. Then again, Mrs. Thurman seems pretty…disturbing. In general." He waited to see what they'd say to that.

Carey skewed somewhat diplomatic, as usual. "I'm glad she didn't raise me."

"She's a fuckin' mess." Alice made grabby hands at them. "All right, bring it all in, egg bake time. Viv's a wreck. For one, she's got that fake smile soldered to her face. You think one of these days it'll start peeling, like a snake shedding its skin, and we'll find her whole creepy grin lying on the carpet over there?"

He grimaced. "You're disgusting, Al."

"And for two, there's something hollow about her. She sat at Cathy and Joe's house, smiled, laughed in the right places, but there was something not quite there about her."

"Like a fish out of water," Carey agreed. "She seemed slightly confused by the whole thing."

"And looking at your parents made her sad, but maybe not even consciously sad." Alice combined her ingredients in a dish and slid it into the oven. "Looking over when they were talking to each other was the only time the smile faltered. Isn't that interesting?"

Carey shrugged. "Singer never talks about his dad, as far as I know. I think they're still married, but he didn't even tell them that he and Jake were adopting until Viv showed up here."

"It's fascinating because I wouldn't tell my folks if we were adopting, but they also wouldn't move across the state to be near the cult I was living in, or follow me home to make sure I was okay again. It's hard for me to reconcile the"—she waved a hand—"the detachment with the over-involvement. Wine, Em?"

"Yeah, thanks. But you think I should bring a lock over, right? I mean, there's no reason not to." A request for approval, a check on his impulses. He almost took it back when he realized how it sounded.

She handed him a glass. "Can't hurt. Unless you have an unrequited crush. That might sting a little."

"Shut up. I do not have an unrequited crush. What am I, twelve?"

"Oh, I don't know." Carey shot an assessing glance at him. "I don't think anyone really ages out of having crushes. When you get older you can choose to do something about them is all that really changes."

Alice handed her man a ginger beer. "Exactly. Like buy a lock for a pretty girl."

"Are you two trying to set me up?"

"You're doing a decent job with that all by yourself, pal."

Carey, though, didn't make it a joke. "When's the last time you were interested in someone who wasn't falling all over themself to—" He broke off, as if considering the many ways he could end that sentence.

"Get all up on your jock," Alice supplied helpfully.

Emery shot both of them dirty looks. "Not something I usually have trouble with. Hi: model. Tattoo artist. Don't need help finding company."

"Fair enough," Carey said. "Is that what you're looking for, though?"

"I'm not ... *looking for* anything." When they just stared at him, he sighed. "Shut up, both of you. I'm not. She needs a lock. I can install one. Why is this a thing?"

Alice kind of snorted and turned away to check on the oven, but Carey nodded. "Maybe it's not. For the record, I think Lisa spent a lot of years trying to be what other people wanted her to be. It's gotta be hard to be back with her mother, or even Singer, even us, and not have that persona to fall back on."

Emery almost asked, *You speaking from experience?* But there wasn't any point in calling Carey out, because he'd just nod. He knew from having a role, fitting other people's expectations.

"Get the woman a lock for her door, Em." Alice offered him the wine bottle, but he shook his head. "I like her. She isn't running with 'pretty, but damaged' as a character to play, and every now and then she has a sense of humor. Way better for you than all those people who act like you're their reward for flashing the right smile, or delivering the right cheesy line."

Approval: granted. Weird that it felt good to sit in the kitchen at Alice and Carey's, thinking about Lisa. He didn't want to seduce her. Maybe this *was* more like a crush than anything else: he wanted to find excuses to spend time with her, listen to her talk. He'd caught himself falling into his usual shtick—charming, handsome Emery, who smiles brightly and makes everyone feel special—but Lisa seemed immune to it.

That was rare enough to be intriguing all on its own.

He raised an eyebrow at Alice. "You think it's narcissistic of me to be surprised she's not all that interested in my charming smile?"

"I think it's entertaining as hell that her lack of interest in your flirty persona is what you find attractive." She nudged Carey. "Can't wait to see how this plays out."

"Don't be rotten. And I think she could probably use a friend who's never seen all the masks she's worn, Em. That would be good."

"It's just a lock. Anyway, is my meal done yet? I don't come here because you two are endlessly amusing, you know."

"Exactly how much are you paying us for room and board? And another fifteen minutes at least, pal. I should make you dance for your dinner."

He rolled his eyes. "Didn't you have a favor you were asking me?"

"Right, yeah, where's your portfolio? I need a picture."

Emery went to grab his portfolio and his camera. Talking about photos and paintings would be better than overthinking lock installation. Definitely.

16

A week after the cult specialist who'd so enjoyed Mother, Lisa woke up to a weird text message from Singer.

Did you order a door lock, installation included?

She almost texted back a question mark, but Mother had driven somewhere earlier and hadn't come home yet, so she risked going out into the house instead.

The living room was scattered with toys at varied intervals while they tried to train Miles into inching along the floor when what he obviously wanted was to half walk, half lean on the sofas. Jake was doing most of the training, it looked like. Singer might have been smirking when he gestured to her guest.

Emery was there. With a Home Depot bag and a toolbox.

"Hey. Figured you might want a hand with this. Hope that wasn't presumptuous."

"Oh. No. I mean—yes, that would be good. You found a lock?"

"Sure. Like I said, it's not like it can't be pretty easily picked, and the door wouldn't hold up to a good kicking, but a lot more people will walk in through an unlocked door to snoop than will pick a lock to snoop, you know?"

Was Mother the first group, or the second? She glanced at Singer.

He considered it. "I don't think she'd break in. Maybe. I don't know."

Not that it mattered. The lock would still make Lisa feel better.

"I don't know how to pay you for that. I don't really—I mean, I have this credit card, but—"

"It's on me. Show me to the door, let's make sure it all fits together before we take it out. I could probably still return it, but why put in the time?"

Show him to the door, right. Her door. To her bedroom.

He's just helping. He's a nice guy.

All true. But he had those damn dimples.

"Lisa's door is the first on the right." Singer turned pointedly to Jake. "Do you think Miles would like popsicles? Or is he too young?"

Jake shook his head. "Whatever you do, don't tell Mom you're buying Miles popsicles."

"Good tip." Singer looked over his shoulder at her and made a face, wide-eyed and insistent.

Oh. Right. Her door.

"Sorry," she murmured. "This way."

Emery followed without speaking, and Lisa was grateful that he didn't try to brush it off or make ridiculous small talk.

"This is—my door." She had a strange, almost irresistible impulse to add, "This is the church and this is the steeple," like that old rhyme they used to do as kids, hands folding into a church, then opening to display all the people inside.

Lisa, focus. Hot guy trying to install something you need.

"Um. Here. I can get the lights." She flicked the hall and bedroom lights on and realized that the side table was still pushed in close, where she left it when she wasn't there for ease of shoving back in place. "Oh god. Sorry. I didn't think— No one ever comes back here—"

"Totally all right." Emery dropped to a knee beside the door. "Yeah, so this lock will work fine." He opened the bag and handed her the plastic-packaged doorknob. It was a regular sort of twist lock, but with a keyhole.

"I could lock it when I left the room."

"I figured there wouldn't be much point in getting you one that you could only lock from the inside. And that it might make it easier for you to leave, if you could lock up."

"Yeah." She put the doorknob down and sat on the side table. Sitting on the bed would feel weird. She had to get into the habit of closing it up, if only to make it less likely she'd crawl back inside in the middle of the day. "I need to get a job, you know? But I haven't worked in … a long time. It's hard to start again. Hard to even imagine it."

"I don't know much about the place where you lived, except that everyone seems happy you're out of there."

"They say it's a cult." She swallowed, watching him slice open the hard plastic with a pocketknife, one long straight line, consistent pressure. Emery's movements were efficient and smooth.

"Was it? I mean, I don't know exactly what makes something a cult, but I'm pretty sure no one wakes up in the morning and decides to join one. How did you end up there?"

Was there a good answer to that? Probably not. But unlike when Mother's specialists asked, Lisa felt like talking.

"It made sense, at the time. The people seemed so nice. And there was a man."

Emery smiled at her. "Isn't there always a man?"

She hesitated. Was Emery gay? Did it matter?

"He was beautiful. Not physically— Well, yes, physically, in a kind of Jesus way, which I guess was probably what he was going for." And she'd fallen for it. Had they all fallen for it? Had Di known what he was doing to them? The other men, Tad, John?

"But was he one of those charismatic guys, like even if he'd been ugly, he still would have been attractive?"

"Yes. Yeah, that's exactly it. Because I thought he was so magnetic. And there was this idea that—I don't know if anyone said it or I just believed it—that if you devoted yourself to the family, you could be like that. Special. God, that sounds so pathetic."

"I don't think so. Everyone wants to be special." He was unscrewing the old doorknob now.

"I guess so. But you didn't follow a guy who looked like Jesus to a farm and live there for three years, Emery."

"Which isn't to say I wouldn't have, at certain points in my life." He shrugged. "I was never without Alice. She's probably the reason I lived this long. I used to drift a lot, but she's never let me get far."

"Is that why you're here? I mean, I can tell you guys aren't from California."

"New Jersey by way of New York City."

They didn't sound strongly like New Jersey, or at least not like the New Jersey in movies.

"And kind of. I always wanted to move to the West Coast, but Alice thought it'd make us soft. Then she fell in love with Carey, and the rest is history." He smiled up at her. "I wouldn't have thought she'd ever leave New York."

"She doesn't sound all that ... New York."

"Oh, she does sometimes, but Alice adapts. When she's with all you California kids, she talks a little slower, with a more laid-back rhythm. Go stand on a corner in Queens with her and you'll hear a different Alice. Actually, it's always the same Alice, but her voice tricks out to match whatever she's doing."

"I always wanted to travel. When I was younger. I would have loved to move to New York."

"Why didn't you?" Emery pulled out the last screw and jiggled the knob until it came loose. "Not that I know anything about your family, really, but it doesn't look like you guys were deprived when you were growing up."

"No. We weren't. I'm not sure. I think I was afraid to do something so out of the ordinary, even though it wasn't, really."

"I'm not a huge fan of ordinary. I'm pretty much never satisfied unless I'm looking at the next shiny thing. But we moved to the West Coast, which I've wanted to do since I was probably six or seven years old. The beaches all looked so clean in the TV shows, you know?"

She offered a smile. "That's why I went to LA for school. I thought I'd be at the beach like every day."

"I dreamed of doing that, too. Is that how it was?"

"Not exactly. The farm—the place where I lived—was on the coast. It was fantastic. We grew our own food, and we had this huge property to ourselves, owned by this rich old couple who gave all their money over to the family. The kids ran around naked as long as it wasn't cold out. I actually helped grow plants—food, you know—with my hands, and it was amazing. I had no idea I could do that." She paused, knowing it sounded foolish, but unable to stop. "I mean, you know, now I think about it and it was straight out of some weird hippie commune dream, but at the time it seemed so … unique. It felt like we were the first people to ever live in harmony, almost like we'd invented it."

"I wonder if that's an element of human behavior. That thirst to be the pioneer."

"Yeah. It felt like we'd discovered a little utopia."

Emery began on the screws for the new doorknob. "That sounds pretty amazing, Lisa."

Was he messing with her? Trying to trick her? *No, be rational, trick you into what?* But he seemed so sincere, and what did *that sounds pretty amazing* mean?

"I'm not trying to recruit you," she whispered, leaning forward until her bangs hid her eyes. They were far too long, but not long enough to pull back.

"Oh, no, I'm sorry." He swiveled on his butt toward her and put down the screwdriver. "I'm so sorry if it sounded like I was mocking you. I wasn't. If some pretty man had serenaded me with all that, I can totally see myself going for it."

She looked at him through the imperfect curtain of her hair. "Are you gay?"

"Bi. Does that bother you?"

She shook her head.

"I, uh, didn't mean to act flippant, Lisa."

"No. I believe you. For whatever that's worth, which isn't much."

"It's worth something to me. I'm almost done here, then we'll test it out. I'll leave the other doorknob, though, because I'm not sure how a lock like this would affect your resale value." He turned back and finished the job while she watched.

Could Anthony have changed out a doorknob? Probably, but he wouldn't have. Could she?

She surveyed the tools, went over the steps in her head.

Yes. She could have done this. It would have taken longer, but she could have done it, if she had to.

Lisa sat back up. Was that foolish? Surely anyone could change a doorknob. Still, the sudden certainty that she could have done this insignificant thing filled her with satisfaction. Probably undeserved satisfaction.

"There you go. Okay, I'll stand outside, you lock it."

"Okay."

The door—her door—shut between them. She flipped the lock and Emery tried the knob. No go. She unlocked it and opened it again. "Thank you."

"You're welcome. Here, try from the outside." He pressed two keys into her palm, and for a second she didn't want to let go of his hand. "Pretend you're going somewhere. Maybe with me. Lock up like we're leaving."

Lisa blushed and slipped out. The keys worked. She tried both, just to make sure.

"I can't— I'm not sure how to thank you for this."

"You already did. I'm glad it helps." He gathered his things and packed the old knob in the Home Depot bag, which he handed her. "You might stick this somewhere."

"Okay."

Emery caught her eye and smiled. "It was cool talking with you, Lisa."

"You too. Thanks for not…judging me."

"I figure judging people mainly demonstrates a lack of perspective, you know? I try to have perspective." He mimed framing something in front of him with his camera. "Anyway, I'll see you around."

"Great." Oh jeez, did she really just say that?

He dimpled at her, and she forgave herself for sounding like an idiot.

She walked him to the door and tried to ignore Jake and Singer, but they were staring at her like she owed them something.

"What?"

"Nothing," Jake said.

"Or maybe something," Singer added.

She held up her two keys, stuck between her knuckles like claws. "Don't make me cut you."

Singer laughed out loud. Jake grinned at him like his laughter was the best thing that had happened all week.

Enough of being out. She waved and retreated to her room.

Yes. The door locked. She held the only two keys right here, in her hand.

After a second she pushed the side table up against it just because it made her feel better.

The memory of Emery's smile stayed with her for the rest of the day. Even Mother's announcement that they'd be going back to therapy didn't dent the reality of that smile.

17

SINGER
32 DAYS WITH MILES

Singer went into work again—and he hadn't volunteered this time, but he also hadn't complained—and circulated the new round of photos on his phone. He endured the questions and excitement with patience, part of his brain worrying about what was happening back at the house and the other part entirely relieved to be anywhere else. He'd left four messages for Brandi, who wasn't returning them, to ask how things were going and when the next court date would be.

When he sat down to actually run the round of reports he only had access to on the internal server, he took a second while the computer was booting up to check for messages again. And to text Alice.

At work. Check on J&M for me?

Sure thing, little brother.

Alice was technically an only child. She'd been mystified and exhilarated to find herself folded into the Derrie melodrama.

Should he tell her to check on Lisa, too? But no, Lisa, at least, would be safe behind her lock. He supposed it would be strange to install one on the master, even though it was tempting. Brandi might have questions at the next home visit if keyed locks started showing up on all the interior doors.

Oh, god. They had a visit scheduled for next week, and it was looking far less likely that Mother would... spontaneously decide to leave. They'd been up front about Lisa ("A temporary guest shouldn't be a problem," Brandi had said, emphasizing *temporary guest*), but Mother moving in might make them look like a halfway house for wayward relatives. How was he going to explain that away?

A throat cleared. "Sorry I missed your arrival."

Singer forced himself back to the present moment. "Hi, Victor. It was a repeat of last time, no worries."

"Kara keeps telling me to quit smoking, so I only do it when I'm here. I'm beginning to think going out every forty-five minutes for a cigarette lowers my productivity." He smiled ruefully.

"Can't quit, though?"

"It doesn't feel like I want to, yet. Aside from the health risks, the expense, and the constant badgering. I guess I don't want to *enough*." He raised his eyebrows. "She keeps asking when you guys are coming to dinner."

Dinner with the Republican Christians and their three adopted children. Kara would be blond with bright highlights and perfectly pressed clothes. The kids would be mixed-race and impeccably presented. Singer wasn't sure how to politely decline until it occurred to him that Mother couldn't possibly follow them to Victor's house.

Of course, they'd be leaving Lisa. But she had a lock now between her and Mother. She'd be fine.

"That sounds great. Our schedule's pretty open, so name the day."

"How about next Saturday? Will Miles be okay for the drive?"

"I think so. He seems—mostly placid. Is that odd, in a ten-month-old? Or, eleven months now."

"Do yourself a favor and don't look at all those lists about what's normal for each age. Maybe they work well for children who, uh, have no challenges, but you can go crazy comparing your kid to them. Kara spent a lot of time on websites that told her Rache was up to this standard or not up to that standard, and none of it was in any way helpful." He shut his mouth, like there was something else he wanted to say and then didn't. "Anyway, Saturday. Early, so the kids are in good spirits. Say, four?"

"I'll make sure when I talk to Jake, but that sounds good, Victor. And—thank you."

"Thank Kara. I'll text you the address."

Singer nodded and went back to his reports.

"A family date!" Frankie crowed.

"Kindly keep your voice down, Frances," Singer mumbled, shooting a look at the guesthouse.

They were eating takeout Indian food around the back table. Miles was sitting on Alice's lap picking at her food while she described it all to him. Emery had taken the seat beside Carey and across from Lisa. Singer reminded himself that despite Mother's presence, he still had a right to have friends over.

It was almost hard to remember back when they'd first been in the house and informal dinner parties had happened all the time. This shift in customs could not be laid at Mother's feet; once Frankie moved out, the house took on more of a "couple" vibe than a "group" vibe, and the

Irregulars had stopped dropping by with quite the same frequency.

"We haven't done movie night in a long time," Singer said.

"Movie night?" Carey asked.

Frankie waved her hand, which was holding the phone she hadn't put away since she set down her fork. "Damn, we haven't done movie night in a really long time. We should do it again, boys. I'll bring the booze. Not next weekend though, because you two have a *family date.* Ah ha ha ha!"

Miles spit out whatever it was Alice had given him. Alice burst into laughter. After a second, Miles grinned and stuck his tongue out again.

"I guess it *would* be a family date," Carey said thoughtfully. "Huh. I don't see why it wouldn't be."

"I like it," Alice added. "Do they have black kids? It'd be cool for Miles to know some other black kids being raised by white parents. That feels like something you'd want to make sure he was aware of."

He glanced at Jake, who was staring at her.

"Whoa, this just got real."

They'd had months to read and research and come up with plans, but so far in the month since Miles arrived, they hadn't put any of it into action.

"We underestimated how exhausting this would be." Singer glanced, again, at Jake.

"Hey, remember when we were all, 'Oh, we'll find a black community center, and we'll get the books and the dolls and stuff.'"

"Or a Latino community center, or an Asian one. I remember."

But parenting hadn't left them time to even think about any of that. Everything that wasn't formula, diapers, adoption, or sleep had been pushed from their minds. And this was with two of them home almost all the time; in another month they'd start back part-time at each of their jobs, an arrangement that had seemed so reasonable when they'd organized it all with their incredibly wonderful, supportive employers.

"That's a good idea." Emery pointed his camera down the center of the table. Singer resisted the urge to wipe food off Miles's face. "I think that kind of thing helps with the potential isolation of adoption."

"Are you adopted?" Lisa asked.

"Oh. No. I guess it's more that I'm invested in weird families. Right, Alice?"

Alice ruffled his hair. "Damn right. Thank god for Mrs. Murphy, or me and Em wouldn't have eaten as kids."

Jake smiled. "Thank god for Mrs. Murphy or we would be heating our bottles in pots of water on the stove. And the microwave hasn't messed him up yet."

The door to the guesthouse opened, and the table fell silent except for Miles, who'd started slapping his hand down on Alice's plate. She pulled everything too splatty out of the way and let him make a mess with what was left of her chana dal.

"Quite the party." Mother didn't slow down on her way into the house.

"She's so uncomfortable," Alice murmured once the door slid shut. "Every time I see her I feel her anxiety."

"Really?" Singer looked at Lisa, wondering if she saw that. He'd never thought of Mother as anxious. He thought of her as well-mannered to the point that her entire personality sometimes felt like stitched-together one-liners interspersed with the branch of passive aggression that sounded like humor and felt like thorns.

Lisa looked a little surprised, too. "I kind of thought that was my role."

"Important difference, chickadee. Your kind of anxiety pulls you in on yourself. Your mom's is the kind that stains everything she touches."

Emery shifted in his seat. "Alice, come on. She's their mom."

"I'm just offering an opinion. Miles, you know what they say about opinions, right?"

Miles brought both fists down again, and lentils jumped from the plate. He laughed.

"Should we be doing colors with him yet?" Jake asked. "Or, like, temperature? I guess I feel like we should be doing educational junk with him."

Yet. The word triggered the little ache in Singer's gut that never went away these days. He was forever tripping over words. And it wasn't always the same word. It clearly grated on Jake, how he refused to speak of the future, but trying to live in the present already felt like too much. How could he add the future to that, too?

"If Mom thought you should be doing any of that, his whole bedroom would be full of toys marketed for learning." Carey shook his head. "I'd enjoy hanging out with him and playing. Mom will have her day. Just wait."

Frankie looked up from whatever she'd been doing on her phone to add, "Yeah, Cathy isn't gonna be the uninvolved grandma, for sure. You'll only wish she was."

Except Singer was providing his family with one uninvolved grandma already. Even now she was probably looking out the window at them, wondering how everything had gone so wrong. Lisa, not wearing makeup; Singer, gay; and his boyfriend's extended family, with Alice (not skinny), and Emery (who had to have Italian blood or something; that black hair/blue eyed combination screamed "ethnic European"), and the little black baby they were trying to adopt.

Had Mother pictured this table surrounded by his blond wife and blond children, and Lisa's blond husband and blond children? Singer thought she probably had, maybe without knowing it. If Miles stayed with them, if they raised him, who would he bring home someday? What surprises would he have in store for his parents, the way his parents had surprised theirs?

If they raised him. Chills stole over his shoulders, down his back. The fantasy, the vision, was potent. He knew exactly why Jake allowed himself to believe. They'd been talking about having a family for years, and now it was so damn close, but Singer still couldn't quite touch it without the fear it would be yanked away.

"So, Frank," Carey said. Meaningfully.

Singer refocused on his guests. Derrie drama was always good for a distraction.

Frankie continued texting. "Shut your face."

"So."

"Seriously, boss man. I will get the kid to kick your ass."

"He can't even crawl."

"I'm a patient woman. I'll wait."

Carey eyed her for a long moment before shrugging. He looked at Jake first, then Singer, a silent enquiry.

Singer shook his head. Jake looked away.

"Huh," Carey said.

Jake knew who Frankie was obsessively texting? Curve ball.

Singer exchanged another look with Carey, both of them silently promising to dig for intel later.

"I will fucking kill you all," Frankie mumbled without looking up.

Carey started to reply, but the door opened to the house and he stopped.

"Lisa? May I see you for a minute?"

The table froze. All except for Miles, who was now eating the lentils he'd been playing with, scooping them into his mouth and making delighted "ba da pah" sounds when they dropped away.

"Sure, Mother." For a second Lisa didn't move, and Singer held his breath.

"Want me to do something really fucked up and draw her attention?" Frankie asked, voice too low for Mother to hear.

"No. But, uh, thanks for the offer."

"Anytime."

Lisa got up and went in, and the sound of the slider shutting was more final than it should have been, as if she were cut off and alone, as sure as she had been with her cult.

"You think she's ever going to eat with us again?" Jake asked.

"And why is your mom so threatened by the idea of Lisa having friends?" Carey made a gesture that Singer assumed referred to the past. "She always had friends in high school."

Alice snorted. "Let me guess: skinny blonde girls with one black girl and one brunette, right?"

"Actually, one Asian girl and one brunette," Singer said. "Though I'm not sure any of those people liked Lisa, so much as what she projected."

"Which, to be fair, was a total bitch skank from hell. Ow!" Frankie looked up from her phone long enough to dodge another elbow from Jake. "Dude, you know I speak the truth. Lisa was a bitch."

"Yeah, it's weird she doesn't hang out with us much, Frank, you asshole."

"Like you can blame me for that—"

Before the whole thing could deteriorate into yet another episode of *Derries Do Drama*, Singer cleared his throat. When that didn't work, Alice said, "You guys, shut the fuck up."

Magic.

He looked back at the kitchen windows, but he couldn't see anything. "I don't think Lisa wants to go back to being that person any more than you want to go back to knowing her, Frankie. But Mother is bound and determined. It'd be nice if——" What? *If you gave her a chance to change.* Not that Frankie seemed to need it spelled out.

"Sure, Singer, you got it. We can offer her the uniquely Derrie brand of love and acceptance we offer everyone else."

"God help her," Jake muttered. Then: "Ow, Frankie!"

Singer started cleaning up around Alice and Miles's plate. He couldn't help but notice that Emery, untouched by drama and memory, kept glancing toward the kitchen.

Good luck, Singer thought at him. *You'll definitely need it.*

18

LISA
61 DAYS SINCE LEAVING GRACE

Apparently the social worker lady had to come periodically to make sure they weren't screwing up Miles too badly. Mother, at least, was out. But Lisa was in, and therefore got to experience every awkward minute of the visit.

"It's so nice that Singer has a sister willing to come help out with his expanding family," the lady, Brandi, said to her.

Singer and Jake both did wide eyes in her direction, so she focused on Miles instead, straightening his funny little onesie. "Uh, yeah. Miles is pretty cool."

Which was the right answer, or at least wasn't the wrong one; the lady smiled and made small talk for a minute about Miles's age group and something about food, but Lisa wasn't really listening. Or rather, she was listening more to the things that weren't being said. This Brandi lady was asking them a lot of questions while not answering any of their questions.

"So is there a date for the next hearing?" Singer asked.

"Not yet, but it's gotta happen within the next two months, so I'll keep you posted."

"Any word from Miles's mom?"

"I swear, Singer, I will call you if anything changes. It looks like you guys are pretty much handling things here." Brandi's hair was professionally highlighted, but Lisa wasn't impressed with the job. Also, her makeup was a bit much. Was she trying to look older? She was probably thirty. Maybe makeup that aged her up to late-thirties-with-a-bad-makeover helped her get taken seriously?

Stop being so judgmental.

Probably true, but she still couldn't stop. By the time Brandi asked them how they were managing their stress levels (and who the hell says it like that?), Lisa had to bite her tongue and poke Miles until he giggled to keep from recommending a new hair stylist.

Singer shut the door after she left and slumped against it. "Tell me when she drives away."

"Did we decide getting drunk was a no-go?" Jake asked.

"We could call Brandi back and see what she says."

"God, don't even *think* that. I know it wasn't that big a deal, but I feel kind of gross."

"Did you notice she said nothing about Marie at all? That makes me nervous."

Jake checked the front windows. "She's gone. Yeah, I noticed. But I mean, what's she gonna say?"

"I was hoping for something along the lines of, 'Health problems make it so there's absolutely no way Marie can ever take Miles again, so don't worry about it.'"

"Oh damn."

Lisa looked up in time to catch the stricken look on Singer's face.

"Oh my god, I can't believe I just said that. I didn't— I didn't mean— I *like* Marie. I don't want her to get more sick, I meant—"

"Singer, it's okay. I know. I want to have it all be decided too. I mean, I'm not wishing ill health on little old ladies or anything—"

Singer winced. "I can't believe I said that."

"Seriously, it's okay." Jake stepped in closer and touched his arm. "Hey, you want security and stability for your family. That's totally all right."

"But I was willing to sacrifice Miles's grandmother's health in order to get it. I feel sick."

"Don't feel sick. I know we can't get drunk, but do you want a glass of wine?"

"It's four p.m."

"Four is almost five. Anyway, I'm having one. Lisa? Wine?"

"No, thank you." Jake walked into the kitchen, and Singer just stood there, still looking upset. She caught his eye. "Hey. I can hang out with Miles for a few minutes if you want. You two could, I don't know, sit in the spa or something."

"Probably right in time for Mother to get home."

She shrugged. "Or take some time alone, you know? You could go out to dinner, probably, if you think he'd be cool with me watching him."

"Oh, no, Lisa. I don't want to inconvenience you—"

"It's not—"

Jake came back in with two glasses and a sippy cup. "For you," he said to Singer. "And diluted grape juice for you, but don't get used to it because your Grandma Cathy will lecture me about the dangers of sugar again, Miles, and I just can't right now." He flopped back onto the sofa. "God. I could use a hot shower. A long one."

Perfect. She opened her mouth to offer, again, to watch Miles so both of them could take a shower (was that something people did?), but Singer beat her to it.

"Go ahead, Jake. We're good here for a while. I think I can manage not to do anything too boneheaded while you're gone."

"When are you ever boneheaded?"

"Never mind. It's fine. Go take your shower."

Jake started to shake his head, still frowning, then stopped. "You sure?"

"I'm sure."

"Because I'm serious. Having Brandi in the house feels weird. You think we'll get used to it?"

"God, I hope not. I mean I guess we should, but is it too optimistic to hope everything is resolved before it comes to that?"

"Probably." Jake glanced over, double-checked Miles (lying on his back playing with a mirror thing Jake's mom had gotten him), then stood up. "I'll be back."

"Take your time," Singer said, tone a little too cheerful.

When the door to their bedroom closed, Singer sat down. Then he poured his wine down his throat.

She frowned. "What just happened?"

"Nothing. What?"

"I don't get why you don't want me to watch Miles. I've done that before, Singer. I'm not gonna hurt him."

"Oh, god, no. No, that wasn't— I know he would have been fine."

"So then why?"

"Because. Because every time we're alone together I'm afraid he's going to see how hard I have to try to be *half* the father he is." He sighed and set his wine glass down, looking at Miles.

"Singer…" She had no idea what to say. She could tell, even when they were annoyed with each other, that they loved one another more than she'd ever loved (or been loved by) anyone.

"It's okay. The visit wore me out, that's all. I'll be okay in a couple of minutes. And with another glass of wine. Sounds good, doesn't it, Miles? I wonder if you have alcoholism in your genes. I guess that's not something I can really ask." He shook his head. "I have to get it together before he comes back."

Lisa wanted to say more, say something, but Miles finally lost interest in the mirror and started doing the squawking thing that meant he was going to start crying if someone didn't distract him.

"You want to try crawling again?" She felt silly talking to him. Not as silly as she felt when she got down on her stomach and looked at him upside down. "Hi, Miles. Can you roll over?"

Miles could roll over. He could roll over and lift his whole body up, head and everything. (He had a big head. That was a baby thing, right? Big heads?) He still couldn't quite coordinate his movements to actually *move*, but when he figured out he was right next to the sofa, he pulled himself all the way up to standing.

Lisa realized she was clapping for him, like a fool. But when he let go in order to clap, then fell back on his fluffy diapered butt, both of them laughed. "Oh no, Miles. You just took a celebratory fall, there."

She looked up to catch Singer's eye, but he looked away, blinking, like he was crying or something. Except Singer didn't cry. And nothing sad had happened.

He should be with Jake. Lisa couldn't even get her own head on straight, let alone figure out what was wrong with Singer's, but if he was crying—that was bad.

"Try it again, Miles," she said. Miles climbed back up, clapped, fell on his butt, and laughed.

Really, though, this kid thing? Kind of cool.

19

SINGER
40 DAYS WITH MILES

Singer insisted on helping with the dishes. He stood with Kara at the windows peering over the side yard of her lovely renovated flat in San Francisco, watching Victor and Jake play with the kids.

"They're very sweet with Miles," he said. "I can't imagine having more than one right now." One of the boys was circling a giggling Miles around on the grass, while Miles tried desperately to stay up on hands and knees. Every few laps he collapsed, and five-year-old Ty would pick him up again.

"I felt like that each time. And then, I don't know. We'd start looking at each other, and…" Kara smiled, a little wryly. "Then we'd get back on the roller coaster. How's the psychological side of adoption going for you?"

"It doesn't feel…real, yet. I guess because it isn't."

She nodded. Kara, contrary to his expectations of a white woman in linen casual with a small cross at her throat, was Asian and appeared to prefer black skirts and blouses. *Judge less,* he scolded himself.

"I remember that. I remember every awful second of it." She glanced over, a little guarded. "A friend of mine says the same thing about labor. Everyone tells you you'll forget this terrible trauma, that you'll look at your child and forget all of it, but she never has. I think it's similar. With adoption. But then, I don't know. I think Victor forgets."

Layers and layers there, Singer thought. "Sometimes it feels like Jake doesn't take it seriously. That we haven't met his mother, that there is no TPR, that nothing can be finalized until some court date months down the road, and that's if everything goes incredibly smoothly and Mom plays along." He tensed. "That makes me sound like … like I disregard her role, and I don't, but—"

"It's your life on pause," Kara said.

"Yes. Yes, that's exactly how it feels. Like I'm running in place, and I can't get off this treadmill until something is finalized."

Outside, Rachel, who was painting something, called Victor over to look at it. Ronnie, the older boy, zoomed past and knocked her easel over. Rachel spun on him, raising her hand, but Victor smoothly inserted himself between them and squeezed her shoulder as he righted the easel.

"Then again, single children are nice, too," Kara said, and if Singer hadn't looked over, he wouldn't have seen the flash of edged humor.

"I have an older sister. Though I'm not sure we were ever as friendly as your three."

"Do you get along now? At moments when they are— less than kind to one another, I tell myself they'll all get along as adults."

A month or two ago, his answer would not have been at all reassuring. But today? Today Singer smiled and said, "I think we're working on it. But yes. I value Lisa's presence. As the only other person who understands how crazy our parents are, if for nothing else." Then he realized that might sound strange and added, "Not that you and Victor are crazy—"

"No, no, I understand completely. I have a sister, too. And Victor—though I love him very much—will never understand what it's like to be the oldest daughter in a Chinese home."

They smiled at each other, and Singer reflected that he hadn't put any effort into making friends, probably not since encountering Jake on a street corner in the Castro and reintroducing himself. ("I, uh, remember you, Singer," Jake had said, blushing intensely. It had felt like the start of every bad romance novel, like bells should be ringing all around them, fireworks exploding in the background. He'd kept all that to himself and said, "I remember you, too.")

Jake had come with an entire ecosystem of family and relationships; Singer hardly needed more. But now, watching him play catch with Victor and Ronnie while Miles picked at something in the grass—this could be good, too.

Kara must have been thinking along similar lines. "We should do this again."

"We really should."

They talked a little bit about adoption in general, and their routes to parenthood more specifically. Singer admitted he was a little intimidated by Marie, partly because she seemed to intensely dislike them (with good reason, he hastened to add), and partly because she was the family matriarch. "I can't decide if I'm doing a creepy racist thing there—like maybe she would intimidate me less if she was white—or if this is just the position we're in with regard to each other."

"The whole process has been a mix of confirming and throwing out the window different stereotypes for me,"

Kara said. "Which I guess means I should stop thinking I understand things before I experience them."

"Actually…" Singer only hesitated for a minute. "Speaking of that, I assumed you'd be white, before we met."

She laughed. "You did not. Does Victor really look like the guy who only dates white girls?"

"No! No, I don't think it was that. It was— There's a rumor he's a Republican. I assume all Republicans are white, isn't that terrible?"

"Well, don't tell anyone at work, but he's having a hard time maintaining his Republican cred right now, with the party doing what it's doing. And *I* am not a Republican. Not that I think the Democrats are that much better, but they do seem slightly less creepy a small percentage of the time."

"You two vote in different parties?"

"We fell in love debating politics in college." She smiled. "When we're struggling with everything else, we can always fall back on the political merits of Bill Clinton's administration. Victor would say the *lack* of political merits."

"I admire your ability to amicably disagree," Singer said, trying to keep a smile on his face.

Kara immediately sobered. "Are you two getting any time alone at all right now?"

Not if I can help it. "It seems like us talking about things when we both know we're coming at them from different angles will just make it all more…painful. Sorry, I didn't mean to spill all of my problems on you, Kara. We hardly know each other."

"It's not all your problems. And I've been there. Or at least been where I was, which was really fucking difficult. Anyway, if you ever want to talk, or even just rant, let me know."

He nodded, abruptly worried that if he said anything more about it, he'd start crying.

Maybe something of that came through in his expression; she took her time drying her hands on a dish towel and neatening the kitchen. "Should we go out?"

"I think so." Singer decided a complete change of subject was in order. "Does Rachel love art?"

"With the kind of single-minded focus that reminds me of Olympic athletes, yes."

"My sister-in-law is an artist. A painter. I've seen her do that, lose herself in her canvas."

"I don't think I have a passion like that, but watching Rache makes me wish I did."

They went outside, talking about hobbies and passions and what differentiated them. And when Jake turned toward them, he smiled, and for a moment Singer thought everything might be okay.

*

Miles passed out in the car on the way home.

"Okay, Jesus was a little intrusive." Jake tucked the barely touched bottle back into the diaper bag at his feet. "But otherwise? They are really nice people, Singer."

"Jesus?"

"You didn't notice Jesus? He was in the bathroom, the hallway, and the kitchen, all different bible verses."

Singer shook his head and internally chalked it up to Jake's Catholic past, the hyperawareness of other people's religion. "Kara asked me if we were thinking about having more kids."

"Yeah?"

He'd expected Jake to be taken aback. Like he'd been. But whatever Jake felt about the idea of more kids, it wasn't that. Singer looked over, at Jake's profile.

"Are we? Thinking about it?"

"I do, sometimes. I mean, not right now, obviously, but later? That was fun, playing. It was fun watching the boys play with Miles." Jake readjusted his seat belt, shifted, steadfastly did not look at Singer. "When we talked, before, we talked about adopting more than one kid."

A coldness he'd been ignoring for days started to steal over Singer's organs, beginning with his stomach, an icy lump chilling him from the inside. "I'm not saying no, I'm just saying it's overwhelming, right now, to imagine it. We don't really have Miles yet. Brandi could call us tomorrow and take him away."

Jake didn't say anything for a long time. They were through San Francisco and over the bridge before he spoke again. "Everything you said is true. This could be our last night with him. I guess it feels like … I feel like I want to love him as much as I can, that even if he leaves us tomorrow, he'll have had that. I don't know. Maybe it doesn't matter. But for him? I want him to have everything, for whatever time we have."

Tears stung Singer's eyes, and he could find no words to reply to that. It seemed incredibly foolish to bet everything on what was so far from certain. Like Jake was inviting heartbreak.

And yet it also seemed incredibly brave, somehow.

The rest of the drive was silent, and Jake put Miles to bed with infinite care. Singer watched from the doorway, seeing them as strangers. Obsessing over how good a father Jake was did nothing to banish the cold, hollow place in Singer's gut. He took a shower, still trying to warm up, and when he came out Jake was pretending to be asleep.

This wasn't going to bed angry, Singer told himself, climbing in without disturbing Jake's side of the blankets. But he didn't think either of them slept well, angry or not.

20

LISA
65 DAYS SINCE LEAVING GRACE

Lisa locked her door. Even to pee. She knew it was ridiculous. She hated the sound it made, the little click, because it always felt so loud. She'd shuffle her feet or brush up against the wall to hide the sound. But knowing the door was locked made it easier to breathe, so she did it anyway.

It was a little after eleven p.m. and she couldn't sleep. She was still refreshing Twitter, though she knew no one was awake. It didn't help. She was actually beginning to think it was messing with her head.

Voices were coming from the front of the house. Probably Jake and Singer. Did she want to go back to her room? But no, she didn't. She wanted a cup of tea. And if they were in the living room, the kitchen would be empty.

Or should have been, except Frankie Derrie was sitting on the counter eating a cupcake. (And one of the swinging doors was propped open, probably from when Jake had been playing with Miles earlier.)

Lisa froze. "Sorry," she whispered.

"For coming into your kitchen in your house?" Frankie, also whispering, waved a hand. "Have a cupcake. We're the beneficiaries of Aunt Cathy's stress-baking habit."

"Thanks." Did she want a cupcake? She couldn't decide. Tea, though. Tea she could manage. She'd was filling the kettle when she heard voices in the living room.

"It's not reasonable, Singer. And that man, bringing a lock into my house— He's no friend of Lisa's. I've never seen him before in my life."

"He's a friend of ours, Mother. And if Lisa wants to be friends with him—"

"Does she know what he is? I heard you talking, Singer. I heard what you said he does for money."

"Mother, he's a tattoo artist. And a photographer."

"He takes *naked pictures of men,* that's what you said!"

Wait, were they talking about Emery? Also, she'd forgotten about his "artsy pictures of nudes" comment. Exactly how weird would it be to ask if she could see them?

Shockingly, something stirred in Lisa's gut.

That is not your gut.

Naked pictures, naked Emery, oh my god, stop.

"They're artistic photographs," Singer said.

"And he also takes them of women," Jake added. "Not that it matters."

"Really good pictures," Frankie whispered. "Seriously good, and I don't even like naked people. You should look, if you're ever at Carey and Alice's. They have a bunch of Emery's pictures."

Oh boy. *Sure, just mention you heard Emery takes naked pictures and want to see them. No biggie.*

"So this is like round seventeen." Frankie reached up for a mug and passed it over. "You want some casserole? Singer made it, so it's good."

Casserole. Lisa was momentarily distracted from her tea. "Singer cooks? Like all the leftovers in the fridge—that's Singer?"

"Right? When he was living in the city he used to produce the wildest dinners out of a toaster oven and a hot plate. Anyway, I know this is probably pretty *Twilight Zone* to you, but I'm glad you're okay. To whatever degree you are. Okay. Or whatever."

In the living room Mother's voice rose, saving Lisa from having to reply. "How can you possibly approve of that lock on her door? She could be doing *anything* in there, Singer!"

Frankie snorted softly. "Lisa Thurman, master criminal."

And that should have felt more like an insult, but Lisa rolled her eyes. "I'm trying to conquer the world with scrapbooking supplies."

Frankie covered her mouth to muffle her laughter.

Mother was escalating. "But why would she need to lock us out, can you at least explain that?"

"If it makes her feel better," Jake said, "maybe that's what's important."

"You aren't a part of this discussion," Mother snapped. "This isn't your home, young man, so don't presume to tell me about what goes on in it."

Frankie muttered, "Shit. Singer's gonna lose it."

"Mother, you're out of line." In their entire lives, Lisa had never heard Singer sound like that, like he wanted to hit someone. Still less that he wanted to hit *Mother*.

"Oh, crap, Singer's really gonna lose it." Frankie jumped down off the counter.

Mother's tone was rising. "Don't tell me—"

"Good night, Viv. I'll see you in the morning."

Jake walked through the doorway and blinked at them for a second before kicking the wedge of cardboard they'd used as a prop. No one spoke until the doors had stopped swinging shut.

"So that was a clusterfuck," Frankie said.

Before Jake had a chance to do anything more than nod, Mother stopped in the doorway, red-cheeked and appalled. She seemed to decide retreat was her best bet and walked straight out the back door without saying anything to anyone.

Lisa wasn't sure, but she thought all three of them may have actually sighed in relief. Despite the fact that Mother was now safely gone, Lisa felt around in her pocket for her key.

The door swung open again. "Jake? Are you— Oh." Singer faltered. "Um."

Jake offered a dismissive hand wave. "I guess getting massively drunk would be out of the question with a kid in the house."

"Clearly we left the necessity of mind-numbing alcohol consumption out of our calculations."

Frankie grinned, but Lisa thought she was forcing it. "You guys want me to proxy for you? I'm always in the mood for blotto."

"Hush, Frances." Pause. "Jake…"

"*Don't* apologize on her behalf. Don't, Singer. I know, okay? I know already, and she's right. It isn't my house."

"It is."

"It's not, but we fooled ourselves for a while, didn't we?"

"Jakey," Frankie began.

"I know, I'm sorry. Sorry." Jake shifted, back against the counter, and Lisa wished she hadn't come out for tea tonight. "I know, but Singer, she's right. This will never be my home."

He sounded so sad.

"Anyway, I'm going to bed. Seriously, it's okay. I'm okay. But I think I'm gonna read for a while." He straightened up and left the kitchen.

"Fucking hell, Singer Thurman."

"I have no idea what to do about this."

Lisa turned around, uncomfortable when both of them looked at her, but she thought about making Abigail laugh that time after they made tamales and she couldn't stop crying into the dishes. This was worse than that, but it was worth a try. "You haven't tried matricide yet."

Signer shut his eyes, and she thought she'd misjudged until he smiled and Frankie burst out laughing. "Oh shit, Lisa, you just made a joke about killing your mother. Fuck me. I'm gonna be laughing about that all night."

Singer shook his head. "Matricide. I'm not sure Jake's thought of that option. Though it's only a matter of time."

"I'm really sorry about—about Mother. I mean, she's here because of me—"

"What? No, Lisa. You were fine. All of us were fine. Mother is—the only one I blame for Mother. Well. And maybe Dad, but he's hard to blame for anything."

"Amen to that," Frankie said. "Viv is something else." She leaned over to turn on the kettle, which Lisa had forgotten to actually do.

Right. Concentrate. Mug, kettle. Tea bag. She found the herbal tea she most liked and wrapped the string around the handle of the mug, carefully ignoring Singer's silence.

Frankie never seemed to ignore *anything*. "You gonna fix this?"

"I'm clearly trying my best."

"Oh, is *that* what you're doing?"

God, this was awkward. Lisa pressed her fingertips to the little window on the kettle. The water was getting hot now. In a few seconds it would start making that sound, that jet-engine-warming-up sound, and maybe that would be a good excuse for everyone to stop talking altogether.

"Good night," Singer said with finality. He pushed back through the doors to the living room, and she couldn't decide if that meant he was going to bed or if he was just hiding somewhere Frankie wasn't.

"Jesus," Frankie mumbled. "Viv's done nothing to placate the household gods around here, Lisa, no offense. Not that it was all candles and rose petals before—both of them can hold up their end of a domestic—but seriously, has she always been like this?"

"Like what?"

Frankie waved a hand. "Never happy. With anything. I mean, the stuff she gets worried about—Christ."

She thought about it, still pressing her fingers to the window, letting the increasingly uncomfortable heat travel up through the nerves of her arms. The kettle was louder now. "She used to be unruffled. But I think she just saved it all up for Dad. He always looked a little … hunted."

That got a genuine smile from Frankie Derrie. "Ha. Yeah. Your mom as a cheetah, stalking her prey. Yeah, I can see that. Hey, is there some reason you're burning the hell out of your fingers right now?"

She'd forgotten about her fingers.

"Here." Frankie turned on the cold tap. "I'll finish your tea."

"No, no, it's okay."

"Seriously? Look, have you met Aunt Cathy? I can't take another maternal interaction tonight, Lisa, just soak your damn fingers."

Lisa wanted to argue more, but all that water was going down the drain. Wasted. While she stood there. She gave in and let the water run over her fingers.

"I'm going home, now that the show's over." Frankie set the mug beside her. "See ya around."

"Good night."

Lisa listened distantly as Frankie opened and closed the front door, barely audible over the running water. It was mesmerizing, watching it flow over her skin. She kept expecting her fingers to turn to snakes in the rush, but they didn't.

21

Things had been somewhat tense in the house, and while Viv didn't feel *entirely* responsible for it, it was inconvenient enough to require addressing.

She hadn't meant to snap at Jake. That had just happened in the heat of the moment when the person who was really responsible was Singer. He should have been paying closer attention to his sister, and he certainly should have taken an interest in the people he was currently exposing her to. This man, Emery, the *photographer* and *tattooist*. If Viv had been in the house, she never would have allowed him through the door, let alone to install a lock and encourage Lisa's antisocial behavior.

For the most part she avoided Jake. But he happened to enter the kitchen when she was having a slice of toast, and it seemed like an opportunity to at least smooth things over. Perhaps an opportunity to understand how everything had spiraled so completely out of control.

"Hello, Jake."

"Hi, Mrs. Thurman. I'm just…making a sandwich." He frowned and turned away, pulling bread out of the pantry.

"Isn't it early for lunch? Or I suppose you likely have your own schedule."

"Uh, yeah." He gestured toward the hall. "Singer's just checking in with work for a few minutes. I'm not sure we have a schedule, really. I guess whenever Miles goes down for his nap, it's lunchtime."

"That makes perfect sense. Have you always wanted children?"

"I guess so. For a while I didn't think I'd be able to have a family, but it was definitely always something I wished for."

Just as she'd expected. It confirmed her suspicion that adopting was Jake's idea, and Singer was merely going along with it. "I didn't realize Singer was interested in children. He always struck me as so solitary when he was a child himself. It's hard to picture him with children of his own."

Jake's eyebrows rose. He carefully arranged turkey and cheese on his bread. "Really? I can picture Singer doing everything. He's the guy who does it all, you know?"

"I see what you mean, of course," she said. Singer had always been extraordinarily competent. "But parenting is more than a task to be accomplished. It's not as simple as being a good student, or a good employee."

"Uh. Well. We didn't really know each other in school. I only ever saw him from afar, mostly when he was in plays with my cousin."

"Yes, Singer had a flair for theater, didn't he? That's the kind of thing I mean. Less of a…job to be done, more of an innate talent. That's how I feel about having children." She smiled and picked up her purse. "Nice speaking with you, Jake."

"You too, Mrs. Thurman."

She left as he was still putting together his sandwich. Of course, young people were notoriously blind when in love. Jake likely didn't realize the extent to which his inclination to have children ran contrary to Singer's disinclination to do the same. Anyone could see Singer had no particular gift in this area. Half the time he seemed afraid he was going to drop the little boy.

Surely Singer understood that the noble thing to do would be to cut ties now, when the child was young, and not saddle Jake with a disinterested partner. Was he really so selfish that he would rather avoid the inevitable confrontation than face the clear facts? He was so very much like Drew sometimes.

Of course, none of it was the baby's fault. And they were throwing an unnecessarily elaborate birthday party for him in a few weeks. Viv mentally mapped local children's shops and considered driving into the city. Miles should have at least a few things that had not been purchased at Target, for goodness' sake. And she might not have many more opportunities to expand his wardrobe.

22

LISA
68 DAYS SINCE LEAVING GRACE

Lisa's only excuse was that Mother should have been asleep, with her earplugs and eye mask. Not lying in wait, ready to spring yet another appointment on her.

She should have been asleep, dreaming of whatever Mother dreamed about. (And here Lisa drew a blank: what images invaded Mother's mind while unconscious? It was hard to imagine Mother letting the polished veneer she preferred to reality slip, even in sleep. Surely Mother didn't dream of snakes that became faces, or beds that became sucking space vacuums with teeth.)

She shivered, and Mother looked over.

"The air conditioning in these places," Mother said. "Almost as bad as the music."

These places, like Mother had seen a lot of shrinks' waiting rooms? Maybe she just meant with Lisa, in the last two months.

"Lisa?"

Mother stood up with her, stood behind her, and the man at the door put out his hand.

"Lisa? And you must be Vivian."

"Call me Viv, everyone does."

Lisa fought an eye roll. Once, she'd been dropped off at home by a concerned parent from some party the cops broke up. She'd been standing there—a little like this, actually, in the doorway—and the other mom had introduced herself, frazzled from talking to the police, pretty freaked out. Mother, reliably, had said, *Call me Viv, everyone does,* and Lisa had caught Singer's eye for a second where he was sitting on the sofa in the living room. He hadn't rolled his eyes (Singer was not an eye roller), but he'd looked at her, then Mother, then her again, like he was saying, *I know.*

Was she supposed to sit down? But Mother was standing there, half in, half out of the room, urgently explaining to the man that she felt it necessary to stay with Lisa for the session, blah, needs me, blah.

He was in his forties, black, hair cut close, maybe like the military, but she couldn't always tell with black guys, polo shirt over an upper body that looked like it wanted to be defined but had gone soft—good shoes, though. If she'd seen him on the streets in Long Beach or Santa Monica, walking back to the office after lunch, she would have approached him with a smile. He would have let her get exactly twenty seconds into her pitch before graciously excusing himself. He would have been one of the ones who told her to have a good day, even if she pushed him into another twenty seconds.

One of Jake's cousins had recommended him, which was probably why Mother was so freaked out. She hadn't personally vetted this one like she had all the others. And already she couldn't control him.

"Thank you, Viv, that's very helpful." He had one hand on Mother's shoulder, leading her back to her chair. "We'll see you in a few minutes."

Then he ushered Lisa into the room and shut the door.

She offered a half shrug. "Sorry. I'm not sure what any of this is trying to do, but you could probably let her in. I don't care." It wasn't exactly true, but it was true enough to not feel like a lie.

He waved a hand at the room. "Sit anywhere. And you're thirty-four years old, Lisa. That's at least fifteen years out from when I'd be comfortable having your mom in on your first session. And twenty years out from when I'd welcome her. Sit. Unless you'd rather stand, but I'm definitely going to sit."

His name was Saul. Saul Smith. It was right there on his degree, from UCLA. So, Southern California, interesting. He might well have been one of her potential recruits once.

She sat in an armchair.

"Do you get a lot of thirty-four-year-olds dragged in here by their mothers?" she asked when he didn't say anything.

"A few. Am I the first person she's dragged you to?"

"Not even close."

"I'm not an expert on cults. Your mother appears to have a dim view of my profession in general, but she seemed especially irritated that I'm not an expert on cults. I take it I was not her choice of therapist?"

"No, my—brother's boyfriend's cousin gave me your name. Sorry."

"For your mother's dislike? It doesn't bother me."

She shifted in the armchair, trying to find a way to explain Mother. "I was gone, you know. She must have been worried." Which sounded weird. Mother worried? Mother—the woman who greeted *I know it's late, but the police called, and there were drugs* with *Call me Viv, everyone does*—worried?

"She should go to therapy," Saul said, deadpan.

"Yeah. Well, sometimes I think she is, and I'm just the excuse she's using." Lisa shrugged. "Sorry, I have no idea what we're doing here. This is probably a waste of your time."

"Do you like baseball? We could talk about baseball until your time's up. I get paid either way."

"Ha. Yeah, not so much. I used to like basketball, but it's been a while." She gestured to the diploma. "Lakers fan, by any chance?"

He nodded. "But it's been a while. Well, you want to give it a shot? Therapy, I mean, not basketball. I could ask some questions, nod wisely, generally give you the impression I have all the answers while mentally planning my fantasy baseball team."

"Is that something you do a lot?"

"No. But not never, either."

They stared at each other for moment that probably felt longer than it was.

"Sure," Lisa said. "Okay."

"Were you in a cult?"

"I guess it depends on how you define 'cult.'"

He—Saul—smiled. "Good point. Let's see." He pulled out his phone, tapped on it, leaned back. "Google tells me a cult is 'a system of religious veneration and devotion directed toward a particular figure or object.' It can also be 'a relatively small group of people having religious beliefs or practices regarded by others as strange or sinister.' Which definition do you think your mother's using?"

"May I look?"

Saul hesitated, then held out his phone, angled so she could read it but not inviting her to take it.

"I guess the second one. I think Mother regards any group of people doing something she doesn't understand to be sinister."

"That's the thing about words. Ultimately, there's always interpretation involved. So, given those two definitions, would you say you were in a cult?"

She wanted to see Google again, but she didn't really need to. *Directed toward a particular figure.* Praise for Anthony Grace. Even now, out of touch for only an hour (she'd refreshed the search on her phone minutes before being called back to the office), her fingers tingled with the desire to see where they were, who was online, what they were doing. Sometimes they mentioned him, always as *He*, like Jesus, like he needed no name, like that one capitalized letter communicated his greatness.

"Yes." Was there something else she was supposed to say? Should she apologize? Explain?

Saul nodded. "And you live with your mother now?"

She blew out a breath, shaking her head. "No. No, I live with my brother, and I live in the old house, but Mother wasn't supposed to be there. He and his boyfriend live there, with this kid they're adopting, and Mother just showed up. I mean, I was with them for five days, you know? My parents. And it was too much. They wanted to … fix me." It was vitally important that he understand she did not move in with Mother and Dad. "And now she's here and she's really screwing everything up. She told Jake—that's the boyfriend—that it's not his house, and he was actually just defending me, so that makes it so much worse. But she won't leave, and we don't know why."

"Hang on, I need a recap. Your brother and his boyfriend live in your parents' house, while your parents live elsewhere."

"Right, yeah. Yes."

"And when you left the cult, you moved in with them. With your brother and his family."

Singer had a family now. It was surreal, but accurate. "Yes. And I think—I don't know—I think maybe it would have been okay, even though they're Derries."

Saul raised his eyebrows.

"These kids we went to high school with—my brother's boyfriend is one of them. And he's got all these cousins who used to hate me, but I don't think they hate me anymore."

"And how does your mother fit into this picture?"

It must look insane from the outside. How much less insane did it seem to her, after living with twenty-seven other people at the farm? Lisa wasn't sure.

"Mother showed up one morning. Without calling. Or maybe she called and we ignored it, I don't know. And since then it's been—" Intolerable. Impossible. "Difficult."

"She moved in?"

"I guess so? At least, she won't say she moved in, and she won't say when she's leaving."

"And who pays the bills?"

"Singer and Jake, I think."

"Not your parents?"

She shook her head. "No. If Dad was paying the bills, Singer would have moved by now, or at least talked about it. But he's still waiting for Mother to leave, so he must think she's going to." She shook her head. "Does any of this make sense to you at all? I mean, maybe I was in a cult, but describing this feels a lot more crazy to me."

Saul smiled, and she decided she liked him. She couldn't quite smile back, but he was okay, he got it somehow.

"Sounds crazy, yeah. But it also sounds like it has the potential to be a solid support network for you."

"Except for Mother."

"She mentioned you have a lock on your door. It particularly disturbs her."

"Yeah. Well, Emery got it for me."

"And Emery is another friend? Or one of your brother's friends?"

"Singer's sister-in-law's sort of brother, I think. He has dimples." Oh, god, did she say that out loud? She blushed. "Sorry, I don't know why I said that."

"Can I ask why you have a lock on your door?"

"I was blocking it with a table. But that only works when I'm inside. I wanted a way to lock it when I left. And Jake—that's Singer's boyfriend—said I should feel safe in my own house. But I don't, really."

"Because you think someone might enter without your permission?"

"Oh. Well. Not exactly."

Saul offered a small smile. "Not exactly?"

"I know Mother would enter without my permission if I wasn't there. But Singer and Jake never would, and I still didn't … feel safe. Before."

"Because of your cult."

"I guess so." She tried to keep her fingers from writhing around each other, but her bones were showing again. They'd be snakes soon, she could feel it.

"Do you worry that someone will come after you, Lisa? From before?"

What's the difference between worry and hope? "It's not gonna happen. People leave. No one person is more important than any other."

"Sometimes feelings aren't rational. You can know your mother means well and still find her presence difficult. Are you afraid they'll try to take you back?"

Bones, white bones, segmented by knuckle joints. Twisting around each other. "I think I more—at first? At first, every time someone knocked I was afraid. And also, it's like I never existed, like I was never there. Sometimes I wish someone would—would try. To make contact. But I know they never will."

"Your mother says you were there for three years."

She nodded, throat dry.

"It's perfectly normal to miss them, Lisa. And if you feel comfortable, with your brother, with his boyfriend, or his friends, talking about it, that would be good."

It didn't seem logical. "They think I was abducted. Forced to stay there. I mean, they know I wasn't Patty Hearst, but they don't get how much I loved it. How much I wanted it. How it felt more like home than here."

"Tell them," Saul said. "If you can. And try to convince your mother to go home."

"Not likely. I don't know what she's waiting for, but I don't think I can do it, whatever it is."

He nodded and looked up at the clock on the wall. "We're done. Feel free to make an appointment for next week." But she saw in his face he didn't think she would. No. No way Mother would pay for a therapist who wouldn't even let her in the room.

"Yeah, okay. Uh, thanks."

Sure enough, Mother promised she'd never have to return to Saul's cold office. "He's a hack. I'll find someone better."

There was no point in arguing. So she didn't. She surreptitiously pulled out her phone and refreshed Twitter again. It wasn't any more real than Mother's world, but at least it didn't require her participation.

23

FRANKIE
COMING CLEAN

Logan was nearly always in a good mood. It was simultaneously one of Frankie's favorite and least favorite things about him. On one hand, it made him reliable and predictable, to say nothing of—attractive. Low-key, noninvasive good cheer was apparently a quality Frankie actually enjoyed, though she wouldn't have admitted it to anyone.

On the other hand, it was a point in Logan's nature that emphasized the gulf between them. Frankie had a reputation for temperamental, incurable nosiness to maintain, after all.

She knew immediately upon starting work that afternoon that today was not a day when she had to worry about feeling like she corrupted him by challenging his seemingly effortless happiness.

After checking in with Izzy in the office—"Get out of here, Derrie, can't you see I'm busy?"—Frankie did a round of the store, gathering a stack of books to reshelve. She ended up at the front checkout desk and sideways bumped into him as a way to say "hello."

He smiled, but it didn't quite light up his eyes. "What's up, girlfriend?"

"I am not your girlfriend."

"I think you're wavering on that front."

She was. "I'm really not. Why do you look all bummed out?"

"I'm not 'bummed out,' Frankie. I'm, like, *contemplative*."

"Oh yeah? About what?" On a normal day she'd knock on his head, pretend it was empty. Not a game for today.

"It's nothing. I'm mostly inventing a reason to feel bad about myself. Sort of."

Frankie glanced around. They had exactly one customer, a regular, who was sitting in the back of the store reading a book about game theory. She definitely didn't have to be in ultra-professional mode, so she shoved the books out of the way and jumped to sit on the counter. Izzy would snap at her if she happened to venture into the store, but she'd looked pretty busy in back. Plus, Izzy snapping was the usual way of things, not something Frankie needed to avoid. After a brief hesitation, she mock-punched Logan's shoulder. "Why're you trying to feel bad about yourself?"

He sighed. "You'll think it's pretty absurd."

"Shoot. Distract me from trying to figure out why Singer's being even more obtuse than usual."

"Wait, he is?"

"Yeah, like I'm no one's expert on relationships, but he's playing this whole 'I don't know what to do, blah blah blah, Jake's mad at me' card right now that's really getting on my nerves."

"Seriously? But are you sure you're not just sort of making it up, because—"

A less gentle punch this time. "I said, *distract me*."

Logan grinned, raising his eyebrows in invitation. "But I love Derries drama. Maybe you should be distracting me."

"Fine. Tell me what exactly you're not thinking about, and I promise I'll come up with something way more overwrought to replace it."

"Okay. Deal." But he paused for a moment, looking almost hesitant. "The thing is, it's silly. And I know it's silly. But I feel lousy anyway."

Frankie was known for rushing in and asking too many questions. She was also known for saying too much, and at all the wrong times. And maybe, with the cousins, she still played that role, if role was what it was.

With Logan, she did something else. She gave him a little bit of space and waited for him to speak.

"You know how I went to that big graduation party for my cousin over the weekend?"

She nodded. "Was it awful?"

"The party was fine. And I'm super happy for my cousin. Med school was a total nightmare, and she's wanted to be a doctor ever since we were kids, so this is a huge deal."

When he started picking at the little bits of tape stuck to the side of the dispenser instead of continuing, Frankie nudged him. "I sense a 'but' in there somewhere."

"I don't know. My parents are absolutely the greatest parents ever. They totally never put pressure on me to have a career, and they always let me know that if I wanted one, they'd support me, pay for school, whatever. They're pretty wonderful. But then I was watching my aunt and uncle, and how proud they are to be standing at their daughter's med school graduation, and it hit me that when people ask my folks what I'm doing, they have to be like, 'Oh, he works for slightly more than minimum wage at a tiny bookstore in a strip mall.'"

Frankie winced, even though she figured that wasn't really how Logan's parents would say it. "Ouch."

"Right." He smiled wryly. "Ouch. I mean, most of the time I'm okay with being an underachiever. Today I'm feeling kind of not that thrilled with it as a life plan."

"Okay. So what *do* you want to do?" She gestured around to the store. "Since apparently the fabulous world of Planet Book just isn't enough for you." For a second she thought she'd said the wrong thing, but his resulting slump didn't seem directed at her.

"That's the thing. Planet Book really *is* enough for me. For right now, anyway. I like the work, and I'm used to Izzy, and I know all the regulars." Logan's eyes drifted away. "And you're here. I really like knowing I'll see you all the time, and if we didn't work together, I might not."

The idea that Logan could leave the store hadn't been real. And probably it wasn't. But Frankie could see that future, too, and he was right. If they didn't work together, she wouldn't find excuses to show up at his apartment. Maybe he'd stop by the bookstore sometimes, but the constant daily experience of each other's lives would fade until they were nearly strangers, occupying that strange twilight acquaintanceship of peers who'd moved on.

She jumped down from the counter. "I don't want that. You leaving the store. Don't do that. I mean, unless you want to."

"Admit it: you'd miss me horribly."

"You wish."

Instead of coming back at her, he just stood there with a slightly crooked smile on his face.

Frankie relented. "I'd miss you a little, but only because I have an appreciation for your work ethic."

"And I'm pretty sure you like hanging out with me."

She decided to ignore that. "What do you want to do really? I mean, we aren't that old, but sometimes I think I'm old enough to, like, have some kind of goal. My cousin Carey always wanted to be a lawyer, and now he is. My cousin Adam was a slacker for years and then just sort of stumbled into massage therapy, and now he's deep into it, like it's the only thing he could ever do. I don't have anything like that."

"Maybe we will later." Logan shrugged. "Or maybe we never will. Maybe that's not something everyone needs. I don't know. But I'm glad I'm not the only one who's happy with the job I have, even if it's not a career. Anyway, now it's your turn. Distract me with Derries."

"Ew. That's gross." But she regaled him with family tales, including how apparently some of the cousins were actually thinking about marriage in a serious way that made it hard to tease them, which was both bizarre and unsettling.

Add "marriage" to "career" on the list of things Frankie was supposed to want, but didn't.

*

Singer and Lisa Thurman walking in just after Frankie's lunch was a little bit of a surprise.

"As I live and breathe!" she called. "Lisa fuckin' Thurman, you're out in the world!"

Logan elbowed her. "You want to watch your language?"

"What?" She gestured to their only customer. "Michael's not going to complain. Are you, Michael?"

Michael half turned. "And voluntarily start a conversation with your boss? No thanks. Curse away. Even if it does demonstrate a lack of imagination, Frankie."

"That's enough out of you," she shot back.

Logan held a hand out to Lisa Thurman. "You almost definitely don't remember me from school. I'm Logan."

"I'm Lisa." Lisa avoided eye contact, which seemed to be her jam these days. It was weird trying to reconcile "Lisa 1.0"—who was desperate to be looked at—with the new version, who seemed to detest being noticed. Still, she shook hands with Logan like a normal person. Which was probably growth.

Sigh. Polite people were so boring.

Frankie focused on Singer. "Where's your family?"

The skin around his eyes tightened. "Out to lunch with Cathy."

"But not you? What're you doing—babysitting Lisa?"

Lisa cracked a smile. Singer didn't.

"Jake and Mother..." He trailed off. "Anyway, he already had Miles packed up before I realized they were going somewhere."

Frankie narrowed her eyes, like maybe she could read whatever was going on if she only looked closely enough. "The hell does that mean?"

To her surprise, it was Lisa who explained.

"She bit his head off for putting away the pots and pans incorrectly, but it was really, you know, more about how she's seething with resentment about being displaced. Mother really needs therapy." At Singer's pointed look, she shrugged.

None of this made a lot of sense, though the idea that Lisa had been to enough shrinks to say shit like *seething with resentment about being displaced* was pretty amusing.

Frankie was just gearing up to interrogate Singer about why the hell he hadn't gone to lunch with Jake and Miles when he spoke first. "So, no dragon lady today?"

"Izzy went home already, so we can assume she's doing naughty things with her new ladyfriend we aren't supposed to know about."

Logan sighed in resignation. "Frankie…"

"So, Izzy has a secret friend?" The wheedling tone in Singer's voice immediately made her suspicious. "Who does that remind me of?"

No, no, no, fuck no. Frankie raised the book she was holding. "Don't make me hurt you with literature, Singer."

"You have a secret friend?" Logan poked her. "Who's your secret friend?"

"Oh my god, no I don't, and shut up." This was going downhill fast. She brandished the book at Singer again. "Shut. Up."

"You've never once hesitated to stick your nose in my business, Frances."

"Because you keep screwing it up. My business is just fine without your interference."

"Too late," Logan said. "C'mon, Frankie, tell me who it is."

"I want to know, too!" Michael called over, because apparently eavesdropping was more fun than the new James Patterson.

"Everyone shut up. You I can fire, and you three I can kick out of the store, so shut up."

Singer blithely ignored her, turning instead to Logan. "Logan, out of curiosity, do you and Frankie text each other?"

Logan—that bastard, that turncoat—grinned. "Yeah, I was thinking I better be Frankie's secret friend." He poked her again. "You keeping me a secret for some reason?"

"It's not like that," she mumbled. Dammit. She should be messing with Singer right now. How the hell had he gotten the upper hand so quickly? "I have, like, work to do. In the back."

"I think Frankie and I should be dating, but she insists it's a bad idea, even though we both *want* to be dating," Logan explained to them.

And maybe it was because of their conversation earlier, or maybe it was because this was the closest to his usual light and cheery self he'd been all day, but she didn't immediately contradict him.

She settled for death threats. Death threats were always appropriate. "I will kill all of you."

Singer raised his eyebrows at her. "Why aren't you dating Logan?"

"Because reasons, okay?" Fucking hell. Juggling omissions was really obnoxious. "It wouldn't work out. And shut up."

And oh, look, the penny dropped. Logan's eyes widened. "Oh, okay. Sorry. I just assumed since Jake knows—"

"No."

He looked stricken, which unsettled her. It reminded Frankie too much of that moment earlier, when he'd talked about not seeing her all the time, like he'd exposed a little more of himself than he usually did. "God, I'm such a tool. Sorry, Frankie. I am now *that* asshole."

"What asshole?" Singer asked.

This was officially beyond what she could handle without outright lying. Frankie made a split-second decision, based on two simultaneously strong desires: to end the conversation, and to avoid it ever happening again. Fuck it. Singer could be trusted with this, even if he was making a wreck of his own life.

She rolled her eyes, as if none of it mattered. "I'm asexual. Okay? I'm not dating Logan because I'm ace and he isn't, so thus, it wouldn't work out. Christ. Can I go on with my day now please?"

Logan reached out. "Frankie—"

"We are *so* not dating now. Jerk." But she let him leave his hand on her arm. It seemed to make him feel better.

Singer, though. He was gonna be a problem. "I think people make that work. Don't they?"

"My cousin's asexual," Michael volunteered from the back corner. "He has girlfriends sometimes. I think they just don't usually have sex."

"Oh my god. This is my nightmare." Frankie mimed slamming a fancy hardcover Dickens collection into her head. "This is that dream where you're naked in front of the whole school, only it's the bookstore, and I'm not na-ked, I just *feel* naked."

Logan's hand tightened. "I had no idea you weren't out to Singer, Frankie. Shit, I am *so*—"

"Shut up." It definitely wasn't worth that much contri-tion, and it wasn't that big a secret. It was just something she hadn't gotten around to telling everyone yet. "Anyway, I trust the Thurman kids way more than I trust Derries."

Singer visibly shook himself, and it would have been funny in a slightly less fraught moment. He opened his mouth, closed it, tried again. "Wait, you didn't tell— *Carey* doesn't know?"

"No, Singer. Because I actually don't want to talk about it."

There. End of fucking discussion.

Lisa looked up. "I get being afraid, but you should go for it. It's not worth avoiding everything that's scary."

"Says the woman who never leaves her house."

"Yeah." Lisa gestured to the store. "Exactly."

Jesus, outsmarted by Lisa goddamn Thurman. Unacceptable. Frankie was poised to attack when Logan's hand slid down her forearm until his fingers interlaced with hers.

She promptly forgot what the hell she'd been planning to say. "Well, thanks for the pep talk, Thurmans. Move along now, unless you're actually buying books."

"You have any books on asexuality?" Singer asked.

Frankie raised the hardcover again.

"I'll just browse." He didn't quite hide his smile. "I knew you had a secret friend."

"I will *kill you in your sleep*."

He waved her off and turned toward the nearest bookshelf.

Frankie started to shake her head, but when Logan tugged her closer, she went. "You're in the doghouse," she informed him.

"Yeah, uh, upon reflection, I think maybe I crossed a line at some point and didn't notice it? Because seriously, I feel like that asshole who keeps asking a woman out when she says she's not interested. I *thought* we were both sort of … playing? But I'm gonna stop doing that now, because I don't want to, like, actually pressure you. That is so not fun."

"Oh, like you could ever make me do *anything*, dummy. Please. You're not in the doghouse for that." She couldn't bring herself to pull her hand away, so she settled for planting the other one firmly on her hip and staring at him.

"I'm still really sorry about, uh, outing you to your family." His expression was so sincerely remorseful she couldn't hang on to anything but the desire to make him feel better. Which was annoying.

She forced herself not to tell him it was okay. Because kind of, it wasn't. But it also wasn't as big a deal as she'd thought it would be, at least not with Singer and Lisa.

Logan shifted on his feet, a motion she felt through their joined hands. "Clearly I should do something to make it up to you. *Black Butler* marathon later?"

"I need a Sebastian."

"I will totally cosplay Sebastian for you, Frankie."

"Go away, you." But he didn't, and it wasn't so bad, standing there close to him. In fact, it wasn't bad at all.

Frankie decided she'd have to make sense of that some other time.

24

SINGER
52 DAYS WITH MILES

The phone rang a few minutes after 9:30 a.m. Singer was contemplating another half cup of coffee with weary obsession; it had been the rare bad night of sleep, and Miles had ended up between them in the bed, finally getting back to sleep around three with his head on Jake's back and his feet tucked up against Singer.

It was the most connected he'd felt to Jake in days.

Brandi was on the phone. Marie was dragging Miles's mom to Social Services for paperwork. If they wanted a visit and they were free, this was a good opportunity. Eleven o'clock. Sorry for the late notice.

He only had to meet Jake's eyes to know their answer. A chance to meet Miles's mother? A chance for him to see her? Of course they'd drop everything.

So he texted Alice the change in plans. (Her response was immediate: *We'll do lunch over the weekend then, and you can tell us all about her. Can you take pictures? I'd love to paint her for him.*) Jake got Miles into one of the complicated and correspondingly cuter outfits Mother had bought for him during one of her frequent shopping trips, which Singer understood as stand-ins for actual engagement.

She couldn't say, "You made me a grandmother." She could say, "I picked some things up for him just in case you need to take him somewhere nice." Implied: *The rest of his clothes are trashy, but these could pass for decent.*

They were out the door in forty-five minutes. A well-oiled machine. Mostly because he and Jake only exchanged the minimum words necessary for each interaction. Singer's entire life was now avoidance. He avoided talking to Jake for fear of a fight. He avoided talking to Frankie for fear she'd see that he was avoiding Jake. Frankie had witnessed minor arguments before, had shared a pot of tea with him in the aftermath of nearly every disagreement he and Jake had ever had, while Jake was off taking a run, which may or may not have been code for smoking pot.

These days he wasn't up late enough for tea, and Jake was neither running nor leveling out his anxiety with marijuana. And Frankie was no longer in the guesthouse. She'd been replaced by Mother, who was never good company, but least of all after a fight with Jake. Not that they'd had a fight. God, what the hell were they doing? Singer banished all thoughts and tried to concentrate on meeting Miles's mom.

"I'm nervous," Jake murmured as they entered the now familiar building, where the air tasted like cardboard dust.

"I think it's happening too fast for me to be nervous." Singer switched the diaper bag to his other arm and added, "Also, I had more coffee than you did. We'll stop somewhere when we leave."

Jake smiled at him for a second, like it was nothing, and Singer felt his stomach roll with disorientation. They'd lost easy smiles, he realized. They'd lost all noncrucial expressions.

Brandi ushered them into a different—but barely—visitor room, and Marie was already there, with a young woman who had to be Miles's mother. She was tall, with sharp features and soft eyes, a hint of baby fat still clinging to her cheeks and neck, though otherwise she was slender.

"Oh my god, look at you! You're huge! Happy almost-birthday, baby!"

Marie, off to the side, muttered, "That's what happens when you miss two whole months of a baby's life. I *told* you." If Miles's mother heard the comment, she ignored it.

"Regina," Brandi said, and despite the vocal disapproval, she was smiling. "This is Jake and Singer. This is Regina, Miles's mom."

"Let me see you, baby!" Regina pulled Miles into her arms. "Mama, he looks fine. He looks just like his daddy." To Jake she explained, "She said you weren't feeding him right, but he looks fine to me. Sorry, I totally didn't hear your name."

"I'm Jake. This is Singer."

They shook hands with her, greeted Marie, and nodded to Brandi when she said she'd be back in a few minutes. Mostly, Singer watched the way Miles stared up at his mother, not quite smiling, but transfixed by her, as Regina recited a nonstop narrative of everything she'd done since she last saw him.

Singer and Jake sat down beside each other on the little two-seater sofa. He could see Marie, beyond, also watching, but Marie's face was set on anger as if at any second it could crack into grief. Singer was uncomfortably reminded of Mother and tried to banish the image.

"I can't believe my baby's about to be a year old. I forgot to bring his presents, but Brandi said maybe we can do another visit soon." She paused for breath. "So how'd you guys meet?"

"High school, actually," Singer said, suddenly self-conscious under Marie's dubious scrutiny.

"Oh my god, were you high school sweethearts? Me and Miles's daddy were high school sweethearts. He's buggin', he's all, 'I don't want no baby, bitch.' So anyway, were you guys like the cutest couple in high school?" She seemed immune to the conversational whiplash, squeezing Miles a little harder until he frowned. Regina laughed, and whatever was burning through Miles's mind switched directions. His smile did not meet his mother's, but answered it.

"Not exactly," Jake said. "Singer was a lot more brave than I was in high school. But we met again, later."

"And fell in love? Aw!"

"Regina, for heaven's sake—"

"I'm not allowed to think it's cute? Mama, it's like, if they're gonna be Miles's parents, then it's nice, it's good they've known each other so long. It's just like me and David. That's his daddy, but he won't grow up and act like a man."

"If *you* would grow up, Miles wouldn't need new parents, Regina—"

But Regina had already turned back, addressing Jake now. "I got this one girlfriend, she had her baby taken away, and she doesn't ever get to see her. That's not what you guys would do, though, right? I mean, Brandi says I can still see him and anyway, it's not like you guys're gonna be his mama, that's me."

"You let them do this, girl, and he doesn't have a mama anymore."

Regina rolled her eyes, and Singer glanced sideways, reading in Jake's face the concern he felt, not on their behalf but on hers. When he looked up again he accidentally met Marie's gaze, and yes, she was afraid, she understood the system so much better than Regina did, maybe better than Jake and Singer. If they legally adopted Miles, he became their responsibility alone. A year from now, two years from now, five years from now, they could spirit him off to another city, another state, and she'd never see him again.

"You will definitely always be his mother, Regina," Singer said. "Jake's sister-in-law would like to do a painting of the two of you for his room. I mean, if—if we end up being his permanent placement. Would you mind if I took a picture of you?"

"Of course! Smile, baby! Say cheese!"

Brandi came back to lead Regina (and Miles) away for paperwork, and Marie sat at the table in the visiting room with them in absolute silence. You could probably hear the clock tick, Singer thought, if there wasn't so much white noise in the rest of the office.

The visit ended without fanfare, and Miles settled into Jake's arms, head pillowed on the hollow below Jake's clavicle, like he usually did when he was tired. Regina giggled and kissed him a few more times, but Marie looked like she'd swallowed nails. Singer couldn't decide if he felt proud that, clearly, they couldn't be screwing it up too badly as parents, or wretchedly sad that their particular path to parenthood seemed laced with quite so much devastation. Surely, eventually, Regina, too, would feel as though he had been stolen out from under her. Even if at the moment she was simply delighted to have snagged trendy gay men for Miles.

They chorused "nice to meet you"s at each other and escaped.

25

VIV
62 DAYS UNTIL STARTING OVER

The afternoon of Miles's birthday party was uncomfortably warm for autumn. Viv had assumed she would be expected to play hostess, but when she emerged from the guesthouse prepared to do so, she discovered that Singer had already taken care of everything. Cathy arrived shortly thereafter (with cupcakes, of course) and immediately involved herself in the remaining setup. Viv looked to Singer—addressing overbearing guests was always tricky—but he seemed to welcome her intrusion.

In some ways, he'd always been a mystery to her. It shouldn't be any surprise that he still was. She finally found a shady place to sit from which she could observe the party like a spectator. It was hard to believe Lisa and Singer had once been this young. She had hosted Singer's birthday parties in this very yard, full of school classmates and organized activities. He'd been a lively, promising child, all laughter and bright smiles. It was difficult to reconcile that memory with the shutdown, tightly wound man he'd become. When had he pulled in? At ten, maybe. Eleven, twelve. That gulf between Singer and the other children growing larger as he aged. She and Drew hadn't acknowledged it to each other, not explicitly, but they hadn't asked him about girls, either.

She had caught him looking at another boy once, in a grocery store. He'd blushed bright red, and she'd asked, too loudly, what cereal he wanted. They hadn't looked at each other again until dinner.

Lisa had been so much easier. She'd grown into the young woman Viv always imagined she would be—a girl a lot like Viv had been. She'd seemed destined to follow the same steady path: college, a husband, a family. A secure future. All of it derailed by *that place*. Now, without a college diploma, without anything approaching a husband or a family, Lisa was practically a stranger. Her interest in this Emery boy, for instance. Sometimes a mother just knows things, and Viv didn't like the way he looked at Lisa. This new Lisa. The old Lisa wouldn't have spared him a second glance, but now? Now Lisa seemed almost flattered by his attention.

It incensed Viv. Lisa was beautiful and smart and should have brushed aside the likes of Emery without thinking. She could have any boy. Surely she saw that. What had that place done to her that she now settled for such an unsuitable young man? Maybe whatever it was, this regrettable dalliance with Emery would get it out of her system.

As long as she didn't get pregnant. One thing this family did not need was more strange children running around.

She spotted Jake with Miles, standing in a group of his family members. It wasn't that she disliked Jake. He seemed like a nice enough boy. But clearly this entire adoption thing was his idea, and Singer was simply going along with it. He wasn't standing with Jake—which would make sense, at their foster son's birthday—he was bustling around, never still for longer than a moment. It couldn't be any clearer that Singer was avoiding the entire thing because he wasn't sure how to end it.

Nothing made sense: Jake, adoption. This Emery. Was all of it somehow her fault? How could her children gravitate toward such extreme points without it being a reflection of how they saw their own family? And if it was … that was even more confusing. She could not imagine how things had gotten to the state they were currently in.

For the first time she wished Drew had come with her. Viv, back straight in her chair (there was no excuse for bad posture), surveyed the yard. The spa was closed, though some collection of Jake's people were using the lid as a tabletop, covering it with cups. Better that Drew not see *that*. But at least he would understand the … incongruence of this gathering. It wasn't merely the surprise of adopted children, or the presence of so many outsiders. It was all of those things combined, along with the raw absence of the orderly future they'd imagined.

"Vivian! We're about to start cupcakes."

She smiled at Jake's mother. "You really must call me Viv, everyone does."

"I keep forgetting." Cathy was shorter than either of her sons, sturdily built, and she spoke in emphatic declarative sentences. "There are more than enough cupcakes for everyone, if you'd like to join in."

"Cupcakes before dinner?"

Cathy smiled easily. "Derrie tradition. Buys us a little bit of time to eat while the kids run themselves ragged. It's so weird to me that we never met when Carey and Lisa were in school, though that's probably my fault. I'm afraid the boys were on their own a lot by that age."

Viv, try as she might, couldn't find any cutting undercurrent to the words. She'd expected Jake's mother to be brash and arrogant—*an ER nurse with a calling* was how she'd described Cathy to Drew—but in actual fact, Cathy had been nothing but kind.

"I don't think I need a cupcake, but thank you for offering." *Please don't linger to chat.*

"Of course. We *are* family now, Viv. Let me know if you need anything." Cathy turned away, ruffling the hair of one of the children who belonged to the Asian woman.

Family. What a loose way some people used the word. No marriage, no official adoption. They were hardly more family than any two women whose oldest children graduated the same year. Cathy was deluding herself. After all, if Singer had been serious about Jake, wouldn't they have at least begun planning a wedding by now? Instead of this indefinite living arrangement in a house that was not their own. She'd have to speak to him. Having one foot out the door was one thing, but involving children was yet another.

Her eyes tracked Lisa, approaching her brother, the two of them speaking for a moment. A ponytail, no make-up, a pair of *jeans* of all things. It was as if she didn't take herself seriously. If she put the smallest amount of effort out, she wouldn't be so enthralled by the first man who showed an ounce of interest.

Viv thought, for a moment, that Lisa caught her eye. She leaned slightly forward. Her children, even nearly un-recognizable, were still an oasis in this sea of strangers.

Then both of them turned away and separated, off to different areas. Singer went to talk with Jake's father at the barbecue. Lisa went to stand with Emery and that rather overweight woman whose tie to Jake's family was murky.

For a moment Viv just sat there, while some heated, unconscionable feeling rose up in her. This was not how it was supposed to be. Who were these people? Why were there so many of them? And how did it come to pass that she sat here, in her own deck chair, in the shade of a tree she'd watched grow for twenty years outside her kitchen window, and no one seemed to realize they were trespassing in her life?

With effort, she dredged up a bland smile, appropriate to watch children with frosting on their hands and faces zoom around the yard. Only a few more hours, as endless as they would seem. Then she could retreat to the guesthouse—her own *guesthouse*—and maybe tonight she would think of some way out of this mess. At least for Lisa. If she would only agree to move back down to Valencia, where Viv could help her, but Lisa wouldn't deign to discuss it.

Viv had tried to live her life well, to follow the rules, but no one had prepared her for this.

A ball rolled over and hit her foot.

"Sorry!" Jake called, jogging up with the baby in his arms. "Really sorry, Mrs. Thurman."

It was on the tip of her tongue, but she didn't invite him to drop the formality. Instead, she handed him the ball, and he handed it to Miles. She smiled slightly at the baby's grin. "Oh, don't mind me at all. Have fun, boys!"

"We will! Come on, Miles. You want to dunk a basket? Let's go dunk!"

Such a tricky thing. She'd imagined, even anticipated, grandchildren. But not like this. Still, one couldn't help but be charmed by the boy's occasional laughter, his wide grins.

Beyond Jake and Miles, Singer stood in the doorway to the house, expression tight and drawn. When he caught her looking he turned away. Why were her children forever turning away from her?

She hid the now-familiar bewilderment and pretended to watch the game of ball, pondering how she could feel so foreign in her own home.

26

SINGER
55 DAYS WITH MILES

It was clear that Miles had no idea what a birthday was, but he was definitely pro-gifts, pro-cake, and pro-attention. Singer could hear his laughter from the kitchen.

"I'm glad Victor and Kara and the kids came over," Jake said as they passed each other on the way in and out of the house. "Because apparently we know no one with kids except Mixie, and she's stationed in Germany."

Singer didn't know Mixie well (she and her brother were in the branch of the Derrie family that had gone to Catholic high school), but he'd liked her and her husband when he met them. "I'm glad they're here, too. Do you think this means we need more family friends?"

"Maybe that just ... happens? Over time?"

Then Alice grabbed Jake for an urgent trike-building consult, and Singer still had a tray of snacks in his hands, so the most normal conversation they'd had in weeks came to an abrupt end.

Why could they only be normal when other people were around? Singer had the distinct impression that it was his fault.

"Hell of a party, Singer Thurman! Let me help."

"By 'help' do you mean 'take all the food,' Frances?"

"Oh hell yes." She spun away with her bounty.

"You could have invited Logan!" he called in retaliation.

Without pausing or dropping the tray, she flipped him off backward. He couldn't help smiling when Cathy scolded her. The presence of non-Derries at this gathering changed the rules. Even now Victor and Carey were talking about something while throwing around a football, and Kara was deep in conversation with Joe at the barbecue. Emery was showing Rachel how to use his camera, to her obvious delight.

Mother, of course, sat primly in a chair, looking uncomfortable with her paper plate balanced on her knee.

"Is it wrong that I kind of want to spray her with the hose?" Lisa whispered, coming up behind him. "Not seriously. But kind of."

"Don't tempt me. Would it kill her to act like she might be enjoying herself?"

"I don't know. It might. If she smiled her face might crack. Uh-oh. We better separate. She's looking at us, and I think she might actually be thinking about coming over here."

"Bite your tongue," he muttered.

Lisa wandered over to stand with Emery (strategically a good idea, since Mother would never approach any group of which Emery was a part). Singer headed for Joe and Kara. They were probably safe.

"It's the only thing they disagree on," Kara was saying. "Victor scoffs at anyone who uses charcoal, and my father secretly thinks only men of weak character buy propane-powered barbecues."

Joe laughed. "Every time all of us get together, there's a fight over who's in charge of the grill. One year it got so bad that my brother Rob brought over a little Webber so he could cook a portion of the chicken 'correctly' for people who had taste. Now, Cathy's family would rather fight about whether or not the UN is overreaching with their new sanctions against whoever, and I can barely keep up. The boys get their brains from her." He smiled at Singer. "How's he doing? Not too overwhelmed?"

"I think by the end of today he might be more convinced that walking is a good goal."

"That was Jake all over. Carey we couldn't keep in one place from the second he realized other people could move around. Jake, though. Jake didn't mind waiting to see what would happen instead of making something happen."

"My sister and I were the opposite," Kara said. "Everyone always praised me for being such a good girl, meaning I mostly stayed quiet and didn't cause trouble. My parents said it was a rude awakening when Kim came along and had a totally different personality."

"Did they think your behavior reflected on their parenting?"

"Exactly. They patted themselves on the backs for three years about what good parents they were, and then from the second Kim could crawl and talk, she never stopped moving. And she still hasn't stopped talking."

Joe nodded. "It's so tempting to take credit for everything your kids do that people find acceptable and to disavow anything they do that isn't. Or to see genetics everywhere. Even knowing your kids are adopted, I can see your husband in the way your older son throws a ball. I think I've been relying too much all these years on heredity, when I should have been looking at environment."

"Oh, there's definitely a mixture," she agreed. "What about you and your sister, Singer?"

"I think we're only discovering how similar we are now, as adults. When we were younger I think we each would have preferred an announcement that we weren't the same species."

"You and me both."

"The Derries were always a tribe of their own," Joe said. "Which I took as proof that blood was thicker than water, but I don't know. You couldn't look around this party and tell who was related to whom, and who technically wasn't." His hand clamped down on Singer's shoulder. "I'm thankful for all of my family."

"Me too," Singer said, eyes catching on Mother again. *I just wish some of them would go away and leave us in peace.*

"Cupcake and presents!" Jake called from the slider. "Everyone to the table."

"Cake before food?" Kara asked.

"Sorry about that." Joe waved his tongs in the air. "Old family tradition."

Singer flipped through the family gatherings he'd been to over the years. "I never noticed that. Usually the cupcakes are out at the beginning, and I guess I assumed it was because Cathy likes cupcakes."

"Oh, there's always a method to our madness, Singer. You're a parent now, and parenting initiates you into a deeper level of family mythology."

"That sounds vaguely ominous."

Joe grinned. "Nah. We're harmless."

The Derries were anything but harmless. Singer made himself smile, but all he could think was that he wasn't worthy to be part of these people, who loved so completely, and that any moment now they'd figure it out.

27

LISA
83 DAYS SINCE LEAVING GRACE

Thursday had been endless and extreme, like a marathon, only instead of running—meditative, physical—it had been mental warfare.

Except, the other side had no idea they were at war.

Ever since Miles's birthday party, Mother had been … escalating. In small ways, maybe—a few more passive aggressive digs about Singer here, undercutting Jake's role in the house there—but after yet another new therapist this morning, Lisa had been her target all day.

"We'll get sushi for dinner." Mother was clearly oblivious to the very real feeling of collapse beginning to crackle along Lisa's muscle groups, as if her body were preparing to protect itself by any means necessary, and that included playing dead.

Mother would take death as a challenge. She had apparently taken joining a cult as one.

Lisa bit off an entirely inappropriate explosion of laughter—a cult! I joined a cult! (was it really laughter if it was torn from your body like a scream?)—and excused herself to her room.

The kitchen door opened at the same time, and Jake, carrying Miles, as usual, almost bumped into her.

"Oh, hey, Lisa. Listen, we're going to my brother's for dinner. Okay?" He glanced over her shoulder, toward the living room, almost as if he understood that she might not be okay.

Then he looked back at her face and added, seriously, too seriously, "Come with us. You've never seen Carey's place before, and Alice is a painter. And I wouldn't mind the company, either."

"Isn't Singer—"

"Yeah. Yeah, of course. And Emery will be there." He smiled.

"I can't do this more tonight," she whispered to Singer's boyfriend (and kid), standing in the hallway of what had once been her home. "I can't tell who's crazier, her or me."

"We're supposed to be there at six. I'll text you when we get close to ready."

She nodded and unlocked her door. She'd make some excuse, maybe about her dislike for sushi, which could definitely be played up, and she'd escape with them for a little while. Any plan was better than no plan.

Alice and Carey had clearly received warning that Singer's crazy sister was coming to dinner. They were all smiles and welcome.

Carey actually shook her hand. Which was funny. "You want the penny tour?"

"Sure." Weird, watching Carey, this Carey, when the Carey she'd known in school had never smiled, except with the Derries. Never laughed out loud ever. He'd been moody and—*dark*, Lisa settled on, though it hadn't been a show, like with some kids. No trench coats, no eyeliner, no boots. She almost thought there was some kind of scandal when they were younger, one of those creepy priest stories, but who knew if what she remembered was real or rumor.

"So our bedroom's at the end of the hall"—to her relief, no offer was made to enter—"and this is my office, here."

Carey's office reminded her of her scrapbooking room. Prepared for use, without actually being inhabited.

"And this is Alice's studio."

She could tell by his voice that it was meant to be a declaration. That in another context, she would be expected to give up at least an "ahh" if not an "ooh."

Then she saw Alice's studio.

"Oh my god."

The smile, the entirely smug smile Carey was wearing, should have annoyed her. But instead Lisa's feet propelled her into the room without any interference from propriety or politeness.

Paintings leaned up against all the walls, some four or five deep. There was a stack of three canvasses on the nearest table, beside a higher stack. The top of the first stack showed an incredible painting of hands twisted around each other, anchored in space by ropes, knotted at the wrist and extending beyond the edges of the canvas. God, god, Lisa thought, wanting to touch it, to verify what her brain was telling her must be true: there are no hands there. But something about it, far more than a photograph, seemed three-dimensional.

"I don't come in here at night, when the lights are off." Carey had stayed behind her, to the side of the door. "She's been working on hands almost since we moved in. One of the cousins has a friend who models for her, and Emery takes the photographs so she can paint from them later."

More hands, a few of ankles, though these were not nearly as well defined, the ropes blurred from far away and almost indistinguishable up close. (Snakes? *Not snakes.*) In the back corner of the room a second table was set up, and this one held notebooks and notebooks. Some, open, were sketches of a young man, bound with rope, in pencil, mostly. A few in charcoal. And then, larger, another sketch. Emery, unmistakable, looking down on a boy, one hand out, hovering just over his bent head, camera in his other hand.

"I mostly stay away from the nudes in this sequence, but that one is … compelling."

The boy was naked, though the rope coiling around his arms and chest almost disguised it.

She gestured to the man above the boy. "It's Emery, isn't it?"

"Yes. He and Alice have known each other for almost their entire lives, and I have to believe that does something for the art. I think all of her work is miraculous, but this series contains some of my favorites." Carey moved to stand beside her at the table. "I don't know where all her Emerys went—there are entire notebooks—and in some of them you can see this look on his face, serious and humorous at once. But that one is a particularly good perspective on—I don't know—the way he watches. Like a heron, very still."

Lisa glanced over.

"Are you impressed? Alice tells me I live vicariously through her. But I can't help but feel weirdly proud, standing here looking at her work."

"Yeah. I think that's appropriate. Wow."

Carey grinned. And that expression was new to him, as an adult. Teenage Carey could never have opened his face like that, shared that kind of smile. "That's the whole tour. Which I basically offered to give you only for this room."

"I can't imagine being able to do this."

"Me neither. The places Alice goes in her head astound me. In a good way." He paused. "Well, never in a bad way, at least. I hope you like pizza. We're having a pizza buffet."

"Stop hiding!" Alice shouted from somewhere else in the house.

Oh god, was she hiding again? She couldn't seem to stop hiding. Lisa turned to the door and froze at the sight of a noose hanging from the ceiling. Her chest seized, throat closing, and she couldn't breathe or swallow and her heartbeat took over her entire awareness—

Carey froze, not quite reaching out. "She meant me. I'm the one who's hiding." Pause. "That's a lasso. A gift from a friend of Alice's before she moved to the wild West."

The words fell around her, out of order, and all she could think was, *I'm dying, I'm dying, the snake is a noose and this is death and I am dead and that noose is proof*—

"Hold your breath. I know it sounds weird, but it works for me. Hold your breath and focus on something until you think you can inhale again. Something real, something tangible, with texture, and scent. Lisa, hold your breath and focus."

Her toes curled inside her shoes, and both of her hands came up to her chest, clenched and crossing, like she was a mummy, dead and buried.

"Lisa. You're here with us, having pizza, and also listening to Alice's crazy ideas about family expansion, which is fitting, since you are an expansion of our family. Focus on something and breathe."

Tears blurred everything, but she could still see the drawing of Emery, looking down, careful and intense and holding his camera, the strap loose around his wrist, and she could feel the weight of a camera strap if she tried, she could feel the swing of it as if the drawing weren't just a moment trapped on paper.

"Breathe," Carey said. "Not too fast."

She looked at the sketch and for a second imagined that she was the one on her knees, that she was the one Emery was looking at like in his gaze even Lisa could be whole.

"You guys ready for pizza?" Alice asked from the doorway.

"We'll be out in a sec." Then, lower, "You good?"

She didn't know how long it took before she could get herself back from the speedy panic in her lungs. But when she did, she nodded, and Carey nodded in reply. No fanfare. No discussion.

One fuckup to another: *You good?*

Lisa wanted to curl up in a ball and cry, but she followed him out to the main room and sat beside Emery, who, whether he knew it or not, had grounded her enough to stop dying.

He smiled at her, and some deep fault line in her shifted, the broken pieces knitting back together.

28

EMERY
54 DAYS SINCE MEETING LISA

Emery liked a good pizza buffet as much as the next man, but it was Lisa's surprise arrival with Jake's family that made the drive out worthwhile.

And she'd sat down beside him. Spontaneously. He could feel her energy in the air even when neither one of them was participating in the conversation around them.

Singer shook his head, absently wiping tomato sauce off Miles's chin. "So, short of matricide, I don't know what we'll do with her."

"Have we ruled out matricide?" Lisa asked.

He shot her a look. Then it softened. "Well. Not completely."

Carey stood up and brushed crumbs from his hands back over his plate. "We can't help you with that, I don't think. But we did talk about something else." He glanced at Alice, who smiled up at him. "Hell, Al. I have no idea how to discuss this."

Things were about to get interesting. This was the pretense on which he'd been lured out to the great beyond, the big capital-T Talk with Jake and Singer.

When Alice opened her mouth to respond Miles let out the kind of belch that Emery associated with drunk frat boys who showed up at the tattoo parlor and tried to goad each other into ink.

The comically bewildered expression on Miles's face made all of them laugh.

"That's gas, from your stomach," Alice said, leaning down.

"Ah?"

"Did he just say 'gas'?" Singer said.

"Or, wait, are we doing that thing parents do, where they think their kid's doing long division and it's just squiggles?"

"I'm writing it down in his baby book as his first word," Alice told them. "This is actually better than we'd hoped, Care. Lisa's here, and Miles is talking about bodily functions."

Carey, still looking uncomfortable, began, "And yet——"

"We are willing to surrogate a baby, if you two would like to conceive but find yourselves unable to because of biology." Alice smirked. "There. Not that hard, Care, if you simply say what you mean."

Ha. She was such an insufferable smartass. Emery caught Lisa's eye, and they shared a look he interpreted as *Glad I'm not involved in this.*

Singer, though, was possibly even more uncomfortable than Carey. His whole body went rigid, but he didn't speak.

Carey shifted on his feet, ran a hand through his hair, and shook his head. "Right, so, I'm making coffee."

"Coward!" Alice called after him. "You would never know it was his idea. Mostly."

"Ah … um …" Jake looked at Singer, who was still sitting there like he'd suffered an electrical shock. "Uh …"

"Listen, this is just something for you to think about. I know how it works from the assisted reproduction standpoint, and Carey's pretty sure he can iron out—as well as possible—the legal side. We don't say any of this lightly, and you two will need some serious time to discuss it. No pressure, of any kind, but we wanted you to know that this is an option."

"Ah," Miles said, to Jake, who smiled weakly.

"Gas, huh? Alice—"

Alice held up her hands. "That's it. Think about it. Or don't."

"Um. Okay. Thank you."

"We have coffee." Carey stuck his head into the room. "Who wants coffee? We also have chocolates with stuff in them. For dessert."

It was probably wrong to find Carey's awkwardness vaguely satisfying, but the man made a habit of seeming unperturbed, and Emery wasn't so noble that he didn't get off on seeing confident people unsettled.

This time Lisa caught his eye and…smiled. It was almost a smile. Really close.

"Coffee?" he asked.

"No. But chocolate would be welcome."

Carey took orders and returned a few times with cups of coffee and two boxes of truffles (which Alice had clearly already picked over for the caramels and cremes). Conversation broke up a little, so Emery was free to turn to Lisa and ask her how she was. A totally normal question. Casual, even.

"Oh. Fine." She selected another chocolate, turning it in her fingers, trying to figure out what was inside through careful study.

"Fine? Is that true, or are you just saying it?"

Lisa's eyebrows rose. "Were you—serious? I figure 'fine' is the standard answer to 'how are you?'"

"I was serious. Like you can give a real answer, if you want."

"Okay. You answer first. So I know what you mean."

He sipped his coffee, reflecting that the universe had exacted quick revenge for how amusing he'd found it when Carey was unsettled. "How am I? I guess I'm … fine."

That earned him a genuine smile. "See? It's not an easy question."

"I'm going to try to answer it. Hang on." He pretended to ponder his life and found that honesty wasn't as difficult as it had seemed. "Actually, I'm good. I like California, and I'm doing work I enjoy, even if it's not the shop I want to work at forever. Considering I only moved out here a few months ago, I feel pretty grounded."

"Grounded," she repeated. Not like she was critical of the idea, more like she was rolling the word over, studying it from different angles.

Lisa's specific attention made him attempt more clarity. "I guess by the time I left the city I was totally sick of it. California's so much … shinier. It'll never be New York, and I miss the speed, the edge, the intensity. I miss feeling like I was standing at the epicenter of the world. But this is so much smoother, like maybe terrible things happen here, but they aren't as ugly as they are there. Is that weird?"

"I don't think so. Or I think maybe the place you know best is always the place where you can see all the shadows."

"That's a good way of putting it, yeah. Maybe I'm only seeing the surface here, but if I live here for thirty years I'll see more of the edge."

"Maybe."

"So? How are *you*?"

Lisa finally took a chance on her chocolate. When he leaned in closer, she held it out so he could see the inside.

"Is that nougat?"

"I guess so? It's good, whatever it was. And not fruity." She finished it off and sat back. "I think I'm sort of deeply aimless, if that makes sense." Her tone shifted, rueful and almost apologetic. "Every day feels like this huge looming thing I have to fight my way through. Sorry, I'm trying not to sound crazy, but even the least of it is probably still pretty crazy." Her eyes darted toward the rest of the house, away from the table. Emery couldn't imagine what she was thinking.

"I don't think it's crazy."

"It feels crazy to me. Like things used to make sense. And now they…don't. When I was younger, I thought I basically had everything together. I knew what was supposed to happen next. Then I went to college it all sort of…faded. Until I had no idea who I was, or what I was supposed to be doing. And then I met my friend Abigail, and she was already thinking about moving to the farm. So we did it together."

"It must have been easier to have a friend with you. I wouldn't be here without Alice, so I get that part. Having a person you can count on makes it easier to be brave."

"Yeah. It was like that. She was excited, thinking it could be home, more than her home. More than here. And I guess it kind of was." She searched his face, and he hoped that she only saw acceptance. After another moment, she continued. "Everything was simple there. We did our routines, worked where we were supposed to work, ate and talked and slept. Now I get hung up on these stupid things, thinking I must look so completely nuts from the outside. Do you ever worry about that? That if people could see you when you were alone they'd think you needed to be committed because you were actually crazy?"

"I try not to think too hard about how people see me." It wasn't a lie. At least not entirely. He'd learned when he first started modeling how to divorce himself from the image of him that other people saw. When he took pictures he came at it from the other side, attempting to show something, to elicit a certain response, a certain connection.

If he were photographing Lisa in this moment, he'd be trying to somehow encapsulate the ways she expressed uncertainty through the constant motion of her fingers, the way her eyebrows dropped inward as she contemplated what she wanted to say.

"I can't seem to stop thinking about it." She took up another chocolate. "Oh, gross. Cherry."

"Here." He popped the rest into his mouth. "I like the cherry ones."

"It always tastes like it's bleeding or something." Lisa shuddered.

"Okay, that's disturbing. I think you've ruined cherry-filled chocolates for me."

"Sorry. But they're really sickening, Emery."

And damn. She'd said his name.

He hid how pleased he was and reached for another chocolate. "I'm going to eat all the cherry ones I can find now, just to gross you out."

"That's mature."

They smiled at each other, and Emery imagined an entire series of photos: *Lisa, with truffles*. He'd have to get a mixed box, like this one, so he could catch the exact expression on her face when she inadvertently bit into a cherry. And definitely a shot of her smile when he teased her, and she teased him back.

29

SINGER
59 DAYS WITH MILES

It started in the bedroom.

Singer had given the kitchen a cursory once-over after they got home from Carey and Alice's while Jake put Miles, already asleep, in his crib. They'd reconvened in the bedroom.

It started with Jake saying, "Maybe we should think about surrogacy. I mean, I never considered it as an option, but I don't know. Maybe it is." Then he'd looked over, with that sweet, goofy smile on his face that made him look younger, and added, "Seriously, the thought of a kid with your genes is kind of amazing, you know?"

My genes. Singer turned away, trying to shield his expression so Jake couldn't see how the idea made him squirm. He started brushing his teeth, but Jake's reflection in the mirror straightened up, as if he could sense how uncomfortable Singer was, as if he could scent it, like a predator.

"What?" Jake's voice was flat. "You don't want to try surrogacy?"

"I didn't say that."

"Yeah, newsflash, Singer, you don't *say* anything lately. At least not to me."

He finished with his teeth and leaned against the sink, a safe distance away. "We talk all the time."

"Jesus. We really don't, and I know you're doing it on purpose, so don't you dare act like I'm making this up."

"We spent the whole day together." It was a lie. Singer's guts twisted, thinking about all the times he'd avoided Jake lately.

"Don't *bullshit me*, dammit!"

"Please keep your voice down—"

"I *am* keeping my voice down." Jake glanced at the baby monitor and stood up. "We need to talk. The living room would be farther away from Miles's room."

"But—"

Jake was already out the door, baby monitor in hand.

This wasn't good. Singer's legs felt unsteady as he followed, and when he sank into the sofa he could feel the strength leave them.

Jake paced back and forth in front of the coffee table, shoulders set. "We used to be able to talk about things. God, Singer, you talked about—about everything with me. I thought that's what we did."

"Tonight, though? We need to have to talk about *this* tonight? I'm don't see why it's suddenly urgent—"

"It's *not* 'suddenly urgent,' it's urgent the way something gets urgent when you don't want to talk about it ever!" He spun to walk back in the other direction, fists clenching and releasing at his side. "I can't figure out if you're pissed, or upset, or— Is this about having another kid? Are you saying you don't want that now?"

"No, I'm not, but I don't know how, with everything that's happening right now, you can even think about having more."

"I don't know how you can look at Miles and not think about the future. Do you really not think about anything? You don't think about what it'd be like to drop him off at school? Or what we'll do if kids make fun of him for having gay dads?"

Singer realized his hands were knotted in front of him so tightly he could feel all of his bones. "I can't do that right now. He could get taken away from us at any moment, and I can't—"

"But that's the reason I have to! We could lose this any moment, but I want to actually *have* it while it's here!"

"I'm just saying I can't do this right this second, Jake, and I resent—"

"*You* resent *me*?" Jake stared at him incredulously, and everything in Singer locked down, meeting emotion with iron control. "You haven't even looked at me in days! It's like you can't stand to be alone in a room with me, and what the hell, Singer? My parents have offered to watch Miles how many times now?"

He made his voice calm. "I don't see why we would inconvenience your—"

"It's not an inconvenience if he's their grandson! Or are you having second thoughts about all of it?"

"Of course I'm not! How could you say that?" *How could you even think it? Are you thinking it? Are you having second thoughts?* Singer's fingers tightened further, until his arms were shaking.

"How could I think anything else? Why do you keep refusing to talk to me?"

"I'm not. I don't mean to. I—I'm so afraid, and you don't seem afraid. I don't know how to talk to you. I don't know how to pretend when all of it could fall apart."

"I thought we said we were a team. When I was scared, you said you were my backup."

"I *am*." Except he wasn't, and both of them knew it. Singer bit down on his cheek.

"This isn't working." Jake, chest rising fast, stood in the middle of the room. "This isn't working. And I don't know what's broken."

This was the moment, in the past, when Singer would have opened his arms and pulled Jake in and promised him that things were never as insurmountable as they seemed. That together they would manage it. They'd always manage.

He let loose just enough tension in his hands to stop shaking, but he couldn't find any words. And despite the fact that he was the one holding back—which he knew, even if he couldn't force himself to stop—he absurdly wanted Jake to be the one who pulled him in, kissed him, told him that everything would be okay.

Jake didn't. "I don't know what to do. I guess I'll ... go to bed."

A door opened down the hall. A whimper. Jake's voice over the baby monitor: "Shh, Miles. Go back to sleep." A huff of Miles resettling. The door closed. Their bedroom door opened. Closed.

Every thought in Singer's head pricked him like a needle. He sat very, very still, and tried not to think at all.

He couldn't be hearing right. He couldn't be seeing right. None of this could be what it seemed like it was.

"I'm not leaving you. I just need a little time to think." Jake, shoving clothes in his gym bag. "I can't think in this house right now. I don't know how you can."

Where are you going? Why? When will you come back? Singer swallowed all of his questions, and the accompanying aching sorrow.

"I love you so much," Jake said as he zipped his bag. Sentiment thrown over his shoulder casually, a toss in Singer's direction, costing him nothing. "I'll take Miles. We'll be at Carey's, okay?"

None of this is okay. Nothing is okay. Singer sat, numbly, on their bed. He needed to say something. His silence was a weight, pressing down on him, growing heavier by the second.

When Jake looked over his expression crumpled. "I love you so much, you have no idea."

That was it. He went to Miles's room. Singer listened to the sounds as he must have packed a bag. Miles woke up toward the end, and Jake's artificially perky voice said, "Hey, let's go see Carey and Alice, okay? You want to? We'll get Alice to show us some more pictures of Manhattan, and Brooklyn, and Queens, all the places we've never been. Okay, Miles?"

Miles babbled. He might know "Carey and Alice" by now. He was always happy to see them.

Singer leaned forward and cried into his hands, listening to the sounds of Jake picking up Miles, of the bedroom door closing, of the front door opening.

It shut again with a muffled *thump*.

Eventually he went to bed.

30

It was almost ten before Lisa could drag herself out of bed, and there was a text message waiting from Frankie: *Wtf happened last night? S is wrecked and J moved out? WTF?*

The message was only eleven minutes old. Lisa went out, tentatively, to the kitchen—for coffee, or to take her teacup to the sink, or any number of other excuses she came up with.

She walked in just in time to hear Mother say, "This could be for the best, Singer. I did try to explain it to Jake as well—"

"It would be for the best if you went back to your own home, Mother, and left me to decide what was good for my family."

"They aren't your *family*." Mother's eyes narrowed. "Signing a few papers doesn't make you a father, and living with someone doesn't make you married."

"Thanks so much for *that* newsflash."

"This is no place to raise a child. It's like a traveling circus here, with all these people in and out all the time."

"Why are you here, Mother? I called Dad, but he won't talk to me. What's going on?"

"Nothing. I have no idea what you mean. I'll see you when you're feeling more civil."

Lisa hid in the hallway while Mother exited, and Singer called after her, "I happen to *like* my traveling circus!"

She only hesitated for a minute before walking into the kitchen and setting her cup in the sink. Singer was leaning over on the counter next to the coffeemaker, head buried in his hands like he was attempting to become an ostrich.

"Sorry," he mumbled.

"It's weird. I like your traveling circus, too."

He turned, and it was almost unbelievable. Singer, who was usually perfectly assembled, mask in place, now had tears all down his cheeks and bright red eyes. "He's gone. I mean, not gone, over at Carey's. But he took Miles, and—I mean—he must be coming back. It seems so stupid. He said he was coming back. He said he needs time. I have no idea if he means a few hours or a few weeks. But he took a *bag*."

If there was an appropriate response to what was probably the most heartfelt and faltering thing he'd ever said to her, she had no idea what it was. Instead, she asked, "You called Dad?"

"And he keeps saying, 'I can't talk now, I'll call back later.' What is he doing down there? He works part-time. I picture him at the eighth hole, telling a bunch of old white men that it's just his fag son calling to whine about his wife."

Lisa blinked. "That sounds nothing like Dad. At all."

"I know. I know. Sorry. It's just that our whole relationship, mine and Jake's, I was the one who knew where we were going. I was the one who knew who I was. Now all of a sudden, he's this great father, this great parent, and it all comes so naturally to him, and I— It's like I'm blind, like

I've lost an entire sense and my body can't figure out how to compensate."

"But, Singer—Jake's cousin lived in your backyard."

"I know it's weird, but—"

"No, I mean— That's not what I mean." She paused, struggling to fit what she understood into words she could speak. "Jake's family *likes* each other. They actually enjoy hanging out together."

"Circus," he murmured.

"Yeah, but it's kind of wonderful, too. And I don't know if it was a cult, where I was—it didn't feel like a cult—but whatever it was, I lived with people, a group of people, and we all wanted the same things. We wanted to feel like we belonged together. I guess we did, for a while. You have that here, only no one's claiming to be a prophet of God."

Singer blinked.

"I'm just saying, that part of it? The part where Jake treats Miles like he's his own? I don't know. I … think that makes sense. These people aren't like us. It's like … they were born with more love than we were. They share it better."

"It is like that. Like he has all this love to give to this baby and I'm … deficient. But I used to be the one who could love enough for both of us. So how do I get more?" He looked across the kitchen at her, like he was really asking, like he wanted to know what she thought.

Lisa shrugged. "I think I'm pretty much beyond repairing. But you already love him. Jake. And Frankie, and Carey, and all the rest of them."

"It's not Miles. I mean, I like Miles. He doesn't feel like an intruder, or false. I just don't … I don't feel like a parent. I feel like he's someone else's child."

"I guess he is. But is it supposed to happen automatically? I mean, I like your traveling circus, Singer, but I don't think they're *normal.*"

Singer vented a startled laugh and shook his head. "No argument there. I'm pretty sure my de facto sister-in-law offered to carry my child. These people are anything but normal."

"Anyway. I just think you gotta give yourself time. I think Jake would, too, if you asked."

"I don't know when talking to him became so hard. Talking to Jake used to be up there with eating and sleeping on my list of things I needed to do to get through the day."

"I don't know." She risked adding, "The last guy I was in love with fucked different women on a schedule and never slept with any of us."

"Have I mentioned lately how glad I am that you're home?"

"Well, thanks. Not that it was all my doing."

"No?"

Lisa shook her head and reached up for a mug, taking her time pouring coffee, going back to her side of the kitchen. "I had this friend. Good friend. Like the kind of girl I would've been friends with here. And she killed herself. So really, it's Abigail. She's the reason I left. Because she killed herself and they said that she wasn't pure enough to go to heaven. That she was weak."

"How awful."

"I keep meaning to try to find her parents. But I don't know what I'd say to them."

Singer glanced in the direction of the guesthouse. "I can't even figure out what to say to our parents, let alone someone else's."

"Anyway, you should talk to Frankie. She sounds worried."

"Oh, grasshopper. By now Frankie's talked to Carey, Alice, and possibly Jake. She'll corner you later. Only after all that will she talk to me. Only when she already thinks she knows what I'm going to say."

"Okay," Lisa said, more than willing to drop it. "Or you could … talk to her now. I'm gonna go back to bed."

"Then I will see you later. I'm thinking tamales for dinner. I suppose we should invite Mother."

"Invite Frankie first."

"Ah." Singer nodded. "And I'll tell Mother Frankie's coming over, thereby saving us the trouble of actually eating with Mother. Very strategic."

Tamales would be good. Tamales also reminded her of Abigail, though she didn't tell the story. Without Abigail, she wouldn't be standing here right now, talking to her brother like they knew each other, like they chose each other's company.

Thank you, Lisa thought. That's what she wanted to say to Abigail's parents: *Thank you. I loved her very much.*

31

SINGER
63 DAYS WITH MILES

Jake and Miles were gone.

The first day had been the worst, until he woke up on the second day. When, on morning three, Singer had reached over to an empty, cold bed, his ears tuned for waking baby noises from the monitor still sitting on the nightstand, he realized that if Jake and Miles didn't come home, he'd wake up like this every day for the rest of his life.

At least he didn't start crying again. The crying had been humiliating. Even alone. Especially alone, crying for no reason but the circular thoughts in his head. No excuse for the tears that didn't seem to stop flowing that first day. *I'm not leaving you. I just need a little time.* But what did that mean?

Jake had dropped Miles off Friday so he could go in to work. But he didn't stay. And Singer had been—bowled over/relieved/terrified by how much he'd missed Miles after two days, how hard he'd hugged him, how much he wanted to hold him. Miles, he thought, had been happy to see him, too. Until he spotted his toy chest and demanded, back arching, to be put down. Even then, Singer had watched, sipping coffee, while Miles pulled everything out, like he was taking inventory, making certain nothing had changed since he'd been gone.

Mother had been scarce all day. So that was a perk.

He couldn't decide whether he should try to get some work done or maybe accomplish something around the house, so in the end he settled for bothering Frankie at the bookstore for an hour and returning home loaded down with new reading material.

Where he discovered Emery, standing on the front porch. Holding a potted orchid.

"Are they not answering? Mother's Volvo is here, and Lisa's always home."

"I hadn't knocked, yet." Light pink tinged Emery's otherwise tan complexion.

"Are we having a garden party about which I wasn't informed?" Singer shifted his bag of books to unlock the door. This was Emery in a new state. He tried to think of whether he'd ever seen the man blush. But no, he was certain he hadn't.

"It's a gift."

For Lisa. Orchid as—friendship gift? Something more? Singer found himself intrigued, despite a contrasting desire to throw himself on his bed and wallow a bit more in depression (which had been his plan when he'd left the bookstore).

"Did you text her? That might work better than knocking."

"I don't have her phone number."

Singer turned. Emery had followed him into the kitchen, set the orchid on the counter, and stood there. "You don't have Lisa's number? Why?"

"She hasn't offered it. I didn't want to presume anything."

"Ah," Singer said, like that cleared it up. When really, it made it more foggy. "Do you want coffee? I'm making another pot."

"Please. Thank you."

Singer waved. "Sure." He texted Lisa: *Discovered a wayward photographer on our porch. Pretty sure he isn't here to see Mother.* There. That ought to both horrify and provoke.

It was lunch, or just after. Singer pulled out sandwich makings and hoped, reverently, that Mother didn't choose this moment to emerge from whatever it was she did in the guesthouse when she wasn't out "shopping." Frankie thought prescription drugs, Alice had a theory about old photographs, but that didn't make sense because Lisa was in the room that probably held those, if they existed. Carey, after some thought, laid out a somewhat detailed description of depression and isolation and the possibility that she was having secret meetings with either a therapist or a lawyer, which had made Singer momentarily feel bad until he recalled the effects of Mother being *less* isolated.

"Lunch," he told Emery. "Take a plate."

"You don't have to serve me, Singer." Emery half smiled. "Where are Jake and Miles?"

Oh, god. Singer fought a vicious wave of fear—what if they never come home? what if, what if?—and steeled his voice. "They're staying with Alice and Carey. At the moment."

Emery only faltered briefly. "I go to my place for a few days and I'm completely out of the loop. On the other hand, I'm sure Alice is in hog heaven, filling notebooks."

"We took pictures of Miles with his mom for her. I haven't seen the sketches, yet."

"Have you seen her other sketches—" Emery broke off. "Hey, Lisa."

"Hi." She looked over. "You okay?"

Singer fought a grimace. When your recently-escaped-a-cult sister checks in with *you*, you know you're in trouble. "I'll live."

Lisa didn't look particularly convinced.

"Lunch? I have turkey, ham, provolone, and something Frankie brought over from Trader Joe's, but I think that was just a dare. It's a meat-free meat product, whatever that means."

"Um … sure. Yes." She looked up at Emery for a second.

"I'll help myself."

"Are you talking about Alice? I saw some of her work when we were there."

Singer allowed himself the blissful sensation of distraction. He hadn't considered that Emery might be serious. Emery had not, to his knowledge, dated since he'd followed Alice and Carey to California. Not seriously enough to warrant entry to the Derrie bush telegraph network, anyway.

"Oh, you did? Amazing, aren't they? Alice is like, crazy good."

"She is. I mean, I don't really know anything about art, but some of them? It was like I could reach out and touch them in space. Not like they were photographs, but … real."

"I know, it's incredible. My work, you know. The restraints."

"Restraints?" Singer asked, beginning his sandwich now that they were both done. Not hugely surprising, that Emery could restrain someone. He'd learned early on not to underestimate either Emery or Alice's random collection of skills.

"Alice is doing a painting," Emery explained. "She needed a model restrained. And one of the Derries had a volunteer handy."

Of course they did.

"He was stunning. Completely beautiful on his knees. And *so* submissive." He shook his head. "A little too tortured, maybe, but the painting should be amazing. Were there sketches of his face?"

"I'm not sure. But there were a lot of notebooks Carey didn't show me."

"Carey showed you?" Emery's blunt disbelief mirrored Singer's exactly. "Really?"

"Is that strange?"

"Carey generally stays away from nudes. Especially nudes in knots. I mean, he likes Alice in knots, but strangers? Not so much."

Singer waved a hand. "Enough oversharing about my pretend in-laws, thank you."

Emery didn't exactly look repentant, but apparently decided not to push it. "Still, *Carey* showed you? Hm. That is really interesting."

Lisa shrugged. "You were in some of them. I don't think I've ever seen drawings of someone I knew in real life."

"Were you uncontrollably aroused by my badassness?"

"Is that an industry term?" Lisa shot back, even as she blushed.

"Damn right. I, uh, brought you an orchid. By the way."

"An orchid?"

"Is that bizarre? I thought having something alive in there with you and the scrapbooking supplies might be good. And you mentioned you liked plants."

Since when did Lisa like plants? Singer finished making his sandwich and stood back to eat it. Or maybe to observe.

"Oh. Thanks."

"I wanted a fern—for the oxygen—but this caught my eye." Emery nudged the little pot across the counter.

It was like watching very young children who didn't yet understand how to interact with people. Lisa set her sandwich down and picked up the flower, turning it in her hand. Pink-tinged petals, glossy green leaves.

"It's … very nice. Thank you. I'll, um, be right back."

Singer watched her leave, then turned to Emery. "Should I be shaking my fist at you and threatening to beat you up if you hurt my sister?"

"Considering she just responded to my pathetic courting attempt with 'it's very nice,' I'm thinking there isn't much for you to worry about, there, Singer." Emery raised an eyebrow. "And do you really think you could take me with your fists?"

"A purely symbolic gesture. My sister doesn't seem like your usual type."

"You know nothing about my usual type. And don't bother asking Alice. Alice will never tell."

Lisa returned, going back to her lunch. "I put it next to the computer. But I think it might be better by the window. It would take a little remodeling."

"Let me know if you'd like a hand. I'm excellent at remodeling."

"According to you, you're excellent at everything, Emery."

Emery smiled. "I really am."

Alice's slightly aloof best friend had a crush on his sister. *Jake will be so amused.*

It all came crashing back. Jake would be amused, if they were still amused with each other.

Singer decided he'd rejected "wallowing in despair" far too quickly and excused himself to his bedroom.

32

SINGER
66 DAYS WITH MILES

They walked into the building just in time to see Marie walking out, backward, arguing with Brandi.

"He is my *grandson*—"

"I've told you over and over again, Marie, unless Regina is here—"

"I don't know where she is! If I did, she would be here!"

Jake raised his eyebrows. "So, Regina isn't here today?"

"I'm so sorry you drove all the way here," Brandi said. "I was *told* she would be here."

Marie, voice cracking, tried one more time. "I want to see my grandson."

"I don't see any reason why you can't." Singer glanced at Jake. "We'll take you to lunch, Marie." Brandi began to object, but Jake was nodding like this was the obvious solution. Even a scrap of Jake's approval—once so common as to be taken for granted—was enough now to warm Singer's spine.

"I really wouldn't recommend that at this stage—"

"I'm sure it will be fine. Marie? Can we take you to lunch?"

Marie's expression did not soften. She hesitated so long that Singer thought, as impossible as it seemed, she might say no. "Fine," she said at last, as if she were conceding defeat. "That would be fine."

"I'm not sure—" Brandi began. Then stopped. "I will contact you to get another visit, with *Regina*, scheduled." The door snapped shut, with attitude.

"Somewhere nearby," Jake said, and Singer conjured an image of himself and Jake riding in the front seat of their crossover, with Marie and Miles sitting in the back. *Walking distance, so I can feel less like a privileged white man, if nothing else.*

"Do you know anywhere around here to eat, Marie?"

"This isn't my neighborhood."

"Right, well, we'll find something, then."

"Do you want to hold Miles?" Jake asked.

"Can't today. Maybe when we're sitting."

"Of course." Singer, then Jake, adjusted their pace to hers.

The diner they found two blocks down was perfect. Big booth seats, quick service, and Miles ate something from all of their plates, standing up next to his grandmother to lean against the table.

"He's getting real big now, isn't he?" Marie asked.

"My mom says not to worry if he loses weight when he starts walking, because he'll be using different muscle groups, but I don't know. I think Regina was right. He's built like a football player."

Marie nodded, sipping her coffee. "His daddy was a damn fool. Could've gone to college for that, but got caught up in drugs. He's the reason for all this." She waved her hand across the table, from Miles to them. "Got Regina into all those drugs and she can't get herself off them. Fools, both of them."

"Marie, can I ask you something?" Jake cleared his throat. "I told you my mom's an ER nurse, right? Can I ask you what's wrong with your back? Why you can't— Why the placement didn't work out?"

For a long second, Singer thought she wouldn't answer. Her expression went steely, almost defiant. Then Miles squawked at his food and something softened in Marie's gaze. When she started talking, she only sounded resigned.

"Car accident, two years ago. Got rear-ended by an *idiot* with no insurance. Whiplash, bulging disc, some kind of joint pain they keep telling me is fixed, even though I feel it every day." She shook her head. "Kept going back the whole first year, but it didn't matter how much pain I was in, they told me everything looked good."

"That's horrible," Jake said, with feeling. (Singer could only imagine what Cathy would say.)

"They *thought* I was trying to get pills." She eyed them, hand smoothing up and down Miles's back.

"Mom says the real danger is all the overprescribing to people who aren't trying to get pills. Doctors will give you Vicodin for a headache and withhold the Percocet you need for chronic pain."

"I hate all of it. I don't want to go through life with a pill bottle in my hand."

"And they didn't try physical therapy?"

She grunted. "Sure, they tried. The insurance gave me sixty days to 'fully recover' from my injuries. That was it."

The reality of it crackled over Singer's awareness: had a car not hit Marie two years ago, they wouldn't be sitting here now. They wouldn't have ever met Miles at all. He fought a shiver. Any gratitude for Miles's placement with them was tied up in gratitude for Marie's injury, her pain. He couldn't be sad about Miles, but he had to beat back rage on Marie's behalf.

Miles slammed a hand down over her potatoes and fisted it, trying to pick up enough to shove in his mouth. Marie smiled and reached out, ghosting it over his head, down his neck.

"Sweet boy. You all take him to church?"

They looked at each other, sharing mirrored stumped expressions.

"We don't actually have a church," Jake said. "Singer's family is agnostic, and mine is Catholic."

"But you don't go."

"I guess my parents still go to mass. My brother and I don't." Jake paused. "The church hasn't always been good to us. I'm not sure I could go back to it."

Singer caught his breath, watching Jake's face.

"Mm-hmm," Marie said. "Children need church. You boys don't know that yet, but children need to have Jesus in their lives."

"Marie," Singer said, hoping like hell he wasn't about to end any chance that he and Jake would ever sleep under the same roof again. "You have a church, right?"

She stared at him.

"Could we bring Miles to your church? It's not something that means much to us, but I think you're right, I think it's important that he have—choices. That he have access to faith. I didn't have that, when I was young." He didn't dare look over at Jake.

Suddenly Marie began to laugh, huge rolling laughter. Miles blinked up at her, and his face crumpled.

"Here." Jake scooped him into his lap. But Jake was smiling.

"Oh, that's funny. Oh, that's so funny." Marie wiped her eyes. "Picture you two pale, pale white boys—oh, that's so funny."

Miles, now safe on Jake's lap, stared over at his grandmother, fascinated by her. He waved food-encrusted hands around and made noise. Singer captured each hand with napkins to minimize the damage while Marie calmed down, still wiping her eyes.

"Well, I grant it might be strange," Singer said. "But it would be a way for Miles to see you without Brandi telling us not to. And if Regina was there, he could see her as well."

"That girl hasn't gone to church in years, not since she turned sixteen and knew better than God." Marie shook her head. "You're really serious about this. You want to raise this baby, like he's yours. He's not your family. He'll never pass as yours."

This time it wasn't an accusation, but a question.

"We can't accidentally get pregnant, Marie," Jake said evenly, as if he were discussing the traffic patterns on the bridge. "We want to adopt. We love Miles. Tell us where your church is and we'll come. Unless you think we wouldn't be welcome?"

Marie and Jake stared at each other for a long moment, and Singer couldn't tell which way it would go. He mopped at Miles's face again and watched as he crammed another chunk of scrambled egg into his mouth.

"Any grandson of mine is welcome in my church," Marie said. "And you two along with him."

"Settled, then. Give us the details."

And Singer's first thought, as he reached into the diaper bag for a pen and paper, was: *at least I'll see them on Sundays.* Every Sunday morning he'd spend with Jake and Miles at Marie's church. That was worth any discomfort.

And Marie's challenging look, saying good-bye to them on the sidewalk. She didn't think they'd show.

But Marie didn't know Jake with a dare. The gauntlet had been thrown down, and there was no way Jake wasn't going to church.

33

VIV
53 DAYS UNTIL STARTING OVER

At long last, Viv thought she might be getting somewhere. Now that it was just Singer and Lisa in the house, everything would certainly improve. Even if Singer had watched the baby one day, he must be seeing exactly how his impermanence was detrimental to the child.

And sometimes distance made it clear exactly what wasn't working between two people. She resolutely turned her mind away from Drew and the house in Valencia.

Tonight she would talk to them. Singer. Lisa. It was time for the three of them to be honest with one another. Last time she and Singer had spoken, he hadn't been ready to hear the truth, but that had been days ago. Surely he'd be more aware now. He might even be able to see that all this was a blessing in disguise, saving him from far deeper mistakes.

And Lisa. If she only had a little bit of time with Lisa, Viv knew she could convince her to see another specialist. *Not* that man who thought he knew better than Viv about her own daughter. Someone else. She'd find the right person, she just needed Lisa to give her a chance.

Resolved and ready, dressed, put together—the three of them might go to dinner, somewhere nice—she entered her own home by the back door. Singer was in the kitchen, which was convenient.

"Darling, don't you think it would be nice if we went to dinner? I was thinking maybe that place in Lafayette we went for your birthday that year, though we don't have a reservation. I'm sure we can get in somewhere."

"Sorry, Mother. We're having people over." He pulled a wine bottle out of the refrigerator and gauged its level before returning it to its shelf.

"People? What people?"

"Oh, Frankie. Emery. I think Carey and Alice are probably staying home."

He said it as if it didn't matter, but she could sense the undercurrent there. "I should imagine, since they have guests."

Singer kept his face in a cabinet, bringing down another bottle of wine, unopened. "Yes, well, in any case they'll be here soon."

"Are you trying to evict me from my own house?"

"*Evict you?* No, Mother. Since you've never shown any interest in spending time with my friends before this, I assume you have no interest in spending time with them tonight. And anyway, I think we'll probably just have a glass of wine and sit in the spa." He glanced over. "I'll tell Frankie to keep her voice down."

The spa. *Her* spa. With—that man in it.

"I simply don't understand why that Emery keeps coming over. I thought you said he was a friend of Jake's." It took everything in her power not to demand Singer call off this—this gathering, these people. She had her own plans, which were undeniably more important than the brash girl and the young man who would almost certainly use the spa as an excuse to—

Viv didn't want to think about it. "Your sister isn't involved in this, is she?"

Singer sighed. "She does live here, Mother. And Emery is her friend, too."

Viv was about to say something to that when Lisa herself slid into the room, along the edges, like she always did now. As if she were trying not to take up too much space.

She only met Viv's gaze for a second. "I like Emery."

"You *like* him," Viv repeated. "Well, Lisa, I hope you'll forgive me if I don't consider your good opinion exactly beyond reproach."

Singer spun toward her, taking half a step forward. "Have you ever had a friend, Mother? In fact, have you seen anyone in your age group since you got here?"

His tone was so … vicious. She nearly moved back, as though even with the peninsula between them his aggression could reach out and touch her. Singer had never been an angry boy, but the expression on his face now was far from pleasant.

Viv marshaled herself. "How would you know what I've been doing? It isn't as if you've been eager to spend time with me since I arrived, Singer, and I really don't know what to make of that—"

"Since you arrived? You mean when you didn't tell us you were coming or how long you planned to stay? How long do you plan to stay, Mother? We're spending time together now, so—"

The doorbell rang. They stared at each other.

Lisa shifted, melting out of the room again. "I'll, um, get that."

The door opened. Viv was still locked on Singer, but both of them heard the low voice, and Lisa's in answer. She braced, but Lisa didn't bring him into the kitchen.

"I hope you know what you're risking having that man around this house," she said tersely.

He rolled his eyes. As if her concerns were a *joke.* "Oh, what are we risking? Why do you treat him like he's a predator? He's a friend, Mother. Do you think I'd have him here in the house—with Miles—if I didn't think he was safe?"

"I honestly can't begin to imagine what you're thinking most of the time, Singer."

He glared at her, but didn't reply.

The front door opened again, no doorbell. "Hello, my lovelies! I come bearing refreshments, hint— Oh, hey, Mrs. Thurman." Frankie leaned insolently back against the counter. "You look real nice, you going somewhere?"

"Just coming in." The lie was quick to her lips. She didn't spare a glance at Singer. "I will leave you to it, then. Have a good night."

The girl returned her smile. "Yeah, you too. Hey, Singer, you want me to get glasses down?"

It burned, the way these people seemed so comfortable here. Viv was on her way to the guesthouse, while that obnoxious Frankie was rooting around in *her* kitchen, pouring wine. And Emery, who was with Lisa—

Viv paused in the doorway to the guesthouse. Were they in Lisa's bedroom? Behind that unseemly locked door? She hesitated, almost tempted to go back inside. But what could she do? Singer hadn't shown the least bit of interest in looking out for his sister, that Frankie girl was useless, and no one had a key to Lisa's room except Lisa, which was hardly safe.

The back door opened and she made her decision, firmly closing herself into the guesthouse.

Their voices grew louder, then hushed. Viv stood to the side of the window, shielded by the curtains, and watched. Singer poured wine into four glasses. Frankie toasted him, and both of them drank. The back door again, and this time Lisa and Emery emerged.

He was smiling at her. They took up glasses of wine as well, for another casual toast, and Viv backed away from the window.

She sank down onto the couch, feeling numb. A burst of laughter grated over her nerves. They wouldn't let her help, but she couldn't abandon them. She was their mother. And yet they kept pushing her away, like very small children, insisting they could do everything on their own when they patently could not.

More laughter; a splash.

Viv dug her earplugs out of her traveling bag and settled them into her ears. She'd just have to think of some other way to get through to them. Or at least to Lisa. Maybe there would be an opportunity later. If she couldn't sleep, there might still be a chance she could speak to Lisa, try to talk sense into her.

It was Viv's responsibility, after all. That's what mothers were supposed to do.

34

LISA
91 DAYS SINCE LEAVING GRACE

They'd finished the wine course and Frankie declared it "hot tub o'clock," which seemed like a bad, very bad idea, and Lisa thought for sure Singer would complain. Singer had yet to enter the spa since she'd come home, though the Derries did with some frequency. But Singer acquiesced with a sigh and went inside, offering Emery a bathing suit.

So. They were in a hot tub.

Singer cleared his throat. "We may have to make a rule about you and the spa, Emery. It feels like cheating on Jake to even sit across from you mostly naked."

"I am not a home wrecker." Emery smiled and stretched his arms out over the rim of the spa, displaying his steamed-and-glistening tattoos. He had a few on his shoulders and back, but Lisa's favorite was the fox on his chest, tail curling around a nipple, looking over its shoulder as if Emery had a spirit animal and it wanted you to know it was watching.

Oh my god, Lisa, stop staring at his chest.

"Damn," Frankie said. "Totally not what I invited you here for, Emery. Though not a bad idea, actually—"

Singer splashed her soundly. The idea of Singer splashing someone was so outside of Lisa's image of him that she tried to remember having ever seen him play a practical joke on someone. Or tease in such a physical way.

"Thank you very much, but I am entirely taken."

"Yeah, except for the whole not getting laid in—"

"New parents often put intimacy on the proverbial back burner, Frances. Not that you would know, having never maintained a relationship of any kind for longer than five minutes—"

"Oh my god! Singer Thurman, you prick. Don't be mean to me or I'll withhold refreshments. Plus, I banged Caldecott for like two months!" Frankie, cheeks flushed from the wine, grimaced. "Fuck, forget I said that. Hell."

Lisa sat up straighter. "You did?"

"Who's Caldecott?" Emery asked.

"High school basketball coach," Singer said, as Lisa was saying, "My first real boyfriend."

"Oh, fuck me. Sorry. Never mind." Frankie waved a hand and turned to root in her pile of clothing. "Pot. I need pot."

"Wait. He and I hooked up right after graduation." Lisa shook her head. "But you were a year behind me. Oh. After I left, then?"

"Not so much, no." Frankie held a lighter to a little glass pipe and inhaled.

All three of them watched her until she breathed again and passed the pipe to Singer. (Oh my god, Singer smoked? That was almost crazy enough to distract Lisa from Frankie.)

"He and I didn't *date*. We just fucked."

"I can't believe he was cheating on me." Not that it mattered now, but still.

"He wasn't. Fuck me." Frankie scrubbed her eyes. "We stopped fucking before you and he started, Lisa."

"But—" That didn't make sense. "How old were you?"

"Sixteen, junior year, and it's really okay. He was an idiot. If anyone was taking advantage, it was me." Frankie held out her hand to Singer. "Give."

Singer passed the pipe back without comment.

"Wait, he was having sex with you when you were *sixteen*?" Lisa would have been a senior. She'd been such a stupid fool, always flirting with him in front of people. "Oh god. Is that why you hated me? Frankie—"

"Nope. It's over. I got nothing but love for you, Lisa. Shit." She moved to repack the pipe, but Singer grabbed it.

"I have this."

"It was going to be my distraction from the looks of pity, Singer."

"Deal with it."

"That's rich, coming from Mr. Head in the Sand."

Singer didn't bother to respond.

"*Anyway*," Frankie said. "Can we get back to how Singer's not getting laid at all? I'm pretty sure passing the humiliation torch is in order. Unless Emery has some secrets he wants to spill?"

"Ignore Frankie." Singer finished with the pipe but didn't raise it to his lips immediately. "I didn't know. About Caldecott. I'm sorry."

"Shove it right up your ass. I don't need anyone to be sorry for me, and definitely not you, buddy. How're things going on the home front there, Singer Thurman?"

Singer sucked in smoke and held it until his eyes watered. "Jake and I have accepted that for the time being our needs, as a couple, are secondary to Miles's needs—"

Oh good, a change in topic away from Lisa's ridiculous adolescence. "But why won't you let anyone watch him?

I offered, Jake said his parents offered—" She shut her mouth over the words. Or maybe she should just give up on talking altogether. "Sorry. Never mind."

Singer looked shifty. But Frankie just looked pissed. "Why the hell wouldn't you? Jesus, Singer. Is this some stupid bullshit about self-reliance, because I swear to god, sometimes you're a fucking fool."

"*Thank you*, Frances." Singer moved to get out of the spa, and Frankie actually reached for his arm.

"Fine. You don't want to talk about it? Fine. But either you want to fix this thing or you don't. You're right, I'm not a fucking expert on this shit. I don't have to be, dumbass, because I've been watching you two for years. You guys blow out, yell at each other, cry, get drunk, and fucking make up. What the hell has changed?"

"We have a *baby*, for one."

"Hence: babysitter. Hell, Lisa and I could keep the kid alive for a few hours, Singer, Christ."

"I was serious," Lisa added. "I actually watched kids at the farm. It—wasn't as bad as I always figured."

"Uh, scratch that, Auntie Lisa can take care of the kid while I illegally download Barney videos and get him hooked on ice cream."

Singer raised his glass across the spa. "So, Emery. Any interesting tattoos lately? Please?"

"Not lately. But I'm sure I can entertain you with some old stories you haven't heard before. Let me think. Oh, Alice loves this one. So like one night this group of guys walk in …"

Emery told a good story, but Lisa found her thoughts wandering anyway. The water felt good on her skin, and it wasn't too cold out. She'd forgotten how pleasantly soft pot made the world, though she needed a lot more of it if she wanted to dull the twinge of humiliation every time she looked at Frankie.

Frankie Derrie slept with the basketball coach. In high school. While Lisa was flouncing around making doe eyes at him during practice. God, her past self was so embarrassing.

Frankie went home early, claiming it was no longer fun to crash on the couch with the specter of Viv standing over her disapprovingly when she woke up. Singer stayed only long enough to take a few last hits off the glass pipe they'd been passing around, then told them good night.

Leaving Lisa and Emery.

It wasn't awkward, being alone with him. Not even in the spa. But she wasn't exactly sure where to look, so she'd defaulted to watching his hands, riding the surface of the water. When he pulled them out and sat a little straighter, she braced, expecting him to say he had to leave, too.

He didn't.

"So, just so we're on the same page, I'm attracted to you. But I'm not— There's no pressure. I really like hanging out with you." He carefully dried his hands on his T-shirt and put the pipe aside, testing the temperature of it before tapping it out over the big abalone shell ashtray, but using his knuckles to keep the noise down. When he was done with the pipe he submerged his hands again, and for a second they flickered, almost squirming.

Lisa's heart skipped. But then they were just hands, fingers, no snakes. She couldn't even trick her eyes into seeing snakes.

"And I understand completely if you're not interested. Obviously."

Not interested wasn't exactly it. "I'm pretty … messed up, right now. And you're—" Gorgeous, considerate, funny, smart.

"A loser with no long-term goals?"

"What?"

He grinned.

"No, just, you're—" This time he didn't interrupt. This time Emery leaned forward, like he was honestly curious about what she'd say. "You're amazing. So. You know. Probably not exactly in the mood for 'recently fled a cult.'"

His eyes widened a little. "Is that how you think I see you?"

"It's how everyone sees me. Mother hardly has a conversation without mentioning it."

"Please believe that my feelings toward you are not even close to maternal, Lisa."

She answered his smile with her own. "You bought me a lock for my door. And an orchid."

"The lock isn't maternal. Singer would have gotten you a lock, if you'd asked. Wait, that's totally running against the point I was making. I don't feel *fraternal* toward you, either."

"I'm pretty screwed up. Mother keeps bringing me to therapists, but there was only one I liked, and she didn't."

"Why not?"

"I think because he was on my side, not hers. Saul Smith. That's a cool name, right? Sounds like he should be a detective or something."

"Wait, your mother will only take you to a therapist who's on her side? That's messed up."

"*I'm* messed up. I was just staring at your hands, reassuring myself they're not snakes."

"Snakes?"

She shrugged. "Sometimes my fingers turn into snakes. I don't know how to describe it."

"That's interesting. I wonder why?"

Why, why, she knew why. At least sort of. "I had a friend. Abigail. She said she used to dream about snakes a lot when she was a kid, was completely terrified of them. When things got bad for her, she'd start seeing snakes everywhere. And it's like, the minute she died, I started seeing them, too." God, that probably wasn't what you wanted to tell someone who didn't, yet, think you were crazy. Unless he was lying. But … no, she didn't want to believe that.

"That's interesting. Snakes. Even as a kid?"

She nodded.

"She died recently?"

"Maybe seven, no, maybe eight months ago now."

"Was it some kind of accident?"

"Isn't every death an accident of some kind, even if the actual accident happened years before? Abigail's accident was intentional. I found her hanging in the kitchen. She loved the kitchen at the farm."

Emery shifted, water surging around them, bouncing off her and rippling back toward him. She braced herself, suddenly certain he was going to put his arm around her, and then what? Kiss her? Hold her down, head under water?

"And then you started seeing Abigail's snakes." He paused, and she went still, waiting for the feel of his skin on her skin.

It didn't come.

"Lisa? You okay?"

No. Not now. Not right now. Do not do this right now. But she could barely breathe, and everything was starting to go dark. *Focus on something,* Carey had said. She picked a spot of chipped enamel, right at the water line, and stared at it. The water, still bubbling, sometimes covered it, sometimes uncovered it, leaving a blurred dark spot where it should be. Breathing came easier when she stopped thinking about it, but the minute she realized it had gotten easier she started thinking about it again.

"How often does it get this bad?" His voice was perfectly calm over the sound of the water.

She shook her head, focused again on the chip, breathed.

He would ask questions, demand answers. The light she kept thinking she saw in his eyes when he looked her way would extinguish and she would just be Singer's crazy sister, growing out her fingernails and thinking about snakes behind her locked bedroom door.

"The mind's a strange place. And childhood fears are the most unshakable, I think. I wonder if she had a bad experience with snakes, or if she just knew they could be dangerous." He paused again. "I'm trying to distract you. I'm not sure it's working."

"It is." She turned her mind away from Abigail's body that morning and thought about her voice, about the way she spoke when no one else was listening. "There were rumors. About Abigail. Some of the girls, our age, thought maybe she was a lesbian. She … didn't really like men. I mean, she liked them fine, but when it was her turn, she'd get one of the girls to cover. Sometimes me. I mean, all of us would go to him. Were … eager … to go to him." She blushed and kept her eyes on the chip. At least she was breathing now.

"That must have put her in a delicate position."

"I guess I didn't think it did? Until Di, who was kind of the highest-ranking older woman, asked a few of us if Abigail had ever come onto us, and of course she hadn't, but you could see even just asking made the others … think about it."

"About every time they'd been alone with her, every time they happened to look over right as she was looking at them."

She narrowed her eyes at him. "How do you know these things?"

"Human nature. Power of suggestion's been documented scientifically, Lisa, you know? So what happened?"

"I'm not sure. But then she started being scared all the time, talking about her snakes, and I told her we could leave, that we could get her help—like, a psychiatrist, or something. But she said as bad as it was at the farm, it was worse outside, that no one ever understood her. And then she died."

"Poor kid. Was that what made you want to leave?"

It would be so easy to say yes. But that wasn't really it. She would have stayed forever, even after that, even after Di's terrible questions.

"They didn't let me hold a ceremony for her. They said she had unnatural attractions. That God had encouraged her to remove herself from our midst to keep us free from sin and she couldn't go to heaven."

"That sounds awful."

"Yeah." She leaned back, looking up at the stars. "And I knew it wasn't true. Not— I mean, maybe she was gay, but it wasn't God who made her hang herself. She was sick. They should have helped, at least tried to help, instead of making her into some kind of *lesson*. After that I stayed for a while, but all of it seemed less … right. In my head. My heart." Tears pricked her eyes, and as she blinked, they fell into the water.

"I wish I'd been able to meet her."

"I wish I'd made her leave with me. I think she'd still be alive."

She expected him to say all those ridiculous things people said, those mindless reassurances, but he didn't. Emery didn't say anything at all. He didn't try to make her feel better, and he didn't get too close, even though she was still crying.

"I'm sorry about Abigail," he said softly.

"Me too."

He left maybe an hour later, after they'd talked about normal things long enough to plaster over the weirdness. She told him more about Saul Smith, and Emery didn't seem to judge her for going to therapy. He actually seemed to think it was a good idea.

It was dangerous to care about his opinion, but she found that she did. No matter how sternly she lectured herself about how she wasn't getting involved with anyone, and definitely not with Alice's almost-brother. Even if she did want to know the stories behind his tattoos. And how his skin tasted. And what it would feel like, inside her head, if she let herself get closer to him.

It should have been awkward to say good night at the front door, but it wasn't. Emery smiled and touched his head, like he was saluting, and told her he'd see her soon.

Lisa felt warmth in her gut, in her heart, in lower places she'd thought would never feel warm again. She stood there for a long time at the window after he'd driven away, thinking about this sensation, letting it travel through her. How long had it been since she let herself feel something without trying to determine if it was the right thing to feel?

"He only wants one thing from you. It's so obvious, Lisa."

Mother. Standing at the still-open slider. Watching her with dark intensity.

She couldn't cry in front of Mother. Suddenly she knew that if she started to cry right now, she'd be back there, at the farm, and it would be the morning of Abigail's death all over again.

"I don't know what we did to make you needy like this, but you should—"

Lisa didn't slow down on her way to her room, fumbling the key out but unlocking the door cleanly and closing it much too hard behind her.

Was she really gone? Lisa shivered, still wrapped in her towel, afraid to move, imagining Mother right outside her door. Waiting to catch her. Change her. Make her what she used to be.

She had no idea how long it took to talk herself to bed, but she was freezing cold and trembling in her bones by the time she pulled the blankets over her head and fell asleep.

35

FRANKIE
18 DAYS SINCE COMING CLEAN

Logan opened his door immediately, even though it was late, and his usual smile slipped as he stepped aside. "Beer?"

"Nah, I've already had more wine and hot tub than I should have been driving on, probably. Sorry, I should have called ahead, I just couldn't go home."

"Frankie, hey." He didn't move, but the loss of Logan's perpetual cheer was enough to stop her cold. "Crash here. Don't go home if you don't want to."

She swallowed and side-leaned into the wall, even though what she really wanted to do was lean into Logan. "I couldn't be around fucking idiot men right now."

"No offense taken." He offered a slight smile, but she shook her head.

"I meant my roommates. You could never be an idiot man like that." Absurdly, tears pricked at her eyes. "Oh my god, I'm a fucking mess. I should not have had all that wine."

"Sit. Watch *Black Butler*. I've been meaning to start back at series one anyway. Let's call out all the close-ups on Ciel's eye."

"Ha. You were gonna propose a drinking game."

"I adjusted on the fly." This time when he smiled, she smiled back. And pushed off the wall.

"Fine. We will *Black Butler*. But that's it. No talking."

"Way to make it clear you need to talk while simultaneously making it so I can't ask questions." Logan flopped onto the couch and reached for the remote.

She followed, taking the other side, inhaling Logan's familiar scent, his space. By the time the credits rolled she knew crying was inevitable. Logan's scent. His presence, as close as she wanted it to be, playful and loyal and all the things she would want in a boyfriend. Which was why it was such a mindfuck.

Better to be home than here, torturing herself.

Logan turned the volume down. "How about I play surrogate for the emotions you're trying not to have? Am I supposed to be sad right now? Or pissy? Full of rage? Or joy?"

"You're supposed to not ask questions," she mumbled. Sniffling.

"That was about *what was wrong*. I'm not asking about that. This is totally different." He poked her lightly with the remote. "C'mon. What am I supposed to feel right now so you don't have to?"

"Hell. Nothing. Everything. I don't know. I'm pissed at Singer, who's apparently decided to detonate his entire life for fucking no reason at all, except he's acting like maybe if he ignores it he'll wake up and everything will be fine, which *never* works."

"Okay. I can be pissed at Singer. Though for the record, he's always been nice to me."

She shot him a look. "You know I can't stand you, right?"

"I know there's more going on with you than you're saying." He turned completely, pulling his legs up to criss-cross in front of him. The show continued in the background, but Frankie, tugged by some strange force field of Logan's attention, faced him.

He didn't look away. "Just FYI, I'm pretty sure you didn't come here because you're pissed at Singer. But if that's what we're pretending, I'm cool with that."

Dammit. Everything would be so much easier if he was…a lot more like Caldecott, so she wouldn't have to care about him. Not caring was easier than sitting across the couch from him and knowing that there was fucking nothing she could say that would change the way he saw her.

"Singer's definitely being an idiot."

"Uh-huh."

So he'd let her get away with it, but she found she didn't want to. Maybe with the cousins she wanted to pretend. With Logan she wanted…something else.

A hard lump formed in the pit of her stomach. "You remember Coach Caldecott?"

Logan blinked. "Uh, yeah. Gym teacher, right? He coached basketball or baseball or something?"

"He dated Lisa Thurman after she graduated."

"What, like the second she wasn't his student anymore he started banging her? That's fucked up."

Frankie focused on the television, which was still playing the show. Sebastian was accomplishing feats of spectacular butlering. Ciel was watching him with a distinctly unimpressed expression. "I had sex with him. Caldecott."

"Uh. Okay. So he was kind of a bastard where, like, ethics and boundaries were concerned."

She didn't say anything. She knew she had to. Because whatever else Logan was, he'd been a good friend, and lying by omission wasn't how she wanted to treat him. But it was hard. Because the second she explained he'd want to think that she was just a little broken and needed to be fixed.

"I was sixteen."

"Shit. I'm sorry. That sucks."

She waited. But that was it. That was all Logan said, and even without looking at him, she could tell his expression hadn't changed. Might have gotten a little sadder, might not. But the sum total of his response was *Shit. I'm sorry. That sucks.* Which was so far from the outrage and overwhelm she'd expected, she didn't know how to reply. So she didn't. She dissolved into tears and buried her face in the back of the couch.

It was so fucking *infuriating* that she was crying when she wanted to be screaming.

"I'm not fucking *sad* right now," she growled through tears.

"Dude, Frankie, I know the difference between rage tears and sad tears. Come on."

She choked on a laugh. "Shut up."

"Was it … shitty? I mean I can't imagine how it could be anything but shitty. He was kind of a lousy gym teacher. Not that the two skills are related, but—"

She kicked him.

"Okay. I'll stop making jokes. It's probably not the most sensitive way to have this conversation."

"This is not a fucking conversation."

Logan shrugged, eyeing her from beneath the fringe of his hair, which she always wanted to push back. Mostly just for an excuse to get closer in a way that couldn't be taken as flirtation.

"What? Why are you looking at me like that?" she asked.

"I need this to be a conversation." He held up both hands defensively. "For a minute, okay? Five minutes. I need us to talk."

"I'm not talking about Caldecott."

"No, I didn't mean about Caldecott. Though if he ever walks into the bookstore I'm going to beat him to death with a hardcover James Patterson."

"Not if I get to him first," she muttered.

"Yeah, okay, you get dibs. And Izzy can have what's left. If she ever found out—"

"How could she possibly? No one knew. Except Jake. Christ. And now Singer, Lisa, and Emery. I gotta quit drinking wine. It makes me say shit."

"Saying shit might not be the worst possible thing, Frankie."

She narrowed her eyes. "Okay, then. Talk."

"All right. Because I've been thinking a lot about this, and I know you keep saying we can't be serious about being together, but I kind of *am* already. And I tried to go out with other people, but I didn't want to be with them the way I want to be with you."

"You mean except for the part where they'd have sex with you?" She'd meant for her voice to sound sharp, but instead she just sounded … tired.

"Yeah, but what's the point of being with someone who wants to have sex with me if I don't want to have sex with them?"

She laughed triumphantly. "Exactly! That's exactly what I've been telling you! What's the point of you being with me when I don't want to do that?"

"You know it's not the same. I mean, I don't want to watch *Lord of the Rings* fifty thousand times, but I like being with you anyway. And I still think you like having me around, even if I don't share your love for Mordor. Or elves.

Or hobbits." He waved a hand in dismissal, then stretched his arm along the back of the couch, not all the way to her, but she could tell it was an attempt at connection. It was so obviously an attempt at connection.

Frankie swallowed the sick feeling in the back of her throat. "If you and I got together, for real, it wouldn't work. Because I don't— I mean I could try, but—"

His nose wrinkled. "Jeez, no."

"Hey, are you trying to say you don't want to fuck me? Because I think I'm offended by that." There. Her voice was better. Less weepy.

"I want so many things that we could actually *do*. Can I at least tell you? I feel like we've been dancing around this for a year and a half and every now and then I take my life in my hands and, you know, stand slightly closer to you at work. And okay, if you don't want me anywhere near you, I swear I can respect that, but that's not what it feels like. Is that— I mean is that actually what you're saying?"

But it wasn't. Not even close. She shook her head slowly.

He watched her for a long moment, as if waiting for something. "Sometimes you sit next to me on the couch, and one time I put my arm around you. You said it was okay, but then you didn't sit next to me again."

"I didn't want— It seemed like that was sort of taunting us with how we can never make this work."

Logan sighed. "Maybe we should try before we decide it'll never work. Just going out on a limb here."

"You like having sex with people. You look at people and think, 'Oh, they're hot, I want to fuck them.' I don't. What part of that do you think is negotiable?" Since she couldn't keep meeting his eyes, she stared at his hand instead, halfway along the back of the couch, well within reach. What if she *could* reach for him? Hold his hand?

Without it being weird or taboo or off-limits? Without feeling like a tease?

"I do like having sex, yeah, but I'm not a horny nineteen-year-old, Frankie. And I have a hand. You know? I'm not going to die from lack of orgasm. You act like 'I enjoy sex' means 'I have sex with anything that moves with no regard to if I actually like the person inside the body,' which is kind of insulting."

"That's how it seems. I mean, I know that's not actually how most people are, but from the outside it seems like allosexuals are into it all the time, with everyone."

"We aren't." His hand opened, palm up. "I'm not saying I'll never think about sex again, or that I want to live the rest of my life without it. But I don't think that's what we're talking about. Right now I just want to hold hands. And cuddle. And for you to maybe admit you like me a little."

She loved his hands. Light brown skin, long fingers, with a black ring on his right pinky that she'd always wanted to ask about but never had. Sometimes she got distracted at the store watching Logan rearrange displays, because his hands were so effortlessly competent. An extension of himself.

"It's only that you could be with anyone in the whole world. And there's pretty much no one for me. So it's easy for you to say 'let's try this' because if it doesn't work out—which it *won't*—then you just move on to the next girl. And I—" She bit down hard on her tongue until the tears receded. "It's not the same for me. It feels like a bigger risk."

"I hear that. And I guess I even kind of agree with it. There's a risk. And maybe it's not equal between us. But there's always a risk. Every relationship is a risk, a gamble. You put up your stakes and you roll the dice, you know? Except it's not random, because we aren't inanimate objects, we're people, and we can work things out. You can watch *Lord of the Rings* and I'll jerk off in the other room and all will be right with the world."

"It's not that easy."

"You know what's easy?" He reached out. "Hold my hand while we watch *Black Butler*. And if you want to sit closer, you should. But definitely don't go back to your apartment tonight."

"Wow. That progressed from 'hold my hand' to 'sleep with me' fast." She held her breath and took his stupid hand anyway.

Logan's fingers closed around hers, firm and confident. "I'm a good bed partner. I don't steal sheets, and I don't kick."

"Is this— Are you giving me your resume or something right now?"

"No. And you can take the couch, which was actually what I meant, though I would personally love it if you wanted to share the bed." He paused. "Queen-sized. Plenty of room."

Her hands were more pale, and her fingers thicker, shorter, but somehow their hands together didn't look as foolish as it seemed like they should. "At some point you're going to want to go from cuddling to kissing to sex. And I won't."

"I know. So that'll probably be hard. But I think a good portion of sex is really just a way for people to be close to each other, and I don't think it's the only way. And kissing's not all one thing, either." He pulled her hand to his lips and kissed it. "Does that gross you out?"

A split second of his lips, dry, on her skin. "No. That was— It didn't gross me out."

"So I could do it again, or no thanks?"

Such a small thing for it to be so monumental. She almost didn't say the thing she was thinking, because it was ridiculous. It was a risk. He might not get it.

"That was the first time anyone ever kissed me and like … knew. Knew to not be all over me."

His fingers tightened, but he didn't speak.

She looked up. "You could do it again. Mostly I think you're cracked and this is gonna end badly, but you can hold my hand. And you can—you can kiss me like that."

"Yeah, okay. And if I ever do anything you don't want, knee me in the balls."

"Like I need your permission for that. Looking forward to it."

Logan reached for the remote again. "We're totally dating now. I'm telling everyone."

"You've been telling everyone we're dating for months."

"Yeah, but now it's for real."

She sighed. "Oh god. This is the worst decision I've ever made. Plus, most people don't know I'm ace so they're gonna think we're all— Ew."

Logan laughed, then clasped his remote hand to his mouth. "Am I allowed to laugh at that? Because it feels super subversive to date in public and not have sex in private. We are subverting the dominant paradigm, Frankie!"

She punched him in the arm. "Can it. And turn the volume up, I like this episode."

"You know you're kind of my girlfriend now."

"I know you're really obnoxious."

"You don't have to tell me how excited you are to be my boo. I can sense it."

"You did not just call me that."

He laughed again and turned the volume up.

She took the couch, eventually, when they'd marathoned most of series one. But it wasn't beyond the realm of possibility that she could sleep beside him in a bed without worrying that he'd take it wrong. Maybe next time.

The fact that there would be a next time made Frankie feel terribly happy, the sort of happy that she tried to fight except her entire body felt lighter with it, more buoyant, even on Logan's lumpy couch. He'd left his bedroom door open, and every now and then she could hear a snore, or a sigh, or a shift in the blankets.

And that made her happy, too.

36

Singer had only ever been to Midnight Mass on Christmas with the Derries. It had in no way prepared him for Marie's church.

They were two of a small handful of white people (they weren't the only ones, though being so dramatically outnumbered was certainly novel; it would be good to do this frequently, Singer thought, because Miles would so much more frequently be the only dark-skinned person in the room). But where he felt even more dwarfed than that was the voices. Marie's fellow parishioners could sing, and sing loudly.

Obviously that there was singing at a black church really wasn't a surprise. Maybe this time he should have relied on the stereotype. He'd have to ask Kara about what church she and Victor took the kids to.

Miles loved every second of it, after an initial few moments of looking around, eyes bulging, mouth agape, over Jake's shoulder. He probably remembered it from when he was younger, the singing, the energy.

And oh, god, Jake looked brilliant. Jake, in his Sunday best, handsome as anything, standing tall beside him, holding Miles in a brand new outfit he kept picking at. Singer felt a surge of pride and straightened his own back to meet it. They might be white, okay, but they were trying to be good parents for him. If they tried this hard to be good partners, they ought to be able to—but no, think about that later.

Marie held Miles to meet her pastor—Brother James, though aside from the introduction she called him "James"—but couldn't keep him in her arms much longer than that.

"You let these strong young men carry Miles, Marie," Brother James told her, kissing her cheek. "I'm so glad to see you smiling, Sister. It's very good to meet you both, and to know who's caring for our baby boy."

"Thank you, sir," Singer said.

"And, um, thanks for making us feel welcome," Jake added, blushing faintly.

Brother James laughed out loud. "Y'all are always welcome here. You let me know if there's anything we can help with."

"Boy needs a barber," Marie said.

"In time, Marie." James winked at Miles, chucked his chin, and moved away.

This was evidently some kind of sign. The next twenty minutes were all introductions and shaking hands and names (some of which Singer realized he could neither spell nor remember how to say). And black women, mostly older than Marie, handing Miles around, laughing when he began to cry, as if they were sharing a joke with him, which somehow pulled him out of his tears long enough to be distracted.

They shifted off to the side when they were clearly un-necessary. Jake leaned in, barely speaking above a whisper. "This? Would not happen if we brought him to mass. I don't mean Miles, I mean any kid of ours." Jake paused for a second. "Maybe any kid of anyone's. This is amazing, Singer. We have to do this. I mean, as often as we can."

"I agree completely."

Shared certainty, Singer reflected, was one of the things he missed most. They stood back, a few feet behind Marie and her extended network of grandmothers and aunties, watching Miles get sleepy, eventually settling on someone's shoulder, eyes heavy, fluttering, finally closed. *Every kid should have this. Every kid should be passed around, in a wide circle of people, kith and kin, who love them, until they're so sated and relaxed they drift off to sleep.*

Sometime later, after a meal served buffet style in a big room off to the side of the church proper, Singer and Jake extracted Miles from a woman called Sarah, who appeared to be one of Marie's close friends.

"Will we be seeing you again, then?" she asked, looking at each of them.

"Same time next week," Jake replied.

Marie laughed. "You sure are determined, I'll give you that." She kissed Miles once more. "All right, then, boy, you'll see your old nana next Sunday. Drive safely home, now."

"We will."

*

Jake somewhat awkwardly invited him back to Carey and Alice's. There were a few bad seconds, when he stood just inside the door, hit with the contrast of how welcome he'd felt in this house when he knew Jake was coming home with him.

Then Carey was there, suddenly, at his side. "How was church?"

"Oddly … positive."

Carey's mouth quirked at the corner—which was, for him, a genuine smile. "It occurred to me at some point in adulthood that there are people with uncomplicated relationships with God. I can't imagine it."

"You mean, people who expect church to be positive?"

"Exactly."

"I don't know, Care," Alice said from across the room, where she was helping Miles peel out of his church clothes. "I'd think it's the people with the most complicated relationships to God who find succor in a place of worship."

"Did you just say 'succor'?"

"Shut it, bub. You want some coffee, Singer? Jake?"

Coffee, yes, then cookies, and Miles falling asleep in his arms, for the first time in days. Singer laid him carefully down in the playpen, set up to the side of the fold-out bed in Carey's office.

"I'll, uh, drive you home," Jake said.

They were alone in the car. Singer couldn't remember the last time they'd been alone together. His heart was pounding, like this was a first date, like what he said now would influence whether or not they'd ever go on a second one.

"You could stay. With us." Jake glanced sideways, fingers lightly tapping on the steering wheel.

"At Carey's?" *In the office?*

Jake shrugged, but Singer could see the tension in his shoulders now, back going rigid. "I miss you."

"I miss you, too. I miss both of you. All day, every day."

"Then why not bring some stuff over? It's not a solution. But it'd be nice to…see you. While we figure one out."

Singer felt a wave of stupid, inescapable anger and bit down on his tongue. "A solution to what?"

"I don't really know. Whatever's going on. With us."

"What's going on with us is you left. You took Miles and went to your brother's house."

Jake was already shaking his head, which made little fiery daggers shoot through Singer's limbs.

"Isn't that what happened? You said you needed some time and you'd come back, but how much time? When?"

"I didn't say that. I said I needed time and that I wasn't *leaving you*. And I'm not. I think about you all goddamn day long, Singer." Jake pulled the car, inelegantly, to the curb. "What the fuck are we doing right now?"

"You tell me. You're the one who left."

"Yeah, because you haven't talked to me, really talked to me, in weeks! I left? Jesus, Singer, you've been gone since your mom showed up, and it doesn't matter that we were in the same house." Jake paused, eyes narrow. "So what, you're waiting for me to apologize?"

"I'm waiting for you to explain it!"

"I can't do what we've been doing anymore. This thing where we're in the same room but we're not. I don't understand what changed, except it has to do with Miles and Lisa and your mom, and you aren't fucking talking to me about it, so maybe it has to do with me, too. Do you even want us to be together, Singer?"

"Don't put this on me. I didn't leave. I sleep, in our bed, every night."

"*Not* 'our' bed," Jake shot back. "Your parents' bed. In your parents' house. Where your parents have made it clear that neither Miles, nor I, am welcome."

"Not my parents, my mother, and the minute she leaves everything will be back to normal."

An extended, painful moment of dead air permeated the car while Jake just stared at him. Then he turned away and restarted the engine.

Singer's heart was pounding so hard it hurt. "Well? Isn't that— Isn't that what you want?"

They were almost to the house when Jake spoke again. "I don't know. I think I want better than normal. I think I want... more. Than that. Than waiting to see what your mother decides to do and going along with whatever that is."

"But..." More? Better? What was wrong with how it had been before? The painful tightness in Singer's chest expanded until he couldn't have spoken even if he'd wanted to.

"Anyway, I'll drop him off Tuesday morning. Did that work okay? With you taking him so I can go to work?"

Singer blinked back tears. And were tears acidic? Because these seemed to be burning. "Of course."

"And you remember we have the visit Thursday with Regina?"

"Yes."

"Okay. See you in the morning. Say hi to Lisa for me."

Singer stood there watching the car drive to the corner, stop, turn left. So, no second date, then. God, how did everything get so messed up?

He went straight to his bedroom (or rather his *parents'* bedroom), stripped off his Sunday best, and took a long, hot shower. When he came out he curled up in bed and stayed there the rest of the day.

37

LISA
96 DAYS SINCE LEAVING GRACE

"No," Lisa said. That was it. She was done. The word "no" had never felt so much like an entire argument as it did right now.

Mother didn't seem to catch on. "We have an appointment."

"*You* have an appointment, Mother. And you should go to it, if that's what you want."

"But— It's— I made it for you."

"No. I'm not going to any more of your hand-picked 'specialists,' Mother. Not a single one of them has been helpful to me at all."

"But what about Susan? She was helpful, and I still don't know why you didn't like her—"

"She was helpful *to you*. Which is fine. You should go see someone if you want to. But she wasn't helpful to me, so I don't plan to see her again. Or any of the other ones."

Mother's eyes narrowed. "Because you liked that man, the one who overstepped. I'm beginning to worry about your relationship to men, Lisa."

It should have hit home—Lisa was already worried about her relationship to men—but it didn't. Somehow barbs thrown by Mother were less and less sharp these days.

"He didn't overstep. He respected me as a person who's different than you."

"Well, since I was the one paying—"

Singer walked into the kitchen (why did all of her fights with Mother happen in the kitchen?) and poured himself coffee. They waited for him to leave, but he didn't.

"Am I interrupting?"

Lisa waited to see what Mother would do.

"Singer, your sister is bound and determined not to accept help from anyone. Don't you think—"

"Since when?"

"Since when what?" Mother asked, in a tone making it clear she was sick of both of them.

"You said Lisa won't accept help, but it seems to me like she's doing better than either you or me, Mother. You're clearly not facing whatever it is that's going on with you and Dad, and I'm clearly not dealing with Jake. Lisa's the one who comes out looking normal from where I'm standing."

Lisa shot him a raised eyebrow.

"Well. Maybe not *normal*, though the standards around here are flexible. But at least Lisa's improving. Has she shown you her orchid?"

Mother was practically shaking (with rage, or maybe just irritation). "*What orchid?* I have no idea what you're even talking about, Singer!"

"Emery brought her an orchid. Very sweet of him."

"Shut up," Lisa mumbled.

"It's not every day I walk up to find an extremely attractive tattooed man on my front porch bearing orchids.

If only." But the smile he forced with the humor was a little weak.

Why was he still hiding from Jake? This was getting ludicrous. It had been two weeks now.

"Are you going over to Carey and Alice's?" she asked.

"I think I'll hang out here today. Thought we could go bother Frankie at the bookstore. That's always good for a laugh."

"I'll get ready."

"Lisa, we have *an appointment*—"

"Mother, I told you: I'm not going. Singer and I are going to the bookstore."

"But there's— We have— Lisa, you can't go through life doing whatever you want!"

Singer gestured, a little violently. "Why can't she? Why can't all of us go through life doing whatever we want, Mother? What else should we be doing? What other people want?"

"I don't understand how I raised such selfish children," Mother sputtered. When neither of them responded, she stalked out through the slider.

"Okay, Mother calling us selfish, that's…" Singer shook his head. "Wow."

"Yeah."

They stood there contemplating for another minute. Then Singer turned to the cabinets. "Coffee in a travel mug for you?"

She'd been really trying not to get into the coffee habit again. Once in a while wasn't an addiction, right?

"Yes, please. I'll, uh, be right back."

"I'll be here."

Lisa couldn't decide if she should feel guilty about not going with Mother. She decided to just run with the not feeling bad thing. It probably wouldn't last, but it was nice for a moment.

*

Frankie and Singer were trading digs at each other's personal lives at the checkout counter, so Lisa wandered through the nonfiction shelves, not looking at anything in particular. She wound up at a table display full of books under the sign "The Road Less Traveled."

"That's Frankie's favorite table." The Asian guy. Logan. Whom she'd distinctly not known in high school. He smiled. "She gets off on the whole 'man turns his back on his life and has adventures that show him how to find meaning in the mundane' thing."

"Really?"

"Yeah, that's her shtick. You know she went to college in the UK, right? She's bored here. I think she's jonesing for adventure."

Frankie Derrie, adventurer. That was a weird thought.

Lisa studied the books. (Classics like *On the Road* next to books with covers that advertised film versions starring beautiful women and mysterious men, and why didn't women ever get to be mysterious, anyway?) "I don't think this is my thing."

"No, it's not mine, either. I'm more kind of 'stand your ground and fight' than 'go on epic quest.' Not that I'm anti–epic quests, but it doesn't seem to be a theme I can readily apply to my life."

"But 'stand your ground and fight' applies?"

Logan's smile twisted at the corners. "Hell yes. Can I help you find anything, Lisa?"

"I'm just looking around. Any minute now they're going to piss each other off and we'll leave, so I thought I'd kind of browse until then."

"Sounds good. Let me know if there's anything I can track down for you."

"Okay."

This being out of the house thing was still unsettling, but she could do it. She could stand here in the bookstore and not constantly think about snakes, or dying, or Anthony Grace. In fact, she hadn't checked Twitter since this morning.

She might have to thank Mother. Avoiding her was apparently the only thing powerful enough to get Lisa voluntarily out of the house.

Another entire table was full of crafting books, and who knew they made crafting books? She flipped through, wondering if she could actually make a scrapbook. All the stuff was sitting there in her room, not being used. But what would she do a scrapbook about? Baby pictures of her and Singer? Definitely not.

Then again, baby pictures weren't a bad idea. And everyone had been taking them. Emery would help. And Alice, too. Huh. She glanced at Singer, wondering what he'd say if she presented him and Jake with a scrapbook of them and Miles. Jake would love it. Singer might get that look on his face like he was too freaked out to even come up with a fake smile.

Lisa couldn't remember how many hearings or whatever had to pass before they actually got to keep Miles, but it probably meant she had some time to work on her idea. If she decided to do it. And why not? It wasn't like she was busy.

Job, job, she needed a job. Was Frankie hiring at the bookstore? Twenty minutes Lisa could do, but eight hours … probably not. She swallowed nerves and reminded herself that she didn't actually have to do this yet. She could coast on Singer and Jake's goodwill for a little longer.

"God, you're irritating, Frances," Singer said. She was already walking toward him when he turned to look at her. "We're leaving."

Logan grinned over Singer's shoulder. "Nice seeing you again."

"You too."

"Don't be nice to Singer, he's on my shit list," Frankie said.

"I wasn't. I was being nice to Lisa."

"Oh. Fine, then. Lisa's not on my list." Frankie waved vaguely. "Try not to join any cults."

That should have been offensive. It wasn't. "Bye, Frankie."

"She drives me up the *wall*," Singer muttered as they walked out. "The nerve of her, lecturing *me* on relationships …"

Lisa didn't have to participate, so she kind of nodded along while Singer ranted.

She probably couldn't make, like, one of those really cool scrapbooks from the books, but with Alice's help, she might be able to pull off a kind of low-level cool scrapbook. Now she just needed to collect some pictures.

38

SINGER
74 DAYS WITH MILES

Regina looked tired. Her eyes were puffy, and her hair was loosely pulled back, but parts of it were coming out of the ponytail, crimped-looking, not straight like the rest, lying limply against her skin.

She smiled when they came in. "Hey, baby. Hi, guys." This time she didn't swoop in to grab Miles. She waved. Jake went to sit beside her on the two-seater, and Regina reached out to touch Miles's cheek.

He didn't hold up his hands to her like he did to Marie. Miles was in silent observer mode. Singer watched his responses, wondering what he sensed when he looked at his mother.

"So he's one now. You're a great big one-year-old, Miles." She played with his fingers, which grabbed at hers and never captured them. "Did I tell you Miles means 'warrior'? Regina means 'queen,' and I thought, you know, I thought he'd need to be a warrior. Not that bein' a queen has ever done a damn thing for me, right? I mean, obviously. My little warrior."

Miles wiggled, wanting to get down. Jake set him on the floor between his feet, and Regina leaned over to watch as he climbed up, fat hands grasping at Jake's jeans, at the plastic of the little sofa, until he found purchase on the ridge of the bottom frame.

"Aw, look at you, baby! You're so big." She leaned back, eyes never leaving him. "You all really take him to Mama's church?"

"We really did," Jake said.

Regina laughed softly. "I'd pay to see that. Were y'all scared?"

"We were not *scared*, Regina." Jake smiled, his tone the same as the one he used to tease Frankie. "But we decided it was a good experience. For us and for Miles. Plus, he got to see his grandmother."

"Yeah, I heard all about it. 'If you showed an ounce of the strength God gave you, Regina, you'd be the one standing there with your boy in your arms.' She acts like I *like* being this way. Like I was a little kid and thought, *When I grow up I want to be just like that meth head hood rat down the block, with no teeth, who don't even remember her family.*"

Until this moment Singer hadn't understood all the warnings against offering money to the relatives of foster kids. Of course they had no intention of doing any such thing, and they were on guard for any attempt to get money out of them. But this was the real danger: not Regina asking for help, but looking like she needed it. He wanted to send her to rehab, if that's what she wanted. His parents could have helped him with anything he'd needed, and Regina's couldn't. Not because Marie didn't work hard, but because that's how it shook out for her. Race and class and circumstance.

Singer had never been stupid. He'd always understood that there was great benefit in being a white man born to well-off parents. He'd always understood that being born into poverty was a nearly inescapable trap no matter how much the feel-good movies tried to act like with enough hard work anyone could make a comfortable living and own a house in the suburbs. Enough hard work and a whole lot of luck.

Regina didn't look like she'd seen a whole lot of luck.

"David—that's Miles's daddy—was a football player. Did I tell you that? He was so beautiful out there on the field. He made varsity sophomore year, he was that good."

"So what happened?" Jake asked.

"Oh, nothing, you know how it is. You make all these big plans and things just don't work out. God, he's so big. He's walking?"

"He's pulling himself along the furniture, anyway. He took one step, fell down, and you could basically see him thinking maybe he'd try again in a few months. He's really fast getting around on the couches."

"We think because he mostly skipped crawling, he's still a little top-heavy," Singer added. "Jake's mom said when they crawl for a while they build different muscles, but Miles went straight to a shuffle-crawl, then trying to walk, so he's still getting used to his balance."

"Uh-huh. He'll get it, though. Right? I mean, not that he's— Brandi said he's fine, but Mama says she thinks maybe I messed him up."

"You didn't mess him up." Jake glanced over, meeting Singer's eyes. "He's not messed up, Regina. Look at him."

Miles had made it past his mother's legs to the end of the two-seater and was now obviously calculating whether he could make it to the closest chair. He teetered, undecided, and didn't look up when Regina touched his hair.

"Did Mama tell you to take him to a barber?"

"She mentioned it. We figured we'd ask her on Sunday."

"I can't even *believe* you two go to her crazy church."

"Well, the food was good," Singer deadpanned.

Regina laughed, a little more like she'd been the first time they met her. "Yeah. Make sure you compliment the slaw. Get on Sarah's good side. She and Mama been joined at the hip since they were babies."

"Thanks for the tip. It was slightly overwhelming last week. I'm not sure how much I tasted, really." Jake leaned over to poke Miles's side. Miles giggled, maintaining his focus on the chair. After a second he wiggled, so Jake poked him again. God, it was so good to see them play. Singer didn't know how he could miss something that made him so jealous, but he did.

"So you guys have, like, a nice house and stuff, right?"

That was an abrupt shift.

"We do," Singer said.

"Good. That's good. When I picture him, it's always nice. And bright. Do you have a backyard? I always picture him in a yard, with grass, and trees."

Singer swallowed thickly. "We have a yard. Though I don't think he likes grass that much right now. Maybe when he can walk he'll like it more."

"He'll probably be a good football player, like his daddy." She eyed them. "You guys play football?"

"Only in family games where everyone knows how much I suck," Jake said. "But my brother used to be pretty good." He narrowed his eyes. "Raiders, right?"

"Forty-Niners! The Raiders are for shit, Jake."

"Raiders or *die*, Regina!"

Both of them cracked up, and Miles craned his neck to see what the joke was. After a beat, he laughed, a little late, which set them off more.

Regina was just nineteen, ten years younger than the youngest of Jake's cousins. But for the bags under her eyes and the way her skin hung off her bones, this could be a fight in the living room between opposing factions of football fans.

"The thing is that they can be so good," Jake was saying. "They'll play three quarters and look good, and then in that last quarter they start giving away interceptions like it's going out of style. What the hell is that?"

"Because they suck, I told you. And they front like they're gonna kill whoever gets in their way, but they can't back it up!"

A knock at the door. Regina slumped against the cushions.

"How's everyone doing?" Brandi asked. Singer might have been making it up, but he thought she was eyeing Regina hard.

"We're good. Raiders or Niners, Brandi?"

"I don't watch football. Did everyone have a good visit?"

When Regina didn't say anything, Jake replied. "Yeah. Miles showed off his mad furniture-walking skills for his mom."

Because Singer happened to be looking in Regina's direction, he saw the way the little muscles around her eyes tightened at the word *mom*. She'd missed appointments and flaked out on drug testing and whatever else she was supposed to do to get Miles back, but she loved him. She missed him. He flashed to drinking in the spa the other night, getting high at least in part because missing Jake and Miles had been so acute there was nowhere he could hide from that feeling. How much worse would it be for Regina, who'd given birth to him and never expected to get him back?

They left the visit subdued and silent. Once they had their customary coffees, Jake cleared his throat. "We'll have to be careful with Regina."

"How do you mean?"

"She's inconsistent. Her mood last time was way different than this time. We have to be careful with Miles, so he understands that she loves him, and that she can't always be reliable."

Singer glanced over. Jake was sitting in the passenger seat, cradling his coffee, staring out the window. "You think we need to tell him that?"

"I think we have to do what's right for Miles, and sometimes that will be saying no when she wants to see him because the last few times she broke his heart by not showing up. And if she wants to see him that badly, she can come to church, Singer. But he's gonna get older and then he's going to know when she doesn't show up. Not that we never let him see her because she might not come, just that we put some boundaries in place so she's deliberate—so all of us are deliberate about their relationship."

Which made sense, but still made something deep inside Singer ache.

"I feel bad for her. She had a football player boyfriend in high school, she had plans, and now she's got nothing."

"I feel bad for her, too. And for Marie. I bet Marie had all kinds of plans for Regina, you know? Our parents definitely had plans for us."

"I'm pretty sure I was supposed to marry a blond woman and have a lot of blue-eyed children."

Jake huffed a laugh. "Yeah, I bet. I think my parents were more invested in my career. Care wanted to be a lawyer since he was little. I was probably supposed to be a doctor or something. But I didn't want my life to be about my job, like Mom's is. I like having an office job I can walk away from at the end of the day."

"Me too. And I agree with you. But all this makes me more determined to keep going to church than ever. He needs to have his"—*people*—"family around, to whatever degree we can manage it."

"We are his family. And so is Marie, and Regina, and Marie's bestie Sarah, who makes delicious slaw." This time Jake glanced over, and Singer felt it, even though he was still concentrating on the road. "Did you get the feeling Marie and Sarah were—*close?*"

"Close?"

"I'm just saying."

"Jacob, if you're trying to tell me that you think Miles's grandmother is a lesbian—"

Jake laughed. "Oh man. I'm making that up, right?"

"I'm sure you are. Really."

"You gotta admit, she didn't even blink at us—"

"Jake. Stop making up stories about Marie."

"Ha. I totally am. Probably I shouldn't do that when he's awake, though."

"Probably not." Singer checked the rearview mirror. Asleep, and safely latched, and yes, he was bigger than he'd been when he first moved in. They'd had to rethread the shoulder braces on the car seat.

He wanted to ask Jake to come home. To beg, if necessary. And judging by the fight they'd had Sunday, which he still didn't understand, begging probably *was* necessary. But he didn't.

Singer dropped his family off at Carey and Alice's house, kissed both of them, and drove himself home.

39

SINGER
75 DAYS AND 19 HOURS WITH MILES

Singer felt slightly more comfortable the second time they brought Miles to church. He wasn't relaxed by any means, but it was easier to hand Miles over to Sarah and watch the way he traveled between people. Kids were always coming up to play with him, and this time when he started to fall asleep, Marie brought him back to them.

"You want to get him in the car so he sleeps on the way to your house?"

"That would be great," Jake said. "Thanks, Marie."

"I've done screaming babies in cars. He's a real sweet thing next to Regina. She was always screaming."

"Yeah, I think we're getting off lightly." Jake took Miles, resettling him on a shoulder.

"That just means he'll challenge you later." She kissed Miles's cheek. "Have a good sleep, boy." She hesitated, not quite looking at them. "Will you be back next week?"

"Definitely. Believe me, Marie, this is way better than the church I grew up going to."

The lines around her mouth released, as if tension she'd been holding since they met her was suddenly a little less. "Damn right it is. This is what worship looks like, boys."

Jake hesitated, then reached for her hand. "We'll see you next week, Marie."

"Good." She turned away, suspiciously wiping her eyes.

"Did you just make our son's grandmother cry?" Singer whispered.

"Shut up, I didn't mean to." Jake looked over. "Did you just call him our son?"

Singer almost stopped walking, only vaguely paying attention to his feet as he followed Jake to the car. *Our son.* He'd said it without noticing. But it felt right, standing here in a black church, where Miles looked like he belonged and the two of them looked like they were lost and needed directions to the John Denver concert.

"Yeah," Singer said. "I did. He is."

"Do not make me cry, Singer."

Things between them, surely at a high point for relationship awkwardness, were one thing. The other thing was this: they had a son together. Somehow those two facts were not mutually exclusive.

"You coming to lunch?"

"Sure."

Lunch. Coffee. Cookies. Carey and Alice's house.

"Maybe we can—talk later, Singer. About everything."

Everything. Singer's stomach knotted. "You say my name more than you used to."

Jake got into the driver's side and didn't look over. "Um. Yeah. Well, I used to try not to. Because Frankie said that any time I said your name it was obvious how I felt about you, and it took a few years for me to figure out that it wasn't actually a secret anymore."

Singer gave that a beat before saying, "So I should blame Frankie?"

"Ha. Yeah. It's totally Frank's fault."

This was the moment. He needed to say something. Ask something. Or maybe confess. No avoiding it, even though he felt queasy, and he didn't want a repeat of their last car fight. But *later* was so seductive.

The sound of Singer's phone ringing interrupted, and he answered before it could wake Miles.

"Frances, we were just talking about you."

"Dude, what the hell is going on at your house right now? Your dad's here?"

"My what?"

Frankie made a loud air sound into the phone. "Your dad. Is apparently here, or at least that's what Lisa said when I ran into her on the way in to torture you. I dropped her off at the shopping center like ten minutes ago."

"Wait, Lisa's at the shopping center?" In Singer's peripheral vision, Jake looked over.

"She was creeping around the side of the house and wanted a ride somewhere, so I dropped her in front of the bookstore. Why?"

"Lisa doesn't go out. At least, not alone."

"Well, now your dad's here, and Lisa's on the run. What the fuck, Singer Thurman?"

"I have no idea. I had no idea Dad was coming up."

"Your *dad's* here?" Jake asked. "Holy shit."

"Frankie, I gotta go. Will you call me if you see my sister?"

"Sure. She looked fine, though. Maybe a little freaked out—"

"Yes, thank you." He cut the line and turned to Jake. "I need to get home. Will you—"

"'Course. You want us to come in with you?"

Yes. No. I don't know. He wanted Jake at his side right now, to face down whatever was going on. With all their misunderstandings, Jake was still solid, was still the person he'd want to have his back walking into any situation that included both of his parents. But Singer glanced at the back seat, where Miles was still asleep, with his head at what had to be the least comfortable angle possible. "No. No, take Miles with you and I'll keep you posted."

"Singer."

Singer shook his head. "I'll call you if I need you, I promise. But if I'm finally going to figure out what my parents are up to, I think it would be best if I did that alone. But text Lisa, would you? It's weird that she's out in public by herself after three months of living in her bedroom and occasionally letting us drag her places."

"I'll see if I can get ahold of her. If I tell Alice, I can almost promise Emery will show up at lunch just hoping to see Lisa."

"Oh, I know. They blush even at the mention of each other."

Jake's head snapped to the side. "You've seen Emery blush?"

"You haven't?"

"Man. Never mind. But seriously, he's hot, right? I mean, it's not wrong of me to notice that?"

"You'd have to be *dead* not to notice that." Singer decided not to mention the tattoos. "I can't believe my father is here."

"Me neither. What do you think they're up to?"

"I really have no idea."

Jake pulled up at the house and idled at the curb. "If you need us, we'll be here in ten minutes."

"Thank you. Let me know if you hear from Lisa."

"I will."

Singer leaned over for a quick kiss. "I'll talk to you later."

"Yeah, the Derries are gonna need an update, Singer."

He'd meant about them—their relationship—*every-thing*—but where would clarifying get him? Singer kissed his fingers and pressed them against Miles's cheek.

"Anyway, let us know what's going on. And take care of Lisa."

"I'll try."

He waved until the car was out of sight, then started up the driveway. The Volvo wasn't here, but Dad's car was, so he'd driven up. What was that, eight hours? Seven? That wasn't an impulsive flight.

Singer braced himself and went inside.

His father was sitting in the living room. A suitcase stood next to the door.

"Hello," Singer said, and waited.

Dad stood up, hesitating before walking over to shake hands. "Hello, Singer."

"To what do we owe the pleasure of your sudden and mysterious appearance, Dad?"

"I'm here to help your sister. Your mother's very worried."

"Lisa's fine." Notice, no *How's your long-term boyfriend? I hear you adopted a little boy.*

"To be perfectly frank, Singer, she doesn't sound fine. Has she really had excessive meetings with a sex worker?"

Oh my god, a *sex worker*? Singer desperately (briefly) wished he'd asked Jake inside. "To be perfectly frank, Dad, no. She hasn't. I'm going to see if there's any coffee left. When did you get in?"

"Maybe thirty minutes ago. Your mother said she'd be home soon, and I wasn't certain who else was in the house."

You might have tried our phones. "Would you like some coffee?"

"Yes," Dad replied after a pause. "Is she here? Your sister?"

"I have no idea, I just walked in the door. Jake and I took Miles to church with his grandmother this morning." He glanced over, but no, no flicker of recognition through the confusion on Dad's face. "She didn't tell you?"

"Tell me what?"

Singer sighed and dumped coffee into the machine. "I don't even know where to start. I'm going to jump in the shower. I'll be out in a few minutes." He smiled, wryly. "Make yourself at home, Dad."

Dad smiled with all due humor in return.

The second he shut the door to the bedroom, Singer pulled out his phone. *Where are you? This is fucking bizarre. Dad's in the house. I have no idea what to think about that. Also, Mother didn't tell him about Miles. Typical.* Then he pulled off his clothes and stepped into hot water.

Dad was in the house. Lisa wasn't. And he had an indeterminate date with Jake to talk.

And he'd called Miles their son without even trying, without thinking about it, without calculating his risk. Singer turned into the spray and stood there until he could face his parents without flinching.

I have a son.

40

VIV
44 DAYS UNTIL STARTING OVER

Viv retreated to the soothing comfort of Neiman Marcus and wandered its wide aisles aimlessly.

She wasn't ready to see Drew. Oh, she looked forward to his presence. If anyone could speak to Singer, it would be Drew, who shared his detachment, his ability to simply remain indifferent to anything that made him uncomfortable.

But in another sense, she wasn't prepared to greet Drew after all these weeks. There were gaps between them, spaces where they no longer met in the middle. It didn't make any sense. Her expectations hadn't changed. Drew was a creature of habit; he could no more alter his understanding of their life than he could his hairline.

Neiman Marcus always smelled the same. She passed the cosmetics counter, with its lights and mirrors and smiling young women. Viv had loved watching her mother get ready in the morning, using her brushes and pencils, sure hands applying layers, smoothing out any imperfections she could see in her round mirror. "The trick is not to use too much," she'd said, words of wisdom Viv had passed down to Lisa standing right here in Neiman Marcus, letting a salesgirl show them the right shades for Lisa's skin.

Lisa, smiling, vivacious, ready for anything.

"Can I help you?"

Viv blinked away memory. "No. Thank you. I'm just looking around."

"That's fine. Let me know if you need anything."

"I will."

She kept moving through the different departments, each of them exactly where she expected them to be, comforting in their predictability. Purses, shoes, then upstairs, through the clothes marketed directly to Viv and her contemporaries.

Of course none of them were the same as those days when she'd come here with Lisa, but in a sense all of it was the same. The same faceless mannequins and tasteful displays. The same draw at the edges of her interest—this particular shade of turquoise, the cut of that blouse. She pulled out a hanger here or there to better see a skirt, a sweater, and each of them made sense to her. Yes, she could imagine wearing this on a crisp day when the weather began to feel more like winter than autumn. She could imagine how she'd feel in it, the way it would fit her mood, how she'd stand.

She put each piece back, moving deeper into the store.

How could each item of clothing change so much and yet the store itself look exactly the same? Everything in place, if interchangeable. The tiled walkways coaxed her along the same paths she'd always walked. A detour to look at a vest seemed preplanned, as if somehow no deviation was truly out of place.

Viv ended up in the powder room on the second level. She sank down on the padded bench and settled her purse beside her. Small and contained, the powder room was slightly separated from the restroom. It felt safe.

She'd sat here during one of those shopping trips—for prom, maybe, or grad night. Some event for which Lisa absolutely needed a new dress, though she'd preferred Nordstrom to Neiman Marcus. After trying on the minimum number Viv would accept before going to another store, they'd retired to the powder room.

Lisa had fixed her hair, straightened her clothes, checked her teeth. She must have been seventeen by then. It was the first time Viv had looked at her daughter and seen a grown woman, even as the woman in question kept up a constant monologue about boys and finals and some coach she never stopped talking about that year.

Self-assured and ready to take on the world. That's how she'd seemed to Viv, watching from behind her. Surely she would have known if that were not the case. There just hadn't been any signs indicating Lisa was anything other than what she seemed to be.

The door opened, and Viv made a show of looking for something in her purse. She slipped out of the powder room after a careful "discovery" of her phone, which informed her that Drew was now at the house.

Words on a screen. That's what they were reduced to. Words without tone, without expression. *I'm here. Where are you? I don't think Lisa is here. Why is Singer suddenly going to church?*

She felt a twinge of conscience as she made her way back through the store. She would have told Drew about the child, and Jake, if she'd thought they seemed permanent. There hadn't been a point once they moved out. Now it would look as if she'd intentionally kept him in the dark, which was hardly fair; if he wanted to be up to date about his children's lives, he could certainly contact them himself.

Viv located her car and headed home.

41

SINGER
75 DAYS AND 21 HOURS WITH MILES

"You want to lock her up. After she's just escaped from a fucking *cult*?" Singer leaned forward on the sofa, fighting a wave of anger.

"Please don't use that kind of language, Singer."

"I think it's appropriate to the sentiment. You can't lock her up, she's thirty-four years old."

"If we had reason to believe she was a danger to her-self—"

"A danger to herself? She's fine. She hangs out in her room, she hangs out with me, how can she possibly be a danger to herself? I'm actually not considered dangerous, unpredictable company. By anyone."

"You brought *that man* into our house, Singer!"

"Really?"

"Viv, hold on. Singer, please explain to me about this person your sister's seeing."

God, there was no way out of this. *I am so sorry, Lisa.*

"Emery's a tattoo artist and a photographer. And a friend of ours."

"He takes naked pictures of men."

"And women, to be clear. He also takes pictures of weddings and bar mitzvahs. Not that I see how his profession has anything to do with either of you."

"We're worried about her well-being."

"In that case, Emery has a reliable income, is trustworthy, has a good sense of humor, and is maybe the only person I've seen her actually relax around without first getting drunk—ever. So I hope that satisfies your incredibly *sudden* parental interest in Lisa's love life."

And that hit scored, on both of them. It should have felt at least a little bit wrong, hurting his parents, but at the moment Singer just felt validated.

"You can't lock her up. You're both completely insane if you think that's a good idea."

"It's not 'locking her up,' it's getting her help. Do you really think she's adjusting well?" Dad spread his hands. "I know it may be hard to understand, Singer, but we've always been invested in your lives—"

"Lisa's, maybe."

"Not only Lisa's," Dad said, while Mother said, "That's not fair."

Singer ran his hand through his hair and stood up, moved away from the sofa, vaguely in search of more coffee. Or something to clean. Or, okay, just to be anywhere that wasn't right there with them. "Listen, it doesn't bother me anymore. But you aren't invested in my life even now. I'm adopting a son, Dad. With Jake. And you've been here two hours and you haven't even asked me about them."

"You—*adopting*— Viv?"

So she really hadn't mentioned it. He thought that made it a little bit better. At least her words hadn't had Dad's seal of approval.

"It didn't seem like it was a permanent situation. They haven't been here in a month."

"Two and a half weeks, Mother. And that's because of you." *Don't think about Jake right now, don't think about Jake right now.*

"Blame me all you want, Singer, if that's what it takes. If it was something you wanted, you wouldn't let me stop you. You never have before."

Oh god. Was *that* what Jake was thinking?

Singer stopped walking. He should drop everything. He should get in his car and drive to Carey's and beg. Because it wasn't that—it definitely wasn't that he didn't want Jake, Miles, their family—but Mother had a point. When had he let her or anyone else stop him from doing anything?

"I want to hear about your partner and your son, Singer, but I also want to get your sister settled."

"In a hospital somewhere? Where would she be more settled than here?" His brain clicked over, and he felt stupidly relieved. He'd deal with Jake. Later. After making sure they couldn't get to Lisa.

"It's more of resort."

"Look." Mother handed him papers. "I love her. I love both of you. I don't know why I can't—why it's so hard for us to connect—"

He was glad she didn't say more than that. To hear Mother lament having failed to connect with her children, when all he remembered was her congratulations when things went especially well—grades, games, his high school performances—it was all so ludicrous.

He'd asked Jake once, and Jake said his parents were busy, they'd hardly ever made it to games or anything like that. "But if I needed them to go yell at some dick teacher for something, they were on it." Singer wouldn't have ever told his parents about a teacher, dick or not.

"It's a lot like a resort," Dad agreed. "But with an emphasis on group and individual therapy."

"And you're going to pay for it," Singer muttered, reading over the very glossy, very colorful brochure, which featured a lot of smiling people involved in activities like volleyball and swimming. "You'll pay for what I can only imagine is an incredibly expensive retreat, where she'll be off healing on her own and you'll never have to see her until she returns, magically better. How long is she supposed to stay at this 'resort'?"

"I resent the hell out of you talking like that, Singer. Your mother and I—"

"Haven't seen each other in two months, so don't even start with me. I'm making some food. You're welcome to eat some, but please stay out of the kitchen."

The doors swung shut, and he breathed, deeply, until he could think again. Thank god Lisa wasn't here. How far would they go? It wasn't like they could actually kidnap her. Still, she was right out of a cult. She already felt terrible about her judgment; how long could she listen to their parents go on about how good it would be for her before she just folded in self-defense? He sent a quick recap by text, then a second text immediately after when he realized the first was probably alarmist: *We'll take care of it. Don't worry.*

The slider opened, very slowly. Frankie's head, not the rest of her. She must have snuck around back.

"What the fuck is happening in here?" she whispered. "Christ, it's goddamn World War III. I could hear it from the porch, so I got scared and decided to come in this way."

"They want to send Lisa to some private cult rehab in the desert somewhere, with volleyball and group therapy."

Frankie's face contorted. "God, she'd fucking hate that. Is she home yet?"

"Not that I know of. She hasn't called for a ride?"

"Nope. Figured she'd call one of you guys anyway. Maybe Jake's heard from her."

Very distant warning bells went off in Singer's head. He'd assumed that Lisa was at the bookstore. "Is Logan working today?"

Frankie blinked. "Yeah."

"Can you ask him if Lisa's there?"

"Well, I could, but he said she left like an hour ago."

"Ask again. Please." She could be walking home. Maybe. "Did she have anything with her?"

"Just her backpack, like usual."

The warning bells were louder now, but Singer couldn't quite place the origin of his sudden deep concern. "How long does it take to walk here from the store? An hour, right?"

"Nah, more like forty-five minutes, remember when I walked to work all the time? Never more than forty-five minutes, and I could make it faster when I wanted to. Singer? Why are we worried about her? She's fine. Right?"

He shook his head, slowly, still thinking it through. "I'm sure she is."

"Yeah, you're so not convincing. Let me call the store and see if she came back."

Lisa hadn't gone back to the store. And Jake hadn't heard from her, either.

She was probably fine. She was a grown woman. She was also outside the house for what couldn't be more than the sixth time since she moved in. Damn. He shouldn't have sent that text.

"I'm calling for backup," Frankie said.

Backup. *Derries to the rescue.* Singer put on a pot of water for pasta and started working on sauce. Where the hell would she go? He had literally no idea.

42

LISA
100 DAYS SINCE LEAVING GRACE

Lisa couldn't figure out where she was now. Except that her shoes were starting to feel painful, which meant she'd been walking for a while.

She pulled out her phone to check the time, then remembered she'd turned it off to save the battery.

She'd started through the neighborhoods, with the vague notion that there was a back way out, that if she walked these roads long enough they would lead to another road, and that one was dark and wound around a creek and would eventually take her to the Central Valley. Though it was beginning to look like she wouldn't be able to keep walking without finding a new pair of shoes.

The first surge of terror and betrayal after Singer's text (*sending me back, sending me back, oh god, oh please, I can't, I must*) had eventually bled away to a dull burn of resignation. Mother and Dad weren't trying to send her back to the farm. They were trying to send her back in time. They wanted to dangle that life in front of her like a dress four sizes too small, force her to put it on again.

She couldn't. Even if she wanted to, she couldn't, and it didn't matter. She wasn't that girl anymore, no matter what they thought.

So there was only this. The road beneath her feet. She'd walk until she collapsed somewhere. She didn't care where. At least it was movement, and she was free.

But her feet. Her feet were seriously starting to hurt. She hadn't thought about her feet.

The worst part of walking was how easy it was to get lost in her head, especially as it got darker. She'd forgotten her mind could do these sorts of tricks, lulling her into memory, making it so real she could smell the lingering shampoo of her friends on Anthony's pillow, feel the slide of sheets over her legs. And then headlights would blind her and she'd remember, no, not there. Both a relief and a loss, a gaping hole where no one would ever touch her like that again. As no one really had before.

Oh, sex, but sex wasn't the same. You could have sex with a sofa in the shape of a person, a person who didn't care or know your name, but what Anthony did was like flying, like being the only two people in the world for a little while, and god, Lisa wanted that feeling back. That feeling of being special, of being everything, she'd wanted it so badly she'd let herself believe it was true right up until he gently kissed her and said good night. Which really meant: go away now.

What would it be like to have all that and fall asleep where you fell, wherever you fell? You might touch his hand, rest against his arm, tangle your legs in his.

Lisa felt like moaning with desire, but bit her tongue instead. Desire, of course, was no good. Desire should be fought, they'd said, because you can't control desire, desire controls you. Desire for food, desire for drink, desire for one person above another person. That was what Anthony did: demonstrate control over his desire. And it allowed every woman at the farm to imagine that he might secretly desire her most, but he had to rigidly control it so as not to hurt the others. Or himself.

What would it feel like to let desire take over? She shivered with wicked excitement at the thought.

A horn honked, just over her shoulder, and the wind from the car passing nearly pushed her off the road. When did she lose the sidewalk? She didn't remember. And ow, the way she'd caught herself from falling awoke a few sleeping blisters. Ow, ow, ow.

Well, there was no place to rest now. *Keep going.* It was very dark here. She must have lost the streetlights with the sidewalk. Very dark, and she could hear cars approach from a distance, sounds echoing off trees and the utter nothing/everything black on the right side of the road. Maybe it was the creek, though she didn't hear water.

And she was cold. She'd been shivering for a while, but her muscles were starting to lock up. Very cold now. Beyond the tree branches overhead, the night sky was deep, endless blue, so dark it turned purple in places. There might have been stars, but Lisa couldn't look straight up for long enough to find them without falling.

So damn cold, and so damn tired. She kept walking.

43

SINGER
76 DAYS WITH MILES

The living room was full of people. Most had coffee mugs in hand, the rest had vodka, and a few were mixing the two. Derrie drink of crisis; nearly everyone was related to Jake by blood.

("Who are all these people?" Singer had heard Dad ask, standing defensively in a corner of the dining room.

"This is what I've been saying. How could she recover in this chaos?"

But Dad had only said, "They seem to really like her, Viv.")

"*Stop.*" Cathy's sharp tone cut through the babble.

The assorted masses (his parents no longer among them) stopped.

"Lisa is a healthy young woman at the prime of her physical strength. If she's outside, she will be cold. She will not *die of hypothermia*, Frankie, so stop saying that."

"Yes, Aunt Cathy," Frankie muttered.

"So we've ruled out former friends and teammates. She wasn't particularly close to any teachers—single exceptions notwithstanding, and not helpful. And none of you remember Lisa working when she lived around here. So? Where else would she go? Singer? Anything you can think of from high school or earlier, any safe places?" She gestured to Frankie, Carey, and Jake. "That goes for you three as well."

"Never that close," Frankie said.

"And I didn't even know Lisa," Jake added. Miles had been carried, asleep, down to the bedroom by Joe, who hadn't returned. Singer wondered if he was watching Miles sleep and thinking about Jake and Carey at that age.

"Carey? You and Lisa were in the same class."

Carey looked over, catching Singer's eye. "She's been having panic attacks."

"She has?"

"She mentioned them to me, as well," Emery agreed. He'd been sitting in the same spot on the sofa, pressed into Alice's side and holding a cup of coffee, since he arrived.

Cathy's gaze landed on Singer. "And I assume she's been seeing a therapist."

"I know she saw one she kind of liked," he offered weakly, unable to come up with a date, or even a gender.

"Saul," Emery said. "Give me a minute and I'll think of his last name. But she said she didn't think she'd see him again because her mother didn't like him."

Cathy's eyes narrowed. "Singer, Lisa's been here for … three months? Four? And she hasn't settled on professional help to navigate the culture shock? To say nothing of the likely unbearable grief. Didn't you notice she needed help?"

"Cath," Joe murmured from the doorway. "Not Singer's fault."

But it was. "I should have paid attention." He shook his head. "I don't know. I was—I should have at least asked her." *They want to lock her up in some Club Med rehab resort, and I never even bothered to ask her if she could use some help.*

"Smith." Emery snapped his fingers. "Knew I could remember. Saul Smith. She liked him."

Cathy rubbed her eyes. "Then when she comes back, she can make another appointment. I'll take her myself. She's been gone since one, you said?"

At least he knew the answer this time.

"Shortly after."

Frankie nodded. "I dropped her off at maybe one thirty, but not later."

"Well, that's ten hours. Unless any of you can think of something, we might as well all get some sleep. She has her phone with her, correct?"

"Yeah, but the charger's still in her room," Alice said. As the only member of the family with lock-picking skills, Alice had been the one to inspect Lisa's bedroom. Singer had looked up from the prior conversation just in time to see a complex set of glances exchanged between the Derrie parents and their sons; Jake had, for a split second, met his eye and smiled. Because of course Carey brought home a girl who could pick locks.

"Would you mind?" Emery began. "I know I barely know her, but if someone could give me her number, I'd like to leave a text with my number, at least. She probably won't call, but it doesn't hurt to try."

"Hell, she's way more likely to call you than anyone else," Frankie said.

Singer considered it while Jake recited numbers. Would she call Emery? He wasn't connected to her family, to the house. Maybe she would.

"Singer, you might look around her room, see if anything looks strange."

"I haven't really been in her room."

"I have," Emery said.

Eyebrows shot up around the living room.

"I installed her lock. And we … hid. For a few minutes. A couple of weeks ago."

"So Em." Alice was still serious despite the humorous looks shooting between everyone else. "You might check it out. I didn't know if what I was looking at was the usual state of the place or not."

"Yeah, okay. Come on, Singer. You're my insurance, entering her space without her permission."

"You think that matters right now?"

"I think it matters all the time."

He followed Emery into her room. It felt wrong to see the door open wide and the light on.

"She had the bed made back into a sofa the last time I was here." Emery stood just inside the doorway. "And the side table was where it is. The computer was the same. Her orchid." He looked around, shaking his head. "She keeps the backpack right there by the window like a go bag for an escape."

"Escape from what?" Mother asked from behind them.

Singer turned, biting off the urge to say, *From you.* "It makes her feel more secure, I think. I don't think she was actually worried she needed an escape." Then again, as already covered, he hadn't really been all that in tune with what she needed, had he?

Mother frowned, and he realized suddenly that before, she'd had smile lines. Laugh lines, even. But now there was no hint that Mother's was a face that had ever held real humor, or joy.

His heart twisted, just a little.

"If you had let us speak to her, Singer, none of this would have happened."

Thanks for making it so easy to be angry at you, Mother. "If Lisa had wanted to speak to you, she would have. Kidnapping her and hauling her away to some group therapy oasis *isn't* the answer."

"Group therapy oasis?" Emery took a seat at the desk and powered on the laptop.

"You should see the brochure. Volleyball in sand pits. Tennis courts."

"Sounds lovely."

"I hardly think any of this is *amusing*—"

It was impossible to stay merciful.

"We don't think it's amusing, Mother. We think it's serious. You might notice that Emery and I and Jake's entire family have been sitting here all night trying to figure out where Lisa would have gone, and why, and how to contact her to come home, and what to do to help her when she does. Where have you been, other than hiding from people who are actively trying to help?"

"I don't see that it's gotten you anywhere, Singer."

He took a deep breath and turned back to the desk. Better to ignore her. Better to avoid engaging.

Emery clicked something, maybe opening a browser. "I am so fucking uncomfortable right now."

"Then why are you doing that?" Mother snapped.

"Because I don't know what else to do. Maybe she's been searching for places to go, or jobs, or bus schedules, or anything that will help us know where she might have gone."

Mother pursed her lips and didn't respond.

"Well, here's something. She uses Chrome, and she's got it storing passwords." He clicked a few more times. "Twitter, Twitter, Twitter. I know you use Twitter, lady, so what are you doing? She follows no accounts. Huh." Click,

click, click. "Wait. She has two saved searches. Dead for the last few hours, but … huh."

Singer leaned over his shoulder, watching as he scrolled down. "What is this? Who are these people?"

"Consistent through the weekdays. A lot of activity from just before five a.m. on until the early evening, locations and times and numbers. Hm."

"Yes, but who are they? It's all the same people."

"Ohh. I think I get it." Emery pointed at the search string. "Praise for Anthony Grace. Anthony is his name. The one from the farm." He craned to look up at Singer. "That's him, I'd bet on it."

Lisa's voice, matter of fact: *the last guy I was in love with fucked different women on a schedule and never slept with any of us.* His hands tightened, nails biting into palms. "I want— I want to—" There weren't words.

Emery nodded. "Believe me, I've considered a lot of possibilities, but it isn't necessary."

"So can you use this to find her?" Mother asked.

"No. Definitely not. Now would be the worst possible time to go around chipping away at her agency and self-direction." The commentary was pointed, but Singer assumed it went over Mother's head.

Or maybe not. She gritted her teeth and withdrew. Good.

After a few seconds, Emery pulled out his phone, opened a Twitter client. "She's calling herself Crazy-Scrapbker. A little long, but she's never actually sent out a tweet, so I assume it only needed to be memorable to her. Okay. So. I'll direct message her, just in case. Most phone clients send a notification unless you change the setting, and she probably wouldn't have thought about it."

Singer watched Emery's fingers on the screen. *Lisa, it's Emery. Forgot to give you my number. 555-3849. Call any time.*

Seriously. Even if it's just to talk about snakes. I mean that, by the way—I keep pretty weird hours. If you want to call, I'm probably up. -E

"Hell. What do you think? Too much?"

"Snakes?"

"Private conversation, and shut up, no, not about that."

"I think it's good. I don't know if it'll work, but it sticks to your theory of not pressuring her to do anything."

"Fuck it." Emery hit send. "The same thing in text ..." He typed a nearly identical message out in a text window and sent that, too. "And now we cross our fingers."

"Excuse me." Dad's voice from behind them. "I don't believe we've met."

Singer and Emery turned at the same time.

"I'm Drew Thurman. Lisa's father."

To his credit, Emery didn't blink. "Good to meet you." He stood and offered a hand. "I'm Emery, a friend of Lisa's."

"I've heard."

"My reputation precedes me, huh? I'm going to hunt down a coffee refill, Singer, if you don't mind."

"Of course."

"Good meeting you, Drew."

Singer fought the sudden desire to grin savagely at the liberty. Dad was a big guy. No one called him "Drew" without being invited first.

"Well." Dad looked at the door where Emery had gone. "He appears to have a good head on his shoulders, which I didn't expect. Bit of a problem with authority, though."

"Do you want to come out and actually meet the rest of my family, Dad?" It was a challenge, more than anything. Singer watched the gears turn and waited for the dry, emotionless letdown.

"I think I would, yes. Your mother's gone to bed."

"Then there's even a chance you might like them." Singer straightened, stretched, walked into the hallway. "Miles is asleep, but we can check on him." The bedroom was dark save for the nightlight by the crib, which highlighted Jake, staring down at the baby.

"Hey," he whispered. Then, catching sight of Dad, he raised both eyebrows just slightly. "Um, hello, Mr. Thurman."

"Please call me Drew, Jake. We didn't meet properly before." Dad nodded toward the crib. "He's a strapping boy. Is that from the mother's side or the father's? Or is that a rude question? I'm not entirely sure how to approach this."

Jake shifted over, and Singer moved to stand beside him. "We've only met his mother, Regina. But she tells us his father was a football player in high school."

"A good one, according to his grandmother," Singer added. And if he stepped a little closer to Jake, Jake either didn't notice or didn't mind.

Dad stared down at where Miles lay, breathing deeply, arms and legs splayed out wide, head tilted. "It's the strangest thing, isn't it? They're so young, so vulnerable. And you promise yourself you'll do anything to keep them safe. And then they grow up."

Jake's hand reached over, barely moving, and brushed against Singer's.

"It was very good of your parents to come over tonight, Jake. We owe them deep gratitude for that."

"Well, Singer's family. There's nothing my parents wouldn't do for him, or for Lisa."

Enough. Singer closed his fingers around Jake's and squeezed. *Thank you, love.*

"Yes. Well. I think I'll thank them in any case." Dad cleared his throat. "It's very … exciting. That you are adopting a son. Children never cease to be sources of surprise for their parents. I'll take care of the crowd, if the two of you would prefer to stay here. This time is very short. Enjoy it."

Then he backed out of the room, and Singer found himself stupidly tearing up. It must be the combined stresses of the day, Jake and Miles still being gone, Mother and Dad, Lisa—

"C'mere. Hey." Arms closed around him. "You know we're gonna find her, right? She'll come home and be safe and we are totally throwing Alice under the bus for picking the lock. Also it's Halloween next month, and we haven't gotten Miles a costume yet—"

"I forgot completely about Halloween."

"We have a little time. And we've been busy, Singer."

Busy not talking. Not fighting. Not meeting each other's eyes. *Or maybe that's just me.*

"I know we're not— I know this isn't resolved," Singer said, slowly, trying very hard to be precise. "But if there is any way— I mean, if it wouldn't be too much—"

"Should we trust your dad to get rid of everyone? I told Carey we were spending the night here."

Everyone else could take care of themselves, but he really shouldn't leave Emery out there without backup.

"I'm pretty sure they'll be fine," Jake murmured. A light tease. "We have to talk. You have to talk to me, Singer, for real. But not tonight."

"Yeah. Yes. I agree."

"Come to bed."

It was the first time Singer had slept well in weeks. He should have felt bad about that—Lisa was still missing, after all—but he couldn't. Not when he felt Jake's chest rising with every breath. Not when he could hear every time Miles moved through the baby monitor.

Home. Family. Yes.

44

LISA
DAY 1 OF GRACE

At some point she stopped walking. It was just starting to get light, and there was a bus stop on a road in the middle of farmland. Farmland? But there was a cow, so it counted.

Where did you think you were going?

I thought this was going to be Antioch. What's past Antioch on this side of Mount Diablo? I wish I had a map.

She fell asleep, for a while, on the bus stop bench. It was like being in a movie, one of those movies where at the beginning the main character's beloved mother dies or something, and then she sets off on a trek across the country, meeting fabulous people, eating exotic food, living off the generosity of strangers. By the end of the movie you'd laughed and cried and felt moved to change your whole life, started thinking about it while you got ready for bed. Maybe you'll take up jogging. Or salsa dancing. Or maybe you'll quit your shitty job and sell your belongings and see the world. Go on an epic quest.

Lisa stretched, tentatively, and sat back down when everything started to go black.

You don't have a job. And you don't want to take up salsa dancing. And nobody died, not recently.

Still, though. This was farmland in the middle of the Bay Area—geography she thought she knew well. Maybe there was a little bit of fairy tale to this morning, even without the drama of a funeral at the beginning of it. Nothing was stopping her from walking to wherever. No one could tell her not to.

What will you eat?

Maybe I won't. I'll be like the mystics and pick moldy bread out of dumpsters, fill an old jug with water and swing it by my side.

You'll be cold again, like last night. And it's only going to get colder.

That was harder. She didn't like the cold. She'd nearly called home, called Singer, asked him to come find her on the side of the road and bring blankets.

But I didn't die. I'm still okay. I'm sitting here, aren't I?

Her shoes, though. Her shoes were the flaw in the plan. I'll need better shoes if I'm going to be a wandering mystic.

Then she got up again, slower this time, and waited for the swimmy sick feeling to pass before she started moving. And yeah, the shoes. The shoes were becoming, with every step, a pressing, aching, bleeding concern.

You can't buy shoes in farmland. No dumpsters or water fountains, either.

Well, shit, Lisa thought, and sank back down again. Maybe I'll take another nap. This grass looks soft.

What if there's snakes?

What snakes? There aren't snakes, Abigail, look around.

Wait.

She took a few deep breaths, panicking more about the idea of panicking than actually panicking itself. Focus, focus. Ants, an anthill, working very hard at dawn, already bringing home little bits of leaves and grass.

Had she been hearing Abigail's voice in her head the whole time? Since she died? When did that voice become Abigail's?

Slow down. Slow down. Everyone talks to themselves in their head, right? It's not that weird. And Abigail's voice is so normal, so comforting.

But for a second, it was almost like she was sitting right here, on this patch of grass, talking about snakes.

Lisa started breathing too fast again and couldn't pull herself back. Her heart beat too fast, she couldn't get it to sync up with her lungs, everything was out of order, and time was slowing down and speeding up and flying apart into pieces, and nothing made sense except dying. Dying, right now, on this patch of grass, next to this anthill, dying, unable to breathe or pump blood or move or think.

It was the worst one by far. She lay there and watched the sky go light and eventually realized that she hadn't died. Lisa pulled out her phone and powered it on, relieved when it had enough juice to start up. It started chiming and beeping and vibrating with missed messages, which was overwhelming but tied her to the world in a way nothing had in hours, not even her aching feet.

Her minutes as a wandering mystic were over.

45

SINGER
77 DAYS WITH MILES

They found Emery on the sofa in the living room.

"Sorry. Felt like I should stay around. Or something." He rubbed his eyes, more harshly than strictly necessary, and shook his head. "I feel responsible."

"For what?" Singer asked, handing him a cup of coffee and sinking down next to Jake in the two-seater.

"Lisa disappearing. I don't know. Maybe I pressured her. I was trying to keep it light, keep it fun, it seemed like she'd had so little of that lately."

"Well, get in line. You're at least behind me, Emery."

"You're all narcissists," Jake mumbled into his coffee. "Lisa left because she wanted to leave. When she wants to come back, she'll come back."

"Thanks for the compassion, Sunshine," Emery said.

Jake shrugged. "When Carey ran away from home, he went to Manhattan and stayed there for seven years. And at the time I thought it was mostly my fault. 'Cause he got molested and I'm gay and somehow that's my fault, that Carey couldn't look me in the eye or talk to me, and that he flew across the country so he wouldn't have to. But it was his decision to leave, and his decision to come home."

Things never said by Derries, not ever. Singer rested his knuckles against Jake's forearm.

"I know you're right." Emery's eyes were deeply shadowed. "But she could go back to them, you know. I was up all night thinking about that."

Singer shuddered. He had decidedly not been up all night. Certainly not thinking about Lisa rejoining her cult.

"I don't think so," Jake said. "She likes it here."

Jake's certainty—in the face of so many question marks—was disquieting.

"How do you know that? That she likes it here?"

"She left her phone charger."

Emery looked every bit as stumped as Singer felt.

"Listen, when she first got here, she packed everything, every time she left her room. I mean everything. I went in there last night. She cleared out the drawers in the desk for her clothes, you know? So she took them with her, but she unpacked them at some point. That's kind of a thing."

"And her phone charger?"

"It was probably an accident, but it wouldn't have happened two or three weeks ago. I'm telling you, she didn't scrub the room when she went. She didn't . . . erase herself. She just went out, like she was planning to come back. So I think she will."

Down the hall Miles started making sounds, waking-up sounds. Not crying yet, still waiting for them to arrive. Like any kid. They'd expected sleeping problems, shattering abandonment issues. But they hadn't wagered on Marie, of course. Miles always seemed to know they'd be there in a minute because for his entire life his grandmother had answered his cries.

"I'll grab him." Jake kissed Singer's forehead as he stood up.

"So," Emery said after a minute. "Jake likes a damsel in distress. Good to know."

"Damsel in distress? I thought he was talking like she didn't need any help at all."

"I was referring to you, Singer. You two seem better. Than you were."

It was so tempting to think so, but nothing had been resolved. More that it had been put off until some future *talk*.

Emery seemed about to say something else—something even more insulting and invasive, probably—when his phone rang. The clumsiness with which he fumbled it out of his jacket, in a pile on the floor with his shoes, somewhat belied his apparent calm.

"Oh thank god. Lisa? Is that you?"

Singer accepted the profound relief as answer enough.

"No, no, not at all, we're drinking coffee. Where are you? I'll bring a travel cup."

Okay. Okay, then. Singer sank back against the loveseat and allowed himself to worry. Now that he knew she was okay. He let it hit him all at once, a vast wall of self-recrimination and loss.

"Yeah, pull up Google and text me—something. Coordinates. A town. A road. Farmland? Uh, are you sure? No, no, if there's a cow, then ..."

A cow? But who cared? She was safe.

"Is that Lisa?"

Singer smiled and stood up, kissing Miles's cheek. When Miles giggled, he did it again. To his surprise, Miles leaned over until Singer took him. And oh god, how right his weight felt in Singer's arms. He fought back emotion. "It's her. She's okay. I mean, she's okay at the moment."

"Good. Okay, Miles, what are we having for breakfast? Should we see what's here? Maybe we need donuts." Jake tugged on Miles's ear and went through to the kitchen.

"All right, hang out there, I'll call you when I get in the car. No, it's Bluetooth. Yes, it's safe. Give me five minutes and keep your phone on. It doesn't matter if the battery dies, I'll find you."

"Thank you, thank you, thank you," Singer said, not sure if he was thanking Emery or Marie's God or what.

Miles, for his part, said something emphatic that might have been "thank you" or "donuts" or anything else he'd just heard.

"I'll be there as soon as I can, and I'll call you in five. Bye." Emery stood up. "Okay, so, you guys find a computer and look up farmland, and call me if you have any leads. She said she started walking through the neighborhoods past Frankie's bookstore and eventually she was on a two-lane road with no sidewalks and then farmland."

"Well, we'll look up a map. You think you can find her?"

"I can find her."

"Are you talking about Lisa?"

Singer didn't know when his parents became secret agents, but they'd successfully sneaked up on him a lot in the last twenty-four hours. He turned toward the kitchen doorway. "She called. Emery's going to pick her up."

"Shouldn't *we* pick her up?" Dad asked. "She's our daughter."

"She's an adult, Dad. She called Emery, so Emery's going." Singer shot Emery a look and added, "Damsel in distress?"

"Hardly. Not unless we've added clear wireless communication to the fairy tale. Anyway, call me when you find a map. Wait—do you have anything warm she can wear? She said she's cold."

"Here." Mother went to the hall closet. "Unless you— No, here." She produced a very old jacket Singer would have sworn had never been in that closet before. Lined leather, but old, dull. Still, he remembered that jacket. It had been Mother's favorite when they were young.

"Yes." He reverently patted it, amused when Miles did the same, then passed it to Emery. "Yes, give her this."

"Thanks."

Jake stuck his head in from the kitchen. "Here. Don't forget coffee."

"Thanks, Jake. Singer, call me when you figure out where she is." And Emery was out the door, arm pressing two travel cups to his body while he pulled his phone from his pocket.

"Where is she?" Dad asked.

"She's not sure." *Drive fast, Emery.* Singer described it again, and his parents looked at each other.

"Brentwood," Mother said. "Though I didn't know there was still farmland out there. When we were young, all of it was farmland, but now it's mostly shopping centers and tract housing."

"You're sure?" Brentwood. He thought he might have driven through it once, on the way to somewhere else.

"You can take Marsh Creek from Clayton all the way out," Dad agreed. "And that's where those neighborhoods past the shopping center lead."

"Okay. Thanks." It only took a second to call Emery and verify the direction he was heading.

Jake pushed through the swinging kitchen door again. "I'm making more coffee, but all we seem to have in the house is bacon. If there are eggs, I didn't see them. I can probably scrounge up some bread if anyone wants toast." He handed Miles a frozen waffle. "Here, kiddo."

Dad shook his head. "We'll go out for something. Just let us get dressed."

"I'd like to be here when she gets home," Mother said to him.

"Then we'll have to dress quickly."

She shot him a dirty look and walked out the back door.

Dad stared after her for a moment. "I honestly didn't mean anything by that."

"So even after years of marriage, you still have stupid miscommunications?" Jake said. "Good to know."

Hell. Dad raised his eyebrows, then waved and followed Mother to the guesthouse.

Lisa's arrival home was anticlimactic. At best.

"I was only gone a few hours."

"Overnight, and we had no idea where, you could have been dead!" Singer clamped his hand over his mouth. "Did I just say that?"

Lisa yawned. "I'm pretty tired." She turned to Emery. "Um. So. Thank you for picking me up."

"I probably could have given you my phone number sooner. Would that have made a difference? Might have saved you a cold night in farmland."

She considered it carefully and shook her head. "No, that was … good. I think. But also, I might be coming down with, I don't know, schizophrenia or something, so you might have actually saved yourself."

"Schizophrenia?"

"Yeah."

"I already called Mom," Jake said. "She—threatened? promised?—to take you back to that shrink you liked. And I don't think I'd argue with her if I were you. She's been a nurse in the ER forever. There's really no convincing her not to do something, if she feels it's health-related."

"Your mom?"

Singer nodded. "Cathy held a command center in the living room last night and interrogated all of us about where we thought you'd go. And I'm with Jake. Do what she says and everything will be fine."

"Huh. That's funny, Singer. You found people who are—nothing like our parents."

God, that was a whole other ball of wax.

"They're probably gonna be home any second, if you want to escape. They said they'd bring breakfast."

Lisa slowly shook her head. "No. Breakfast sounds good. And I feel better. I kind of freaked out, and thought I was dying. And then I didn't. And I'm ... okay with that."

Okay with not dying. Singer wanted to ask more, wanted to know what that meant, and how long she'd been okay with dying, and how he didn't even notice.

Then Miles started waving his hands angrily at Lisa, and she frowned and bent down to see him.

"What?"

"Arguh marga fubba!"

"I think he's mad 'cause he hasn't seen you lately," Jake translated. "You say, 'Hi, Aunt Lisa.'"

Miles waved his hands and cursed. At least, that's what it sounded like.

"Oh. Uh." Lisa tentatively put out her arms. "Ugh, Miles, you are way heavier than you look."

Miles resumed talking to Lisa, but not as angrily.

"Oh yeah?" she asked, glancing at Singer.

"Bubba argh dadadadada."

"Did he just say 'dada'?"

"Alice swears he has been, but I don't buy it," Jake said. "I'm gonna text everyone, let them know you're okay."

"Everyone?"

Then Mother and Dad walked in, with bags from the store, and Singer watched them catch sight of Lisa, Lisa and Miles, and maybe they weren't the greatest parents, but both of them looked so utterly exhausted, so viscerally relieved by her presence, that he started forgiving them. A very little bit.

"Well, I'm glad you decided to come home," Mother said, clearly trying too hard.

Lisa met his eyes as she turned, and he thought: a very little bit. But it was enough.

46

LISA
1 DAY SINCE FINDING GRACE

She was tired. Very, very tired. Not too tired to say yes when Emery offered—bashfully—his apartment to her.

"I can sleep on the futon. It's small, but it's … quiet."

Meaning not full of parents and relatives. *Yes.*

She was too exhausted to do more than snap her seatbelt shut before she fell asleep against the window.

"We're here. Lisa?"

"'Kay," she murmured.

Emery's apartment was one big room with a loft bed and a kitchen in what must have once been a closet. He hadn't been expecting company: clothes were draped over both kitchen chairs, and a trunk stood open, spilling what appeared to be coils of rope into the room, as if he'd set them aside while digging for something else.

"It's not much, but it's better than sharing a house with a bunch of people, which is what I can actually afford. Every time I'm taking pictures at a wedding I remind myself that this is what I'm paying for."

"Privacy?"

"And the ability to have a guest over."

She blushed. "Oh." She looked around, mostly to keep from looking at Emery. "What's all this?"

"Bondage gear. I had a shoot last weekend for a local dominatrix."

"Wow." Lisa didn't touch, but just staring was sort of enough.

"Sometimes I like that sort of thing, but it's not a deal breaker. And I can take you home if that makes you uncomfortable."

It took a minute.

"You mean, *not* for photo shoots?"

"Yeah."

She thought about all those sketches in Alice's studio.

"Is this where Alice did her drawings?"

Emery's eyes lit. "Wait, did you see those? Did you like them? And no, that was in this gorgeous playroom that I can't even describe, but it was amazing. I wish I had something like that. But seriously, did you like the sketches?"

If there was a neutral way to answer that question, Lisa didn't know what it was. "They were very nice." Then she looked up and both of them laughed. "I don't honestly know what to say. Alice's drawings were incredible, and you were very— There was a drawing of you, which was very compelling. But I don't know anything about, uh, that kind of thing. Before the farm I just did what everyone else did, and it was mostly pretty lousy."

"In a sense, I lucked out." He sat down on the futon. "I managed to skip a lot of the lousy. I was modeling, and you kind of knew there were … other options. I did some fetish shoots, but I wanted to get behind the camera more."

"That didn't bother you?"

"People making me look sexy and taking my picture? Not so much."

She rolled her eyes. This was familiar, like banter was a language she was only a little bit rusty speaking. "How old were you?"

"Eighteen, nineteen. I was modeling as a teenager, not glamorous modeling, really bargain basement stuff. But I'd mess around taking pictures on my crummy little point-and-shoot, and one of the photographers—who was also not exactly thrilled to be doing bargain basement work—showed me how to use a real camera. And the rest is history."

"Is that what you want to do? Career-wise?"

"I want to do everything. I love tattooing. I love doing art on skin, it's a crazy rush when it's good."

"Huh." She leaned against the ladder to the loft. It was built-in, sturdy. Could you use the ropes over there to tie someone to a ladder like this? Probably. Not that she was volunteering.

Then again, not that she *wasn't*.

"I don't have any tattoos," she said, because it felt like it was her turn.

"I can get you a deal if you want one."

"I'll, you know, keep that in mind."

"So. You want to go to sleep?"

She did. She also didn't. "I'm not sure. I don't really want to stop talking to you."

"That's good. I mean, I don't really want to stop talking to you, either."

She shot him a *look*. "I told you, I'm fucked up."

"I'm not worried about that."

"What're you worried about?"

He held her gaze for a long second, like he wasn't quite sure if he should answer. "I worry that you've only known intimacy as a somewhat disregarded by-product of very heteronormative sex, and that you think that's what I'm interested in. I'm not. At all."

"You don't want to have sex with me?"

"Well, I wouldn't say *that.*"

"Uh-huh."

"I would like to know you better. Deeper. More intimately. Whether or not sex is ever a part of that."

What on earth did that mean? The confusion must have shown on her face, because Emery just kind of sighed.

"Or maybe I've jumped the gun. I could have waited to mention it."

"No. No, I'm done playing games. I don't know what you want from me, exactly, but I'm definitely done trying to guess what's going on in other people's heads. So, I don't know, tell me what that means. Tell me about a time you had this intimacy thing, without sex. 'Cause I don't get that. At all."

"Will you sit? Not that I mind you standing, but I'm going to get a crick in my neck."

She could sit. She could, she found, do a little bit better than that. "I might fall asleep," she warned him, as she lay her head back against the futon to look at him. "You can get closer. I'm not afraid of you."

"Good. I'm glad. Okay. So, the boy in Alice's sketches? He's a good example. Because restraining someone that vulnerable is a totally intimate experience, but I would never have sex with him."

"Why?" She yawned.

"Aw, he's sweet, but he's taken twice over. I'm surprised they let me play with him, though I think there was some sort of Derrie alchemy involved in that."

"Derrie alchemy's a good term for a lot of unexplainable things." *Like me, right now, sitting here with you.* "And that's intimate?"

"Well, think about it. You create this space where someone can open up to you, be vulnerable with you, and you have to hold them in your hands, metaphorically, so they can find this release they're looking for. Yeah, Lisa. I'd definitely call that intimate."

She smiled and closed her eyes, turning toward him, not touching. "Is that what you want to do with me? Hold me in your hand?"

"Maybe more than metaphorically."

"Yeah, all right. You can hold me." She opened one eye and yawned again. "Clothes on, though. No pictures."

"No pictures," he agreed, and moved in closer. "You want to go up to the loft?"

"I think I'd fall off if I even tried to climb that ladder right now." She expected him to come back with something dumb, like, *Don't worry, I'd catch you.* He didn't.

"Here is good. Let me get a blanket."

The blanket was warm, and Emery's arm pressed against hers. She wanted to thank him for answering his phone. And for picking her up on the side of the road. But really, she just wanted to fall asleep, right there, with someone she liked beside her.

47

SINGER
80 DAYS WITH MILES

Mother and Dad finally went back to Valencia on the Thursday after Lisa's overnight in farmland. Their presence in the guesthouse was still obtrusive, but in another sense, Singer was grateful; Jake and Miles were back, but they could hardly work out all of their issues with his parents potentially walking in at any moment.

He and Jake had reached a sort of temporary truce. They wouldn't push it while the guesthouse was occupied, but all the things they hadn't said still hung over their heads, and Singer found his momentary resolve to iron everything out had waned. Maybe if they pretended long enough that everything was fine, it would be. That possibility seemed so real that Singer almost believed it.

The entire situation reminded him of Kara's comment about life being on pause; Miles's next court date was fast approaching, at which point a judge would either terminate parental rights or not. He and Jake had both established an additional two months of half-time work at their offices, so each of them would go in two days a week and work from home a few hours during the rest of the week.

They'd be apart during the days, but at least they'd have dinner together. At least they'd sleep together.

True to form, Frankie waited all of fifteen minutes after he texted her to let her know Viv had flown the coop to stage a spontaneous invasion.

"Oh, hey, where's the party?" She walked into the living room and brushed him aside. "Jeez, look at that, it turns out I brought it with me. Care and Alice are stopping off for Thai. Miles! What's up, kid?"

"And why are you here?" Singer asked, making his tone severe (Jake huffed laughter).

"Singer, you wound me. Lisa! Get your ass out here! Your boyfriend's coming over."

Lisa's door opened. Frankie laughed.

"Is your boyfriend coming over?" Lisa called.

"I do not have a fucking— Goddamn everything. You two have been spending way too much time with Derries."

"When's Emery going to be here?"

"I'm not telling you because you're rotten." Frankie pushed through the swinging doors to the kitchen. "ROT-TEN!"

Lisa smiled at him. "I'm glad Emery's coming over. And I'm really, really glad Mother's gone."

"Me too," Jake said. "Man. I've never spent so much time around someone who made me feel like I'd done something wrong when I, you know, didn't do anything wrong."

"Here's what I don't get: did she never make me feel that way before because I did what she wanted, or is she just getting more critical in her old age?" Lisa asked. "Or was I really that eager to please her? Maybe I was."

Singer shook his head. "Mother will never change. But Dad might. At least, he seemed … a little more supportive than he used to be."

"He did?" Jake glanced at Lisa, setting Miles down with his toy box.

"Well. Since the baseline of his parenting before was 'pays the bills and makes an appearance at dinner most of the time,' offering a second of … commiseration surpassed my expectations."

Lisa whistled lightly. "You had a *moment* with Dad? I'm jealous. I'm not actually sure we've ever been alone in a room together."

"He told us that children surprise their parents."

She grinned. "I guess he should know. Anyway, I'm gonna go bug Frankie."

"Sounds like fun," Jake said. "Miles, you want to go with Aunt Lisa?"

"Yeah, c'mon, kid. Let's go get baby germs on Frankie, okay?" Lisa scooped Miles up like it was nothing, like she was comfortable with him in her arms.

Singer hesitated, not quite sure he wanted to keep talking about Dad, but curious what Jake's read was. "You didn't think my father was trying to be supportive?"

"Yeah, okay, I do think that. I liked him, even. But seriously, your mom moved up here thinking she could help Lisa, and she obviously wasn't happy about it—ever—and we didn't really welcome her, but she stuck with it. I'm definitely not Viv's biggest fan, but I feel like if one of your parents should get points for being parenty, it should probably be her. Anyway, they're your folks. I just think that Drew said one nice thing one time and you're letting him off the hook, when most of the time he's your model for how *not* to be a dad." Jake smiled crookedly. "But for real, next time one of them decides to move in with us, I call Drew. I'm not sure I could take close encounters with Viv again."

Singer offered a smile, still trying to decide if he was letting Dad off too lightly. It was possible. It was hard to feel merciful toward Mother, though. He was still considering it when Emery's car pulled into the driveway, with Carey's right behind it. "Thus ends our brief moment of peace," he said dryly.

Jake stepped forward and kissed him lightly. "It's Miles's bedtime. Should we herd them all outside?"

"If it's warm enough, that sounds good."

"I'll grab plates."

It felt right, having people in the house. It felt like their house again, and he wanted this. He wanted to feel like they had a place, like his family had a home. He wanted it more than he'd ever wanted to play the leading man, more than he'd wanted a cute apartment in the Castro instead of a closet with a hot plate and a toaster oven. If determination counted for something, the situation between him and Jake would be better immediately, without any additional effort.

But it wasn't.

48

SINGER
84 DAYS WITH MILES

Kara called while Singer and Miles were sitting in the backyard—now free of Mother—playing with the hose.

"That's so subversive," she said. "Aren't you afraid someone's going to report you to the police for wasting water?"

"Technically we have a garden we don't water. So we're … watering the garden."

She laughed. "I literally bought vegetable plants last spring so I could justify letting the kids play in the sprinkler. You think we'll see an El Niño this year?"

"I think if we do it'll be a catastrophe for anyone living on a hillside, and if we don't it will be a catastrophe for everyone."

"Exactly. I'm nominally calling to see when you three would like to come over for a playdate."

Singer adjusted the direction of the water so Miles wasn't spraying it straight up over his head. "Oh, any weekend day works for us. We're both back at work part-time."

"Victor told me. How's that going?"

"It's good. It will be strange when we're back full-time, but half time feels doable."

"Then you're doing better than Vic did. I went back full-time when he still wasn't quite ready to leave the house."

"To be honest, it's been a relief," Singer admitted. "I never thought my job would be the most relaxing part of my day, but it definitely has been lately."

"I've always wondered if people with life-saving jobs had the same response, or it's just those of us in safe little office bubbles."

"My mother-in-law is an ER nurse. I think she understands, even if she didn't exactly feel the same."

"My mother stayed home with us. I think *we* would have been relieved if she had gone to work."

"Mine, too. And I know she worked at some point, but not until we were in school." Strange to think about Mother interviewing for jobs while he was at kindergarten.

"Do you have childcare for Miles arranged for after you're both back full-time?"

He dodged an errant spray of water and adjusted the hose again. "Jake's sister-in-law is looking forward to taking over during the weekdays."

"That's great."

"It is." He wasn't sure what else to say. A slightly expectant pause fell between them, and he started brainstorming ways to end the conversation. Propose an actual day for their next family date, maybe?

"How are you and Jake doing?" she asked. "Feel free to tell me to mind my own business."

Singer swallowed, touching the curls at the back of Miles's head. "It's not easy." He couldn't confess that they'd lived apart for three weeks, could he? But before he'd assessed the risk, he already was.

"I felt so lost without them," he said, at the end of what had to be a barely coherent babbling of the last few months. "But I still can't reach out to him and it's breaking us, Kara. It's the two of us in reverse, like we're back at the beginning, only this time it's me who can't touch him, and neither one of us can bridge the gap. We had this one good night, and I thought—at least I hoped—that maybe it would be enough, but there are so many things I know we have to say to each other. Oh god, I'm so sorry I just poured all of this on you when you were only being polite—"

"I wasn't only being polite. I meant it." She sighed. "I know how it is. Or maybe I'm projecting, but it's *hard*, Singer. And no one tells you how hard it's going to be on your relationship, how you have to change everything about how you communicate, how you relate to each other. Vic's getting Rache into these terrible video games and sometimes I think about the way you gain points, gain skills, gain weapons. No one tells you you'll have to level up so much when you become parents."

Singer nodded, switching hands so the hose could follow Miles's scrambling around in the grass. "It was hard in the beginning, when he was afraid to be out. But little by little he did it. He was so brave, and at the time I mostly thought he was making too big a deal out of everything. His family is intensely close. They would never have turned on him for being gay, you know? I didn't realize how much he risked because I only saw it in terms of how much he had." He shook his head. "Now I'm part of it, part of them, and I'm absolutely terrified they'll find out I'm a fraud, that I can't do this."

"You aren't a fraud. Just because you aren't living up to your own expectations—even if you never live up to your own expectations—you aren't a fraud. You're one of the people Miles can rely on to look him in the eye, to pick him up when he's hurt, to respond when he talks. Singer, that's it. That's all you need."

"His grandmother was giving him all that long before we ever came into the picture."

"Don't get me started on how we could be supporting families more than we are now, and maybe keeping some kids out of foster care. You know what pisses me off most? The people who look at my family and tell me how wonderful I am, how heroic, what sacrifices I've made to 'help' these 'poor children,' as if my kids are characters in a morality play. I want to hurt those people, Singer. This is my family, not a Hallmark Channel Christmas special."

"I've only seen that at a distance, but I'm already braced for it."

Miles sprayed himself in the face again, freezing for a split second to decide if he was more frightened or delighted. To Singer's relief, he settled on delighted and did it again.

"What makes me more qualified than someone else to be his father, Kara? I used to think we already jumped through enough hoops, but now I feel like everyone should have to jump through more than this. What really makes me a better parent than his grandmother, who misses him so much I can *taste* it when she looks at him?"

A pause, then Kara said, "You want me give you the cheerleader answer? Or the real one?"

"The real one. Please."

"Nothing. Absolutely nothing, Singer. You aren't more qualified. You're just the guy with the job."

He choked on a laugh. "What was the cheerleader answer going to be?"

"Yeah, I was hoping you wouldn't pick that one because I have no idea. The point is you're just like everyone else. Maybe you thought you were going to be better than everyone else. I thought I was going to get pregnant the first time we tried. Then the second. Then the whole first year. Then with assisted reproduction. Then with one awful cycle of IVF before we turned to adoption, and it still felt like giving up, Singer. Starting down the path that led to my kids felt like defeat for months, maybe years. Every time things got hard I told myself that if only I'd gotten pregnant, things would have been easier."

That was a heavy load to bear. Singer couldn't think of a damn thing to say.

"But then I realized we're all the same. All of us. The parents who have no problems conceiving, the parents who use assisted reproduction, the parents who have their kids taken away, the parents who voluntarily surrender, the parents who are grandparents and aunts and uncles, and the parents who adopt. We're all equally unqualified, and our kids need us anyway. Do the job. There's no glory in it, most of the time, but I wouldn't give up this family for any family I could have had in a different way, no matter how hard it was, how many tears I cried, how many times I hated myself, or hated Vic, or god help me, hated my kids."

Singer swiped at his eyes. "Thank you," he said, voice breaking. "I'm so sorry. But I really needed to hear that."

"That's the speech I wish someone had given me, in the black moments, when I felt like we were at a dead end."

"I don't know what to say to Jake. For the first time I actually feel like maybe I can do this, maybe I can be a parent, even if I'm kind of a lousy one, but there's still all this stuff up in the air with Jake, and I have no idea where to start."

"Start with what you said to me. But do it soon. And I can't believe you got away with living apart for three weeks. How'd you manage that without your worker finding out?"

"I don't know. We had a visit in the middle, but I was here with Miles and Jake was at work. I guess it's all looked normal to her."

"Lucky. Well, fix it if you want to fix it. And be honest with yourself if you don't."

"I do. I have to."

"Good. Do that. Then call me so we can set up another playdate now that Miles is walking more. The boys are excited to teach him soccer."

"I'm not sure he's up for soccer yet."

"They'll figure it out. Talk to you soon, Singer."

"Thanks for calling. And yes, soon." They said goodbye and hung up, and Singer caught Miles's attention. "Cheese?"

Miles said something long, and Singer's ear couldn't pick out "cheese" in it, but there might have been an "ee" sound in the middle.

"Yes, cheese," he said. "Let's turn off the water and go inside for cheese and crackers."

He shut off the water, making certain it was all the way off (he really didn't want to add to the drought, but Miles loved watching the sunlight make rainbows), then bent down to pick up a very wet, very naked baby.

Who refused to be picked up.

"You want to walk?" Singer asked.

Miles reached up again, and Singer offered his hands, which Miles used to pull himself, unsteadily, to his feet.

"You know, Nana says she thought you'd be walking by now." Could Marie walk like this? Holding onto Miles's hands while he tottered in front of her? Probably not; this might be worse for the back than carrying him was.

Miles, having made it with the aid of Singer's fingers all the way to the slider, collapsed onto Singer's feet. And hiccupped.

"That was a good workout, little man. Come here." This time there was no protest at being picked up, and blatant enthusiasm at being deposited in his high chair, pulled up close to the counter.

It was a good half an hour later before Singer realized he'd just executed an outdoor activity, a transition inside, a snack for both of them, and a reheated cup of coffee for himself, all without screwing up.

He decided to go for broke.

"Let's take a nap, Miles."

A nap was accomplished, eventually, and by then he seriously needed another cup of coffee.

49

EMERY
82 DAYS SINCE MEETING LISA

Emery lingered over the paintings in Alice's studio, slowly circling toward the table where she'd almost definitely be keeping the photograph he wanted to see.

Maybe not *wanted*. Needed to see.

He hadn't quite made it there when Carey found him, stepping inside the door and to the side, as he always did. Leaving room for escape.

"It's a great picture."

Emery turned. "How did you know what I was doing back here?"

"You and Al are a microcosm of my family's currents and countercurrents. She feels guilty for using a picture of you that you don't like; it's not a leap to imagine that's what you're in here contemplating. She said she can't start the painting until you blow up the shot for her, but the sketches are probably here somewhere. It really is a good picture." Carey's voice lifted a little, as if asking.

That wasn't exactly what he wanted, either. Emery allowed his gaze to scan the worktable and pick out the most likely location. She'd have the photo out, but she'd have covered it up.

He shifted a few notebooks until he found it.

"That's the bitch of the whole thing. It's a *fantastic* picture. The dominatrix knew what she was looking at and captured it on film." He held it out. "What do you see?"

"You and two friends of Will's who make me uncomfortable." But Carey took the four-by-six and studied it. "Tell me their names?"

"The black one is Eddie. The white one is Leo."

"Right. This is good. I'll eventually see them again, so it'll be good to know their names." He studied the photograph. "This was after you did your scene, right?"

"Yeah. How'd you pick that out?" In the photo Eddie was nude, though the shot only showed his upper body. It could have just as easily been taken before.

Carey shot him a raised eyebrow. "I'm familiar with blissed-out-from-ropes face, and this kid is wearing it. And the way you're looking at Leo is not your normal expression, Em."

He took the picture back. "That's what pisses me off. And it's exactly what she was talking a picture of: his mastery and my desire."

"Your desire to be mastered?"

"No. My desire to be seen. Which Alice wants to paint so the entire world can—" He broke off. "This would be easier if she was a lousy painter."

"And she has her teeth into this one. Would it be trite of me to ask how things are going with Lisa?"

Emery replaced the photo beneath the notebooks and resumed a more casual perusal. "Good, I think. We have fun. And it seems like she can relax around me, even when we're alone, which I worried about at first."

"She always put on a good show, back in school. I remember wondering how much energy that took out of her, because putting on a merely mediocre show took a lot out of me."

When Alice had first introduced him to Carey, he'd seen that side. The one he was most likely to show his brother and cousins. Oldest cousin Carey, who had it all together, who could be relied upon to save the day. Who'd fled across the country to escape the obligations of the role, and inevitably brought them with him.

Now, leaning up against the wall of Alice's studio, Emery could see the man underneath. The Carey who struggled more, but didn't flinch if you told him how you really felt.

"I just don't want to pressure her. Or influence her."

"What makes you think you can?"

"C'mon, Carey. Last time she liked a guy, she joined a cult for him."

Carey shrugged. "She joined a cult because it felt like a place she could call home. When it stopped feeling that way, she left. Lisa's arguably demonstrated more backbone in the last three months than I have in the last three years."

"You're in a committed relationship with Alice; nobody worries you lack backbone." Emery smiled to show he was teasing, but Carey's expression remained serious.

"Alice might have said the same things about me that you're saying about Lisa. Did she?"

Alice had said a lot of things, had probably shared a hell of a lot more than Carey would have wanted her to, but never did she act like he didn't know his own mind, or needed her to safeguard his ability to speak it.

"You know she didn't." He let his weight rest on the table and turned the whole thing over in his head. "But I—I don't want to be yet another jerk in her life who only sticks around when she's happy and doesn't want her otherwise."

"So you decided you'd be the jerk who only wants what's best for her and decides he's the conservator of that? Or am I missing the nuances of your position?"

"You should have some sort of handicap for domestic arguments. Fighting with a lawyer is obnoxious."

"I haven't passed the bar in California yet. I think right now you're just fighting with a friend."

Emery crossed one leg over the other and refrained from crossing his arms as well. Then, almost an after-thought, he pulled *that photo* out again, staring down at his own face as if it could tell him something.

"Em, what're you trying to protect her from?"

"This." He tapped his face. "That I...need things. Want things. Not—you know. Not sex. That's so far from the point it's unrelated. But when we're together I want to take it to deeper places, and maybe she doesn't."

"Or maybe she wants to be with a man who trusts her enough to let her see that. Vulnerability can be a gift, and if it only goes one way you're doing it wrong. That's a di-rect quote, by the way. Alice is far more persuasive than I will ever be."

"I don't want to burden her." He met Carey's eyes across the room. "You never feel that way?"

"What, that I don't want to pour all my neuroses on Al-ice? All the time. I feel that way all the time, but I don't act on it." His lips quirked up in a wry smile. "Mostly. I *try* not to act on it. Because, as she's pointed out to me at length, it's her choice to be with me, and she chose freely. Do you think Lisa's doing anything less?"

"No. And Singer still likes me, so clearly he doesn't think I'm taking advantage of her."

"Lisa doesn't need saving. Or at least no more than the rest of us." Carey gestured at the photograph. "You should show her that. I don't know, Emery, maybe consider letting her *see* you."

"You're kind of an ass. I have no idea why Al likes you so much."

"Asked and answered. Anyway, I'm making more coffee, if you want any."

"Okay. Thanks."

Carey left, and Emery only looked at the photo for another moment before tossing it carelessly on the top of the stack. Alice would find it that way and know he'd been looking, and if she felt a twinge of guilt for using an image he specifically disliked, well, good. A little guilt wouldn't hurt.

The painting, when she was eventually done, *would* hurt. But maybe it was the good kind of hurt, the kind that revealed something important. Emery wasn't convinced yet, but since there was no stopping Alice once she got rolling on a project, he should probably figure it out.

Vulnerability. The trick was letting someone see you and not hating them for whatever they saw. Since he couldn't imagine ever hating Lisa, that might be a good place to start.

50

SINGER
89 DAYS WITH MILES

"I now call this official Thurman House meeting to order." Jake raised the bottle, which caught the back porch light and glittered. "Wine, anyone?"

Singer's phone vibrated. Frankie. *I can't believe you jerks are having a house meeting without me.* "Is it strange that Frankie's annoyed that she's not here?"

Jake handed a glass of wine to Lisa. "Is it strange that it wouldn't be strange to me if she was?"

"That's weirdly true." Lisa glanced between them. "I thought you guys weren't drinking with Miles around?"

"We're not *getting drunk* with Miles around. Big difference. Plus, we have church tomorrow."

Singer seesawed his hand. "And we're using Thurman standards for *drunk.*"

"What's the difference?"

Jake grinned. "Well, Lisa, since you ask, Derries basically consider everything this side of belligerent to be 'slightly intoxicated.' And 'I've only had four beers' is how we express a desire to be the designated driver."

"That seems ... juvenile."

"Oh yeah. These days it's all a big joke, but we're lucky we all survived to adulthood. I mean, I don't want to talk shit, but you weren't exactly pure as the driven snow in high school either, right?"

"Ha. No. I, um, once puked in the side yard."

Singer swiveled so fast that his wine sloshed against the sides of the glass. "That was *you*? Dad thought it was me! And I didn't even drink back then."

"Sorry, Singer. I told him it was the cat from down the street."

"He gave me an entire lecture about honesty and owning up to my mistakes." He sat back, feeling the injustice of it slide into the past. "I can't believe that was you."

Jake shook his head. "If it wasn't you, who did you think it was?"

"I didn't even think about it in those terms, to be honest. I just felt ... wronged." He blinked away the memory—they'd been in the living room, and he'd fought waves of guilt and embarrassment, which was hardly fair since he really *hadn't* puked in the side yard.

"You want me to call Dad and tell him it was me?" Lisa was smirking, which also wasn't fair.

"Oh, hush. And anyway, of course he believed you and not me. It makes perfect sense, even though I was always the more reliable one."

Her mouth dropped open. "Wait. Am I the favorite? Do they have a favorite?"

"Well, they wouldn't have moved to Southern California to rescue me." He'd made his voice light enough to fool Lisa, but Jake shot him a distinctly not-fooled look.

"Okay, and what's the deal with that? When I, you know, moved to the farm, they were these normal retired people who like ... traveled, or whatever. Now Dad is working again—part-time, but they clearly don't need the money—and Mother sits in the house, only leaving it to go shopping for things she doesn't need. What happened?"

Singer topped up his wine, thinking about it. "I think it was like, they started taking those trips because that's what people who could retire early with all the money they'd ever need kind of … were supposed to do. But can you imagine spending that much time with either one of them?"

Both Lisa and Jake shook their heads, Jake with feeling.

"And then you moved to the, uh, farm, and suddenly they had a goal, a reason to go places and do things. When you were inside, Mother went to a lot of support groups and—actually, I'm not sure exactly what all of it was, but she seemed busy. I guess maybe when you came out she stopped."

"Wow," Jake whispered. "That's kind of tragic."

Lisa raised her hand. "Speaking as the obsession she replaced all that with, I want it noted for the record that it wasn't a cakewalk for any of us."

"No, but still. It's sad, don't you think?" He swirled his wine and stared through the glass.

Singer would have given anything to know what he was thinking. "What is?"

"I don't know. Like, it's easy to look at Viv and think, *That lady has everything.* And maybe she kind of does. But since she's not even a little bit happy, I guess I feel sorry for her."

"No one on earth has ever felt sorry for Mother," Singer said.

Lisa tentatively raised her hand.

"You have not."

"You didn't go to therapy with her! It was sad, Singer. She cried."

"If Mother is a pitiable figure, it's due to her own actions."

Jake reached for the wine. "That's pretty much true of everyone, though, isn't it? I mean, when it comes to people like us, who were born with advantages. When we fuck it up, it's our fault. Doesn't mean it can't also be kind of sad."

That was an opening. Singer could feel it slipping through his fingers as he sat there, thinking about Mother and responsibility.

"Anyway, Singer, you called this house meeting. What's the agenda?"

He cleared his throat, banishing any rash ideas of confession and forgiveness. "I hereby propose we move. As soon as possible." Since both of them were staring at him and Miles was apparently sleeping peacefully, he began an in-depth study of the wood grain on the top of the table. Then, when that wasn't diverting enough, he added, "Lisa, I know that things will be a little up in the air for you until you settle in more, but I'm sure you can stay with us as long as you need to." He glanced at Jake.

Who was watching him enigmatically, no longer the transparent young man he'd been when they ran into each other as adults. "Of course she can stay with us, though I don't know how Brandi will feel about that." He shrugged. "I think it's only important that Miles has a room, and I'm not sure we can afford a three-bedroom. But yeah, of course you can stay with us, Lisa. You're family."

Family was such a tricky thing. Singer had no idea if that was a passive aggressive dig at him or a genuine expression of support for Lisa. Or both.

After a pause, Lisa nodded. "I definitely think we should move. And if you guys don't mind me hanging out a little while longer, that's…really good. I don't think I could live with Mother and Dad again, even if they were here." She shuddered, tugging her sweater in around her shoulders.

Jake reached out, clamping down on her arm. "Seriously, that's never gonna happen if you don't want it to. Carey and Alice have a nice sofa bed, and you just know Emery would find all kinds of excuses to show up if you were there."

"Shut up." They grinned at each other, and Singer looked away.

He'd meant this to be … something. An olive branch. A move in the right direction. A sign he understood Jake's fears, that he wasn't willing to wait for the next time Mother decided to invade. He was taking the bull by the horns, dammit, so why was Jake smiling at Lisa right now? Why had he seemed so … unimpressed with Singer?

He cleared his throat again. "I'm glad that's settled."

"So which one of you is gonna call your parents to tell them they'll have to take over the mortgage?" Jake's raised eyebrows were clearly a challenge.

"Must we?" Lisa seemed to be considering the idea of just abandoning the house and letting the late fees pile up until Mother and Dad noticed.

"Fine." He hoped his tone of grievous self-sacrifice wasn't lost on them. "I will call them tomorrow."

"Call Dad's phone in the morning when he's at work," his sister advised. "Straight to voicemail."

"Did you just set me up?"

"Hey, you're the reliable one, right?" She lifted her glass in a mock toast. "You said it, not me."

He sighed.

Jake nudged him. "Do you want me to defend your honor? I'm pretty sure Lisa just got over on you."

I want you to do more than nudge me with your elbow when I thought we were going to have a serious conversation. "No. I can handle leaving Dad a voicemail while he's at work all by myself, thank you."

A fleeting smile in response. "That's cool. I wasn't actually gonna fight Lisa, anyway. More wine?"

They finished the bottle, though Jake lagged a little behind, which was unexpected.

Silent commentary on Singer's own willingness to numb his senses? Or just the prudent action of a parent who didn't mind drinking a little less in order to be a little more aware? Singer didn't know, and tried to drink enough so he didn't care.

51

LISA
17 DAYS SINCE FINDING GRACE

As far as first dates went, Lisa thought this one was probably going to be good.

"There's one more thing." Emery glanced at her in the passenger seat. "We have to stop by Alice's for a minute."

She shrugged. "Okay."

"I had to print off a few photographs for her, so I told her I'd drop them by when I was on my way to your place, but then I was running late—"

"It's fine. Emery, really, I don't mind."

"I mind. I don't want to be one more guy in your life who prioritizes everything else before you."

She rolled her eyes. "Guess we'll find out. But you already went out of your way to install a lock on my door, so you're starting with some credit."

"Credit. Yeah, all right. I'll try to stop whining about my own lack of reliability now."

Lisa couldn't decide if he was trying to hide how stressed out he was or if he was trying to display it so she'd ask why. Not that it mattered. She was pretty much done

with trying to anticipate and meet other people's expectations. "You don't like these pictures?"

He tapped the steering wheel. "She's using my least
favorite one. I didn't print it because I don't like it, but she
wants to paint the damn thing. Sorry. I just said I'd stop
whining."

"Why don't you like it?"

"Because I'm in it and I didn't take it."

"You didn't take it?"

"No. The dominatrix I was doing the shoot for grabbed
one of my cameras and took a picture of me talking with
her boys. I didn't even realize she'd taken it until I devel-
oped the roll."

"And it's a bad picture?"

They reached Carey and Alice's house and pulled up
outside.

"I'll show you."

He pulled his big portfolio into his lap and searched
through for a second, then handed her a picture, larger
than normal.

And wow. She'd seen Emery and the black guy on his
knees in a different picture, but there was a white guy, too,
skinny and pale and tall. In the picture he was standing
with one hand on the black guy's head and one hand holding onto Emery's forearm. Emery's head was slightly tilted,
and his lips were soft, like he was just beginning to smile, or
like he was waiting to be kissed.

"It's not a bad picture," she said.

"No."

"But you don't want Alice to paint it."

"She wants me. Only me."

Lisa looked up, trying to find clues in his face. "It's a
beautiful picture of you. Why do you hate it?"

"It was an unguarded moment. I don't like being caught on film when I don't know I'm being watched."

She raised her eyebrows.

"Okay. It was a hot moment." He tapped the photo. "The two of them are sexy as hell. Working with them reminded me why I used to enjoy BDSM. This moment was …" He paused. "This moment was electric on my skin, and I resent it being captured from the outside like this."

"It reveals too much."

"Yes. Exactly. Which is why the dominatrix took it, and why Alice wants to paint it. Anyway." He put it back in his portfolio. "This shouldn't take long."

They walked up to the house, and Emery knocked and rattled the doorknob. "Little pigs, little pigs, let me in!"

"Not by the hair of our chinny chin chin!" Jake pulled the door open. "Hey, guys. Alice is in her studio, Emery."

"Thanks."

Emery walked down the hall. It seemed to make sense for Lisa to stay with Jake and Miles in the living room. She only thought about it for a second before closing the door and walking over so she could squat in front of Miles.

"Hey," she said to Jake. "What're you guys doing here?"

"Singer's at work. We got bored."

Miles, sitting in the middle of a circle of toys, waved his hands around and talked to her.

"Oh yeah? Then what happened?"

He kept talking, and Jake laughed, drawing his attention. Then he started talking again.

"I thought he was crawling?"

"Yeah, this is actually the first time he's stayed still since we got here. And it's not crawling, exactly, it's more this weird sideways shuffle thing. But it gets him places he can't follow a table or a couch."

"Miles, you gotta show me. I feel like we haven't hung out in days." Oops. She probably shouldn't say stuff like that.

Jake leaned back on his elbows, stretching his legs out so he could poke Miles in the stomach. (Miles laughed and immediately engaged with the foot monster.) "Yeah. Your brother's making me nuts, no offense."

"None taken. What's his deal?"

"I have no idea."

She looked over. "Seriously?"

"I don't know. I think I'm not…transitioning well. Like, for years he did all the things, and now I do, like, more of the things. So I might be expecting more than is really reasonable? Except he just…it's like he thinks I moved back in, and now we just need to find a house, and everything will be fixed, poof, done. When all I really want is for him to actually *talk* to me. Hell, I don't know. Anyway, dick move, telling you my problems with him."

"Not really. I mean, you aren't saying anything mean. And I get not knowing where someone's coming from or what they're thinking. I feel like that pretty much all the time."

"With Emery?"

"With everyone. I'm constantly wondering why you're being nice to me, if you're trying to get something from me, if you'll start making demands unless I do enough back for you." She swallowed. "I don't know how to describe it. I'm always waiting for people to turn on me."

"Well, I don't know if this is good news or bad news, but you're part of the family now. You could leave the country and we still wouldn't let go. Just ask Frankie." Jake's feet attacked Miles from both sides, rolling him in between until he shrieked. "Sorry, bud. Too much?" When Miles raised his hands, Jake grabbed him. "Isn't it weird to think that it's all random? You and I went to high school together for a year. Singer and I for three years. And I never talked to either one of you until Singer and I bumped into each other in the Castro one day."

"Really?"

"I was staring at my shoes because I was afraid I'd see too much gay if I looked up." He offered a rueful smile. "Let's get some food going, little man."

She followed them into the kitchen. "So what happened?"

"We bumped into each other, Singer dropped the book he was carrying, I apologized without seeing him, and then he said my name, so I had to look up." Jake's face smoothed out. "He thought I wouldn't remember him, but I did. Actually, I kind of remembered him a lot better than he remembered me."

"That's a great story."

"It's probably not that simple. He had to wait for me to come out to the family, and even after I had, I wasn't exactly winning Gay Man of the Year, you know? I still don't really know how to be gay like other people."

"Um. You mean … what? You don't have a rainbow sticker on your car?"

"I don't always relate to things I'm supposed to relate to. TV shows, movies, books. They don't feel like my experience, you know?"

"Well, I think that's everyone. But some people want to see themselves in those places, so they try to mold what they see to fit, or they mold themselves to fit what they see. I did that for a long time."

"Huh. Here, go see Aunt Lisa." Jake passed off Miles (who immediately tried to explore her teeth with his fingers) and turned to the fridge. "Okay, I see what you're saying. So what do you do now?"

"I freak out and can't breathe and feel like I'm dying."

"Yeah. Good times."

"I definitely don't see people like me on TV, Jake. Like, here's the hero's sister, who just left a cult, who can't figure out if the hot guy who asked her out actually likes her or is only waiting for her to relax enough so he can mess her up."

Jake shut the fridge and turned toward her. "He's not. And also, dude, you're not the hero's sister. It's *your* show, Lisa. You're the hero. You did some stupid shit, and it sticks with you, but you still have to live your life."

You're the hero. It was hard to wrap her head around the idea.

"Anyway, where are you and Emery going for the big first date?"

"Shut up, Jake."

"What? What'd I say?" He grinned and went back to poking around for food. "Miles, how about some pasta? The spiral kind you like playing with?"

Miles couldn't have actually understood, but he definitely knew he was being addressed; he replied, and this time she was sure he said something that sounded an awful lot like "Ake."

"He just said your name. Did you hear that?"

"He was making sounds, it's not like—"

"Miles," Lisa said, catching the kid's eye. "Is that Jake?"

"Ake." Okay, so it didn't have a real distinct "ck" at the end, but he was clearly repeating Jake's name.

"Holy shit. He's totally saying your name right now."

"No, he's not—"

"Alice!" She probably shouldn't interrupt them, but this was kind of a big.

"Yeah?" Alice called back.

"Did you know Miles is saying names now?"

"Lisa—" Jake began, but Alice's whirlwind arrival in the kitchen overran him.

"Wait, what? He said a name?"

"He totally just said 'Jake.'"

"Ake, Ake, Ake, Ake," Miles agreed.

Alice burst into laughter. "Oh my god, you *are*! Miles, boy, you're talking."

"You guys, can we not make a big deal out of this? Please?" Jake reached out, and Miles dove into his arms for about half a second (squawking "Ake!" again) before demanding to be put down so he could shuffle along the perimeter of the kitchen, leaning up against the cabinets.

"Why?" Lisa asked. "It's cool."

"Because I wanted him to say Singer's name first. I know that sounds stupid, but I thought it might help him feel, like, more important. Or something."

"Hon, no. This, we celebrate. So will Singer."

"I hope so."

"Of course he will," Alice said.

Lisa wanted to think so, too, but she also thought Jake might be right. Which was pretty annoying.

Emery stuck his head in. "Lisa? You want to go?"

Right, they were going on their date. "Oh, yeah. Sure." She knelt down beside Miles and pointed to herself. "Lisa. That's me. Really easy name to say. Lee-suh."

Miles crinkled his nose at her. After a second he babbled a bunch of sounds, none of which were even close to her name.

"Okay, fair try. Next time, buddy." She patted his head and got up.

"We'll see you later." Jake hesitated, then gave her a quick hug. "You're the hero. Don't forget."

"Yeah, all right."

Emery quirked a smile at her as they walked out to the car. "You're the hero?"

"Apparently. So, where are we going?" She could do dinner in a restaurant. She'd been psyching herself up for it. She'd even talked it over with Saul, whom Jake's mom had taken her to see on Monday. He'd been more interested in rehearsing different ways of saying *I need you to take me home right now please* and talking over early warning signs for panic attacks with her. But no. She could do this.

"We have a few choices, but I'll be honest. My preference is we pick up something and take it back to your house or my apartment. What do you think?"

"That sounds great. Your apartment, not my house."

"Mexican?"

"You know any good Ethiopian? I haven't had Ethiopian since—in years."

"How do you feel about a drive? I know a great Ethiopian restaurant, but it's in Berkeley."

"Perfect." The car felt safe. "Thanks, Emery."

"For what?"

Lisa thought about it for a long moment. "I guess for not trying to fix me. I mean, assuming you're not just pretending you'd rather eat in than go out."

"God. No. I mean, feel free to always tell me if you want to eat in, because I'm usually a safe bet. I love being around people, but I just worked a couple of insanely long shifts and now I want to hibernate for the winter."

"We could reschedule—"

"Oh, no, not at all. You don't exhaust me. You aren't demanding anything from me. Don't get me wrong, I love Alice, she's family, but sometimes it'd be nice to be able to walk away."

"Been there, done that, and it is for a little while. Then it just feels very alone."

"Which is probably why I've never done it permanently. Sorry, Lisa. I didn't mean for our entire date to be a downer."

"It's not. Miles said 'Jake.' That pretty much made my whole day. Not that our date isn't also cool—"

He laughed. "Miles said 'Jake.' That's awesome. All right, let's hit Berkeley and pick up some food. Do you have a music preference?"

"I have no idea. Whatever."

"Cool."

She didn't recognize a single song he played, but he kept it low, like a soundtrack to their drive. This time they slept in the loft, and he'd been serious about not having sex. It didn't even come up. They held each other, both of them in Emery's old sweats, and despite her fears of snakes and nightmares (and possibly Emery), Lisa slept.

52

LISA
19 DAYS SINCE FINDING GRACE

Now that they were officially moving, Singer was packing. Now that Singer was packing, so was everyone else.

Lisa took a break from poking around in boxes (her entire life had been boxed up and stacked in the garage, apparently, with Dad's blocky "LISA" on all four sides of each box) and found Frankie in the kitchen, making coffee at five p.m.

"You too, huh?" Frankie asked.

"Me too what?"

"Well, you're covered in a layer of dust, and you're sweating like a pig. I assume you've been in purgatory trying to decide what parts of your life you want to keep and what parts you want to throw away."

"You mean the garage? Yeah. I didn't see any of your stuff in there, though."

Frankie rolled her eyes. "Yeah, I hid it behind other stuff, hoping Singer wouldn't notice."

"Why didn't you hide it at your parents' place?"

"Because then I'd have to talk to them, obviously. Come on, coffee. Brew fucking faster. No, wait, what am I talking about? Brew slower so I have an excuse to not dig through shit I don't want. Where's the happy family?"

Not so happy, Lisa didn't think. "They're at ice cream. That court thing they've been waiting for happened on Thursday, and it's taken them two days to figure out if they're allowed to celebrate it or not."

"Wait, you mean it's for real? Miles is theirs?"

"I guess not quite. The social worker came out Wednesday for a home visit and said that basically the judge was probably going to order Miles to be available for adoption, or something."

Frankie's confusion mirrored her own. "He wasn't already?"

"Yeah, I don't really understand how it all works, and asking Singer just made everything more confusing. Anyway, the next soonest they'll have another court date is in six months, and Singer said sometimes it doesn't happen that fast."

"And *that's* when it'll be official?"

"I … think so? But I'm not sure. Maybe."

"Christ. This fucking thing is exhausting." Frankie pulled two mugs down and poured coffee into both of them. "Here. Fortify yourself, Thurman. We're going in."

"I was thinking about taking a break."

"You saying my company's not relaxing? Don't make me go in there by myself. Plus, I may need help moving shit around. Last time I had an accomplice."

"Who?"

"Logan." Frankie brushed past. "Hurry the fuck up."

If Frankie had moved out almost a year ago, and Logan had helped her, then this thing between them wasn't as new as Lisa had assumed it was.

"Can I ask you something?"

"As long as I can throw my coffee at you if it's out of line."

"Why'd you have sex with Coach if you don't want to have sex with anyone?"

"See, you're calling my bluff. That's so fucking out of line you should be screaming in agony and dripping coffee all over the floor right now. Sadly, I'm not actually throwing my coffee at you. Christ al-fucking-mighty, this garage looks like a tornado hit it."

"Jake thinks Singer's freaking out and it's manifesting in the garage."

"Oh, he's not wrong. I oughta bang their fool heads together a few times, see if something shakes loose. I think I hid my shit in this corner, though I might have … spread it around a little."

Compared to the neatly stacked, uniformly sized LISA boxes, the rest of the garage did look disorganized and chaotic. Lisa, not quite ready to go back to work yet, sipped her coffee and watched Frankie shift things this way and that.

"Caldecott was ripe for the picking. He loved all the attention he got from teenage girls, he loved that it made him kind of a stud to the boys, and he was easy to play."

"So you manipulated him into having sex with you?" Lisa let *I call bullshit* flavor her tone.

"Well, okay, I was pretty screwed up in the head. Listen, I didn't get that I was that different. I thought everyone was making it up, you know? When people talked about sex, I just assumed that they were saying they wanted it because it was cool, but mostly they felt like I did."

"Which was what?"

"Hell, I don't know. Vaguely grossed out? I didn't want to kiss people, and I sure as hell didn't want to get naked and, like, interface with their bits." Even now, she sounded kind of disgusted by the idea.

Lisa hid a smile in another sip of coffee she definitely shouldn't be drinking this late.

"But then I started to work out that some people really *were* into it, they weren't just making it up to be cool like the Lisa Thurmans of the world."

"I was pretty embarrassing."

"You were a teenage girl. Anyway, I thought I'd give it a shot, see if I was missing something. And I knew that if I fucked Caldecott he couldn't tell anyone, so it'd never get back to the cousins what I'd done."

"Except it did. It must have."

"Well yeah." Frankie backed out of the boxes and reached for her coffee. "The first time I managed to do it, and after like seven showers, I kind of felt normal again. But the second time ... I don't know. The second time felt worse, and it never got better after that. So then he called me to stay after practice one day, and you know him, he thought he was being cute with it, like we had this secret. But I wigged, and Jakey was on his way over to catch a ride with me, so I dragged him to the car and completely lost my shit. Which sucked, because he thought something way worse had happened than me forcing myself to fuck Caldecott."

This was no longer a funny anecdote about younger Frankie's sexual misadventures. Lisa gripped her mug tighter. "Shit."

"Yeah. I barely got him to not rally the cousins to go after Caldecott, which would have been wasted on him since he was seriously too stupid to get how fucked up it was, but I had to tell Jake why I'd done the whole thing in the first place."

"You told him you were asexual?"

"I didn't know there was a word for it. I just knew that I never ever wanted to have sex again. And not because he took advantage of me or some shit. I wasn't traumatized over that. I was—I guess I was a little traumatized that I'd done it to myself, if that makes sense."

"That makes sense. Every awful thing that's ever happened to me was something I did to myself."

Frankie nodded, raising her coffee. "Cheers to that, Lisa Thurman. Why trust other people to fuck you up when you do such a good job without them, right?"

"So I still don't get why you won't date Logan, if he knows you don't want to have sex with him and it doesn't bother him."

"It's a pretty big fucking incompatibility gap. And I can't— I thought maybe I could try—but I can't."

"God, Frankie. No."

"Some people can. Some people can be ace and have sex sometimes. A lot of people, actually."

"Yeah, because that would be super hot for him, you just doing it because you felt like you had to."

"Worked for Caldecott. Was he really shitty in the sack? Logan asked me the other day, but I feel like I can't give an unbiased report. I assume your experience must have been better than mine."

Lisa shook her head. "I actually thought, you know, older man, he'd be so much better, but he was just an older version of a teenage boy, out for his own pleasure, kind of like mine was an afterthought. You did not choose well if you were trying to enjoy it."

"I wasn't. Trying to enjoy it. I was just trying to figure out if everyone else was completely batshit to be interested, and it turned out, they were. Anyway, how's Emery? He's got to be good in bed. I mean, look at him."

"You look at Emery?"

"Hey, just because I don't want to have sex with people doesn't mean I can't tell when they're hot. Anyway, you've heard my story, now show me yours."

"We haven't had sex."

Frankie's eyes widened. "No shit?"

"Yeah, it's weird. He, uh, said he wants to be intimate, but he doesn't—like, that doesn't have to mean sex."

"Wait. You're sure he's not ace?"

Lisa thought about the bondage equipment and the picture of the man who held onto Emery's forearm and made his face go soft. "I'm sure. I thought he was, y'know, kind of biding his time, figuring if he was patient, eventually he'd get me into bed. But I don't know. He seems to actually . . . I think he likes me."

"Oh shit, Lisa, yeah, no, we already knew that." Frankie laughed. "Oh my god, you and me. We're so fucked up. Logan says the same shit and I shut him down. Ha. Plus, fucking *look* at Emery. If he wanted to get laid, I feel like that would not be a problem. Of course he likes you."

"I'm not sure anyone ever really thought I was likable. Before now, I mean. I knew I could put on a short skirt and makeup and do my hair, and then they'd all look at me, but I'm not sure any of my friends, any of my boyfriends, actually liked me. You know?"

"You were a bitch. But that wasn't your biggest sin. You were untouchable, like nothing rattled you, no one could hurt you. So yeah, they wanted to be around you, but no one can relate to the girl who never seems to have a bad day, Lisa."

"Is that why you like me now? Because I have bad days?"

Frankie carefully put her coffee back on the ledge of the utility sink. "Who the fuck said I liked you now? Get your ass over here and help me move this shit."

Derrie alchemy. Lisa'd never been insulted, cursed at, or ordered around so much in her entire life. When she and Frankie finally emerged from the garage after hunting down five boxes Frankie admitted were probably only half of her stuff, Lisa realized she'd also never felt so strongly that she belonged.

53

EMERY
91 DAYS SINCE MEETING LISA

Escorting Lisa to Carey and Alice's was fun. Emery ran around the car to open her door for her and bowed over his arm.

She grinned. "You're kind of a goof."

"Should I … apologize?"

"Nope. I don't think everyone gets to see your great big goofball side, so it makes me feel special."

He straightened, caught in a moment of surprise. "Oh. Actually, that might be true."

"I like it, so you better not stop." Lisa brushed down the front of her clothes. "I look okay, right?"

"You want me to answer that objectively?" He pretended to regard her outfit. "I pronounce you officially 'looking okay.' Maybe just slightly better than 'okay.'"

"Just slightly?" She reached for his arm, hooking hers into it. "I know I basically bought all the same clothes I usually wear, but it feels different."

"Because now it's intentional." They walked up the driveway, passing Singer's crossover. "I think intentional looks good on you, by the way."

"Objectively?"

"Oh yeah."

He knocked twice before walking into the house. "Hello?"

"Hey, lovebirds!" Alice kissed his cheek, then Lisa's. "Party will be relocating to the living room when everyone gets the hell out of my kitchen."

"Sorry!" Jake called. "C'mon, Miles. Aunt Lisa's here."

Singer followed on Jake's heels, but his expression was tense. "I have to tell you something, Lisa. I spoke to Dad tonight."

"You did?" She grabbed Miles when he held out his arms. "Whoa, far out, Singer."

"There's— There's news. I have to tell you something." He took a deep breath.

Emery moved closer, hoping she'd understand his nearness was in the spirit of *I'm here if you need me*, not *I'll rush in and take care of everything*.

"I don't even know how to say this, but it seems like … they're getting a divorce. Mother and Dad."

Lisa burst out laughing, then quickly covered her mouth. "Sorry! I thought that was a joke!"

"Why would I make a joke about our parents getting divorced?"

"I don't know, but it's kind of … it's not a little bit funny?" She giggled, which made Miles giggle.

"How is it *funny*?" Singer asked, crossing his arms over his chest.

"Well, they've been unhappy for years, Singer. It's not a shock that they're finally breaking up."

"That's what I said," Jake mumbled. Singer spared a withering glance for him, but he only shrugged.

"I fail to see how our parents getting a divorce makes sense *at all*. So they're just going to start over as single people? They're going to *date*? They've been living together for thirty-five years, and what, they're just giving up?"

Lisa sat down, Miles in her lap, and picked up a stuffed elephant for him. "Giving up what? Being stuck together because they're afraid of the unknown? Jeez, Singer. I thought I was kind of unfair to them, but that's harsh."

"I didn't mean— That wasn't—" Singer frowned. "You think they were that unhappy?"

Emery had barely interacted with the Thurman elders at all, but even in a few exchanges here and there, "unhappy" was in the top five words he would have used to describe them. He carefully kept his mouth shut.

"How unhappy do you have to be to get divorced? Plus, you were the one who said that their plans didn't live up to their dreams. I just think thirty-five years is long enough to earn the right to make a choice about whether they want to stay married without everyone judging them." She made the elephant poke Miles in the belly until he laughed.

"I'm not *judging* them. I'm just a little shocked." He shook his head. "I'm going to make sure no one needs help in the kitchen."

Lisa waited until he was gone to whisper, "I know I'm a little bit crazy right now, but how can he possibly be surprised?"

"I know," Jake whispered back.

Emery stretched out on the floor and pulled out his phone, activating the camera so he could get some pictures of the elephant-poking game. Pictures at Alice's—wherever she happened to be living at the time—always had the advantage of good artwork on the walls in the background. He twisted in order to frame Lisa to the side of an angular painting of the Williamsburg Bridge, the cool grays and blues of the painting complimenting her new mahogany top.

Miles, of course, was in a red-and-blue striped shirt that didn't really go with anything, but Emery decided he liked the effect of garish kids' clothes for casual family pictures. Or even portraits. You could always tell when a kid had been dressed in stiff formal clothes against their will.

"I don't know what his deal is." Jake glanced toward the kitchen. "But it really wigs him out that your folks are breaking up."

"He's such a traditionalist sometimes." She smiled for the camera. Or maybe for Emery. "By the way, not that we're getting married, but I *so* don't believe in 'till death do us part.' Nope. 'Until we get sick of each other do us part,' maybe."

He lowered the phone. "Not quite as musical, but I agree. We live in a world that changes so fast we can barely keep up, and our lifespans are constantly extending. Anyone who vows until death today doesn't even know how long that is."

"Aw, you guys." Jake leaned back against the diaper bag and didn't quite look at them. "I think it's kind of romantic. The vow itself, I mean. But I wouldn't stick with it if it was making me miserable."

"So then what's the point?" Lisa asked.

"I don't know. I think there's something powerful about looking at another person and telling them you'll spend the rest of your life with them. Even if you have no idea how long that will be, or what will change in the rest of the world. Like you're saying that no matter what, the two of you will weather it together."

Emery met Lisa's gaze, confirming that however potent that dream might be, neither one of them was counting on it. Or even interested in it.

She reached out to mess with Jake's hair. "That's sweet. And you're kind of a sap."

"Don't tell my cousins."

Emery shook his head. "For the record, I can't keep secrets from Alice, so if she asks about your sappiness, I'll have to tell her."

Jake laughed. "Yeah, okay, Emery. But you don't keep, like, any secrets from Alice?" He glanced at Lisa, then back. "Like, *any*?"

He flushed and raised his camera as a shield. "Get your head out of the gutter, California."

"Ha ha ha, awesome. I just made both of you blush. My work here is done." Jake stood, stretching, and dropped a kiss on the top of Miles's head. "I'll be right back."

Then it was just the two of them and the kid.

"I, uh, don't tell Alice everything."

"You trying to say there's something to tell?"

He looked up. "You trying to say there isn't?"

Miles squawked, demanding the elephant come back to life. Apparently something had distracted Lisa from her game.

Emery smiled. She smiled back.

"I'm pretty good at secrets, but I don't think this is one." She paused for an elephant-related adventure up Miles's back to the top of his head, then sliding down the front of his body as he grabbed for it. "So, Em. How are you?"

He'd asked her that in this room before. The gleam in her eye made it clear she remembered. "Oh, fine. You?"

"So good. Like tonight? Not in general, necessarily. But tonight is really good. Even if moving is a total nightmare, even if I'm sleeping on Singer's couch for years, as long as there are nights like this one I think I'll be okay."

Which was amazing, and he was happy for her, even if none of it directly had to do with him. And that was the rub: he didn't like the feeling that his happiness was far more directly influenced by Lisa than hers was by him.

But only a coward would keep *that* a secret.

"I'd like to revise my answer."

She grinned.

"I'm doing really well. I have a job that I like, and a boss who's mostly stopped picking on me, and Carey has basically tricked the Derries into treating me like I'm part of the family, which has been hilarious to watch." He reached out to brush his knuckles against her knee. "And there's this phenomenal, astoundingly brave woman in my life, who seems to like me a little."

"A lot," she whispered.

He held his fingers to his ear as if getting a message in an earpiece. "Excuse me, I'm informed that in fact she likes me a lot. So that's … scary and thrilling and I haven't looked forward to the future like this ever. It used to be I looked forward because where I was in the present was so bad. But I'm really good right now, and I'm still excited for whatever comes next."

It was all so silly and foolish when spelled out like that. But Lisa leaned up, and he met her in the middle for a kiss.

"Good," she said. That was it. And it was so much more than enough.

Jake returned, dinner was delivered to the coffee table, and Miles had to be restrained from shoving everything in his mouth at once. When Emery sat close beside Lisa he wasn't worried that she would misinterpret it as anything but what it was: closeness for closeness' sake. Because each of them felt good when beside the other.

54

LISA
26 DAYS SINCE FINDING GRACE

It was good to be back in Saul's office again. This was the third session since her stint in farmland, and the first time she'd had the courage to bring up the thing where she maybe might be hearing voices.

"Did you actually think Abigail was there with you, in the field?"

Lisa pushed back in the little sofa and studied all of Saul's degrees and diplomas, the straight lines and satisfying rectangle shapes of them on the wall. "No? No. I mean, only after I'd started thinking I was going crazy. But no, it was a voice in my head—not a voice like I thought someone was talking to me, just my own head playing devil's advocate. I think."

"Sounds pretty normal to me," Saul said. "Now, if you start seeing Abigail or anyone else, or if the voices sound less like you and more like auditory hallucinations, call me. Anytime, day or night, and tell the service to get ahold of me."

"Uh, okay."

"Lisa?"

"Hmm?"

He waited until she looked at him. "I'm serious. If anything like that happens, I need you to call me so we can sort it out. Even if you're not sure what's going on. Okay?"

"Yeah. Okay."

"Good. So, your brother's boyfriend's mom is sitting in my waiting room?"

She kind of laughed. "I think she's basically adopted me. I'm just glad it's not my mom."

"See, now that sounds like a support network," Saul said. "I think that's the first time I've seen you smile."

"Yeah, I guess I . . . not like I woke up one day and got happy, or something. But things seem a little bit better right now."

Saul shut his notebook and put it aside. "That's excellent. I don't want to rain on your parade, but you know this is just the start, right? And that not all of it's going to be easy. Getting your confidence back, fitting in your skin, now that you're figuring out who you are—not easy paths, Lisa."

"I think I know that." She thought, again, about waking up on that bus stop bench. "It's not that I think everything's great. It's more—I guess I decided it's worth trying for."

"I'm glad to hear that. Next time you can tell me more about the photographer."

She flushed, momentarily confused. But then he grinned, gently teasing, and she realized it was okay. "Shut up."

Saul's grin widened. "I'll see you next week. Call if you need to."

"Got it."

Cathy was waiting with an iced coffee drink for her and no invasive questions.

"Thanks for driving me again." It was still hard to work out how she should handle all this attention from Jake's family.

"Anytime."

This is where, if this was that movie with the transformative ending, Cathy would say, "I always wanted a daughter," and we'd hug.

Instead, they got in the car. And Cathy said, "Now. What are we gonna do about the boys?"

So this is what it's like to be on the inside. This is why they're all so crazy. And also, why they're all so wonderful.

"We have a couple of irons in the fire, Lisa, and we'll need your help for most of them."

"I'll definitely help if I can." Not that she knew what that meant.

"Oh, I'm counting on it. Let me fill you in."

The Derries were terrifying when they thought they knew what was best for you. Lisa had heard the stories before, but now she was privy to the inner workings, and it felt good. A support network, yeah. She still didn't know how to help with the plot to fix Singer and Jake, but she was glad there was one.

Now that she was part of the circus, she really didn't want to give it up.

55

SINGER
109 DAYS WITH MILES

It was a conspiracy. Clearly. Of massive, impossible proportions.

"Jake's mom and dad picked Miles up ten minutes ago," Lisa said.

"But didn't Mother say they'd be right back with more boxes? How can they be going to dinner when the whole point of them coming up this weekend was to clear stuff out of the house?"

Frankie, sitting on one of the counters and swinging her feet into the cabinets below, laughed. "Yeah, Lisa and I lied our asses off, and they're going, too. We said you guys were hosting a couples date with your friends from the city." She grinned. "We *meant* your friend from work and his wife, but if they took it to mean you guys are like raunchy gay swingers—hey, bonus."

Singer cringed and rubbed his eyes hard. Ow, headache. "Frances—"

"Don't fucking Frances me, buddy. This is happening. You should go track down loverboy, but Lisa and I gotta fight the good fight over at Cathy and Joe's."

"And you're saying my parents are there? At Cathy's house?" He appealed to Lisa, who smiled.

Frankie jumped down. "Yeah, you owe us. Love you." Where other people might hug, Frankie punched.

"You too." Singer rubbed his arm. Maybe he should ask her to punch a little harder. Might distract him from the headache.

Lisa waved. "Good luck."

An epic plot by their nearest and dearest to … what? Fix everything. One evening wasn't going to fix everything. It couldn't.

Carey once told him that everything important was down to a series of small decisions. Maybe that was overly simplistic, but maybe it was the only thing to do.

He made a small decision. And opened a bottle of wine.

Jake came out from the bedroom a few minutes later. Bare feet, old jeans, maroon T-shirt just slightly crooked on his shoulders. God, when was the last time Singer had looked at Jake and *seen* him?

"We've been had, Jacob. It's a conspiracy." Singer handed him a glass of wine.

He frowned. "You mean my folks taking Miles?"

"Your parents have taken Miles, Frankie, Lisa, and my parents. And I'm sure Carey, Alice, and Emery as well. They're having a dinner party without us."

Jake's expression went from defensive to concerned to—amused. "Wait, what? And where are we supposed to be?"

"Either hanging out with nice Christian straight people or trading sex partners for the evening. Frankie indicated she and Lisa had left the details to Mother and Dad's imaginations."

"Oh god. Singer."

"Yes. I keep vacillating between feeling very annoyed with all of them and, well, it's how Derries show their love. So there's that."

"And what are we actually supposed to be doing? Assuming my parents didn't engineer this whole thing so we could have sex."

Singer adopted the most dry tone he had. "I think it's safe to assume that was *not* their intention. Or, actually, maybe it was. Which is—"

"Ew. So much worse." Jake shuddered. "Anyway, so?"

For a moment Singer faltered, nearly losing his nerve. "There are some things we need to talk about. I propose we do so in the hot tub. With wine."

"You don't think we might be distracted?"

Singer couldn't quite meet the gleam in Jake's eyes. "No. And I'm sorry it's taken me so long to … get here. To this point. Thank you for not giving up on me."

Jake swallowed and lifted his glass. "Drink to not giving up on each other."

"I think toasts are supposed to be more … hopeful. Than that."

"We've been setting a pretty low bar lately."

Singer tipped his glass toward Jake's. "To not giving up."

They drank.

"The hot tub?" Jake asked, raising an eyebrow.

He was willing to be playful. Willing to forgive. It was more than Singer deserved, and he was suddenly seized with a sharp, desperate fear that he couldn't do this, he couldn't start any conversation that risked Jake not looking at him just like that. "Did your parents fight in front of you? When you were kids?"

"Fight in front of us? Well, uh, I mean, they didn't always agree on stuff. Is that what you mean?"

"I don't know. Maybe." But it wasn't. "My parents never fought in front of us. Maybe the skin around Dad's eyes would go tight, or Mother would press her lips together, but Jake, they never said anything in front of us that indicated they held different opinions about anything. I ... don't even know what that's supposed to look like. Frankie said, a few weeks ago, that this is how we are, that we get mad and we fight and we get drunk and make up, and I didn't know we did that. I can't remember what we'd even have been fighting about."

"Are we going to fight right now?" Jake asked after a second.

"That's not what I meant. I don't want to fight with you."

Jake shrugged. "Sometimes it makes things easier. I mean, I feel like I have so much to say to you, and it might be easier if I was pissed instead of this thing where sometimes I look over and you have this expression on your face like your heart is broken and you just keep taping it back together. And I want to go to you, but I'm so afraid if I do you'll turn away from me."

It was exactly what Singer had wanted, over and over again. "I wouldn't. I would never turn away from you."

"But ... you have. A lot. Which is a thing we gotta talk about." Jake caught up the bottle of wine. "The hot tub was a good idea."

Then they were in their bedroom, pulling on their suits, and it was like any other day, except more quiet, and Singer was far more nervous.

"Have you ever hot tubbed with Emery?" he asked, holding his towel in front of himself. (Jake always draped his over his shoulders.)

"Uh, probably?" Jake shot him an incredulous look. "Why?"

"No reason."

"Uh-huh."

"Only that being so close to naked with someone that good looking was slightly surreal."

"You trying to say Emery's better looking than I am?"

Oh, hell. "No, I—" But Jake was rolling his eyes. "Shut up. No. But I wished you were there, too."

"So we could ogle Emery together?"

"Really. Shut up."

*

Singer topped up both of their wine glasses and settled into the water, trying to remember all the things he needed to say, trying to put them in some kind of order in his head.

Maybe he didn't have to say *everything*. Some of it was so humiliating. Now that he could be with Miles and not constantly obsess over how he was screwing it up, maybe he could skip some of that.

Except then he looked at Jake, who was watching him across the water.

"I'm so sorry." That was a good start. Or at least a start.

"For ... what?"

Singer frowned, picking at a chip in the side of the spa. "Do you want a detailed list? I've been terrible lately. I'm ashamed of myself."

"Okay. And not a detailed list, but some idea what we're talking about would be nice."

Jake had the right to ask, of course, but Singer still felt a defensive flare of anger. "We're talking about me, and you, and whatever it is that's going on between us."

"So…" Jake shifted in the water, sitting up straighter. "So it's not about Miles? I mean, you…you're okay with Miles?"

"Okay with him? What do you mean? Of course it's not about Miles. I mean, I guess some of it is incidentally about Miles, but not really—" Singer broke off. "Did you think I didn't want to…to keep him?"

"Oh my god, Singer, you *weren't talking to me*, I thought everything. All the thoughts anyone could have, I had them, lying on the pullout at Carey's house. Did you want to break up with me? Did you want to give Miles back? I had this conversation with your mom where she was like 'Oh, Singer never wanted kids' and I brushed it off, but then I was lying there, and you were here, and I started thinking, you know, did I talk you into it? Maybe you didn't want kids, maybe I only thought you did, and now you realized you really didn't, and you couldn't tell me about it."

Singer gaped at him. "You had a conversation with Mother?"

"Right? It was this totally normal, innocent conversation, or at least I thought it was. But talking to her's like being bit by a snake with really slow-acting venom. It just kept working deeper and deeper into me all the time, thinking you didn't want kids and you'd be happier alone—"

"Happier *alone*? I would *not* be happier alone. And of course I wanted children. We talked about that a long time ago, remember? Not about us having them, but about children in general."

"Yeah, but I don't know, the way she talked I started thinking maybe I sort of pressured you into it or something, like you were reluctant and I made assumptions."

"Jake, I filled out all the paperwork. I coordinated all the appointments. How could you think I was somehow ambivalent?"

"Jeez, I don't know, could be because you looked freaked out every time you had to be alone with Miles for five minutes, and you were always looking over your shoulder at me like you were afraid I'd catch you doing something wrong. Everything your mom said—or actually didn't say, more implied—started making a lot of sense."

Mother. How could she try so deliberately to undermine Singer's relationship with Jake, with Miles? With people he'd *chosen* to be his family? Except...of course that was exactly why. He'd chosen people who weren't her, who were nothing like her, and she wanted them gone.

"I'm sorry about Mother. She was wrong about everything."

"The problem wasn't Viv, Singer. The problem was that when I was all twisted in my head because of her I couldn't ask you what the hell was going on because you weren't talking to me. But I wouldn't mind some kind of explanation now."

It was only fair, even if it felt ugly and nauseating. Singer sank deeper into the water. "I want Miles. It's so much harder than I thought it would be, but when you two were gone, it was excruciating. I don't know how many times a night I'd listen for him over the monitor when he wasn't there. I tried so hard not to feel so I could wall myself off from the pain of losing him, but I felt it anyway. It's not Miles. I always, always wanted children. Mother didn't know because I wouldn't have ever told her, or maybe she didn't care, but you didn't talk me into it."

Relief was etched in the shadows on Jake's face. "Oh thank god."

Singer wished he felt relieved, instead of more and more impaired. "But wanting to be a parent isn't the same as being one, don't you get it? I'm not...good, at this. I feel like we went into it and I committed to being better than I am. I feel like maybe I deceived you, or deceived us both, into thinking I'd be a good father, when the past few months have pretty convincingly demonstrated that I'm not."

"Seriously?" Jake stared at him for a long moment, only the jets breaking up the silence. "This whole fucking thing has been about you being insecure as a parent? Jesus, Singer, we *read books* about this. It was in every stupid class we took. You may not bond right away, you won't feel confident right away. They told us that over and over again, who'd you think they were talking to?"

"*You.* You, I thought they were talking to you." Oh god, Jake's face. Singer couldn't stop now, not with that look on Jake's face. "You were so nervous the whole time and I wasn't, I thought everything would work out, I thought it was going to be fine, but the second he got here you were great, you were amazing and I— I could wash his bottles. I could do that for him. But he goes to you when he's upset, when he needs comfort, and I've watched him, Jake, he's not as screwed up as I expected, either. He attached to you, he's attached to Marie—"

"You're such a fucking idiot sometimes."

Singer ran out of breath.

"God, I love you, but you are so fucking stupid sometimes it kills me." Jake drained his glass, set it aside, then splashed Singer so hard he inhaled spa water and coughed painfully until his lungs were clear again. And whatever was left in his glass was no longer drinkable.

"Yeah. Uh. Sorry. That may have been a little … much."

Cobbling together what was left of his dignity, and pushing stringy wet hair out of his eyes, Singer politely inquired, "You were saying?"

"You! God, you're such a jerk. So basically, in your vision, you thought Miles would be a wreck of a kid, and I'd be a wreck of a husband, and you'd hold us all together with your dishwashing skills and your excellent diction?"

"Did you say 'husband'?"

"What? Was that wrong?" Jake glanced away, maybe blushing, hard to tell in bad lighting. "I mean, in my vision of the future, that's true. Not, like, tomorrow or anything."

Singer ran it all through his head again. "No, I think you just proposed to me. Making this the strangest fight, by far, that we have ever had."

"You want me to splash you again?"

"Do you have rings? A date in mind? A wedding planner?"

"Shut up, Singer! Can we get back to the part where me not sucking as much as you expected was apparently such a glaring disappointment that I spent three fucking weeks on Carey's lumpy sofa bed? Jesus!"

"I didn't tell you to leave, you did that all by yourself. You can't run to Carey's whenever you're mad at me, Jake."

"Don't act like that's all it was! Every time I tried to talk to you, you changed the subject, you did everything you could to avoid ever talking to me about anything. And then your mother was there, constantly, making me feel like you were just biding your time until we broke up. How long did you want me to hang out while she said this wasn't my home?"

"I told you this was about my mother—"

"No, Singer, no, it's not. It's about you. And me. And Miles. And if we're actually a family, even if we're slightly less completely screwed up than we were in all your hopes and dreams."

"Hey!"

But Jake couldn't be stopped.

"Because if we're a family, and I feel like we are, then we need to make that real. That's why I went to Carey's.

Because if you and me and Miles were living in the spare room at Carey and Alice's, they'd still make us feel at home, Singer. They'd still make us feel like a family. And that's— We haven't had that. Maybe for the first few days, but not after that, and maybe not even then." Jake swallowed, shaking his head, wiping his eyes with wet hands. "So yeah, I'd do that again. Because fuck this, okay? I'm not doing—this."

"We're already moving. We've already decided." Singer topped up both of their wine glasses (because three might *almost* be enough for this conversation). "I don't know what we're fighting about. What did you want me to do? Run after you?"

"Yeah, maybe I did. Or call me. Or ask me what we should do, we, *us*, together. Singer, you didn't do anything. I mean—" Jake downed half his glass and set it aside again. "What were you doing, for three weeks, while I was trying to figure out the difference between despair and rage, 'cause I was really mad at you, but I was so fucking sad I was almost out of my mind. If Miles hadn't been there I wouldn't have gotten out of bed. Care would have put me on a fucking suicide watch."

"I understand exactly." Smelling Jake's pillow. Over and over again. Like he was dead, not just a few blocks away.

"So why didn't you *talk* to me?"

"I thought you wanted me to stay away."

"That's a fucking cop-out. You not talking to me started way before I took Miles to Carey's."

Singer winced. "I'm sorry."

"I thought you'd come with us, Singer. I thought it was clear that's what I wanted when I told you that in the car. Why didn't you talk to me, way back in the beginning, if you've felt like this the whole time?"

"I'm sorry. I was so ashamed, and so useless. I'm not used to feeling that way. And then when you were gone I missed you so much. I had no idea I could miss Miles like that, viscerally, that I'd think about him all the time. I'd see his toys and cry." He cleared his throat. "I had no idea that I could feel so empty, when I thought you were gone, when I thought the rest of my life I might wake up without you."

"We should definitely never do that again." Jake held his hand out to be grasped.

That weight, under water, was so welcome, so vital.

"You can't hide everything like this again. Because then I start making stuff up, and it's bad. I was so convinced you hated me, that you resented Miles, that I was going to have to try to get you to lie to Brandi so I could keep him, but then I'd be a single father, and you'd hate me even more." He shook his head. "And like, what would my parents say? Frankie would lose her shit, Carey would give me that look, like the entire universe fell on his head again—"

"I know. I'm sorry."

Jake squeezed. "But why didn't you just *talk to me*? I don't understand. I talk to you when I get messed up, and you make me feel better. You didn't think I could help? You didn't think it mattered what I thought?"

"No. No, it was— I thought if I told you how hard it all was you'd realize I'd been a fraud the whole time. I'm not used to not being able to do something, or I guess, I'm used to pretending being good enough. It always has been before."

"You pretend with me?"

It would be so easy to say no. The bone-deep desire to lie was nearly impossible to ignore.

Jake squeezed his hand. "I can take it. You're the first person I never had to pretend with. I get how it is, Singer. And probably I needed you to be the guy who was totally certain all the time, but that was years ago. You don't need to do that anymore."

"I pretend sometimes. I'm sorry. I know it's dishonest, but it just feels … necessary. To get through the day. I pretended with Miles all the time, at first. I didn't feel anything for him."

"I still don't get that. I mean, we read all those books. Don't you remember what they said? Sometimes it takes time. Alice says that's true, even if you give birth to a kid, even if you're pregnant for ten months, you don't necessarily bond right away. You could have told me."

"No, I couldn't. Because I didn't want to think about it. I didn't want to say it to myself. You were so good with him, immediately, like you'd never done anything else, and I couldn't."

"Yeah, well, I was going into kindergarten when the twins were little. A lot of that shit comes back. And anyway, you said 'at first.' What about now?"

Singer let the hand Jake wasn't holding play over bubbles. "It's better. I still don't feel—competent. But I'm not as terrified as I used to be. And I used to think, you know, maybe he could sense my ambivalence, that I had no idea what I was doing, that I didn't know how to connect with him. I thought he must know how much better you were because he always chose you, you were the one he wanted to pick him up, you were the one who could get him to stop crying."

"Jesus." Jake shifted closer in the water and touched his jaw.

"It was really hard to pretend all the time." Singer's voice had dropped so low he could barely hear it himself. "It's better now. I'm not constantly wondering if I should smile now, or touch him, or if this is when I'm supposed to tickle him."

"God, really?"

"It was like being in a play and not having a script." *Now he'll leave me. Now that he sees how horrible I am at this, that I reduced fatherhood to acting.*

Jake's hand lightly smacked his cheek. "Don't ever do that alone again, dummy. What's the fucking point of this if you're feeling like you have no script and I'm feeling like you hate me?"

"But it might not be enough, otherwise. I mean—"

"What?"

This was the worst part, the deepest fear. The thing that kept him from talking to Jake when Jake was the only person who mattered. "You like that I'm capable. I mean, I think that was part of the attraction, when we got together. You weren't sure how to be out, and I looked like I had it all together, and that was… You liked that, about me. What if we can't get beyond that? What if I stop pretending and you realize maybe I'm not the person you thought you were with?"

"You mean, my boyfriend, who passive aggressively doesn't clean the toilet if he thinks I'm not doing my part to keep the bathroom clean? Or how all the booze in the house mysteriously disappears if you think Frankie and I have been overindulging? Were you pretending with all that, 'cause hey, you could totally let up now."

"I'm being serious."

"I don't think you should worry about the evolution of our relationship, Singer. I feel better, right now, than I've felt in weeks. Don't you?"

"Yes." And this time it wasn't a lie. "Yes, but it can't be that easy."

"No, you got some shit to work out. Not me, I'm totally together. So I guess we're switching places."

"Jake."

"Singer."

They stared at each other.

"We need to do things differently," Jake said. "You and I need to reconnect, you know? In our own space. And we are absolutely letting my parents take Miles whenever they want. I need to be able to have a glass of wine once in a while."

"When you were gone Frankie got me drunk and high," Singer confessed.

"Oh, you fucking asshole. I would have *killed* to get high."

"Sorry."

"Listen, when you don't ever want to be alone with me, I start to seriously worry about us, and I can't take that right now, with Miles and parenthood and everything else. Right now I need us to be solid."

"I just knew I couldn't keep up appearances, if you were looking at me. I knew I'd embarrass myself and you'd be disgusted and—"

"Disgusted by what? You not being perfect? Singer, I don't know how blind you think I am, but I actually already knew you weren't perfect."

"Maybe I didn't. I don't know. It felt like you'd be so sick of me, if you saw how hard it really was. You're such a good dad, and I struggle so much to even look like a mediocre one."

"Hey." Jake leaned in closer. "I'm not your parents. And maybe you haven't noticed, but my family doesn't understand perfect the way yours does. It has, I guarantee you, never occurred to anyone except Carey that other people thinking you were okay meant you were actually okay."

"And probably not around Alice." Not with the way Alice accepted Carey wherever he was, if he wanted to stand close but not touch, or sit across the room and exchange glances.

"Yeah, no, I really can't see Alice going in for his act. Singer, I can't do perfect. I can't even do halfway normal. And if that's what you need—"

"No. No, no, please, I can't go back to that. I mean, that's what Mother wanted, you know. She wanted to be here, with Lisa and I, and she wanted us to do what we used to do. She wanted us to be who she wanted to see. And Lisa just can't, right now. And I don't want to. Ever."

"Okay, then," Jake said, like that was a decision. Like they'd come to some kind of conclusion.

"Okay then—what?"

"So we work it out."

"Just work it out? Does that mean we're done fighting?"

Then Jake pulled on his hand, and in the beginning it had all been Singer, because Jake was nervous and uncertain. But now he was pulling Singer in, leaning his forehead close, murmuring words against his lips. "I love you, stupid, and you absolutely can't pull this shit again. Next time we fight first, so I can stop fighting with you in my head."

"Deal," Singer whispered back.

"By my calculations we have at least another hour before Lisa gets back, and that's if she doesn't spend the night with Emery. My parents made me promise they could keep Miles overnight. So..."

"We can make up in the bedroom, right?"

"I think that would be ideal, yeah."

Singer wanted to give in to the levity, but he couldn't. Not yet. "Jake...I'm sorry. I thought I'd be better co-parent material."

"You didn't sell me a lemon, Singer. We'll learn. I can't cook a casserole. You gonna leave me?"

"No, but you never acted as though you could."

"Another deal, then. I'll take the first ten years. You don't have to be good for ten years. But once puberty hits, it's all you. You get the dating questions and the body changing questions"—Jake shuddered—"and all the rest of that. Deal?"

"Deal. The bedroom?"

They were both exhausted, emotionally drained, and momentarily awkward. It wasn't the most mind-blowing sex they'd ever had. But settling into each other, after, to sleep? Very possibly the most loved he'd ever felt.

They'd pick up Miles in the morning and head over to Carey and Alice's for some serious house hunting. Time for a fresh start.

Singer groaned.

"What is it?"

"When we move, we're in for another home visit."

"Ugh." Jake waved a hand. "Fuck it. Last time she let us go with my cousin living in our backyard and Lisa's long-term 'visit.' It'll be fine."

"Yes. It will." And maybe it was just hormones or chemicals or relief talking, but for the first time in a while, Singer believed it.

56

LISA
36 DAYS SINCE FINDING GRACE

Lisa was sitting on Emery's couch reading a book about scrapbooking. Or at least looking at the pictures. She doubted she could make something even half as amazing as the pictures in the book, and they weren't exactly her goal. She didn't want to make a scrapbook of some idealized version of Miles's life, which seemed to be what most scrapbooks were. But maybe she could balance it so when he looked back he'd know how hard he'd worked to get where he was.

She wasn't at all sure she could do that with a scrapbook, but she could definitely try.

One of the sample pages toward the back of the book had a photo of a young girl with light brown hair, holding what looked like an Easter basket. But her eyes, her eyes stared right into the lens of the camera, and she wasn't quite smiling.

God, she looked like Abigail. That expression, like she was hiding so much of how she felt that you could only scratch the surface.

Emery had been picking through shots from the most recent wedding on his computer. He was trying to assemble a collection to print and a larger digital collection to give the couple on a flash drive. She didn't realize she'd been sitting there staring at the picture of the little girl for so long until he touched her arm.

"You okay? You haven't moved in like half an hour."

"Oh. I'm okay. Just thinking, I guess."

He closed his computer and shoved it under the futon. "Yeah? About Miles's scrapbook?"

"A little. And this picture. This is exactly how I would have pictured Abigail as a kid."

"Really? I like her eyes."

"Abigail's were more green, but they were similar in other ways. Like you never saw beneath the surface." Lisa reached for whatever it was she wanted to say, and Emery didn't fill the space. "I don't know. I miss her. I wish I could introduce her to you. But I know she's dead, and it's still hard to— Sometimes it's hard to let go of the idea that I could tell her about Miles, or you, or the Derries."

"I'm sorry she's lost to you," Emery said. "Now would be a good time to get religion."

"I wish I could. I wish I could believe she was a spirit, that she wasn't just my memory of her voice, you know? But that doesn't feel right either." She looked up. "I thought about trying to find her parents, to thank them, or to tell them that she didn't die unloved. That I loved her."

"You decided not to do that?"

She shook her head. "There were reasons she left home, same as there were reasons you did, or Alice, or me, for that matter. If it was reversed, if she showed up to tell Mother she'd loved me, that wouldn't make Mother feel better."

"If you randomly told my parents you loved me, they'd laugh and slam the door." His voice was low. "I know what you mean. Even if you found them, even if they weren't awful, it wouldn't necessarily make you feel like anyone understood her loss."

"Yeah. So maybe no one but me ever will. And that's sad, you know? Because she was good, and I miss her. And maybe because she's the first person who ever looked at me and wanted to actually see me, not just whoever they needed me to be."

"I think I get that. Being seen can be a gift."

"It was, I think. Though it pretty much makes it impossible to go back to who I thought I was." She closed her book and turned so her knees rested against his thigh. "Can I ask you something?"

"You can ask me anything." His nose wrinkled. "Okay, forget I just sounded like the lead in a romantic comedy."

"Uh, yeah, I think there's not a lot of danger of this turning into a romantic comedy, Emery. Can I look at your portfolio?"

He blinked. "Totally not anywhere I thought you were going. Of course. I never really get tired of showing off my genius, I don't know if you've noticed."

They unfolded from the futon, and she waited for him to set the portfolio out on the rug before she started looking through it. If the picture wasn't here, that would make this harder, but Emery usually kept copies of everything he gave to Alice. He said he liked to know what she was working from, and she must have had something to make that sketch in her studio.

And here it was, strikingly familiar even though Lisa had only seen the drawing.

She pulled out the photograph of Emery with his hand out as if offering a blessing to the boy in ropes kneeling before him.

"Oh, that's a good one." He took it and tilted it to the light. "It's a little insulting that you picked out a picture I didn't take, but I'll forgive you, since you have a good eye."

"I like looking at you," she said, watching his face. "How careful you look here. Like you're standing between him and the world. As if you tied him like that to protect him."

Emery's eyebrows rose. "I don't need ropes for that, Lisa."

"Maybe not. But I might. Could we—if I asked you to—could we try something like that? I want to feel safe. I want to trust myself to know what that is, even if it's a man."

He stared at her for a moment longer, then nodded. "Tonight? Or in the future?"

"Tonight." *While I'm still thinking of Abigail, while I can still hear her egging me on in my head.* "I mean, if that's okay. And I don't— I don't know how this changes other things. Sex. I don't know if this means sex to you, but you said it doesn't, so—"

"Definitely not tonight. And it doesn't. They can play together, but they don't have to. Do you want ropes? I have other things that can bind people."

"Ropes. Ropes is how I, uh, pictured it."

The serious lines in his forehead smoothed out. "You've pictured me tying you up in ropes?"

"And you haven't?"

"Oh god, don't make me answer that, please. I plead the Fifth."

Good. Good, it wasn't just her, it wasn't some dumb thing she made up like it would be the answer to her everything.

"Also, you can keep your clothes on." He stood up, put away his portfolio and dragged out his tub of stuff she didn't understand.

"I don't want to."

"Don't want to what?"

She swallowed. "I don't want to keep my clothes on."

He swiveled on his heels to look at her. "Listen, I don't want you to think, for a second, that I object to seeing you naked. But ropes is a whole lot of contact, and it might make you feel incredibly vulnerable, which is what it sounds like you're going for. Do you really want to add nudity to that?"

"I think so. I think that's kind of the point."

"Huh. Then how about you keep your underwear on? For me, not you."

"But why?"

"Fact of the matter is, if I do this right it's going to massively turn me on, and I don't want you to notice that and think there's any chance I'll try something while you're tied up. I think a barrier would be good."

"Oh." *Oh. Oh god.* She blushed. "Sorry, I didn't think— I mean, I guess it's not really fair to ask you—"

"To be turned on and not have sex? Yeah, actually, that's totally fair. You might be turned on, too, you never know. Can I trust you to control yourself?"

"I kind of doubt it will come to that, but yeah. I promise I won't try to take advantage of you, Emery."

"Thanks."

And oh boy, those were definitely ropes. One long piece? Multiple lengths? She was a little distracted by their similarity to snakes, though she'd never seen a neon purple snake.

"Lisa?"

She looked up.

"You can stop me anytime."

"I know."

"Okay. Good."

"So, uh, how does this work? Am I supposed to take off my clothes now?"

"I'm not quite ready yet." He put the ropes down on the coffee table and drew her to her feet, holding her hands. "How modest are you?"

"Modest? I didn't used to be."

"I'm thinking about a harness. It wouldn't incapacitate you; you could sit down, stand up, move around, even put your clothes on and cut it off later. But you'd be stunning in one, and I assume if you're looking at that picture, you aren't trying to start small."

"I want everything," she whispered. The boy in the picture had been clothed in lines of rope like a shield, like a force field.

"Let's start with this." He brought her hands to his lips and kissed her knuckles. "It stops when we say it stops. If you don't like it, tell me."

She pulled their joined hands to her own lips, a clumsy return kiss. "I'll tell you. I'm a little worried they'll turn into snakes."

"I have scissors, Lisa. No matter how far into it we are, I can have them off you and away from your skin inside thirty seconds."

"And they're neon, so that … helps."

He smiled. "Good."

"So how does this start?"

"With your shirt. But wait." Emery dropped her hands and pulled off his own shirt, tossing it on the futon.

And oh god, the fox inked on his gorgeous chest. It was staring at her, but this time it made her feel as if she were under its protection, not outside of it. Lisa pulled off her own shirt and stepped forward, kissing the side of his smile.

"That wasn't in the script," he murmured.

"Sorry. I'll get myself under control in a minute. Or three." But god, the feel of his hands sliding up into her hair made her want to stay suspended in *now* forever.

"Three." He kissed her, soul patch tickling her skin. "Two …"

"One. Okay." She leaned her forehead against him. "Tie me up, Emery."

"Oh god. I mentioned I'm pretty turned on, right?"

She looked. She couldn't not-look. And yeah, he was packing something in those jeans.

"Stop. You'll make me blush."

Lisa giggled. "Sorry."

"You still want to do this?"

"Oh yeah. Definitely. More than ever."

At first it was awkward. Partly because she had to hold two ropes at her shoulders ("Trust me, it will all be worth it when you feel it at the end," he said), but mostly because she was far too *aware* of everything. Horns honked down the street; someone walked up the stairs with jingling keys to their apartment on an upper floor; kids on the corner shouted insults; radios blared out of car windows; a scuffle outside the door included a yap and a sharp *"SHHH!"*

She could hear the motor in the fridge, and the way the toilet ran intermittently. She could feel every air current against her skin, only underwear and bra still on.

She wanted to think she felt safe with Emery because he was safe to be with, but the real truth was she'd felt safe enough with all of them, with every one of the men she'd been with. She wondered briefly if Frankie had felt safe with Caldecott, then banished the thought.

The harness, so far, was disappointing. Far from the woven work of art she'd seen in Alice's drawing, this was just a series of knots down the front of her body. And Emery touched her carefully, but she didn't think any more or less carefully than he'd touched the boy in the picture. He could probably tie up anyone and touch them just like this.

The last knot landed above her pubic bone, and this time he looked up from where he knelt.

God. No shirt, on his knees, at her feet.

"I have to get kinda touchy for a minute," he said. "Is that all right?"

"Touchy?"

He held up what was left of the incredibly long rope he was using (even doubled over, it seemed to go on forever). "I'm running this between your legs. Don't worry, it won't chafe."

Chafing. She hadn't yet considered worrying about chafing.

Lisa slid her legs just a little apart. "Okay."

"Tell me if it's too uncomfortable."

"I will."

It wasn't uncomfortable. In fact, even through thin cotton, it was arousing and grounding all at once. The background noises receded, and she could feel the ropes now. Emery did something behind her and pulled them around, stringing each side through the top knot he'd made above her breasts. Then around back, forcing him to move in close, and through the front ropes, pulling the lengths between knots into diamonds.

Lisa lost herself to the feeling of tug and tautness as the ropes seemed to find their own perfectly balanced tension against her skin.

She realized she'd closed her eyes, that the only sensations she could still feel were his hands, his ropes, and occasionally his breath on her skin. He was on his knees again, tying the last of the knots with the last of the rope. She waited for him to speak, but he didn't, so she kept her eyes closed and swayed slightly as if there were a draft. She was upright, but her body was fluid; standing with the floor against her feet, but also floating in space, in ropes that both buoyed her up and tethered her down.

She was naked, and somehow the ropes held her securely and at the same time set her free.

When Lisa at last opened her eyes, he was gazing up at her as if he could never get tired of the sight.

"Sorry," she whispered. "Do your knees hurt?"

"Who cares about my knees?" he whispered back. "How do you feel?"

Birds soaring, waves crashing, dolphins shooting through water, cheetahs speeding over the savannah.

"Powerful. I feel powerful."

He grabbed her hands again and held them to his lips, just breathing for a long moment, eyes still raised to hers. Then he stood up and stepped in.

"May I kiss you?"

"You better."

Kissing a man who'd tied ropes around her body should have felt like giving something away, but instead it felt like creation, like between them they made something new——a fire, or at least a spark.

He leaned forward to speak directly into her ear. "You look hot in neon purple, by the way."

"It goes so well with black matching bra and panties."

He laughed. "It really does."

What had started out steamy and just a little bit kinky wound up as a brief wrestling match, after which both of them collapsed on the futon.

"This rope rubs in interesting places," Lisa panted.

"Tell me more. You want it off yet?"

She slid more completely under his body. "Not yet. Can I spend the night?"

"Definitely. And I meant it, earlier. We've done this now. We can do it again. It's not a step on the way to something else."

She nodded, feeling generous. "Unless we want it to be."

"Unless we want it to be, yeah."

Sex would be good. God, could they have sex with the ropes? No, right? That would rub both of them wrong. Though Emery probably knew some way to do it so they could.

As much as Lisa wanted the outcome of that—of knowing she could have sex with a good man, of knowing she wasn't so broken she couldn't bear his touch—what she wanted more was to rub against his glorious muscles with ropes between them and kiss.

She reached up to kiss the fox on his skin. "Eventually, yes. To everything. Tonight I want to stay in this space in my head where all I can feel is strength."

"Hell yes," he said. "Let's do *that.*"

So they did. Not as a consolation prize. Not as something she was willing to offer in the face of what he really wanted. They kissed and rolled around and took it up to the loft when they nearly rolled off the futon for the fourth time, and when Emery untied her, much later, she felt as if she were being stroked and petted and soothed, that every touch sank into her skin, leaving behind an invisible layer of protection to guard that precious sense of power she'd only just discovered, a tiny fire burning that she could still feel even without the ropes.

57

SINGER
117 DAYS WITH MILES

Moving was a nightmare. Singer was thankful for the army of Derries who'd volunteered to help, but between the twins picking up lunch—then getting lost on their way to the new house where everyone was gathered to eat—Cathy and Carey arguing over the organization of furniture in the moving truck, and Frankie's general derision, he was pretty close to over the entire thing.

And it was only just beginning; once they got everything to the new place, they'd have to unpack.

He stood beside Jake in the center of the kitchen. "Moving is endless."

Miles called, "Ake!" Both of them looked over.

"You agree, Miles?" Jake asked.

"Ake."

"Yeah, us, too, buddy. I think this calls for a nap. Or something."

"How can we nap? They'll all be back any minute now for more stuff—"

"It takes fifteen, twenty minutes to get over there, then they have to unload, then they have to drive back. We have a little bit of time." Jake nudged him. "Grab the kid."

It had initially felt stilted, Jake handing off parenting duties like he was making a point. But this was Jake, and he wasn't really making a point. He was trying to help in the most bludgeoning way possible.

Singer scooped Miles out of his high chair and made a mental note to hose it down before they brought it into the new house. "Maybe I should take this outside and clean it so it'll be dry before——"

Jake laughed. "You think our landlords won't give us an extra day or two to move out if we need it? Seriously, everything's under control. Plus, let's give Mom the food safety jobs. She'll whip up some kind of white vinegar miracle thing and she'll like doing it."

"I just don't feel like we should——"

"Hey." Jake stepped right in front of him so he couldn't go anywhere but back. And he didn't want to. "Miles is pooped."

Singer ran his hand down Miles's back and Miles sighed, putting his head down. "I don't think he likes moving, either."

"Nope. Why don't we go lie down with him for a few minutes? I bet he falls asleep."

"You think we'll get another nap out of him today?"

"Maybe. I know I could use one."

Miles's room had been completely dismantled, and Alice was in charge of recreating it in the new house. The committee had decided it was the most important room to have settled by the end of the day.

Their bedroom was all boxes and half-open drawers, but the bed was still there, and made. No side tables, and one of the dressers had been moved out already (Singer's; Jake's still had clothes hanging out of it and junk on top).

"Here," Jake murmured, flipping back the comforter and blanket and sheet, moving the pillows to the sides so Singer could lay Miles down in the center of the mattress.

It seemed perfectly natural to follow, stretching out, with both of them bracketing Miles. Miles kicked his legs and put up a token protest, then curled to his side facing Jake and closed his eyes.

They watched. Singer reached out, lightly resting his hand against Miles's back, feeling his breaths. He wouldn't have done it at night, or if this was the only nap, but if it didn't work out, they'd just get back up. They didn't *need* this nap, and it made him bold.

"We, uh, forgot to change his diaper," Jake breathed.

Singer winced. "He's going to leak everywhere."

"And all the rest of our sheets are in a box somewhere in Pleasant Hill."

They looked at each other. Jake grinned, slowly, the expression stealing over his face as if the more he thought about it, the more amused he was.

Singer couldn't help but smile back, his muscles mirroring Jake's involuntarily. "There isn't anything funny about this."

"It's a little funny. And I think that means we should bite the bullet and move the bed next."

"I'm not the reason our bedroom is last on the list, Jacob."

"Hey, your whole side of the vanity is a mess."

Singer looked over, ready to defend himself, but Jake's muffled giggle pulled his attention back. "You're such a liar."

"Made you look."

Miles heaved a huge breath and flipped to his back, eyelids fluttering. For a second neither of them moved. Then he settled again, deep breaths resuming.

"If you wake him up, you have to clean the bathroom," Singer whispered.

"If you wake him up, you have to *let me* clean the bathroom. Without supervision."

Singer narrowed his eyes at Jake's triumph. "You wouldn't."

"Oh yeah. I'd leave hairs in the drain. And I wouldn't get the mirror streak-free."

"It's not *clean* if— Never mind." Singer turned back to watching Miles sleep. He was walking all the time now, but he was still stocky; he seemed to defy gravity as he trundled through the living room.

"Can you see his heartbeat?"

He tilted his head down, and yes, there, faster than Singer expected. "That's amazing."

"I know. Like, I get how the human body works, and it's objectively miraculous, but then I look at him and it's even cooler."

Singer glanced up. "Thank you for not giving up on me."

"I tried to, but it didn't stick. You're pretty hard to give up on, Singer Thurman. Oh my god, wait, speaking of not giving up on people, I haven't told you my evil genius plan yet! What if Lisa and Frankie moved in together?"

"What? That's crazy."

"I *know.* It can't possibly work, except it might. And it would be *epic.*"

"It really would be."

"And anyway, I love Lisa, but none of us are going to be comfortable with her on the sofa bed in the living room for long. And I'm not so sure moving in with Emery is a great call, though he'd probably let her."

Singer wasn't so sure that either one of them would go for that. Taking things slow seemed to be working exceptionally well at the moment, and Lisa was in no hurry to repeat past mistakes. "But she and Frankie? That would be …"

"*Epic*, I know. I'm telling you."

He hesitated before offering, "I'll miss being at the epicenter of the Irregulars. I'll miss the circus, I think. You know. With the new house and everything."

"Singer. How long have you known my family?"

It sounded like a rhetorical question, but out of curiosity, Singer did the math. "I met the Derries freshman year of high school. So … eighteen years?"

"You think there's, like, any chance we won't always be in the middle of a circus?"

"Hm. Good point."

Down the hall they could hear the front door slam open.

"Boys, we're back!"

Both of them winced. Miles's eyes opened wide, and his hands clenched into tiny fists.

"Miles, it's okay," Singer began, while Jake said, "Shh, shh, it's all right."

It was no use. Miles started to cry. He reached for Jake, who pulled him to one shoulder and shot a *See what I'm saying? There's no escaping the circus* look at Singer.

In some other part of the house, Cathy was scolding Frankie for yelling in a house where babies were present—apparently unaware that her voice was just as loud—and Singer could only smile. He reached out to pat Miles's back as he whimpered tiredly.

"Fucking Derries," Jake muttered.

Singer leaned awkwardly over to kiss him. "I wouldn't have them any other way. I think it's time Frankie learned how to change a diaper, don't you?"

Jake laughed.

58

VIV
STARTING OVER

Viv Thurman stood, tall and dry-eyed, in the house where she'd raised her children.

She needed to call a cleaning service and double check with the local agent she'd engaged to make sure there was nothing else to do before she drove home.

Home was such a tricky word. This had been her home, for thirty-six years. Now that the pain had passed, she found herself strangely at peace with selling the house. It was empty of everything except a few pieces of furniture the real estate agent thought properly staged it, just enough to let new people, potential buyers, imagine themselves here in the future.

Like they had, she and Drew. It had been only the third house they'd looked at, but they'd been able to see their future in it immediately. They'd stood right here in the living room and pictured evenings spent drinking wine and reading books. They'd stood in the empty bedrooms and tried to imagine their children.

Always two. They had always pictured themselves with two children, one for each bedroom.

Never divorce, though that, too, was becoming more familiar, a word that with repeated use became less vivid, though not quite bloodless. Viv had imagined they'd sell this house when they were ready for assisted living, though at twenty-three she'd thought sixty was at least a decade beyond old.

She inhaled, probing the softest parts of herself for grief. They wouldn't grow old in this house.

One more once-over was all it really needed. A final vacuuming, a final wipe of the counters, a final sweep and mop of the floors. Viv again contemplated calling a service. It made no sense to be sentimental about this last step before locking up and leaving, but she found herself reluctant to turn the job over to strangers.

She dialed Lisa's number instead, not at all certain she would answer.

"Mother? Are you all right?"

Strange how a woman could stand in her old house and bid it good-bye without shedding a tear, but the sound of her daughter's voice made her suddenly want to weep.

"Mother?"

"I'm here." She cleared her throat. "I'm at the house. I don't— I'm not sure—"

"Are you crying?"

"No. Certainly not." Viv dabbed at her eyes with her sleeve. "I need to clean the house before I head back down south. Would you— Are you busy?"

Lisa's voice was tentative. "You…want me to come over and help you clean? We would have done a better job, but we thought you would probably hire people."

"Yes, of course that's what I should do." And it would probably be a relief. What on earth had she been thinking, to consider doing it herself?

"Unless … Mother, do you want me to come over and help?"

"I'm sure you're busy," Viv began.

"Uh, yeah, not really. You mean, busy being a shut-in with serious paranoia issues? Anyway, give me like half an hour and we'll be over. Bye, Mother."

She'd hung up before Viv could say anything. Like *Thank you* or *You aren't a shut-in* or *Who's 'we'?*

She stowed her sweater and purse on the sofa and went in search of a broom.

*

The first words out of Lisa's mouth were: "Derries to the rescue, Mother."

Viv frowned, then was gently—but firmly—pushed out of the way.

She'd feared that the "we" in question was that boy, Emery. But it wasn't. By the time they all trooped inside, she almost wished it had been.

"Mother." Singer kissed her cheek and put down a mop bucket full of spray bottles, cloths, brushes, and sponges. "Have you started? If you'd told us you planned to do everything yourself, we would have done a much better job."

Jake, with Miles in one arm and a bag of toys in the other, passed them. "Hey, Mrs. Thurman. Do you have any requests for food? Derries only work if you provide a meal for them. Fair warning, it'll probably be pizza if you don't tell me something else."

Raucous laughter cut off any chance Viv had to reply.

"And beer! We work for food and beer!" Frankie waved. "Hi, Mrs. Thurman. Nice to see you. I'll volunteer to do my former abode, since I can basically clean the whole thing in like twenty minutes." She picked out a spray bottle and a roll of paper towels. "Text me when the food gets here!"

Singer made a grab for her supplies and missed. "Frances, other people may need paper towels."

"Other people can walk their butts out to the guesthouse, then. Ta!"

The baby made a noise that mimicked her, and Jake grinned. "Do us a favor and do not start copying Frankie, Miles. I'll do something nontoxic while he plays."

"The vacuum is in the car." Singer held out his arms, and the baby went to him. "You and I will assess the jobs that need to be done while Jake gets that, okay? Let's start in our bedroom. Or I guess it's just the master bedroom now." They walked down the hall.

Viv took a shaky breath. "They are so…loud."

"I know, Mother." Lisa patted her arm. "Should we get Chinese? Would that be good? Or Indian?"

"I couldn't possibly eat right now."

Lisa pulled out her phone. "I'll tell Carey to pick up Chinese."

"All right."

Jake bustled back in with the vacuum, Singer returned with what he was calling a "plan of attack," and Lisa took the baby while Singer wrote out a list, assigning tasks to all of them.

Viv realized she was largely redundant right around the time Jake's brother and his girlfriend arrived. She could have called Lisa from Valencia and asked her to arrange for the house to be cleaned, and the entire group of them would have converged just like this, loudly, irreverently. Competently, for all their noise and bluster. The house was nearly clean by the time they descended upon the food.

A pizza as well as Chinese. And an assortment of paper plates and plastic utensils. The girlfriend, Alice, offered Viv first pick of Chinese food, and she found herself eating even though she hadn't felt hungry.

Jake offered her a seat on one of the sofas beside Singer, but she found an excuse to do something in the kitchen long enough for all of them to settle into their places. They talked over one another, filling every corner of the house with their voices and laughter.

The house still felt warm, awake, alive. Not hollow.

It was hard to remember being that young, laughing that freely. Viv wasn't sure she ever had, really, though it was always possible that she'd decided such unfettered emotion was somehow unbecoming, that it wasn't suited to her role in life. When she looked back, she could see places where she'd restrained herself, times when she might have embraced sentiment, or even passion.

Could a woman her age learn how to feel passionate? Probably not, but Viv thought she might try. It was frightening to be starting fresh now, when she'd thought everything would be established, the shape of her days more or less unchanged. But it wasn't without a certain thrill, she acknowledged. Anything could happen.

Across the room Singer happened to look over at Lisa, both of them smiling, and Viv had to turn away briefly to dab at her eyes again. She'd raised her children in this house, and they'd grown into people she hardly knew. But that, too, might be remedied. Both of them could laugh. Both of them could claim friendships steadfast enough to rally for a spontaneous house cleaning.

She pulled a chair from the dining room a little closer to the group spread out over the floor and the sofas and returned to eating her food. She had no idea what they were talking about, but it didn't matter. Every now and then Singer would say something, or Lisa, and the baby rounded the table, happy to eat bits off of everyone's plates.

They all packed up to go later, leaving the house in perfect saleable condition. Lisa gave her a hug and told her to drive safely. Jake and Singer were the last to go. On impulse, Viv grabbed Jake's hand as he was chorusing "Good night, Mrs. Thurman" and said, "Please call me Viv. Everyone does."

He smiled widely. "Good night, Viv. Text Singer when you get home safe."

"I will." She kissed the baby's forehead. "Take care of them."

"I'll do that." He walked out, slipping past Singer, who was staring at her.

"Mother, I…" But he couldn't seem to find words.

She kissed his cheek. "Good night, darling. Thank you for helping today."

"Of course. You won't drive tonight, will you?"

"No, I have a hotel room. I'll leave first thing in the morning."

"All right." He hesitated, then kissed her cheek. "Goodbye, Mother. We'll have to plan a visit soon, if you've decided to stay in Valencia."

"I think so. For now, anyway."

Singer nodded. "Maybe after the adoption is finalized."

"I look forward to it." Both of them paused, and in that pause, that shared moment, Viv understood that she hadn't said anything but the absolute truth. Singer and Jake and the baby would come visit, and she would look forward to seeing them.

Sounding a bit hushed, Singer murmured, "Well, good night."

She found she couldn't say anything at all, and so kissed him again, and locked the door behind them.

EPILOGUE

SINGER
389 DAYS WITH MILES

The Family Law Center in Martinez was an eye-pleasing mix of glass and steel, angles and curves. They stood in the entirely unseasonable summer rain, and Singer focused on the architecture until he saw Marie and Sarah walking slowly down the block. Well. Marie was walking slowly. Sarah was clearly trying to contain herself.

"I'm telling you they're gay," Jake murmured. He waved.

"They're friends. People who don't grow up surrounded by Derries have *friends*, Jacob." Singer knelt down. "Miles, do you see Nana?"

At almost two years old, Miles was a big tumbling kid, and when he started running down the sidewalk Singer felt the same certainty he always felt: this is the time he falls flat on his face. But before he could, Sarah swooped in and grabbed him. She kissed him, then held him out so he could hug Marie, even though Marie relied more on her cane in bad weather.

He scanned the street, but no sign of Regina.

"Do you think he's going to notice she isn't here?" Jake asked.

Singer gestured to the huge collection of Derries and hangers-on. "I don't think so. I'm glad Marie's here, though."

"Me too. That makes it feel real."

Both of them kissed Marie, careful not to act too enthusiastic just in case it brought up old wounds.

"For God's sake, you can smile," she snapped.

"We're so completely excited," Jake said. "You couldn't get her to come?"

"She was high." Marie shook her head. "I thought it'd be best if she didn't, in that state."

"I offered to duct tape her mouth shut, but Marie said no," Sarah added, bouncing Miles. "Good lord, all these people belong to you two?"

"I have kind of a big family, sorry."

"Marie!"

"Incoming," Jake mumbled.

"Your mama doesn't scare me," Marie mumbled back, though Singer thought she was putting on a brave face.

"Then you don't know her well enough yet. Mom, can we not—"

"Hush, I'm saying hi to Marie. Marie, can you believe how big he is? Did you get the photos? How's your back?"

Cathy had found Marie on Facebook and, over their strong objections, sent her a friend request. Jake and Singer were a little surprised when Marie accepted it.

They stepped to the side, and Lisa walked up. "This is my high school nightmare. There are Derries everywhere I turn."

"Don't I know it," Jake said. "Should we run?"

"You wish. How're you guys holding up?"

"This can't actually be happening. I feel like we've been waiting forever."

"I thought we'd wait longer," Singer said.

"My brother the optimist." She opened her mouth to say something, then stopped and smiled instead. "Hey, Emery."

"Am I late? Sorry, there was traffic on 680."

"We haven't gone inside yet."

They didn't kiss when they greeted each other, but they linked hands, which was almost more sweet. Not that Singer was evaluating the sweetness of Lisa's relationship.

Okay, maybe he was. She'd never had sweet before.

"Mother said to tell you good luck, by the way. I think she's under the impression there's a test, or something."

"Dad texted to say congratulations—on Tuesday."

Lisa rolled her eyes. "Nice of them to pay attention."

Cathy raised her voice to call out: "Everyone waiting outside the courtroom, we'll be out when we can. Everyone coming in, let's go."

Lisa snickered. "Ha. Your mom's nervous, huh, Jake?"

"Did you pass her car on the way here? She's got *trays* of cupcakes in it. She's happy it's cold out so they won't melt."

"Ha. Where's the little man?"

It took a second, and even though Singer knew there was no chance of Miles getting lost or kidnapped when literally surrounded by Derries, he still panicked for half a breath.

"Carey has him," Jake said.

As Singer found them, Carey was hoisting Miles onto his shoulders while Miles giggled.

"He's in such a good mood." Singer kept his voice low. "I had nightmares where he got totally overwhelmed and cried all day."

"Pretty sure that's gonna be us, Singer."

"Good point." His phone buzzed. A message from Kara. "Hey, Kara and Victor say good luck, and Rachel made us a picture." Singer swallowed, then held it out for Jake to look.

"Our first family portrait," he said.

Two beige men and one brown baby.

"Oh god, Singer." Jake brushed a kiss to his cheek.

"I know. You think we should go in, so they know we're here?"

"I doubt they can miss us. And yeah, let's do this."

Singer sucked in a deep breath. "Is it weird that I still don't feel ready, even though we've been waiting forever?"

"It only feels like forever. And it only feels like we're not ready for this."

"Right. It's all an illusion."

Jake grinned and kissed Singer's other cheek. "Not all of it." He turned away and called, "Hey! Give me back my kid!"

Miles, alerted, said, "Hey! Ake!"

Even strangers chuckled.

After the flurry of being outside with everyone, the courtroom itself felt almost calm.

"I just got nervous," Jake whispered, shifting Miles to his other arm.

"You weren't nervous before?"

"I guess I wasn't nervous enough."

Miles grabbed a handful of Singer's shirt. "Er," he said urgently.

"What? You okay?" They stopped walking (and perforce everyone behind them stopped walking, too).

"*Er*," Miles repeated.

"I'm right here," Singer said, closing his hand over Miles's fist.

Miles put his head down and didn't let go.

"This is a little like dancing," Jake murmured as they carefully started walking again.

"We should dance more often."

"Quit being punchy."

Singer fought a wave of hysterical laughter and tried to make his face serious, but shuffling along beside Jake and Miles made it hard.

They sat at the plaintiff table with their attorney and scooted their chairs close enough so Miles could hold onto both of them.

"I'm going to puke," Jake whispered.

"You can't."

"But—"

They shut up when the judge rearranged some papers. Minutes ticked by in a slow-motion blur of swearing to tell the truth and agreeing about their names and birthdays.

This can't be happening. This can't be real.

When asked if they wanted to change Miles's name, Jake glanced over, a silent *You talk.*

"Yes," Singer heard himself say. "To Miles Thurman Derrie." No hyphen. Regina hadn't given Miles a middle name, so they did. Singer's name. And Lisa's.

He swallowed hard, and Jake reached over. The warmth of his hand sank into Singer's skin.

The judge's voice washed over him, conferring on them the status and responsibility of permanent parents. Singer followed the words and knew what they meant, but he didn't tune back in until the woman said, "Congratulations, gentlemen. And congratulations, Miles."

Singer kissed Miles's head, and Miles turned toward him.

"Er?"

"Love you."

"LOVE YOU," Miles repeated, unnaturally loud in the hushed room.

Everyone laughed.

Miles looked around, then buried his face in Jake's neck again.

"Pictures," Cathy said.

Right, pictures with the judge. Adoption rite of passage.

They arranged themselves, Singer slightly behind Jake on his Miles side. After a second of hesitation he put his hand lightly on Jake's waist.

Miles started talking, and Singer caught "tacos" and "doggy" and possibly "cupcake."

Jake laughed. "We'll get to cupcakes later, bud. Right now we're doing pictures."

"Say cheese, Miles!" Cathy called.

"Cheese!" Miles called back to his grandmother.

"You think he thinks she means food?" Singer whispered.

Cathy gestured imperiously toward them. "Marie, get in there, we're taking one of you, too."

Were they supposed to monopolize the judge's time like this? Not that she seemed to be complaining.

"Cathy—"

"Don't Cathy me, lady. Get in the picture."

"Don't argue with her," Singer advised, holding out his other arm. "She always wins."

Marie grumbled, shifting her cane to a better position, but she was definitely pleased to be included.

"Say cheese!"

This time Miles wasn't messing around.

"CHEESE CHEESE CHESSE CHEESE CHEESE!"

"I think he's hungry," the judge teased.

In the pictures they'd all be smiling. Singer felt the curve of his own lips tugging at muscles sore from smiling all day.

He swallowed again.

"You're supposed to be the one crying," Jake muttered in the chaos following pictures as they were gently herded out of the courtroom.

"Give me our son."

In all the pictures taken by the people who waited outside, Miles would be in Singer's arms. He felt suddenly self-conscious and turned his own face into Miles's.

"I am not crying," Jake chanted. "Not crying, dammit."

"Liar."

Then the Derries (and hangers-on) swarmed them, carrying them outside, where the rain had miraculously paused. The front steps were lined with a picnic of buffet-style cold cuts and rolls and fruit platters, with various tubs of store-bought potato salad and egg salad and pasta salad.

"You know, with whatever your folks spent on this spread we could have started Miles's college fund."

"If you think they haven't already, you don't know them very well."

Singer paused. "Good point. When do you think they're gonna tell us?"

"Today, maybe. Or they might wait until his birthday. Miles, do you want to go to college someday?"

"Cupcake!"

Jake laughed. "Who has cupcakes? The man of the hour wants cupcakes."

"The man of the hour can eat some vegetables first," Cathy said, holding out her arms. "Come here, my strong boy. Come sit with Nana and Sarah and me while we dissect the joke that is our health care system."

Singer caught her eye. "Everything okay with Marie's treatment?"

"I'm trying to get her to let me pay for the physical therapy out of pocket. There's no earthly reason why she should be in this much pain."

"Good luck," Jake said.

"Oh, I'll win. She just doesn't know it yet."

They waved, and Miles waved back for a split second until he saw Marie's plate. Then he dove for the food.

"So the thing where my mom's trying to push her do-gooder agenda all over Marie—should I be worried?"

"I think Marie loves it when rich white people tell her what to do," Singer replied. "Oh my god, I can't believe we just laughed at that."

"I hope she at least understands that it's a nurse thing. Damn." Jake swiped at his eyes again. "Singer, we're parents. I mean officially. Legally. No one can take him away from us."

"I know." But that wasn't what he really wanted to say. "Jake, I— Thank you. For having enough faith for both of us."

"Only until puberty. Then it's all you."

"Right."

Frankie whistled at them. "Hey slackers! Settle a bet for us."

"Oh god," Jake muttered.

"We'd rather not," Singer called back.

Frankie rolled her eyes but didn't push it, releasing them from the obligation to get involved. She was gesturing wildly with one hand while the other was loosely in Logan's grasp. (She never said "boyfriend," but Logan had reached boyfriend status in the family anyway.)

"He might not want to go to college," Jake said.

"What do you mean?" Singer pulled his attention back from Derrie-watching.

"I don't know. Only that he might not be interested in college. I mean, we all went, and it's not like I'm using my awesome literary analysis skills at work. And you majored in *philosophy*, so—"

"Don't mess with me about Neitzsche."

"I'll, um, try not to. But you know, maybe by the time Miles is older there will be stuff he wants to do."

Singer almost brushed it off, but there was something behind this. More than college. "What're you thinking?"

"I'm not sure. But you know how people act like having a kid is sort of this sacrifice? That it places all these limits on what you can do?"

"You mean like all the drinking and wild parties we used to throw?"

"Yeah, you always knew when movie night at Thurman House got out of hand because people would start insulting on the catalog of Jennifer Aniston."

"I love Anniston."

Jake grinned. "I know you do. And no, I mean, I look at him, right now, and I feel like our world has expanded a thousand times, Singer. I feel like our family didn't just grow by one person, it grew by an entire dimension that didn't exist before Miles."

"Sometimes I feel like he makes us more of a family than we were before," Singer said. "Or than we could have been without him." *Not crying.*

"Yeah. Me too. And, um, I think we should keep thinking about surrogacy, but I could do this again, too. Which I know sounds crazy to say when we kind of just got done with it, but—"

"No, I know." Because right now Miles's two grandmothers were talking like they were friends, despite everything. The system was so fucked up, and yet it had built this family Singer didn't even know he needed. And Miles was theirs, so incredibly, inevitably theirs.

Jake cleared his throat. "So anyway, I had this idea. Um."

"Are we going to Disneyland? Because I could seriously use a honeymoon from—everything. Especially if we're going to start it again at some point."

"Well, um, actually…" Jake reached for his hand and held it. "I was kind of thinking we should make it even more official. Our family. And I'm pro-Disneyland, for the record."

"Didn't we just do that?" Singer almost said something else, something flippant, but the look on Jake's face stopped him. Wait. They couldn't really be saying…this. "Oh my god. Jake."

"If you want me to get down on one knee, I will, but then they'll be all over us. We should get married, Singer."

"I thought that was at some distant point in the future because it doesn't matter what some piece of paper says."

"It doesn't. But then, I don't know, I didn't think it mattered having someone tell us we're fathers when I already feel like a father, and it does. It matters." Jake gulped and added, "I didn't get rings. I didn't want to do anything without you, and I don't know if gay people do engagement rings, so I didn't. But I— I want to do this. With you. And Miles."

"When? We're sitting at a courthouse right now, so—"

Jake squeezed his hand. "We should do it in secret, like we're going to the bathroom. Sneak in, sign some papers—"

"Jacob. We cannot get married in secret. Your mother would *kill* us."

"Anyway, I kind of think we should have a party. But I don't want this to be me asking you to marry me, Singer. I want this to be like everything else we've ever done. Us doing it together."

"They'll all think it's my idea, you know."

"Yeah, that's funny. They all think adopting was your idea, too. I kind of like it. Makes it more, I don't know, private, that my entire family doesn't know *all* the details."

"Did you just say the Derries don't know all the details?" Lisa asked. She sat down on the step below theirs, with Emery beside her.

"Jake and I have some secrets left."

"That must be nice," Emery said. "Wonder what it's like."

Lisa hit him. "We have secrets, too, you know. I keep a list. In my head."

"Of our secrets?"

"And other stuff."

Singer held up the hand Jake wasn't holding. "Don't want to know, thank you very much."

"Aw, look, you guys are being cute in public. That's— cool." She narrowed her eyes. "You guys are being cute. In public."

"Lisa," Jake said, pitching his voice low. "Can you keep a secret?" He glanced up at Singer for half a second.

Singer nodded. Telling Lisa first felt right, for some reason. To say nothing of subversive.

"I'm pretty sure. Why? You guys kill someone?"

"We're getting married."

Emery slammed hands over his ears. "I'm a horrible liar! Alice is going to know I know something now!"

"Oh god. You guys are getting married." Lisa leaned up to kiss Singer's cheek. "Congratulations, little brother."

"Thank you."

"What *the fuck* is going on over there? Hi, is anyone else seeing some weird-ass shit right now?" Frankie Derrie, bringer of chaos.

"Jake?" Singer said, raising both eyebrows.

"Miles." Jake scooped Miles up from where he was picking the celery out of the macaroni salad on Alice's plate, and when he held out his arm, Singer was already moving toward them. Another pointed *You talk* look.

Singer cleared his throat. "Jake and I are getting married. At some point."

"Oh for fuck's sake, what kind of obvious shit is this? Like we didn't—*oof*!"

Carey raised the arm he hadn't just used to elbow Frankie, holding his water bottle. "Cheers to the happy couple and their son."

"CHEERS!"

The circus roared approval, and Miles raised his voice to keep up, not even bothering to form words.

Jake hooked Singer's neck and pulled him close. "Cheers, Singer."

He should have said "Cheers" or "I love you" or any number of other things, but now Singer was actually crying, and all he could do was wrap his arms around his family and hold them tightly.

AUTHOR'S ACKNOWLEDGMENTS

I would not have written this particular book if I had not grown up in a massive extended family. All the love to my grandparents, aunts, uncles, and especially my cousins.

More specific thanks to my ma, Ellen Dunn, for reading an early version of this book and helping me flesh out the various tensions and relationships between families in the system, social workers, and families fostering and adopting kids. I'd also be remiss if I didn't point out that in an actual situation, Miles would have more than one worker. I've somewhat compressed the human side of social services for the purposes of fiction (but the timeline is dead-on accurate for the state of California). Additional thanks to Fresno County for putting a flowchart on their website, which pretty much everyone should use because it's rad.

Other early readers to whom I'm grateful include Iben Mylius, Roan Parrish, and Liz Jacobs. General Wendy talked me through a number of Google Hangouts while I wrung my hands over this book. I am, as always, in her debt. Although she may never forgive me for the first draft

I sent her. In my defense, I like introducing a dozen characters in the space of the first three pages, so I really don't know what the issue was! *cackles*

My eternal gratitude to Lennan Adams of Lexiconic Design for overhauling the cover in my design hour of need.

I wrote the first draft of this book in 2013. And trunked it for two years, until Alexis Hall asked me to pitch him something for Brain Mill Press. So I…pitched him this. Well. For a somewhat loose sense of the word "pitched."

Very lucky authors have great editors. Only the spectacularly fortunate among us land an editor like Alexis Hall. Perceptive as hell, diligent, and with a remarkable gift for peeling back the layers of a story to expose what's underneath. Dude's a motherfucking genius. This book was a tough journey on a number of levels, and I wouldn't have made it to the end without Editor Hall at my side. And occasionally at my back, prodding me with sticks when necessary.

Mad props to my bro, who came up with the title after I fumbled through a very bad description of what I'd tried to write.

Last, but certainly not least, my housemates M, C, and E always make me laugh. An invaluable quality. All the love.

ABOUT THE AUTHOR

Kris Ripper lives in the great state of California and hails from the San Francisco Bay Area. Kris shares a converted garage with a toddler, can do two pull-ups in a row, and can write backwards. (No, really.) Kris is genderqueer and prefers the z-based pronouns because they're freaking sweet. Ze has been writing fiction since ze learned how to write, and boring zir stuffed animals with stories long before that.